D0356391

The Counter

The Man Too Good For Vegas

The Counter

♣ ♦ ♥ ♠

A Novel by Kevin Blackwood

WOODEN
PAGODA
press

This book is a work of fiction. Names, characters, places, and incidents either are products of author's imagination or are used fictitiously. Any resemblance to actual events or locales or persons, living or dead, is entirely coincidental.

All rights reserved. No part of this book may be reproduced or utilized in any form or by any means, electronic or mechanical, including photocopying, recording or by any information storage and retrieval system, without permission in writing from the Publisher. Inquiries should be addressed to:

Wooden Pagoda Press
1056 Green Acres Rd.
Suite 102-132
Eugene, OR 97408

ISBN 0-9717273-0-9
Library of Congress Card Catalog Number: 2002100750

Copyright © 2002 by Ruth Wood

Cover Illustration by Bruce DeRoos
Page Design and Composition by PageCrafters, Inc.

Printed in the United States of America
First Printing: 2002

Visit our website at www.kevinblackwood.com

ACKNOWLEDGEMENTS

SPECIAL THANKS TO:

The late Glenna Grey for encouraging me to write this novel.

Randy Alcorn, whose work inspired me to begin this book.

Greg Davis and Dan Pegoda for your input and friendship.

Eric Weber and Mike Peterson for technical assistance.

Denise Nash for your excellent critique.

Curt and Mark for valuable direction and advice.

Mickey, Cheryl, Gene, Rose, Laura and Dave for reading early versions.

To my loving parents: Malcolm and Marian.

And most of all to my family—thanks for your patient support through this long process. This novel is markedly better because of the tremendous help and editing skills of my wife.

AUTHOR'S NOTE

It is not my intent to offend the many hard-working employees of the casino industry with any of the fictional depictions in this book. Many dealers are friends of mine and have to do a thankless job in an extremely difficult profession.

Visit www.kevinblackwood.com for:

• Purchasing additional copies

• Information about the author

• Post comments or read reviews

PROLOGUE

Like a neon mirage, Sin City rises from the desert floor in a surrealistic shimmer. It lures tourists into a glitzy fantasyland of pyramids and pirates, but these façades mask an ugly truth. The gigantic temples of chance only exist for one purpose—to suck money like a vacuum cleaner from fat wallets.

While European casinos don't let anyone through their doors without a proper coat and dress shoes, Vegas clubs will stand just about anything. Men can play bare-chested in swimming trunks—as long as they're rich, and as long as they lose.

The casinos love most system players and gladly welcome the hordes descending on Las Vegas hoping for easy money. These gamblers, many with visions of *Rain Man* dancing through their heads, come in steady streams to help pay the light bill of the city that never sleeps.

The most popular table game is blackjack because it yields sharp players a slim advantage. However, only the best card counters succeed while the rest fill the casino coffers. In fact, the game's colossal profits fueled the growth of the city. Yet, rather than reward the few individuals who could legitimately triumph, casinos hypocritically kick out these skilled patrons.

Few businesses in the world could get away with such an injustice. When gifted blackjack players honestly beat the odds using only their brains, casinos treat them like convicts—a policy equivalent to McDonald's throwing out any customers smart enough to take advantage of a free burger coupon.

One man determined to overcome these obstacles even though the house is always supposed to win. Raven Townsend resolved to make a million dollars and become the only thing casinos feared. He'd be the predator instead of the prey.

CHAPTER ONE

♣ ♦ ♥ ♠

If it had not been for a single, vacant parking space, all the events that transpired that evening would have been avoided.

As Raven Townsend slowly drove past the impressive Greco-Roman face of the Palace, he knew their garage would be jam-packed on a Friday night. He decided to let fate determine his fortune. If he could park, he would play. He wondered what Pastor Cook would say if he knew that his former protégé had begun to base his decisions on the flip of a coin or the random turn of a card.

Raven almost hoped that no space would be available. He was somewhat hesitant to play blackjack at the Palace again after his last visit. That time he won more than $20,000 before they barred him—not for cheating, or for being drunk or rowdy—he'd simply beaten them honestly, using only his unique mental ability. It still made his blood boil thinking how unfairly casinos treated skilled players.

He turned his red BMW convertible onto the ramp leading to the top floor. Usually he parked in valet to avoid door dings, but tonight he might need a quick escape. Much to his surprise he found an open spot and cautiously backed in next to an old, beat-up Chevy.

As the elevator began its smooth descent to the casino level, Raven wondered if the observation had already begun. The bigger casinos had all converted to high-tech video surveillance with as many as a thousand cameras watching everyone, everywhere. Raven dismissed their threat. It had been seven months since he was eighty-sixed—a long time in a business where pit bosses see thousands of faces each day, and he remained confident they'd never detect him in this disguise. Besides, he never backed down anywhere to anyone when he thought he was right, and he still had an unfinished goal driving him through life. He wasn't the first gambler hoping to make a million in the casinos, but he was one of the few in the world who had a realistic chance.

His skill at the tables forced him to use many different names in order to survive. His given name was Randolph Townsend, although only his father normally used that name. Some called him Randy, but he preferred the name his mother had chosen to honor their Indian heritage and his jet-black hair—Raven.

He hardly recognized himself in the mirrored walls of the elevator. An expensive blond wig and mustache completely changed his appearance. Stylish pants and a leather bomber jacket projected the image of a hip young executive. A classy pair of shoes would've finished the look, but he never compromised on footwear—he wore sneakers on all occasions, whether playing Frisbee or attending a wedding. His face easily blended into a crowd and his light olive complexion gave him the versatility to fit in with a wide range of ethnic groups.

Only the large, dark intense eyes remained recognizable—always alert as they observed the world from under a thick set of eyebrows. A mischievous glint flickered in them now. One of the world's best card counters was back.

The doors of the elevator opened and abruptly the serene quiet ended. Raven walked with self-assurance into the cacophony of sights and sounds. He knew the sharper floor supervisors usually worked near the main entrance, so he instead headed for the tables near the back.

A stunning redhead in a skintight dress walked by, reminding him of the culture shock he experienced on his first visit here. Despite new clubs rising up around her, the Palace always remained the hot place to be and to be seen in Las Vegas. Tonight he hoped the slow parade of bronzed goddesses might help to distract the enemy.

Raven circled the blackjack tables like a wolf might scout for a weak or crippled animal. He studied the pit bosses searching for anyone who might identify him. Most dealers were too busy to detect card counting. The floor supervisors and the dreaded sharp eyes manning the overhead cameras were the foremost threats to him.

He watched a $100 minimum table, counting the cards from the six-deck shoe. A loud cowboy, with a ten-gallon hat and thin hairy arms, sat next to a cute, young brunette who looked half his age. She wore a silver sequined dress with a high slit exposing a shapely tanned leg that brushed against the older man's thigh. Each time he won a big bet she'd bounce up and down and move in closer, as if she preferred the cowboy's lap to her chair.

A bunch of small cards came out; Raven scanned the pit once more, recognized no one, and slipped into the middle seat.

"Howdy," the cowboy said.

"Howdy yourself," Raven replied as he pulled a thick wad of bills from his brown fanny pack.

"Where you from, partner?"

Raven pretended to be busy counting out $3,000 in fresh Ben Franklins to buy his chips. He was here to make money, not conversation.

"I'm from Dallas. Oil business. You live around these parts?" The cowboy wasn't going away, so Raven decided to change the subject to something safer.

"So how are the cards running here, any luck?"

The Texan let out a good-natured chuckle, his deeply lined leather face amiable. "Yep—all of it bad luck. I'm down about two grand. We need another player to change the run of cards. Let's gang up and beat these jackals."

"It's us against the house," said the brunette, "so maybe we can all work together."

"That's the idea," the dealer chimed in. "Now if this were poker and you were a new player, you'd be fresh meat. That's why I like dealing blackjack—it's friendlier, more camaraderie. Good odds, too, especially if you count cards." The dealer, an athletic-looking man with a full head of thick curly hair, slid thirty black $100 chips across the felt to Raven. "Good luck to you."

"Thanks." Raven stacked his chips and shot a furtive glance at the dealer. The man's unbuttoned white shirt revealed a gold chain and he exuded confidence. *But how sharp was he? I certainly don't need extra scrutiny tonight.*

The brunette asked the dealer, "Does card counting really work?"

"Sure it does, lady."

"How?"

"Future odds change depending on what cards have been previously played," the dealer explained.

"How could anyone keep track of that?"

"It's possible to count the high cards to determine the probability for the next hand."

The brunette remained unconvinced. "But doesn't the dealer have the same chance to get the good cards?"

"Yes, the house actually wins more hands than the players, but an expert changes his bet and plays at the right times and comes out ahead."

The conversation unnerved Raven slightly, and he made a quick visual sweep around him to see if he was already being watched. He assumed the dealer was just trying to show off and would be oblivious to the fact that one of the world's best card counters sat right under his nose. The dealer's chitchat slowed the game to a crawl, and Raven considered moving to another table, but just then the count shot up. He felt an adrenaline rush—pushing out big money would attract attention, but Raven didn't hesitate and jumped his bet to $500, won several hands, and then raised it again to $1000. He won the first two thousand-dollar bets, lost a nineteen against a dealer's twenty, then was dealt two sevens.

"You shouldn't split those cards," the cowboy advised. "Best you can do is make seventeen. I only split aces and eights, just like Wild Bill Hickock."

Raven had memorized the correct play for every situation depending on the count. He never went by a hunch and often the best play was the opposite of other players' advice. He split the sevens.

"Unbelievable," the Texan groaned.

Raven caught a three on the first seven, doubled down on his $1,000 bet, then caught a two on his second hand. He hesitated, winked at the oilman from the Longhorn State and slid another thousand on the felt. The dealer busted. Raven used both arms to pull in all the chips and chuckled to himself. *Blondes do have more fun.*

♣ ♦ ♥ ♠

Directly overhead, the ever-present eye-in-the-sky zoomed in on table sixteen. Dark glass bubbles in the ceiling obscured the direction of the camera lens so no one below knew when they were being watched. The larger casinos had surveillance rooms that resembled Houston's mission control with enough video equipment to cover every table and every player. Their cameras were powerful enough to read the serial numbers on dollar bills.

Frank Dunkirk, swing shift head of security, deftly maneuvered the monitors. He had a flattop haircut and always wore a suit and tie. He adjusted the focus so every detail of the blond man's face looked sharp. The mysterious player betting $1,000 a pop appeared to be in his late twenties, just over average height, and extremely fit.

Management jobs at the Palace carried immense prestige and were highly sought after. Frank had turned down an offer to work for the CIA after his military service, since protecting casinos paid far more lucratively than protecting the country. He maintained a meticulous work record, was highly disciplined, and always took care of business. Therefore, it really stung his pride when someone higher up in the organization saw the need to hire an outsider to help him do his job.

Frank picked up the phone and paged Howard Goldberg, who had a consulting contract with several Vegas casinos. The clubs called him in to evaluate suspicious players or to investigate a big hit. Howard had an uncanny ability to recall facial detail, a valuable asset in the detection of undesirables.

For many years Howard had been a high-stakes pro, counting cards on his own and with several teams, but now he used his inside knowledge to benefit casinos. Card counters rarely ended up working for their old "enemies" because they usually believed in the righteousness of the cause—beating the gambling establishment at their own game. But Howard never viewed it as "us versus them." He got into blackjack because it looked like a great way to make money. When the game became too much of a grind, he simply moved to the other side of the table without any guilt. Either way, it was just a job.

Frank looked up just as Howard entered the room. Howard sported an earring on one side, and his trendy clothes set him apart from regular casino employees. Frank rolled his eyes, "Still haven't done anything about that damn ponytail, Goldberg?"

"Can it, Frank. Save the speech for your own people." He knew the ex-Marine wanted everyone to be a company man, but Howard never let anyone own him. "Where's the fire? I was on my way to the Clapton concert when my beeper went off twice—this had better be important."

Frank nodded. "It is. We got a guy down there in Tommy's pit hitting us pretty hard, spreading his bets from black to bumblebees. Anyone you know?" He focused the camera on the yellow and black $1,000 chips. They were stacked in a neat row almost as high as the black $100 chips.

Howard shook his head. "Don't recognize him, but he acts like a player. Look at how he handles his cards and the precise order in which he arranges the chips. You can tell he's played a lot of twenty-one."

Frank nodded. "You got that right. Just a few minutes ago a looker in a drop-dead cocktail dress stood behind his table, and he never even noticed her. In the pit, Tommy salivated like a rottweiler, but this guy didn't even bat an eye. He acts way too focused to be a tourist."

♣ ♦ ♥ ♠

Tommy wore the bored, detached look common to pit personnel at the more prestigious casinos. He wandered over to Raven's table, signed a marker for the dealer, and positioned himself in the best vantage spot to view the big screens in the sports book.

"Damn." The cowboy slapped the table after having lost five hands in a row. "What's going to cool off this dealer?"

Raven had won $8,500 in just thirty minutes, so the dealer was chilly enough for him.

"I'm going to tear up the cards if I'm dealt another stiff," the cowboy threatened. His face flushed red and his ears twitched.

The dealer calmly dealt the next round, and the Texan lost the last chips from his $5,000 credit line. He angrily pulled out his wallet and slammed a large stack of hundred dollar bills on the felt. "Play the cash."

Unfazed by the huge bet, the dealer yelled the customary words to the pit, "Money plays to the limit."

The cowboy was dealt a sixteen. He slowly sucked in his breath before hitting, drew a ten and lost. He had completely tapped out. Raven had a fifteen, but stood knowing that many face cards were left in the shoe. The dealer busted.

The Texan sat stunned for a moment. All the color drained from his face. Then he leaned over to the brunette and whispered something. She shook her head.

"Forget you," he said in a loud voice and stormed off.

The young woman acted as if nothing had happened and sidled closer to Raven. She smiled at him knowingly. "I'm bringing you luck, aren't I?"

Raven expressed no response, not wanting to give her any encouragement. He realized she was a chip hustler, girls who cozy up to high rollers in hopes of getting a piece of the action by convincing them they somehow contribute to their good fortunes. Her brown, seductive eyes grew larger each hand he won, but insincere Vegas women like her didn't interest him. Soon he had amassed an impressive stack, about twelve grand. Raven knew this was enough to make any experienced pit boss sweat, and as he expected, a suit soon walked over.

"Hi, my name's Tommy. You're giving us some great action." The supervisor extended a hand in the friendly manner marketing had taught him.

Raven knew many card counters were flushed out by the intimidating power of the pit boss, but Raven never displayed any sign of fear to alert them. He returned the handshake, left-handed—a quirk he used to keep people off balance—but declined to give a name, simply saying, "And I'm glad to meet you."

Tommy continued undeterred, "We'd love to take care of you. The Palace has the best shows in town—all the headliners. Let's get you rated, and I'll set you up in a booth right up front."

"No thanks, I won't be playing very long." Raven stopped to glance at his watch. "Actually, I have to leave real soon." *Before you're on to me.*

The brunette tugged at his shirtsleeve, "Excuse me, but what does he mean by getting rated?" *Yeah, right, like she doesn't know.* Raven smelled her strong perfume as he quickly sized her up. She had an attractive figure, but her face wore the hard look of a woman who lived in the casinos.

Before he could answer, Tommy stepped up to the plate and leaned in five inches from her nose, "Sweetheart, rating is a way for us to track players. We log in how long they play, how much they bet, and how much they win or lose. This rating is used as a basis to give away comps."

"Oh, I see," she said, dismissing Tommy with an artificial smile. Then she whispered in Raven's ear, "If they were rating for hunks, I'd give you a really high score."

Raven squirmed uncomfortably and focused on the cards.

Tommy persisted. "I can set you up for two. Why don't you give me your name?"

"Thanks, but I think I'll just play a few more hands— then I've got to go." Raven ignored the brunette—this town was the least likely place to find the kind of woman he wanted. Rather ironic, he thought, because Las Vegas has more wedding chapels than any place in the world. He sighed and leaned back in his chair.

♣ ♦ ♥ ♠

In the surveillance room, Howard and Frank argued over what needed to be done with the young man who was fast becoming rich, courtesy of the Palace.

"Look," Howard said, "he could be a player or he could be someone just riding a hot streak. I say track his betting and play decisions with the computer software program and see how he checks out. If he's not a player, he should end up dumping all his winnings back in the rack."

Frank grimaced. "Come on, Howard, you know as well as I do that it'll take the computer thirty to forty-five minutes to determine if he is using a counting system. If he's smart, he'll be long gone by then."

Howard glanced at his watch; he had already missed the warm-up band.

"Hey, I told you it's nobody I recognize."

"You've been a big help," Frank said sarcastically. "I'll talk to the casino manager and see if we can't pay you more for all your expertise."

Howard grimaced. "Okay, you win, Frank. I'll stay just a few more minutes and see if we can flush him out. Call Tommy and have him ask the guy where he's from—that may trigger some memories."

♣ ♦ ♥ ♠

When the phone rang in the pit, Tommy answered and immediately looked at Raven before turning away—not a good sign. After hanging up, Tommy headed straight for him. *Rats, the wig's not working.*

"You sure you don't want to get rated? We've got some great gourmet restaurants—I just need your name and address. Are you local or from out of state?"

Raven decided to trust his instincts, take his winnings and head for the door. "You know, Tommy, I appreciate your offer, but I think for once I'd better quit while I'm ahead."

He stood up, but then decided to play one more hand to look relaxed. The cards hit the felt, first a jack followed by a six. Raven thoughtfully rubbed his nose as he often did when nervous and mentally scanned through the matrix he'd memorized. *Surrender or hit the stiff?*

The brunette dragged on a cigarette, cast a coy look at Raven and asked the dealer, "Where's a good place to eat here?"

"If you like Oriental food, you're in for an authentic treat," said the dealer.

She frowned. "I never liked eating with chopsticks. Any other suggestions?"

The dealer proceeded to review all the places to dine at the Palace. Raven drummed his fingers on the felt. *Does this guy really need to give so much detail on the caviar?* He desperately wanted to turn around and see if anyone from security had been alerted, but chose to appear cool and nonchalant.

The brunette, however, was in no hurry and delayed the dealer with another question. "Which restaurant is the most romantic?" She threw Raven a sultry glance.

"That would be our French restaurant. Fabulous ambiance and the best gourmet food in town. Get there just before sunset and you'll catch an incredible view."

"Sounds perfect. This may be an evening I'll never forget." She brushed Raven's leg under the table with her foot. He normally felt awkward around women, but this one was obnoxious and he shot her a warning look while pushing away the offending foot.

The phone rang again. Sweat materialized in small beads on his forehead. Finally, the dealer dealt the card; Raven busted his stiff, losing the last bet.

All that delay for nothing. He shook Tommy's hand and turned to leave.

♣ ♦ ♥ ♠

Upstairs surveillance scrutinized every aspect of the nameless gambler to determine whether he was a fox or a fish. Howard suddenly bolted out of his chair, "Frank, right there, zoom in on his arm. No, not the right arm, the other one shaking Tommy's hand. His watch, can you focus on that Rolex? That's it! Do you see it?"

Frank didn't understand Howard's sudden excitement. "I don't see anything, just a gold Rolex watch. Nothing unusual about that. It even has the correct time. What's the problem?"

"Look at the second hand. Do you see what it's doing?"

"Yeah, it's moving forward one second at a time. Correct me if I'm wrong, Howard, but I thought the purpose behind Mickey's big hand was to keep track of the seconds."

Howard inhaled deeply; now wasn't the moment for a power struggle. "Frank, the second hand on a Rolex watch does a continuous sweep. That second hand is clicking forward one second at a time. That's not a real Rolex."

"Okay, it's a fake. So what? You want to arrest him for buying a knockoff watch? I don't see the connection between..."

"Listen, Frank. Randolph Townsend wears a fake Rolex. Remember?"

Frank stared at the screen. "I don't know, he's about the same size as the Raven, but this guy looks an awful lot different."

The subject in question ran his fingers through his hair. To the casual observer it would have meant nothing, but to Howard Goldberg's trained eyes, it was the final confirmation.

"Did you see that? His hair just moved. He's wearing a wig! He's trying to do some bogus disguise and make us look like buffoons up here. Call Tommy and tell him the Raven has returned." Howard hit the door running, his heart racing in the excitement of the chase. This time they had the fox cornered.

Raven headed to the cashier's cage, but the brunette followed him and grabbed his arm. "Listen fella, I brought you all kinds of good luck. The least you can do is share some of your winnings with me."

He had no time for this. "Lady, there's no such thing as luck, and I don't like gold-diggers."

"You cheap ingrate," she hissed.

"I've got to go." *Happy hunting, sweetheart.* He pulled his arm away and rushed off.

She shouted after him, "I hope you lose it all back."

The phone rang again. All Raven's senses went on full alert. He'd cash the chips out later. For now, he needed to leave fast. *Good thing I parked the car facing out for a quick getaway.*

He made a beeline for the back elevators but suddenly froze. Two security guards spotted him. One whipped out his walkie-talkie as they approached. *Rats.* Raven slipped behind a row of slot machines, then broke into a brisk walk in the opposite direction. Plan B. He'd retrieve the car later.

Raven kept glancing over his shoulders.

So far so good.

He took another quick look. *Darn. More blue uniforms.*

He broke into a sprint with the guards in hot pursuit. People stopped to watch as he serpentined around tourists like a quarterback with the ball. He slightly bumped an elderly lady and spilled her bucket of tokens. He wanted to help her, but knew he couldn't stop. He shouted an apology and continued his mad dash for the front entrance, stopping abruptly to avoid crashing through the glass door. Raven turned, cast a parting glance at the guards, and stepped outside.

"Mr. Townsend." Raven stared in disbelief, as his old nemesis, Howard Goldberg, stood with hands on his hips blocking the way. "I'm surprised to see you again. I'm sure you remember our last meeting?" Frank and two new security guards soon joined them.

Raven decided to mask the apprehension he felt over seeing his blackjack career ending right before his eyes and responded with humor. "I don't have that good of a memory, but didn't we both audition for the Chippendales last month at the MGM?"

Howard laughed, "Very funny. Actually, I think you have one of the best memories in the world."

Frank stepped in. "Enough of this bullshit, Howard. Let's cut the chitchat and take care of this piece of work."

Raven felt trapped, but knew he hadn't broken any laws. "I haven't done anything illegal, and you know it."

Frank dismissed his argument with a wave of the hand. "Take him to the back room," he ordered the guards.

"That's false imprisonment. You can't do that," Raven said. He would not be intimidated. Besides, ever since two of his good friends were beaten within inches of their lives in a casino back room, he had a healthy fear of going behind closed doors.

Frank whispered to Howard who shook his head. "We'd like you to come with us so we can see some ID. Surely you don't have a problem with that."

It was a problem. He had $32,000 on him, and he trusted no one, not even the Palace who had a reputation for class.

"I know my rights. It's unfair to detain me against my will." Raven spoke loudly to gain the attention of the small throng of people stopping to watch the incident.

"Life's not supposed to be fair," answered Howard. "If it were, Elvis would still be alive and all the impersonators would be dead."

Frank didn't see the humor in the situation and maintained his stony expression. "Come on Howard, let's get this over with."

"Why won't you let me play twenty-one?" Raven asked, playing to the growing crowd. "You bar me for being a winning blackjack player, though I beat you honestly at your own game. The palace probably makes over a million dollars in profit every day from gambling, yet if someone takes the time to read a book on card counting and is bright enough to win, you throw them out. Why don't you put up a sign that says, 'Using Brains Inside Casino is Criminal Activity?'" Someone in the crowd chuckled.

Howard nodded. "Frank, you know he's right about being illegally detained. Read him the trespass act and have security escort him out of here."

Frank grudgingly consented.

Raven persisted, "Come on. Why won't you give your reason?" He wanted them to admit the truth in front of their paying customers.

Howard took a frustrated look around and then leaned forward. "Raven," he whispered, "you're just too good for Las Vegas."

♣ ♦ ♥ ♠

Raven worked his way down the crowded sidewalk along the Strip, incensed at the injustice of being treated like a felon. This part of the business was the most difficult to deal with—he hated the scrutiny and the harassment.

He stopped to watch the synthetic volcano erupt in front of the Mirage and noticed an older woman in sunglasses. She wore a bright pink visor and looked totally transfixed by the drama, rapidly taking pictures with an old Nikon. A balding, pudgy man in Bermuda shorts stood next to her.

"Pretty amazing, ain't it, Sis? When the Mirage opened, this man-made volcano attracted worldwide attention."

"I can see why," she said.

"Yep, but like everything else in this city, it's just an illusion. Eight-foot wide pipes supply 400 million BTU's per hour of natural gas to provide the theatrics, and the scent of pina colada is piped in to mask the smell of gas so tourists like you can imagine they're in the tropics."

She frowned at him. "Well, it works. We don't have anything like this in South Dakota."

"Yeah, but it's all fake—and like a flytrap. Look at Caesars. They got one-way moving sidewalks that bring people in. But just try and find your way out. Eighty-five percent of all visitors to Las Vegas will gamble, so the casinos do anything just to get you to walk through their doors."

"Be quiet, Harold. Just let me enjoy it." She snapped three more pictures and turned to her brother. "Honestly, I think you've lived here too long."

Something about the woman touched Raven. Her face reflected pure delight, amazement and awe. He tried to see the volcano through her eyes with no success. How did he get to be so jaded? As a teenager he collected the offering at Camden Hills Baptist Church—now he collected chips in Sin City. The volcano flared in a radiant orange climax and played out its last, precisely timed rumblings. He could still feel the heat as the flames died out. When it came to his soul, was he playing with fire? Life had been worlds apart back in Maine.

Chapter Two

♣ ♦ ♥ ♠

Raven leaned against the railing of the Vinalhaven ferry. He welcomed the ocean spray on his face, and the wind in his long, shaggy, dark hair. He was seventeen, and it would be his last summer on the island with Uncle Colby and Aunt Ethel. Maine felt too confining for him— he wanted to escape and explore the whole world. Next year at this time he hoped to be heading off to college. As he listened to the churning water rush by, he relived the times he'd spent roaming his uncle's eighty acres, land owned by the Townsend family for generations.

He'd been only eight when his mother died and that first summer he found solace exploring Colby's secluded property. From then on, his father grew more distant each year and continued to send him to Vinalhaven as soon as school ended, not knowing what else to do with him. Though Raven thrived amid the wide-open spaces of the island, he harbored a deep resentment toward his father for taking so little interest in him. Colby always treated him affectionately and Raven wondered why his father never acted as warmly.

As the ferry docked, he spotted Uncle Colby, prompt as usual. He greeted Raven with a crunching bear hug and drove him across the small island in an old rusted Ford pickup. Both windows were open and the familiar smells and sounds of the Atlantic rolled in across the bay. A foghorn blasted in the distance and a flock of seagulls screeched loudly to be heard over its din.

Colby parked next to his sturdy two-story cape cod style home. Several chickens scampered over; mistakenly thinking it was feeding time. Colby booted the leader with his right foot and the rest of the flock wisely stayed off the porch steps. Ethel gave Raven a warm embrace and made both of them take off their muddy shoes. The unmistakable aroma of freshly baked blueberry pie emanated from the wood stove. Raven downed three pieces and a large glass of raw cow's milk before his aunt was satisfied that her favorite nephew wasn't in danger of starving. Then he politely excused himself to head outside.

The air felt cool as he hiked through the woods and the familiar rush of freedom surged through him. His favorite retreat lay in a remote location near the south end of the property. Here the ground sloped steeply to a clearing where ancient oak trees and large boulders, arranged as if in formation, provided shelter from the Atlantic storms. Sifting through the soil around the stone ruins, he would imagine himself an archaeologist searching for artifacts. From this vantage point he could also watch the white sailboats in the bay and dream of ancient civilizations.

When he came within sight of his goal, he stopped, surprised. *Who is that in the clearing?* The entire nine summers he'd come here, he had never encountered another human being. As Raven drew nearer, it became apparent that the intruder was not a boy, as he'd first thought, but a girl with short hair. *Uh oh. What do I do? Moose I can handle, but women?*

She sat perched on his favorite rock; one hand shielded against the sun, and hadn't noticed him. Her black hair stood out in striking contrast to her red, flannel shirt. *What do I say? Hello? How's it going?* He practiced, mumbling to himself. Instead, when the telling moment came, he blurted out, "You're trespassing."

Startled at first, she recovered and hugged her long skinny legs tighter to her chest. "So?"

"This is my uncle's property." Although Colby Townsend had never put up any signs, any native Mainer would know not to cross the stonewall fences onto somebody's land.

Her blue eyes danced defiantly, "Too bad. I like it here."

Raven marveled at the captivating color of her pupils. The light shade reminded him of blue jays in its tone. He struggled to keep his stoic composure and not let her read his thoughts. "What if I make you leave?"

She raised an eyebrow. "You can't."

Raven stood stiffly and thrust his hands deeper into his jeans. He measured in at a Popsicle stick shy of six feet and didn't have a particularly muscular build, but he always tried to exude confidence. He hoped girls interpreted his coolness as mysterious and intriguing rather than aloof and unapproachable. "You might want to—this place is haunted."

"They must be well hidden." She pretended to look around for evil spirits under the rock. "Or maybe it's siesta time for demonic apparitions right now. Besides, you don't seem afraid."

Raven relaxed his posture slightly. "No, I'm not. This is Townsend land and Townsend men are as tough as wolverines."

"So you must belong to the long line of macho Mainers I've heard so much about—the type who fear nothing."

Raven squared his shoulders, "Yep, that's us. Not a coward in the entire clan."

She gave him a dubious expression. "Right. And not even these ghosts who haunt this place scare you?"

"No, but," Raven winked, "we're also very fast runners."

"I think I'll take my chances then. You can't really believe there's Indian spirits floating around, do you?"

"No, Viking."

"Vik—?" She giggled, "The guys with the horns?"

She held two fingers to her head in mock imitation. "Ooh, I'm so scared."

Raven grinned at her comical gestures.

"Do you live here?" she asked.

"Just summers—I stay with relatives and work at the bowling alley."

"I heard about candlepin bowling. Is it true they manually set up the pins knocked over after each frame?" She brushed back her bangs with long delicate fingers.

"Yeah, the ultimate career—picking up deadwood."

Raven scanned the area. "Unless Scotty beamed you down, I'm not sure just how you materialized out of nowhere."

"I'm visiting my grandmother—she lives up the road a few miles. It was such a nice morning; I decided to explore and just kept going. Incredible view here."

Her voice had a refined quality to it and Raven soon learned her name was Cynthia Bradford, that she'd just turned sixteen and hated boarding school. Her older brother and sister were already in college. She lived in Connecticut and had vacationed in Europe twice. Her father was a bigshot lawyer in Hartford and her family tree stretched like a caterpillar all the way back to Governor Bradford on the Mayflower. One thing was very clear—her lifestyle stood in stark contrast to his. He had never met anyone as so-phisticated as her before. Yet it surprised him how he felt so at ease, given his usual shyness with girls, and he made a mental note to warn Uncle Colby in case she came back onto their property. Colby exuded friendliness to those he knew, but had a different mentality when it came to strangers.

And Raven did want her to return. This was his first opportunity to show someone else the unique and mystical spot he had explored for years. "Ready for a tour?"

"Of what?" Cynthia asked. "Your collection of beer cans?"

"So you think all Maine teenagers get drunk and drive pickups?"

She grimaced. "Seems that way. At least from the ones I've met so far."

"Well, I'm more interested in archaeology than Anheuser-Busch. So if you can set aside your stereotypes for a moment, I'll show you some fascinating ancient ru-ins."

Her frown melted away into a cheerful expression. "Okay, you're on." Cynthia scrambled down from her rock, and he led her to the center of the stone formations.

"See this? During the ice age, the glaciers dragged huge boulders over the entire state of Maine, but these look more like a design." He pointed to faint imprints in the ground that suggested foundation lines of three buildings between the megaliths and the ocean.

"So, Indians built this place?" Cynthia asked.

"I found a bunch of arrowheads, and those large mounds over there definitely came from the Indians. They loved the clams, lobsters, and crabs around this island as well as the fish." Raven paused. "But, I don't think they built this."

"Really? Then who did?" she asked.

Raven hesitated; not sure he wanted to be laughed at again.

"Oh, I know," Cynthia howled. "Vikings!"

"Hey, it's just a theory, but I looked up some stuff in the encyclopedia." Raven spoke with mounting excitement in his voice. "The foundation lines would correspond to the pictures I saw of early Nordic long houses—and I found this."

He pulled a bronze ring pin out of his pocket and handed it to Cynthia who examined it closely. "Looks old, but what exactly is it?"

"Early Scandinavians used them to attach the cloak at the shoulder."

Cynthia rolled it around in her hand. "Interesting theory, but I'm sure there are other explanations for this pin."

"The last couple of years, I've spent hundreds of hours digging here," Raven said, growing more animated. "I love exploring and nothing got me more excited than finding this pin. It means I'm right."

Cynthia looked skeptical. "I can't believe Vikings lived here."

"I plan to research it more, but it seems possible to me."

They wandered back to the lookout rock and sat down. Cynthia pointed to an old oak splintered and charred by lightening, "Maybe that tree got zapped by Thor's hammer rather than a thunderbolt." Her eyes sparkled impishly.

"You're making fun of me."

"No, I'm not," Cynthia giggled. "Okay, maybe a little."

Raven began to explain more of his hypothesis to Cynthia, when he stopped suddenly, transfixed by a large spider on her shoulder. She looked at him, puzzled. Raven leaned slowly across her body and carefully maneuvered his right hand up her arm, positioned for a quick and surgical strike.

Cynthia leaped from the rock as if a bee had stung her. "How dare you, Raven Townsend?"

"What?"

"Trying to kiss me—the nerve!" She glared at him.

"Huh? What are you talking about?"

"I'm saving these lips for the one I intend to marry." She tossed her head.

Raven exploded in laughter. "Hey, I was just trying to save you from..." He paused, amused at how funny she looked when her eyes spewed indignant fire.

"From what?" Cynthia demanded.

Raven started to point out the arachnid, but it had fallen off during the commotion. "There was a spider perched on your shoulder. Besides, Miss Prim and Proper, why would I want to smooch you—I'd just get stuck in those braces."

Cynthia's face turned beet-red. "What audacity. I'm not used to being treated this way."

"Maybe you've been reading too many fairy tales," said Raven.

Cynthia refused to sit back down and stood defiantly with her hands on her hips. "You're not exactly Prince Tactful. Besides, I don't read fairy tales."

"Why not?"

"I prefer old classics or the Bible."

Raven looked at her thoughtfully for a moment. "Some people consider the Bible a book of myths."

"Well, they are wrong. It teaches the truth."

"Townsends don't go to church." He regretted the words the moment they'd been said and hastened to add, "But I've always believed in God. When you look at the stars or the ocean or even these oaks—you just have to accept someone made them. And even the purr of the cat is more amazing than any machine man created."

"I'm going to First Baptist with my grandmother this Sunday. Want to come?" Cynthia asked.

"I'll think about it, although it can't be any more boring than the bowling alley."

There really wasn't much else to do on the isolated nine by fourteen-mile island, so despite his misgivings, he attended Vinalhaven Church throughout the summer. Before long, much of this Christianity business began to make sense, but something still held him back from an all-out commitment.

Cynthia talked Raven into attending camp the last week of the summer. There the last vestige of doubt suddenly vanished. He wanted to make his life one that mattered. He gave his soul to God and later in the week, was baptized in the frigid lake.

The two of them hiked up the hill on the last day of camp. They barely reached the top when they realized they needed to head back down, since many parents were already arriving. Raven led the way.

Cynthia was animated. "I'm excited about seeing my mother and father again. It's been almost two months."

"Sounds like you really missed them," Raven said.

"Oh yes. There's no one I admire more than my parents. They've never wavered in their faith. And they have such a storybook marriage. Just like I hope to have."

"So I should start calling you Cinderella instead of Cynthia?"

She smiled warmly, "Not exactly. But they never kissed anyone else and I think that's more special than some fictional fairy tale."

"Really? That is amazing. So that's why you made such a big deal out of saving your lips that first day we met?" Raven asked.

"Precisely. Until I meet the man I intend to marry, they are off-limits."

Going down the hill took only ten minutes. There were still so many things Raven wanted to say. He felt close to this animated girl, but they had never even so much as held hands. His thoughts abruptly ended when Cynthia broke into a run and threw herself into the arms of her mother. Her dad leaned against the hood of a gold Mercedes and smiled at Raven in a guarded way. Her family acted warm and close, ingredients foreign to the Townsend clan. Cynthia promised to write and the luxury sedan drove away on the dirt road, leaving Raven in a cloud of dust.

CHAPTER THREE

♣ ◆ ♥ ♠

Old mansions with Greek columns and manicured lawns stood like sentinels along the oceanfront of Raven's hometown. Some had been built for sea captains as far back as the 1700's. For generations these relics of Camden aged gracefully, despite the elements hurled at them by the sea and Maine's frigid winters. Typically owned by "flatlanders," a term used to describe anyone from outside the state, the upper crust of the eastern seaboard vacationed here to flee the muggy heat of the big cities.

Raven knew his father didn't think much of the summer aristocracy. A rugged, headstrong man and suspicious of the "easy life," William Townsend believed the wealthy couldn't comprehend the virtue of hard work or the true value of a dollar. Above all else, he was fiercely independent, considered religion a private affair, and had no use for any organized church.

Raven started attending Camden Hills Baptist Church regularly. People there treated him kindly and they felt like family. He accepted the church's unwritten code—it made sense to avoid drinking and smoking and he didn't care much for dancing anyway. He heard that some Baptists considered cards to be tools of the devil, but it didn't seem to be a universally shared taboo. This relieved Raven since his happiest childhood memories were of playing cribbage and rummy with his friends and usually winning.

He worried over how his father would react to Raven's summer conversion, but William avoided the subject. Finally, one day in March, Raven arrived home from school to the familiar sight of his father splitting kindling by the woodpile. A tall, sinewy man with bristly gray hair that screamed for a comb, he wore a threadbare shirt and suspenders. His father called to him and Raven came over. William's bushy eyebrows drew together as he scrutinized his son for a moment.

"I'm hearing talk about you bragging to people with some hair-brained idea you're going to find Noah's Ark. What's gotten into you, Randolph?"

Raven had never liked being named after some long forgotten grandfather, but he knew his father would never call him anything else, so he had quit fighting over that years ago. "Nothing. Just planning ahead for my career after college."

"College!" William exploded. "No Townsend ever needed no fancy education and no Townsend ever left Maine."

"I want to serve God in archaeology. Pastor Cook believes that's my calling."

"Your calling," William snorted. "God helps those who help themselves and it's damn hard work. That's how I got ahead. Pulling myself up by my own bootstraps."

"Yeah, right. Looks like you didn't pull quite hard enough then," Raven said as he looked around at the weathered clapboard house with the sagging clothesline and the dilapidated barn and inhaled the pungent smell of manure.

William's steel blue eyes narrowed. "You watch your mouth, Randolph."

"Dad, I can't see working like a dog on the farm the way you have all your life with so little to show for it."

"You can't get something for nothing. You still got to work."

"That's why I want an education—so my hard work will pay off."

"Noah's Ark? You gotta come down from the clouds. How you going to afford college, Randolph?"

"I could get a basketball scholarship."

"Come on, you're too short to make it that far."

Raven's throat constricted. "How would you know? You never came to any of my games."

"Games ain't life." William slammed the ax violently into the wood. "And you think you're earning a ticket to heaven with this church stuff, telling people they're all going to burn in hell because they don't act like you. People don't want to hear that. You catch more bees with honey than vinegar. Everybody knows you can't baptize a cat."

Raven felt his teeth clenching involuntarily. He never liked to be criticized. "I haven't been telling people they're going to burn in hell."

William split two more pieces of maple into kindling. "Son, have you ever heard the story of the elephant and the mouse?"

Raven groaned. *Another one of dad's notorious animal parables.*

"An elephant and a mouse crossed an old, rickety wooden bridge together. The structure creaked and swayed from the weight. Upon reaching the other side, the mouse remarked to the elephant, 'Boy, did we ever make that bridge shake.'" William waved the ax in Raven's direction. "You people down there at Camden Baptist take yourselves far too seriously."

At this point Raven wished the baptized cat from earlier had eaten the mouse.

"You're wrong about our church and Pastor Cook, Dad." Raven knew one of the Commandments said to honor your father and mother, but he couldn't just lie down while his church got run over by this misguided tirade.

"Those people are giving you too many new-fangled ideas. Let me tell you something Randolph. God ain't doing nobody's work for them, and the only destiny you have will be controlled by you, not God."

"Stop trying to tell me what to think," Raven shouted. He turned abruptly and strode into the house. Ever since his mother died, his father had been impossible to live with. Under no circumstances would he stay on the farm. He would find a way to be a success and make a lot of money someday. That would show the old man.

♣ ♦ ♥ ♠

The senior graduation party was already well underway on the back field of Nickerson's farm when Raven parked his 650 Triumph, then picked his way across the grass to the bonfire, careful to avoid the empties and the cow flaps. He was sure other graduates around the country celebrated at hotels like the Hyatt, but here were Maine's finest—trying to look cool in a cow pasture.

Most of the class congregated near the fire, bodies gyrating to music blaring from large speakers set in the back of an old truck. Raven dubbed it 7-11 music; seven words repeated eleven times—trite stuff, nowhere near the artistic quality of the rock he preferred.

He had not planned to come at first because of his convictions against the excesses of partying, but at the last moment he decided to say farewell to his friends. He scouted around for one, but it was difficult to recognize faces in the evening shadows. Raven noticed a solitary figure in white standing under an apple tree, and thinking it Becky Sheldon from church, walked over to join her.

He ducked under a branch. "Hi Beck..." *Oops, wrong girl.* "Jennifer—didn't know it was you..."

Jennifer Ross, easily the cutest young woman in his class, looked stunning in her snowy dress and with her long blonde hair reflecting in the moonlight. Her only flaw was a slight cosmetic imperfection in her teeth that her braces had failed to bridge. When she was eight, the Taylor twins had decided to use her as a wheelbarrow, with each boy grabbing a leg. They eventually let her go and she landed on the sidewalk, mouth first. The result was a slight gap between her two front teeth and a guarded attitude around boys. At least until high school. That mind-set changed fast when she had met Butch Jackson.

A romantic vision, thought Raven, but Butch was not one to upset. *Maybe I'd feel a little less heat back at the bonfire.* He turned to leave.

Jennifer grabbed his elbow and stopped him. "Hey, I hear you got a basketball scholarship to Wheaton College. Congratulations."

"Thanks," Raven muttered while looking down at his shoes.

"I'm not surprised. I remember all the times I've watched you dribbling the ball down the road for hours, even on snow and ice." Jennifer used her hands to mimic Raven's flamboyant no-look, behind-the-back pass.

Raven looked at her with wide eyes. "You did?"

"Sure, and I thought you were crazy, but all that dedication paid off, didn't it?"

"Hope so."

"Wheaton—someone said that's the college Billy Graham went to." She looked at him quizzically. "You want to be a preacher—or a missionary?"

"No, an archaeologist," Raven replied.

"Well, Mr. Harmon is going to hate to see his best math student follow God. I know he wanted you to go to MIT."

Raven laughed. "I won't tell him then."

"I'm sure you'll succeed at whatever you do. I've never seen anyone more driven. When you decide you want something, everyone else better get off the road."

"I'm not that bad, am I?" Raven asked.

"No, it's good. Wish I were more like you." Jennifer turned to face him fully.

Raven nervously looked around. "Where's Butch? I thought you two were inseparable." As a star quarterback, Butch had the most imposing physique of anyone Raven knew, and he didn't want to tangle with him.

"He got into some macho beer-guzzling contest. Last I saw, he was puking his guts out. Heck of a way to celebrate, don't you think?" Jennifer said, "So what does a good Baptist do for fun? Don't all those rules take the zest out of life?"

"Come on. You don't think reading the Bible and praying all day long is grabbing all the gusto possible?" His words rang hollow. *I'm with a beautiful woman and I have to sound like Saint Francis of Assisi.*

She gazed wistfully at the moon and stepped closer. "Honestly, don't you have *any* regrets about missing out? Do you really think dancing is wrong or do you just believe what you're told?"

Raven had wondered the same thing lately. *Was it really my faith or did I just convert to impress a sixteen-year-old girl who I'll probably never see again?*

Jennifer's demure eyes flickered. "Well, I have regrets. All last year I used to wish you'd show up after a basketball game and dance just once with me." She paused and looked at him shyly. "Are you surprised?"

Surprised? Shocked would be a better word. His face began to flush and he suddenly had difficulty breathing. He tried to utter a response, but no audible words escaped his mouth.

She touched him again on the elbow and let her hand rest there. "Know why I wanted to dance with you?"

Raven shook his head.

"Those intense brown eyes fascinate me." She held his gaze for a moment. "There's something intriguing about you. I'm not really sure what—maybe a wild side you're not showing."

Jennifer's green eyes continued in their efforts to cast a spell on him, but he wasn't ready to capitulate. The music suddenly blared louder and Raven put his hands over his ears and made a comical face. "That decibel count's so high, the sheep might suffer permanent ear damage."

She giggled and laid both hands on his shoulders. "Would you dance with me now? Just one time?"

"I can't, Jennifer," Raven said though his knees shook. *Am I an idiot or what?*

"Okay, so dancing is out." A playful glint appeared in her eyes and her hands caressed his neck. "Are there any rules against kissing?"

His pastor had warned him to flee from temptation, but her face was so close...and her lips so inviting.

Out of the corner of his eye, Raven noticed Butch staggering towards them, two sheets to the wind, but still upright.

"What the hell's going on here?" Butch tried to focus on the two of them as he bobbed back and forth.

Jennifer didn't miss a beat. "Raven was just telling me his plans for school."

"I'm leaving next week for Chicago." Raven hoped this information would help.

Butch swayed like a pine tree in the wind, his speech slurred. "So, Maine ain't good enough for you, huh, Randy?"

"I'm certainly not going to stay here and work in the processing plant with you."

"You're too big for your britches. You'll end up broke like your old man."

Raven tensed at the mention of his father. "That's exactly why I'm leaving."

Butch scoffed, "Everyone comes back—especially anyone with Injun blood. You'll be running home to the teepee first sign of trouble."

This attack crystallized Raven's decision to leave Maine. He hated this town and bigots like Butch. Many had called Raven's mother a squaw and she definitely looked Indian. But the family birth records had been lost years ago and no one could ever officially prove her heritage. Consequently, Raven grew up with the taunts of prejudice without being able to reap any of the financial benefits available to Native American Indians. *For years I've put up with this stuff. No more. It's an insult to my mother's memory.*

Raven's rage poured out like hot lava. He screamed, "Don't ever expect to see me again."

"Like hell." Butch mocked. "You'll be crawling back here before Christmas."

Raven's face contorted in angry spasms. He desperately wanted to impress a clear picture of the significant destiny God had in store for him. The image of white mansions along the ocean came to him. He shouted, "That's where you're wrong. I'll *never* return unless I'm a millionaire."

Butch snickered and yelled to his classmates, "Do you hear that, everybody? Randy Redskin here says he ain't coming back unless he's rich enough to buy up our town." He staggered back to the bonfire.

Raven knew before long the whole class would hear about it. He hated nothing more than to be the brunt of jokes. If only he hadn't lost his temper and made a fool of himself. It'd be difficult to ever face his friends again.

♣   ♦   ♥   ♠

The barn smelled warm and musty a few days later as Raven went about his morning chores. He didn't like either end of the cows but he especially detested shoveling manure. His cat, Blackie, sat on a hay bale; Raven stopped to stroke her ears when the barn door flew open and William entered, his face a thundercloud. "Whose motorcycle is that?"

"Mine," Raven said.

"Someone give it to you?"

"I bought it," said Raven.

"Where'd you get the money for that?"

Raven didn't answer for a moment, then replied. "God helps those who help themselves."

William Townsend cringed over hearing his own words being thrown back in his face. "Ever since the church fire you've been acting different—like you're hiding something."

Raven prickled. He did have something to conceal, but wasn't about to share it here. Not with the most unforgiving person on the planet. "Why would I talk to you, Dad? Do you ever care about what's important to me?"

"I care when my boy goes around making a jackass out of himself—bragging he's going to be a millionaire to people." William dug his pitchfork into the hay and hurled it into the cow stall. "Now is your call from God or the dollar bill? I don't know if you want to be Moses or the next Rockefeller."

Raven fired back, "I won't be either if I follow your example. The only thing I'm going to inherit is that big Townsend nose." A stillness as icy as a Maine winter lingered for several minutes.

William finally responded. "I expected you to take over the farm."

Raven retorted, "Do you think I want to end up like you? Chained here to hard labor the rest of my life? You've never even set foot out of the state."

They worked in silence for a while. A solitary Canadian goose flew overhead, honking earnestly, desperately searching for the safety of the flock. Raven finally said, "Whatever happened to you anyway, Dad? Before Mom died you used to take me ice fishing…we'd go hunting together. Why did that all stop?"

William's lips pressed together in a firm line; he pitched the hay hard but said nothing. *Way to communicate, Dad.* Raven threw down the shovel and headed for the door. "That's it. I'm gone."

William yelled after him; "You won't last more than six months. You're not too good for Maine—Maine's too good for you."

Raven swiveled around, his eyes blazing. "I'm never coming back." He stormed out, went to his room and began packing.

CHAPTER FOUR

♣ ♦ ♥ ♠

Raven fidgeted in his library chair, unable to keep his mind on Egyptian history. His fingers drummed on the table. The basketball scholarship had covered his expenses through all four years at Wheaton College, but three terms of graduate school depleted his savings. Barely enough money remained to complete his second year and he needed a Ph.D. from the University of Chicago in order to get anywhere in archaeology. But he feared taking a part-time job might sink him academically.

Tired of dwelling on his financial worries, Raven wandered over to the magazine rack. He found an old issue of Sports Illustrated and thumbed through it. An article profiling a new breed of gamblers caught his attention. None of the three individuals interviewed—a sports bettor, a poker player, and a blackjack player fit the traditional stereotypes for gamblers. In fact, two of these men had been educated at Harvard and Dartmouth, and each one applied only a serious mathematical approach to their respective games.

Raven could see they weren't gamblers in the true sense of the word, but astute businessmen who took advantage of an edge, only placing bets when they were the favorite. He stared out the library window reflecting on what he had just read. Then revelation struck him as if he had decoded some ancient hieroglyphic text—Raven could have been the blackjack player. He always dominated card games involving skill, and most of his friends wouldn't play against him anymore. Yet here was a game that rewarded expertise and discipline with huge financial payoffs—and a place to put his unique memory to work. Better yet, maybe this was the answer to his money problems.

He spent the rest of the day in the library's gambling section. As Raven leafed through the books, he realized most were worthless. For every game of chance known, numerous books with systems on how to beat that game had been written. He saw no mathematical way craps, roulette, or the lottery could be mastered.

However, blackjack differed from other casino games because the future depended on the past. In roulette it didn't matter how many spins occurred after the number five was last hit—five still wasn't due and had no more chance of coming up on the next sequence than it did two hours ago. The same held true for craps. The shooter may have been hot—but on the next roll, there was still no greater chance of the dice totaling seven than on any previous rolls.

But in blackjack, the composition of the deck changed rapidly as cards were played and removed. In a one-deck game, if three aces came out on the first hand, the chances for a blackjack on the following hand declined dramatically. Unlike any other casino game, the past impacted the future in blackjack, and that twist made it exploitable. It all made so much sense to Raven. Now, he just needed to find the right book to get started.

One title jumped out at him—*Easy Riches in Blackjack*. The author claimed to be a highly successful player and asserted that untapped riches lay waiting at the blackjack tables. Raven read on, occasionally stopping to digest a new piece of information. If the numbers presented were accurate, he'd easily make a lot of money playing blackjack part-time and cover his nut for grad school.

All the way home, a battle raged in his mind. His hopes rose in excitement at the potential he saw in card counting, then plummeted with doubts. Would he have the aptitude to become a professional card counter? He guessed he did, but how could he know for sure? Would he have what it took to make it on a world-class level? The problem of putting together a bankroll also ate at him. How would he scrape up the money? In the shadows of the practical questions lurked a moral question: Could he justify gambling in light of his Christian beliefs?

Back in his run-down apartment, he hung up his coat, tossed the blackjack book on the counter, and headed to the refrigerator. He pushed aside some moldy cheese before discovering the donut that time forgot. In the twenty seconds the microwave took to revive the dried-out pastry, he made up his mind. Despite his reservations, it was one of the easiest decisions he had ever made. Blackjack provided the potential of huge paydays and a way to live the American dream—he could get free hotel rooms, free shows and free meals at gourmet restaurants. The book said he might even fly first class to casinos around the world once he became a high roller. The lure of easy money and the enticement of glamour and adventure proved irresistible for someone tired of eating bologna on stale bread.

He carried the donut into the living room where Joel West and Tim Reynolds sat on the vinyl sofa, eating pizza and watching TV, their feet propped up on the rickety coffee table. His roommate, Joel, was sprawled shirtless on the couch like a tanned Tarzan, his long, blond locks framing a face chiseled in Wild-West ruggedness. *There lies the campus heartthrob.* Raven gazed at the six-foot, six-inch forward who starred with him on the Wheaton College varsity; routinely slam-dunking Raven's lob passes.

Tim, on the other hand, looked studious as ever with his wire-rim glasses, conservative buzz cut and serious expression. *The only sport he might have lettered in was Scrabble.* The contrast between the two friends amused Raven—Joel lit up any room he entered while Tim fumbled for the light switch.

Raven wondered how his peers would react to his dramatic discovery. He walked over to the tube and turned it off.

Joel leaped from the couch. "What do you think you're doing? In case you didn't notice, we were watching Star Trek."

"Yeah, yeah. I hate to interrupt such an exhilarating moment, but I've got something important to bounce off you two," Raven said.

Joel still protested. "What's so significant that you butt in right when Kirk is about to kiss the Romulan vixen?"

Tim laughed, "Joel, the captain of the Enterprise always gets the girl cause he's a babe magnet; now if Spock were enjoying a romantic interlude…"

Hands on his hips, Joel feigned indignation. "Great. Now I'll never be able to watch this show again since you've given away the secret plot line."

Raven stood in front of the television and faced them. "I just came across the most incredible concept—the casino game of blackjack can be beat by skilled card counters."

"So?" Joel sat back down and stretched his long legs across the coffee table.

"I think I could be one of those people," Raven said firmly.

His two best friends from his Wheaton College days stared at him in disbelief.

Tim reacted first. "Are you crazy? You're out there where the buses don't run. How can you even consider gambling?"

"Money, Tim. I'm just barely making it through grad school. Blackjack is no different than any other job, except it pays a lot more."

Tim looked skeptical. "Yes, but in a casino? Raven, there's no way you can place yourself in that environment and come out unscathed."

Joel wasn't sure whose side to take. He came from a long line of pastors and evangelists. His great-grandfather had even been one of the founders of Wheaton College. "What about your dream of archaeology? My family would shoot me if I veered off my mission in life to become a gambler," Joel said.

Raven didn't like being double-teamed in basketball, and he didn't relish it here. "It's not like I'm turning my back on God. Blackjack is only a means to an end. When the time comes, I'll just walk away."

Joel frowned. "I like the potential of making big bucks, but something about your idea still sounds wrong. Dead wrong. Gambling and Christianity just don't mix."

"That's the beauty of it. I'm not really gambling."

Joel brushed his long blond hair out of the way. "You lost me there."

"See, I've got an edge. So it really isn't gambling—I'm the favorite—a far cry from someone who gambles away his paycheck every weekend with no realistic hope of winning."

"Look," said Tim, "I know you're got a phenomenal mind for math, but it sounds like you're rationalizing to me."

Raven switched gears. "Tim, if I wanted to be a missionary, I would go to where the sinners are, right? Jesus always hung out with the dregs of society."

"Give me a break, Raven." Tim shot back. "Jesus didn't hang out with sinners to make money."

Joel tried to bridge the gap between the two positions. "Raven, maybe it's not necessarily wrong for you to make money gambling, but do you really think that's how you want to invest your life—winning money off other people?"

Raven grabbed the last slice of pizza. "Card counters don't play against other customers—only against the casino. There's even a certain nobility in taking money from the wicked and putting it into the hands of the righteous."

Tim rolled his eyes. "Sounds pretty convoluted to me."

Raven stopped pacing and sat down in the threadbare olive recliner, facing his friends. "Gambling just doesn't carry the stigma it used to. Look at Vegas—it's become a tourist town catering to families."

"I agree that the stigma is less of an issue in our generation," Joel said, "but that doesn't mean it's been eradicated."

"It is for me. I just can't see any other way to pay for my education." Raven said.

Joel shrugged and shook his head. Tim started to speak, but Raven decided the conversation was over, grabbed his coat and headed for the store to buy a deck of cards.

♣ ♦ ♥ ♠

The next two nights, Raven practiced with crisp, new Bicycle cards on the wobbly dining room table. He practiced learning the simple count explained in *Easy Riches in Blackjack*. The count allocated plus one numbers to the little cards and minus one numbers to the tens and aces. Whenever the count went positive, the odds improved for the players. Soon he felt confident of his abilities and decided to unleash his new abilities on the unsuspecting blackjack world that weekend. Harrah's owned two riverboats in Joliet, a twenty-five minute drive away—he'd find out quickly whether or not he was a player.

As Raven pulled into the casino parking lot, the riverboat gave two short blasts and began pulling away from the dock. He quickly parked and sprinted to the boarding area just as the vessel stopped a short way out on the river. He waited to see if the boat would return soon but nothing happened.

Great. What do I do now?

A portly man with a spare tire around his gut caught his eye. He sat near the coffee machine and waved Raven over.

"Too late, young man. Might as well keep me company while you wait for the next one. My name's Walter by the way." He pulled out an empty chair for Raven.

"Thanks," said Raven as he sat down and introduced himself. "How long is the wait?"

"Two hours 'til the next sailing," the man said. Grinning at Raven's bewildered expression, he added, "Welcome to the world of riverboats, son. Government restrictions allow boarding only at certain times."

Raven frowned. "Are you serious?"

"Yes, indeed. The only way casino proponents hoodwinked people into allowing gambling here was by convincing them that riverboats would avoid the evils of land-based gaming. Return to the idyllic era of Mark Twain, they said. What a load of crap. As if six feet of water can cleanse gambling and transform it into something reputable."

This was all new to Raven. "Really? I assumed I could just walk on anytime."

"No, that would be way too easy. What's really laughable is that often the vessel doesn't even leave the dock. But they still lock their doors and won't allow any one on until the 'cruise' is over."

Walter got up to refill his coffee. "They actually prefer not to sail and will use any excuse to stay docked. Might claim the wind or rain will threaten voyage safety so they can stay put. Sometimes they take a 'ghost cruise'—pull a few yards away and sit the entire time."

"Like they're doing now. Looks pretty ridiculous."
Raven shook his head.

"You got that right. When they do depart, they often just drift aimlessly. In some places, such as the Ohio River, they're forced to stick to the Indiana shoreline—they don't dare stray into Kentucky's territorial waters where gambling is illegal. Other states, like Missouri, created ponds connected to the rivers by shallow waterways in order to be legal. People called them 'boats in moats.' They never sail anywhere and don't even have captains."

"Does seem pretty far removed from the days of Huck Finn," Raven remarked.

"All kinds of wacky rules in this industry. Iowa, for instance, established loss limits on all their boats and restricted the maximum amount of chips a gambler could buy to $200 per day—wanted to protect the good farm folk from losing all their pigs in one sitting."

Raven chuckled in amusement as Walter continued. "The restrictions of that law killed business and left tax revenues far below projections. Eventually many ships went under or simply moved to states with higher limits, leaving several communities with empty wallets after having coughed up large sums to develop riverfront gambling. The huge influx of tourism and money that had been promised never came about."

Raven stood up and stepped over to the window to watch the ship sitting on the water only a few yards away. Other people now slowly filed in for the next voyage. He walked outside for a while and then rejoined Walter. "So what's your story—how'd you get to be so knowledgeable about riverboats? And if you're such an expert, why did you miss the sailing?"

Walter chortled. "I'm a bus driver. Come here twice every weekday with a group from various retirement homes around Chicago."

"So you don't gamble?"

"Exactly. You have to be dumb as a stump to cash your paycheck here—been around these places too long. I observe it everyday, how fast people's perspectives change when they enter the casino. It's a surreal environment and it pumps everyone's adrenaline levels up a couple of notches. As soon as people rush on board, all the energy of the place overloads their senses."

Raven had trouble envisioning senior citizens in walkers knocking over people to get onto the boat, but it created an interesting mental picture.

Walter set down his coffee cup. "But the odds—everything is designed for the casinos to take money in, not give it out. On the bus ride over, you sense the excitement, and people are pretty chatty. A couple hours later, the euphoria wears off and the same people now have long faces while standing in line at the cash machine. Hate to say it, but few return home winners."

Raven thought about explaining why he expected to walk away with a fat wallet. But he didn't want to blow his cover, so he shifted the conversation to small talk. Eventually the doors opened to the boat and everyone in the lounge scurried into position. Raven thanked the bus driver for his time and helpful information before joining the crowd pouring into the casino. He noticed how the pace quickened and people's eyes widened as they surged onto the boat just as Walter had said.

Once inside, he drank in the bustling scene. *What a sight. So many gamblers testing fate. Bet not one of them has ever taken the time to read a book on blackjack.* He felt like the only sage on a ship of fools. Radiating with confidence, he wondered if the casino would detect this new threat to their bankroll.

He sat down at the nearest blackjack table and laid down a twenty-dollar bill. The dealer quickly dropped the bill into a slot and wished him good luck. His confidence faded as he fumbled with the chips—the enormity of the venture suddenly overwhelmed him. The dealer shuffled and Raven sat stunned before the hundreds of cards. At home he had practiced with only fifty-two cards—according to his book, single deck was the best game to play.

Meekly he asked the dealer, "How many decks are you using?"

"Six decks, and they're dealt out of this shoe." She pointed a long, manicured fingernail to the card-feeding container on her left.

"Really? I thought shoes were only for your feet." His tablemates laughed at the greenhorn.

The first four or five hands, Raven made some mistake on each play, bringing a rebuke from the dealer.

"Don't touch the cards."

"Please scratch the felt with your hand for another card."

"Don't yell 'hit me' as if you're in some stupid movie."

Raven grew visibly embarrassed as others around him groaned. *They're thinking I'll cause the whole table to lose.*

The first hour felt like a blur. Raven lost track of the numbers every time a cocktail waitress interrupted him. He found counting in the real world much harder than playing in the serenity of his living room. He struggled to maintain his concentration when the slot machines clanked out their big wins or whenever craps players screamed in delight. Raven wondered if it was even physically possible to count cards in a casino without being deaf. Though slightly ahead, he hardly felt like a winning player since he hadn't accurately kept the count through even one shoe. A sobering fear replaced the cockiness he experienced on entering the boat: *Maybe I'm in way over my head.* He cashed out his chips and decided to take a short break.

The top deck lay empty. He walked out into the cool fall air and inhaled deeply. It felt good to get away from the smoke and noise. After ten minutes, he felt ready to try again and went downstairs.

He scouted for a quieter table and found one on the lower deck, away from the staccato interruptions of the slot machines. Raven nervously bought in for another twenty bucks, knowing his thin wallet left little margin for error.

He reviewed what he'd learned from the book. The whole premise of card counting consisted of betting more when the count became positive from an abundance of small cards having been played. To gain an overall advantage, the experts bet very small on negative counts, and increase their wagers when the count rises in hope of snagging the many picture cards remaining. Raven knew the larger the spread between these small waiting bets and the bigger top ones, the greater the edge. Betting five bucks on a negative count and twenty-five on a positive gave a one to five spread. Dropping to one buck on the low end, and jumping to twenty-five bucks when it was juicy gave a much stronger one to twenty-five spread.

Raven hadn't given a lot of thought to money management, and began with a two to twenty spread. He relaxed and found it easier this time to keep track as the count slowly rose. Tentatively, he put out five-dollar chips, then increased to ten dollars a hand. The count kept going straight up and Raven hit a hot streak. Soon he was betting twenty bucks a pop and his confidence soared as the chips began to accumulate into huge stacks. Within an hour he was up $300.

Wow! That's more money than I ever earned any day of my life, and I raked it in without even breaking a sweat. With this new skill he'd acquired, surely all his financial problems would melt away.

He felt like a completely different person—he had experienced similar transformations in basketball. Off court, Raven tended to be somewhat reserved and self-conscious around people, yet when he ran through the tunnel and in front of the screaming crowds, he became his idol, Pistol Pete Maravich, playing to the fans for attention.

Winning exhilarated him, especially knowing why he won. He was skilled, obviously the most proficient player on the boat—a heady feeling. When others began commenting on his good luck, he hinted that he knew what he was doing. To show off during high counts, he informed his tablemates that a lot of picture cards would come out on the next round. He even confidently predicted his hit cards as he won nearly every hand.

Although he started with a top bet of twenty dollars, he decided it wouldn't hurt to go a little higher, so he switched to twenty-five dollar chips, called quarters. He figured since he won so much with his small bets, he could win even more with larger bets. The other players at the table became his fans as they marveled at the piles of chips he amassed. He reasoned they would be even more impressed if he could turn the stack of red five-dollar chips into a mountain of green twenty-five dollar chips. But the cards turned slightly, and he began to lose a little bit back. He decided to bet more, and promised himself he'd quit once he reached his high water mark of $600 again. The top bet now became fifty dollars and his first hand was a blackjack for seventy-five dollars. He glanced at his watch and figured if he won a few more hands at fifty bucks a pop, he could be home by nine with $600 in profit and still have time to do his homework.

Suddenly and inexplicably, the cards turned cold. The psychic way in which Raven had turned all his stiffs into winners earlier now became a frustrating series of busting hand after hand. The few times when he did catch a card and make 20, the dealer inevitably stroked out a five-card 21.

He was crushed.

In less than two shoes, he went from nearly $600 ahead to actually being behind. His face flushed and once again he had trouble keeping the count. When it finally ended, Raven had completely tapped out. Not a chip remained in his huge mound. The "fans" who praised him just an hour ago fell silent. He was just another loser, lucky for a while, who crashed back to earth like everyone else.

Raven slowly got up from the table, shaken, a flood of questions bombarding him.

What went wrong? Is counting really a viable way to win or just another bogus scam? It seemed so easy at first. I won just like the book said. Did the casino start to cheat me?

As he drove back to Chicago, he came up with another explanation for what happened: God was trying to tell him something. Raven reluctantly concluded his roommates were right—gambling was immoral; he had disregarded wise advice and plunged in anyway. God let him experience a humiliating loss in order to prove a point. Raven learned his lesson and vowed never to gamble again. He'd find another way to finance his Ph.D. because card counting would never work with God looking over his shoulder.

He told no one about this secret foray into the world of gambling. When Joel asked him why he didn't practice anymore, Raven mumbled something about blackjack not being practical and he decided to forget the whole thing. Joel's knowing smile hurt Raven's pride—he hated the words "I told you so"—and Joel's expression said as much.

CHAPTER FIVE

♣ ♦ ♥ ♠

A couple months passed and Christmas approached. Joel had Raven drive him to the airport for his flight home. They both leaned toward the middle of the car to catch what little heat emanated from the vent.

Joel said, "Raven, I can't believe you're staying in this ice box over Christmas. Why don't you mend the fences with your father and head home?"

Raven stared straight ahead at the traffic. His pride and bitterness awoke from their dormant state. "There's nothing left for me in Maine. It's colder there than here, and I don't need my old man telling me what I'm doing wrong."

"Maybe you're being too harsh."

"And maybe you don't know my father. We didn't have any of that close, loving family stuff like you." Raven fiddled with the controls, trying to coax out a little more warmth. "He should be happy that I've buried the hatchet enough to call him once a month."

Joel shook his head and grinned. "You buried it all right—in the middle of his back." He cupped his hands together and blew on them. "Sure I can't get you to come home with me?"

"Appreciate the offer, but I've got to get some seasonal job over the holidays." Raven barely had the money to get through the next two months, let alone two more years of grad school.

"Okay, although I don't see how anyone can work over Christmas."

Raven figured Joel couldn't understand anyone working at all. Though Joel grew up in a family with twelve siblings, he had never known financial hardship. Joel's dad had the soft hands of a banker; years of physical labor gave the Townsend men rough calluses. Raven's grandfather had died from working in the marble quarries on Vinalhaven. That traumatic event hardened William Townsend, strengthening his distrust of anyone with money.

Raven saw Joel off at the gate and returned to the campus library to wrap up his term paper on Noah's Ark. He found numerous historical accounts of people viewing the Ark, including several in the last century. He crosschecked those reports with weather records—every instance occurred in an exceptionally hot summer. Raven concluded the boat must be hidden by ice and snow, only visible when the covering melted.

He collected his books to leave. On a lark he tossed the backpack onto the table and wandered over to the gambling section. He had some time to kill and decided to take a retrospective look at where he had gone wrong.

Easy Riches in Blackjack was checked out. He wondered if some other gullible young student sat at home dreaming of wealth. Raven knew better now. The game wasn't easy to beat.

He turned to leave, but a flashy title caught his attention: *Million Dollar Blackjack* by Ken Uston. Raven immediately recognized the name—Uston was the subject of the old Sports Illustrated magazine article that inspired

Raven's ill-fated attempt at gambling. The title of the book intrigued him—would Uston make the outlandish promise that anyone who read his book would become a millionaire? Raven had learned how difficult plundering the casinos could be. Though cynical, he had nothing planned for that night, and in one decisive movement, grabbed the book from the shelf and took it home.

He finished the volume in one sitting. Uston claimed he had won millions from casinos and explained how. The light turned on halfway through the book when Raven realized that the main reason he had lost was because of poor preparation. Maybe God wasn't a cosmic killjoy after all— the supernatural policeman who had foiled his endeavor. It had been his own fault. Raven had overbet in relation to his bankroll—no wonder he tapped out. The other book had painted far too simplistic a portrait of "beating the bad guys," and running to the bank filthy rich. It wasn't realistic to practice for only two nights and expect to become a winning blackjack player. Without a moment's hesitation, Raven re-dedicated himself to card counting.

♣ ♦ ♥ ♠

With Joel gone over the two-week Christmas break, Raven practiced undisturbed for ten hours each day learning a new, more complex count. Rather than the simple plus-minus system, he memorized a level-two advanced point count. The tens and face cards all counted minus two and the four and fives were plus two. The other small cards were valued at plus one and aces were tracked separately. Though harder to master, Raven intuitively recognized it would be superior in the long run. He used flash cards to learn the nearly two hundred matrix numbers and drilled himself relentlessly.

Every night he ended his training session by simulating two hours of casino play—dealing himself cards and using chips. He recorded the results in a log—only if he beat the house in a controlled setting would he ever set foot back in a casino. While practicing, he played loud music, or had the television blaring in order to discipline himself to focus despite background distractions. He placed an empty pipe in his mouth to prevent a fatal habit—lips mouthing the count—and learned to keep a separate side-count of aces using a system of sixteen various foot positions.

Uston said everyone on his blackjack team counted down a deck by flipping the cards rapidly while keeping a running tally in less than twenty-five seconds. The elite players on his squad clocked in at a scorching fifteen to twenty seconds. Raven worked three hours a day on that one exercise. His first attempts were laughable—he barely broke sixty seconds and only a few times ended back on zero at the last card. Simply the physical act of flipping through the cards in less than twenty seconds looked like an impossible task, but Raven thrived on challenges. Everyone had always told him no one under six feet would get to the next level in basketball, yet somehow he made it to college and flourished there. He thought of nothing besides blackjack for two weeks. The hard work paid off as first he reached the goal of counting down a deck in less than twenty-five seconds and later shaved it down to seventeen seconds. He had arrived.

♣ ♦ ♥ ♠

As Raven walked up the ramp of Harrah's riverboat—the scene of his previous disaster—he wondered if anyone would remember the bumbling beginner who lost all his money a few months earlier. The blank stares in the pit revealed no sign of recognition—hardly surprising since hundreds of nameless gamblers came, saw, and got their butts kicked every day.

This time Raven came prepared. His records showed he consistently beat the game—at least at home. Now he wanted to do a trial run in the casino by simply back counting the tables without playing a hand. If he could manage that successfully, he'd be ready to bet money the next trip.

He stood near the entrance and surveyed the bustling casino. He picked a crowded table in the middle and moved close enough to see each card played. The distractions hardly fazed him and he easily kept pace with the fastest dealers who threw around cards like they were getting paid by the hand, rather than by the hour.

The next night Raven returned again—this time for real. The critical test would be to keep the count while playing the hands and betting with chips. He selected an end seat on a two-dollar table. He focused intently on the cards and spread from two to twenty dollars according to his prearranged plan. He felt completely in control this time around—he had no compulsion to overbet, and was unconcerned with impressing others at the table. He came to make money and it worked.

For the next month he played every weekend while juggling his school schedule. Of those eight sessions, six were winners. Unfortunately, he wasn't making much money. The books told him to expect to win about one-fourth of his maximum bet. Since his top bet was only twenty dollars, the expected return stood at only five bucks an hour. While it felt good to succeed and to actually beat the casino, such meager wages weren't going to cut it. To make any serious money would require a radical step.

Raven had nearly $5,000 tucked away for his education—once those savings ran out, he wasn't sure how he'd afford the university. Over and over in his mind, he toyed with taking a calculated risk—of using his tuition money for his bankroll. With five grand he could bet up to fifty dollars and expect to win about a hundred bucks a day. If he did well at the outset, he could increase his top bet as the bankroll grew and realize an even greater return.

At least that was the theory. The reality contained complex elements on a deeper level. First of all, the personal risk in taking such a step scared the wits out of him. Raven had been independent since he was eighteen and had worked hard for every penny. If he lost his hard-earned nest egg, he'd be forced to drop out of grad school. He hated being laughed at and feared becoming the object lesson in someone's story about what not to do in life.

Raven didn't know if he could handle facing his college friends if he, with a reputation for frugality, had squandered his savings in a casino. Nor would he be able to tell his father, who had difficulty parting with money, and always lived in great trepidation of losing it all. This genetic fear of failure got passed down to Raven and terrified him more than anything else.

He continued to weigh the pros and cons of risking the five grand. In the end he made his decision in a highly unscientific way for a logical mathematician, and deeply unspiritual for a Christian—he flipped a coin. Heads, he'd play it safe. Tails—he'd risk it all. The Walking Liberty half-dollar Raven carried in his pocket ever since finding it as a kid hovered for a moment before tipping over to the eagle's side. It came up tails. Raven stuffed the coin back in his pocket and prepared to put it all on the line.

♣ ♦ ♥ ♠

Raven worked every Friday and Saturday trying to put in as many hours as possible at the riverboat casino, and he soon saw the dark side of the gaming industry. Many regulars gambled away their paychecks week after week. Raven wasn't immune to the compulsive forces that tug at the very soul while gambling, but he was able to shut off a part of himself, remaining detached and unemotional.

The major difference between him and other casino patrons was the longer he played in good games with an edge, the more he would win. For most gamblers, the more they played, the more they lost. Professional card counters understood this concept, but few were as disciplined as Raven. He always approached every situation in life with logic—the perfect ingredient for becoming a world-class blackjack player. He slowly became a machine at the tables, unfazed by bad luck or losing streaks.

In the long run all the little things evened out; there was no way to predict when he would win or lose, or which table to play. Many people gambled all night to try and get even. Raven considered that irrational. The cards had no memory. They didn't know how much you had won or lost that day and the casino would still be open for business tomorrow. No amount of positive thinking or metaphysics could change the cards or their outcome.

After nearly two months of playing at the new chip level, he was up only four hundred dollars—better than losing, but a long ways from the success stories in Uston's book. The sessions were like roller coaster rides—some moments he flew high and other times he felt as if he were falling off a cliff. Yet he still retained faith in himself and in his system. On a blustery March evening, he soon found out that huge swings weren't always bad.

An enormous crowd swelled the riverboat for Saint Patrick's Day; many of them hoping the luck of the Irish might rest on their dice and cards. Raven fought through the masses and began another grinding weekend of full tables and slow play.

The first few shoes ran cold and Raven estimated he had dropped about a hundred bucks. Two players left the table, speeding up the game. Suddenly the count shot up and Raven quickly went to his top bet of fifty dollars. He won the next ten hands. By the end of the shoe, he stood over six hundred bucks ahead.

Finally, things were turning around.

The hot streak continued and by eight o'clock that night, he passed a thousand dollars. Euphoric, Raven got up to leave and cash out his first big win when an elderly pit boss came over to greet him.

"Congratulations, son. Nice win. Have we been rating you?"

Raven gave him a puzzled look. He had read a little about rating in Uston's books, but wasn't quite sure how it worked or if he should keep a lower profile. "No, I never got around to getting a player's card," he replied.

"Well, I've noticed you in here a lot and it's really for your benefit. We track how much you bet and you get comps, or complimentaries, based on your play."

Raven thought that over. "Okay, I guess I'll try it."

The pit boss flashed a kind smile. "Good. For starters, how does dinner in our steakhouse sound?"

Raven went straight to the restaurant and scanned the menu—it seemed too good to be true that he could order anything, and as much as he wanted. No one knew it was his twenty-fifth birthday, and he felt as if this first comped meal was a secret gift. He chose the most expensive item, the steak and lobster, and savored every bite.

Nothing tastes as delicious as a free meal.

He had made one grand in a single day, his first real breakthrough in blackjack—more money than he had ever made in weeks at any other job. His feet seemed to float as he glided out of the casino wondering if life could get any better.

♣ ♦ ♥ ♠

Joel and Tim were embroiled in a chess game when Raven entered the apartment, the grin of a Cheshire cat pasted across his face.

"What's with you?" Joel asked.

"I just had the best birthday of my life," Raven said. "Check out this wad."

He pulled out ten hundred-dollar bills and waved the Franklins around as he danced on the sofa.

Joel's face lit up. "No way. Tell me you didn't win all that."

Raven kissed the C-notes tenderly and placed them back inside his wallet. "It's the truth. My first $1,000 day." He paused. "The first of many."

Tim didn't share Raven's enthusiasm or Joel's amazement. "I'm glad you won, because I honestly thought you would lose your shorts with this crazy idea of gambling."

Raven bubbled with energy, "I told you guys this isn't gambling. I'm the favorite because I have the advantage. Today proved that and changes everything."

Tim folded his arms. "Consider me still a skeptic. What exactly does this change? No matter what you want to call it, I'm still calling it wrong."

"Look. If I play blackjack every day this summer, I may solve all my grad school money problems."

Tim's face saddened. "You can't be serious, Raven. A lot of guys want to be movie stars or famous athletes, but those industries just chew them up and spit them out. Very few retain their integrity. The casinos will do the same to you."

"Tim, you don't need to worry about me slipping off the path. It's just hard to say no to such an incredible opportunity," Raven said. "Do you remember our favorite teacher?"

"Of course. He gave us the assignment to lie on our backs and gaze at the stars. Great lesson for keeping our perspective in life," said Tim.

Raven nodded in agreement. "Exactly. And he gave another example of perspective I'll never forget. He said the best way to appreciate anything is to see it in contrast. Like a diamond against black velvet."

Tim scratched his head quizzically. "I fail to see any connection between that analogy and gambling."

Raven laid his winnings out in a neat line on the coffee table. "You guys know my background, right? My family didn't have indoor plumbing and I never got to take a shower until I played basketball in high school."

Joel chimed in, "How could we forget that?"

"Good, because the contrast between my poverty and this opportunity is as great as that white diamond against the velvet. I, for one, am not going to pass up the chance to change my life for the better."

Tim shook his head in defeat. "I know how strong-willed and determined you are, but heed one last warning from a friend. Be careful the sparkle of the diamond doesn't blind you from your real goal in life."

"That will never happen," said Raven confidently. "I guarantee in a few years you'll see my picture on the cover of Biblical Archaeology Review, with one foot resting on Noah's Ark."

CHAPTER SIX

♣ ♦ ♥ ♠

The windy city skyline rapidly grew distant in the rear view mirror as Raven attempted to keep up with the faster vehicles on I-94 in his old Dodge Dart. He blocked out any disdainful stares from other motorists by imagining himself somewhat like a secret agent entering a foreign country undercover. After all, who would suspect the driver of this bucket of rust was actually a walking data bank with an uncanny ability to recall numbers?

He reflected on how his decision to risk all his savings had paid off—proud over doubling his original $5,000. Now he could plunk down a hundred bucks on the big counts. Though his friends discouraged him, the next logical step was to gamble full-time over the summer. The success of the last six months tempered his apprehensions about venturing into new territory. Self-confidence flowed through his veins. The gambling establishments of Minnesota had no clue that a new menace headed their way.

♣ ♦ ♥ ♠

He experienced a jolt of culture shock upon entering the Mystic Casino. The place was huge and much glitzier than the drab riverboats in Illinois.

Raven was also puzzled to find no Indians working there. He had assumed the dealers and other staff would be Native Americans. Either the tribe had hired an outside management team to run the casino or the Indians were all hidden behind the slot machines, concealed better than they were at the Little Big Horn.

Raven's attention immediately shifted to an elderly lady a few feet away who let out a squeal louder than the echoing bells booming from her machine. She had lined up three sevens and hit a jackpot. Raven edged closer and peered over her shoulder to see how much she had won.

Her demeanor shifted from excitement to distrust as she covered her coins from Raven. "Listen sonny, if you're looking for a handout, you're barking up the wrong tree."

Raven was apalled that she'd even think such a thought. "No, Ma'am, I certainly don't want your money. I'm just new here and a little disoriented. Trying to find my way around and—"

She loosened her death grip on the slot tokens. "Well, you look young and innocent enough. I thought you might be some shifty polecat trying to take advantage of a senior citizen."

"Not at all. Happy to see you win. Anyway, if you could point me to the blackjack tables, I'll get out of your way."

Her eyes softened slightly, "Is this really your first time here?"

Raven nodded.

"Well, welcome to paradise. Mystic is one of the largest casinos in the world. This place has over a hundred table games, but you should forget blackjack and try the slots. A couple of thousand machines just begging you to take their money."

Raven realized his first impression of the lady being grouchy missed the mark. In some ways she reminded him of Aunt Ethel. She had the silver flaxen hair and the same type of bifocals sliding down the bridge of her nose. He felt a sudden impulse to help her escape the casino, knowing she'd be unlikely to keep her jackpot if she stayed too long at the one-armed bandits. "Sure looks like the machines paid off for you. Maybe you should take your winnings and head home? Unlikely you'll stay lucky if you keep playing."

She chuckled loudly, "By gum, you're sounding just like my husband. Henry's always saying no way anyone can beat these Injuns. Always complaining 'bout how much they're making here and not having to pay any taxes. A little over a decade ago, most of these Redskins were welfare cases living in trailers. Now every man, woman, and child in their tribe gets half a million in cash yearly, plus a trust fund providing free college education. Just ain't right."

Raven harbored no animosity toward their affluence. He would much rather see the billions Americans fritter away in gambling go to Native Americans than to buying a new yacht for Donald Trump. He wished his own lineage hadn't been as cloudy and he could have participated in some tribal gravy train—free tuition sure would've helped him. "I guess it's only fair after all the years of injustice that the tribes can legally thumb their nose at the IRS and the government."

Her eyes narrowed again with suspicion. "You're a handsome young man, but I'm guessing you got some Injun blood in you. I know it's none of my beeswax, but are you a member of the Madewakantons?"

Raven immediately recognized the name of the Dakota tribe who ran it. He had always been fascinated by Native

American culture and voraciously researched Indian ways in an effort to understand his own roots.

"No, but I do know a little bit about them," he said. "The Dakota Indians went through the same calamity that beset nearly every tribe in the Americas as white men rolled West. In 1851, Chief Shakopee and the Dakota Indians were pressured into giving up twenty-four million acres of land for just pennies an acre.

"This happened even though, like most Indians, the Dakotas had no concept of land ownership and were unaware of what they were signing. And if the injustice of duping the savages out of their rightful land wasn't enough, the white men added insult to injury when they reneged on the corrupt treaty. When starving Native Americans pleaded for provisions, the rather unsympathetic Indian agent told them to eat grass. The tribe rebelled, slaying hundreds, including the agent, who was killed by stuffing grass down his mouth and throat."

The lady sat stunned by this discourse. "Sakes alive. How did you know all that? I've lived in the Twin Cities my whole life and have never heard any of those things."

"History major, Ma'am."

"You betcha. Well I'll have to tell my Henry. Maybe he'll quit wishing they all moved back to their teepees and be a little more sympathetic to them."

"He might want to, because the ghosts of these brave warriors are rising up to wreak their revenge. The Indians realized long ago they couldn't defeat the combined forces of the U.S. Army in a war, so they changed their strategy and engaged the forked-tongued race on a different battlefield. With casinos, many tribes found their 20th century buffalo. Gambling not only allows them to be self-sufficient on their own land, but the money comes from the wallets of the white man, the same race that swept through the plains a century earlier, claiming manifest destiny. Well, now those roles are reversing as the descendants of those defeated tribes are taking back the plains, one chip at a time."

"So you think the redskins are going to regain their land?" she said.

"No. I don't think that will ever happen. But they could become a force economically with all their casinos."

"Well, I guess I'd better do my part to stop their spread and take some more of their money." She turned and started pumping in her tokens, five dollars at a time.

"You sure I can't talk you into quitting while you're ahead?" Raven asked.

"Don't be silly young man. I've got to strike while the iron's hot. I played here every day last week and didn't win once. Now I'm so far ahead, there's no way I can lose today."

He wished he could have convinced her to leave with her profit, knowing the longer she played, the more inevitable losing became. But he was realistic enough to know most gamblers checked their logic along with their coats when they entered the casino, and nobody was a winner until they made it out the door. Raven excused himself and headed in the direction she had pointed for the blackjack tables.

He quickly noticed the house used only four decks of cards. He had gotten comfortable playing against six decks and it would be an adjustment to factor that into his equations, but fewer decks were better.

The casino personnel acted friendly, and Raven soon got all his meals and his hotel room comped, an immense help in keeping down expenses. A smile curled across his lips while reflecting on the decision to play full time over the summer. *Not only are they offering an attractive game of blackjack, but they're also giving me free room and board while I beat their brains in. Is this a great job or what?*

Since everything was free, Raven felt drawn like a lemming to the most expensive items on the menu. He ended every meal with a huge portion of pie or rich banana splits, and began putting on extra weight for the first time in his life.

♣ ♦ ♥ ♠

He'd been there a few days when a lanky man in black-rimmed glasses jumped into his table with double $1,000 bets. At first, Raven thought it coincidental that the angular high roller arrived just as the count shot up to plus sixteen. Without watching the cards, Raven didn't see how he'd be aware of the count, yet the flashy high roller played all his hands correctly; even their insurance decisions matched.

Raven watched with fascination as he floated around the pit like a politician at a fund-raiser, showing polish that could only come from years of playing. The high roller would never be mistaken for Adonis with his lithe body, yet he exuded a certain debonair style with his gregarious manner. His acorn eyes looked both studious and mischievous as he casually took in his surroundings.

During the next couple of days the high roller consistently jumped in and out of tables like a bee flitting from flower to flower. Raven wanted to play as many hands as possible out of the shoe when it was rich and whenever this interloper hopped in and played two spots, it ate up a lot of the good cards.

Raven had never spotted another pro all the months he had played in Joliet. The very nature of card counting stood out to the trained eye since average gamblers bet similar amounts every hand and anyone who spread their bets dramatically caught the sharp eyes of other counters.

Soon Raven realized that the high roller *always* showed up on high counts and he suspected it wasn't an accident. Before long he figured it out—the gal two spots to his left evidently signaled whenever the cards ran hot, giving the high roller the count with her chips since they never communicated verbally. Raven scanned the rest of the pit and detected at least two other tables where attractive female confederates counted down shoes. He noticed that these gals wagered small amounts, allowing them to blend in and attract no attention from pit bosses more interested in their looks than their play. Raven marveled that not only had he met his first fellow card counter, but he also had witnessed a very proficient team in operation.

♣ ♦ ♥ ♠

At dinner Raven ate alone as usual in the casino restaurant. Bored, he began to observe the other patrons and tried to imagine their lives. One older couple caught his attention. They picked at their salads, yet not once spoke a word or even looked at each other.

Did they have nothing left to say?

The husband strained to see the numbers on the keno screen, while the wife simply stared off into space. His musings stopped abruptly when his wandering eyes zoomed in on a shapely redhead in a nearby booth.

Wow! How come I never met anyone like that in church?

Mesmerized by the mass of cascading red curls, Raven at first didn't notice her dinner companion—the high roller from the casino. He looked out of place next to such a beauty. His ruddy complexion, bird-like head, and oversized black-rimmed glasses made him appear very scholarly. But the only subject he wanted to study was the hourglass figure sitting near him. He looked the type who seldom dined alone, as his suave, easygoing manner created an engaging and confident personality coupled with deep pockets, which more than made up for his physical deficiencies.

He wondered if the redhead was one of the girls from the blackjack team, but she didn't look familiar, and she had a face not easily forgotten. The high roller took off his glasses, noticed Raven gawking, and waved. Embarrassed, Raven quickly buried himself in his meal and tackled the end cut of the prime rib. He had only taken a few bites when he heard a commotion and looked up as the redhead slapped her dinner companion and stormed out of the restaurant, leaving diners startled momentarily into an uncomfortable silence.

The high roller now had the full attention of the place. Unperturbed, he returned Raven's stare with the flash of an impish grin, finished his cheesecake and left. On impulse, Raven got up and followed him to a bar, then hesitated at the entrance—he'd never been in a tavern or lounge before. He argued with himself for a moment. *Would it be wrong to go in there? Alcohol is such a taboo.* Finally, he concluded it would be okay—the drinking was wrong, not the locale, and he had no fear of succumbing to that vice.

He found the high roller sitting alone at a corner table. "Sorry to interrupt. Mind if I join you for a moment?" Raven asked.

"Have a seat." He extended his hand to introduce himself. "My name is Marco Antonelli, although in the casino I'd prefer you call me Ronald Sinclair, since that's the name I'm using here." Judging from his clipped, rapid speech, Raven guessed Marco hailed from the East Coast, probably New Jersey.

"You sure spiced up the atmosphere in the restaurant— I didn't know entertainment was included with dinner," Raven said.

"My lady friend and I had a little misunderstanding regarding our plans for the evening. She seemed to doubt my sincerity."

"Too bad—looked like a nice girl."

Marco shook his head, "I'm not looking for Miss Right, I'm looking for Miss Right-Now."

"Oh, I get the picture." Raven squirmed uncomfortably in his chair.

Marco noticed his uneasiness. "What can I say? Hard to keep this dog on the porch—it's just the way I'm wired." He grinned and shrugged helplessly. "What about you? Any chickadees tucked away somewhere?"

Many girls Raven met seemed to say goodbye before he even got to hello. "No. Most of my relationships have been plutonic."

Marco raised his eyebrows. "Excuse me. Don't you mean platonic?"

"No, plutonic. They all treated me like Mickey Mouse's dog."

Raven had hoped to talk to this high roller and possibly learn more about his team operation, although they obviously had little in common. "Why did you tell me about your false name? Aren't you worried I might expose you to the casino?"

"Well…" Marco paused, "I'm a pretty good judge of people, and I don't think you're the type who'd do that. Besides, we're in the same business."

Either I've been far too obvious in my trade, Raven thought, *or Marco is one very sharp individual.* "How could you tell? You were so busy hopping around from table to table, and my bets are so small compared to yours—to be honest, I didn't think you noticed me," said Raven.

"Nah, it's easy to tell. You're a pretty good player, although you're a little tentative on firing the money into play on real high counts." Marco's accurate assessment floored Raven. After his first disastrous experience in Joliet, Raven had indeed become gun-shy about betting huge stacks of chips.

"Yeah, I know I need to be more aggressive. Just started playing in January. So far, I've only done it part-time, working around my school schedule, but it's gone well. I've already doubled my bank." Raven knew he didn't have to share this information but felt a need to impress Marco.

"Really? That's great. Where did you learn to count? A tutor? Or one of those seminars?"

Raven hesitated, "No, I taught myself after reading Ken Uston's book."

Marco's eyes registered astonishment. "Wow, that's rare for someone to teach himself from a book and become a winning player. I'm impressed. You must really be disciplined."

Raven's face radiated with pride and he rubbed his nose self-consciously. He liked people's approval yet felt awkward accepting it. He coughed and cleared his throat. "What about you? How did you learn to play this game?"

Marco inhaled deeply and Raven prepared for a long explanation. "Some fellow students taught me to play when I was at MIT. Have you ever heard of the MIT blackjack team?"

Raven's blank expression indicated he hadn't, so Marco continued. "The team is comprised primarily of MIT students or alumni. They're cocky as hell and think they're the cream of the academic elite across the nation. We had some real sharp players, guys like Keith Vandertaft, who went on to help develop the Windows program for Microsoft."

Raven let out a low whistle of respect. "Sounds like a great pool to draw from in forming a blackjack team, but you're talking in past tense. Aren't you with them anymore?"

"Hell no. They had a lot of talent on the team, but most were math geeks with great theoretical knowledge—not a practical handle on actually playing the game." Marco rolled his eyes in disgust. "I grew frustrated over how passive they were in the casino—they talk like experts but don't have the balls to put big money on the table."

The waitress came by; looking harried and frazzled while trying to balance the drinks on her tray. Marco immediately lit into her, "Where the hell's my Jack Daniels? I ordered it ten minutes ago and all I've gotten are these stale pretzels. Get your ass in gear and start earning your money, babe."

It chilled Raven to see how quickly Marco shifted from a friendly demeanor to outright rudeness. Raven tried to redirect the conversation away from the flustered waitress. "So, Marco, you evidently left the MIT team and put together your own operation?"

The Italian shot a last look of contempt at the departing waitress and answered. "Yeah, that's right. How much do you know about team blackjack play?"

Raven nibbled on one of the pretzels and shrugged. "Not a lot, really. I read about Uston's teams in his book. Sounded similar to what I think I see you doing. He was the big player or BP, and would station card counters at different tables. They would call him in with some type of signal when the count was high."

"Correcto! Actually, it's rather ironic. The casinos switched to multiple decks to stop card counters from exploiting the single deck games; however, the shoe games create situations where once the count is high, it'll usually stay advantageous for several decks. By having a team call me in only for those situations, I end up playing a stronger game than is possible in single deck."

Raven broke in. "Interesting. So now you only bet money when you have an edge and never play any hands in negative counts?"

"Right again. And I've taken Uston's big player concept and added a few refinements. I only use girls as spotters, since the gambling world is so sexist, they don't expect women to be a threat."

"So the gal at my table counted down the shoes, signaled when it was rich, and communicated the actual count number to you in some non-verbal signal—I'm guessing with her chips. Is that right?"

"Yep, her first bet whenever I jump in is exactly what the count is. Clever of you to notice that," said Marco.

"Pretty elaborate set-up."

"Not really. The blonde at your table looks like your typical cute coed, just here to have fun and meet those Minnesota farm boys, but she's extremely sharp and is one of my best players. She's the one who told me about you and was so effusive in her praise, I assumed you were an experienced player."

The waitress returned with the whiskey and timidly broke into the conversation, "Is there anything else you two need?" Raven figured she wanted this party to move along and free up the booth for some nicer people.

Marco continued his train of thought while dismissing the gal with a wave of his hand, "So you've never played in Las Vegas?"

"No, I've only played here and in Joliet." The idea of going to Nevada suddenly appealed to him, though the thought had never before crossed his mind.

"Well, if you ever get out there, look me up. I just finished building a home—it's got an Olympic-sized swimming pool and a small putting green in back."

Raven continued munching on the free pretzels. The roof of his mouth felt parched from the salt and the conversation. He longed for something wet, but didn't know if they sold anything other than liquor in bars. He thought about leaving to get something to drink, but Marco's world mesmerized Raven. He wanted to know more, but didn't want to wear out his welcome. "Look. I must be boring you with all these questions."

Marco gave a wry smile. "Nah. I'm always interested in hearing what I have to say."

Raven chuckled and felt free to proceed. "So you just moved to Vegas?"

"Yes and no," Marco smiled.

"What do you mean?" Raven asked, baffled.

"For the last two years I've been a man without a home—unless you count my suitcase." This didn't seem to illuminate the issue much more, but Marco clearly enjoyed tossing out one bite at a time.

"Where did I live?" Marco stopped to take a long sip from his whiskey. "In the enemy's lap." He set his glass down and went on. "I moved from casino to casino every three or four days. For instance, I might play at the Mirage just enough to get RFB for a few days, then drive down the street to the MGM."

"Hold on, what's RFB stand for?"

"Complimentary room, food, and beverage."

"Ah, now I remember that term from Uston's book," Raven said.

"After a few months of bouncing around the gambling world, I'd start over with the first casino again." Marco leaned forward. "I get all my lodging, meals, and booze for free. Once on my birthday, I even bought lunch for everyone in the deli and charged it to the casino. Pretty good deal, don't you think?"

"Incredible," Raven said. "I can't imagine that kind of life."

Marco continued. "And I still haven't told you the best part."

"It gets better?" Raven asked incredulously.

"It sure does. I wasn't satisfied with just getting comps; I wanted to figure out a way to add hard cash to my winnings in the casino. One day it dawned on me like a revelation—I could do it with airfare reimbursement."

Raven's face failed to hide either his puzzlement or his fascination. "Airfare reimbursement? What's that mean?"

"Any legitimate high roller expects to get RFB. And if his average bet is a couple hundred dollars per hand, he knows that the bigger casinos will also pay for his airline ticket."

Marco stopped for a moment as his eyes followed a long-legged brunette gliding by in a mini-skirt. *He has the concentration span of a flea,* Raven thought, *but rather than label him ADD I'd diagnose him SDD—skirt deficit disorder.*

"As you were saying…" Raven prompted.

It took a second for Marco to shift gears before he went on. "Anyway, to a casino, a big bettor is just a big loser. They're willing to give him comps and reimburse his airfare to keep him gambling at their establishment. They don't want him to walk away and blow his money in a different club."

"All of that makes sense, but how did you get cash for an airline ticket if you didn't fly there? From what you've said, it sounds like in most cases you simply checked out of a casino before driving down the street to a new one."

Like the only kid in class to know the right answer, Marco's eyes gleamed with smug arrogance. "That's the beauty of it. I never did fly, so it was all pure profit."

"How?" Raven was losing patience with this drawn-out explanation.

"Let's say I played at the Mirage for three days. At checkout, I talk to my casino host about getting my airline tickets picked up. Since I met the standard requirement of playing at least twelve hours over three days and had an average bet over $500, the host doesn't even flinch when I hand him two first class tickets of $1200 each, Cleveland to Las Vegas, for me and my 'wife.' He reimburses me $2400 in cash, just like that." Marco snapped his fingers for emphasis. "I'm no different than any other high roller, except, as you pointed out, I never got on the plane."

Raven nodded thoughtfully. Though fascinated by Marco's ingenuity, the deception troubled him. "How do you get these tickets?"

"I have a nice travel agent friend." Marco grinned broadly. "After the casino gives me my cash, I return the airline tickets to the travel agency for a full refund."

"You're kidding." Raven said, shocked at the audacity of this final twist.

"No, I'm not," Marco said. "I give the agent comps to shows or gourmet restaurants a couple of times a month to keep her happy, and I pocket almost five grand extra each week."

Okay, he's not a choirboy, but the plan is absolutely amazing in its simplicity and cleverness. Raven shifted in his seat over the ethics, but quickly did the math in his head; astounded at the number he arrived at. "Over that two-year period, you made about $500,000 just off airfares which you never flew. That's incredible."

"Yes, I suppose it is. And that half million was in addition to the money I won at blackjack. I've made more money than the President these last few years."

Raven's curiosity about Marco's finances rose. "I don't know why you are telling me all this since we've just met, and I don't want to pry, but I'd love to know how much money you've made in blackjack." The words had barely left his lips when Raven regretted them. People in New England rarely discussed finances with anyone, even their close friends. But the loquacious Marco looked unfazed by the request. He appeared the type who could start up a conversation in an empty room.

"To be honest, I've probably been the most successful blackjack player in the game over the last five years," Marco said, failing in his pretense to sound modest. "There's maybe only about 2,000 players in the country making money over the long run counting cards. Of those, about 1,000 make a decent living off the game and use blackjack as their primary source of income. Out of that 1,000, probably close to fifty are highly successful, making at least $100,000 a year. Perhaps five out of those fifty make it real big, winning at least half a million a year. At the very top, you'll find only one or two individuals in the world who clear over $1,000,000 a year." Marco dramatically stopped to take another sip of his drink and let those facts sink in. The bar became surrealistically devoid of sound as Raven waited for the punch line.

"I've won at least a million bucks each of the last five years," Marco whispered in a low, but clear voice.

Raven's eyes widened. *A million a year. Unbelievable.* He thought of all the summer aristocracy on the coast near Camden. They had been so remote and unapproachable. Yet here he was, sitting with perhaps the most successful blackjack player in the world. It all seemed beyond belief. He had simply hoped to pay for college counting cards; he'd had no inkling anyone made that kind of money in the business.

Having clearly established his credentials, Marco gave him some advice. "As I said earlier, I'm a very good judge of people and I firmly believe you can make an almost unlimited amount of money. But it's not easy and you'd have to make gambling your dream."

Blackjack wasn't Raven's passion, just a means to an end, but he saw no need to mention this.

Marco went on. "The first thing you've got to do is spread more."

Raven looked slightly bewildered. "The only thing we used to spread in Maine was cow manure. I assume you're not suggesting I need to fertilize the farmlands of Minnesota."

Marco laughed so hard some liquor shot out his nose. "No, what I mean is you need to spread more aggressively between your low bets and your high bets. And you also need to spread your play around to different casinos. For instance, how long have you been playing here at Mystic?"

"Nine or ten days, but I see no reason to leave. They love me here, and I'm sure that I'm no threat to them," stated Raven.

"That's where you're wrong. You are dangerous and they know it. I thought you got a lot of heat today from the pit. There are many other Indian casinos around this state, and the games down in Mississippi and Louisiana are tremendous. I'd recommend you try them before you get booted here." Marco clicked his fingers for the check.

Raven thanked Marco for a memorable evening and they made vague promises to meet again if Raven ever ventured out West. He didn't see any problem in playing longer at the Mystic Casino and secretly wondered whether Marco only wanted to get him out of the way to reduce the competition.

♣ ♦ ♥ ♠

Raven had always been a sound sleeper. Lately, however, a thread of restlessness began invading his nights. He wondered if the stress from laying all his finances on the line, day after day, was taking its toil on him. The fluctuations were huge and could grind down even the most hardened of individuals. But Raven always considered himself a machine, immune from such emotional assaults. Inwardly, he wished anxiety from his vocation was causing the insomnia, but he secretly feared a nearly dormant memory had arisen to attack his sub-conscious.

He struggled a long time to fall asleep, since his head still whirled from the momentous meeting with Marco. Once he finally passed through the gate separating the two worlds, a kaleidoscope of multi-colored visions began to bombard his psyche, all taking him back to his native state of Maine. Each subsequent dream became more real and ominous than the previous one. The last one brought back a recurring nightmare of fire, and his narrow escape years ago from the burning church.

The haunting images felt so real and frightening that Raven's tongue became dry as a bone from the imagined heat, and he bolted upright in the bed. He vividly remembered that fateful day, just two weeks before his graduation from Camden High School. He had gotten up early one Monday morning to pick up Sunday's offering and take it to the bank. He assumed the church would be empty, as Monday morning was the pastor's golf day.

He hiked through a shortcut in the woods to reach the isolated house of worship. Suddenly, he experienced an eerie premonition of something wrong. He heard loud crackling noises and looking up, he saw the church—his only real home—nearly covered in flames.

He sprinted across the open meadow to the front door of the white-steepled house of God and stopped in his tracks. The wood building crackled from the advancing blaze. Raven felt compelled to try to save the sanctuary, but the inferno had already reached a terrifying intensity. He summoned his reserves and rushed in. The suffocating heat made his lungs scream for air.

The entire structure heaved and groaned as it fought to withstand the fire. It was a losing battle. Raven knew that it would fall apart in a flash so he decided to save any valuables. Burning boards started falling all around him.

The fire trucks arrived twenty minutes later—already too late. Raven angrily wondered why it had taken them so long to respond. The venerable church, built when George Washington presided over the nation, had breathed its last. The conflagration had been fanned by winds blowing straight off the ocean and not a single stick of wood could be saved. The fire chief gave a blanket to a soot-covered Raven Townsend, who crumpled on the lawn in front of the remains—exhausted and unharmed, but forever changed by the choice he made that day.

♣　♦　♥　♠

Raven collapsed on the sheets for more than an hour, lying perfectly still, drenched in sweat. He couldn't close his tired eyes, so he finally gave up and got up. He wearily worked his sleep-deprived body into yesterday's clothes and headed downstairs, hoping a little gambling would block out the memories.

Marco was nowhere to be seen. *Probably still sleeping,* Raven guessed, having surmised that Marco didn't have to worry about respecting girls the next morning because he never got up before noon.

Raven recognized a few faces from the day before, folks who evidently had made a night of it. One platinum blonde in her fifties still sat at the same table. Her ashtray contained a huge stack of cigarette butts and her eyes had the glazed look of multiple margaritas. The arrangement of gold and diamonds gaudily displayed on her body could have projected prosperity, but her weary face betrayed that image. Most certainly a country club existed somewhere in the twin cities where this woman was envied, but here, she was just another loser.

To escape her heavy smoke, Raven chose a table on the opposite end of the pit. He started playing and immediately became aware of a young pit boss frowning in his direction. After several tense minutes, he assumed he was just paranoid because of Marco's comments the night before. In the few months Raven had played blackjack, he'd never experienced the heat described in the blackjack books. After all, with the average casino blackjack table earning over $200,000 per year, his small bets certainly weren't going to make much of a dent in the bottom line, so why should anyone care?

He figured wrong.

Within five minutes, a flurry of activity occurred in the pit when a new suit showed up. The supervisor's beady eyes bore down on the table. Raven decided he wasn't imagining things. Nervously, he corralled his chips and headed for the cashier's cage. *Just because you're paranoid doesn't mean they aren't really out to get you.*

As the clerk began the pay-off with a stack of fresh bills, Raven felt his heart accelerating. When he first visited the riverboats in Joliet, he feared getting thrown out, but the longer he had played without any incidents, the more he became convinced the blackjack books exaggerated casino harassment.

Suddenly he felt a tap on the shoulder. He whirled around. The beady-eyed pit boss and two security guards faced him.

"Hi, Mr. Townsend. My name is Rex Ahlsten. I'm the casino operations manager here. Could we please see your ID?"

Dazed, Raven removed the Illinois driver's license from his wallet.

Ahlsten scrutinized the picture ID. Satisfied it wasn't a fake, he handed it back and said, "Mr. Townsend, your blackjack play is no longer welcome here at Mystic Casino. We're going to read you the trespass act and escort you off the property. I assume you are familiar with the trespass act?"

"Uh, no..."

Ahlsten seemed amused by this answer. "Mr. Townsend, I think we can cut the act. I'm sure you've been barred many times and know the drill. However, for the record, the trespass act states that if you ever come back on our property, we will have you arrested."

Raven stood paralyzed as shock and confusion welled up inside him.

Flanked by the security guards like a criminal, Raven was forced to walk out to his car. He noticed them snicker slightly when they saw the old Dodge Dart. As he drove off the casino grounds, the guards stood immobile until he was out of sight. *A little overdone,* Raven thought sarcastically, *like I'm going to suddenly turn around and rush back to the tables for one more bet.* Several feelings raced through his mind and a choking anger rose within him. *How could the casino do this to me just because I'm a winning player?*

Another thought unsettled him even more: *Was it possible that Marco Antonelli had alerted management?* After receiving no heat for ten days, it seemed odd that the morning after meeting Marco, Raven had been thrown out. The answer to his question remained elusive and his anxiety grew over the next week as he got barred from two other Minnesota clubs. Had he been betrayed, or was he just too obvious as a card counter? Either way, the time had come to leave Minnesota for greener pastures.

CHAPTER SEVEN

♣ ♦ ♥ ♠

Rain tumbled down in buckets, battering the windshield of the Dodge Dart. Raven strained to see the darkened highway as the weather steadily worsened. He knew he should stop for the night, but his head still reeled from the recent events in Minnesota. The injustice of the situation gnawed at him.

How could casinos bar him for skillful play? He had done nothing illegal, yet they treated him like a crook.

He fiddled with the radio dial. Just outside Louisiana, he found a great station. Song after song spoke to his heart. The thumping bass lines from Neil Young's *Cinnamon Girl* banged in time with the wipers, bringing a broad grin to Raven's face.

Lightning cracked across the sky, illuminating the countryside. Maybe it was a portent. Raven knew the Romans always looked for omens to predict the future, searching for signs in the heavens. Immediately the rain receded and the summer mugginess of the Deep South returned. He rolled down the windows, and the fragrant bayou air filled his car. Up ahead in the distance loomed the faint outline of a large casino, framed by sycamore trees in the morning sun. He had arrived at the Swamp.

The Swamp originally existed for bingo and modestly supplemented the local Indian tribe's coffers. But when it became the only land-based casino in the entire state of Louisiana, it might as well have been a printing press for twenty-dollar bills. The lack of competition yielded obscene profits. The entire complex was paid off in less than a year, rather than the five to seven originally projected.

This one-way flow of money didn't discourage the local population where gambling stood as a cultural heritage. The number of customers grew steadily, with more and more people bringing in their weekly paychecks. The unofficial slogan among employees became, "We've got what it takes to take what you've got."

Raven worked his way through the crowds for an overview of the casino layout. Spartan in its simplicity, with no clanging slot machines in sight, the quiet ambiance of the Swamp reminded him more of a warehouse than a casino. This delighted Raven. He never gambled because of décor or atmosphere—he only cared about profit potential.

He found a spot at a nickel table and bought in for five hundred. There were many more Native Americans working at the Swamp than any of the Minnesota casinos. They displayed pride over their tribe finally prospering. Gambling brought to the Indians what over a century of federal programs never had—self-respect and self-sufficiency.

Raven played for four hours, cashed out with a small win, and headed back up the freeway to a cheap motel. As he slipped beneath the sheets and tried to get comfortable on the lumpy bed, he wondered how long he would last at the Swamp. Minnesota had transformed Raven from a naïve, wide-eyed college student into a combatant. He couldn't view blackjack as just a game anymore—it had become a battlefield where only the strong survived. More determined than ever, he fell asleep, resolved to beat the system.

The next morning, Raven rose early to meet the enemy, and found a small grouping of four tables with single deck blackjack next to the six deck games he'd played the night before. *Wow! How did I miss that?*

Originally, he'd learned to count using a single deck, but he'd never seen one in a real casino. He quickly grabbed the only seat left. The dealer pitched the cards from a hand-held deck and the players actually got to pick up the cards and touch them. *This feels just like home,* he thought.

Eleven hours later, Raven, heavily weighed down with chips, pushed away from the table and cashed out. *Unbelievable! Single deck blackjack and no heat.*

With his playing stake now over $15,000, he could bet up to $150 a hand. Raven calculated his expectancy to be seventy-five dollars an hour because of the favorable rules. If he kept winning, he would soon have a bankroll big enough to average $1,000 in profits every day.

♣ ♦ ♥ ♠

Four days passed without attention from any supervisor. This place looked too good to be true. It appeared the entire pit was asleep at the wheel. *They obviously didn't use the best parts of the puzzle when they put together this crew,* he thought. It reminded him of a joke Marco told him that if you lined up all the pit bosses in the world end to end, it would be better to leave them that way.

The bubble appeared about to burst when a stout-looking man in his fifties tapped Raven on the shoulder. He looked out of place in his rumpled suit—a redneck trapped in the wrong set of clothes, someone who preferred blue jeans and the comfort of his pickup rather than the confines of the pit. Raven returned the handshake with his left hand, waiting for the ax to fall.

"How y'all doing? I'm Harry Read, the casino manager."

Raven scrambled for a pseudonym and drew a blank. "Randolph...Randolph Townsend." He immediately regretted giving his real name—a very stupid move after what happened in Minnesota. Next time he'd be better prepared.

"Rudolph? Like the red-nosed reindeer?"

"No, Randolph." *Like you missed Sesame Street the day they studied the alphabet.*

"Okay, Randy, I got it now."

Raven remembered Butch calling him Randy Redskin and wondered if that might come next from this pit boss. "It's Randolph, not Randy, but I prefer to be called Raven."

Harry wrinkled his nose and gave a patronizing smirk. "Sure. I wanted to let you know we've been watching you for the last four days. You've been doing real good here, Randy. You must like this single deck game?"

Raven cringed at the massacre of his name and guessed at the sequence that would follow. He would get complimented on his skillful play and then get shown the door. It probably didn't matter that he used his real name since the gig was up. But he summoned up his bravado for one last ploy. "I play single deck because there's not the long shuffle like you have in six deck, although I lose just as fast in either game." Raven kept a straight face and tried to sound convincing. He locked gazes with his adversary until the pit boss blinked.

Harry coughed twice, exposing a cornrow of teeth yellowed by years of smoking. "Randy, do I look that stupid to you?"

Raven suppressed the urge to answer yes. It already struck him that Read was an odd surname for someone who looked as if he had never read a book in his life.

Harry went on, gathering steam. "Look Randy, we both know why y'all are playing this table. It's easier to count cards with one deck than six. Ain't that right?" He displayed the condescending look of a cop catching a speeder.

Raven wasn't going to roll over and play dead. "Card counting. You must be kidding. Don't you need a photographic memory for that?"

Harry snickered. "Mr. Townsend, we here at the Swamp think everyone's got a photographic memory. It's just some players forgot to put the film in."

Raven had no idea what that meant and had tired of this little game. He started picking up his chips to cash out.

Harry acted surprised. "You done for the day?"

Now Raven smiled for the first time. "Yeah. I think it's time to get out of Dodge."

"Let me comp your dinner before you head out," said Harry.

Taken aback, Raven hesitated, wondering if this was a trap, but figuring he had little to lose, he accepted.

Raven ordered chicken wings for an appetizer. They went down so fast, he went ahead and got the crab legs smothered in butter. After a few days of cheap burgers, everything tasted good. Between bites, he pondered Harry Read's comment on memory.

He remembered how fellow students always assumed he had a photographic memory, yet he'd never bothered to correct them, preferring their admiration.

Harry Read appeared unexpectedly just as a Native American waiter brought the entrée. No "hello" or "may I sit here," the pit boss just grabbed a chair like he owned it and barked to the server, "Wolf, get me a cup of black coffee and a pack of those cheap cigs your squaws make."

He cackled over the last line and turned to Raven. "Don't ever drink tea on a reservation. You know why?" asked Harry.

Raven stared at him, thinking *there's no such thing as a free lunch.* "No."

"Coz Injuns who drink too much tea drown in their own teepee." He laughed robustly again at his own wit. "So Townsend, how's the food?"

Raven sensed he needed to tread carefully in this conversation. "It's great, but I didn't know pit bosses ate in public restaurants."

"Yeah, I eat here a lot. They have a separate diner for employees, but there's too much damn minority help working there for the food to be any good." The waiter returned with the coffee and certainly heard the racist remark, yet he acted unfazed by Harry's behavior, and moved on to his next table.

Raven glared at Harry and said, "That was rather rude."

Harry dismissed Raven's concerns, "Son, I learned a long time ago that the most important thing in life is sincerity," Harry winked, "and once you learn how to fake that, the rest is easy."

Raven steered the conversation to a safer topic. "What's your favorite food here then?"

Harry patted his pot-bellied stomach. "Seconds." He chuckled and grabbed a huge chunk of bread. "Anyway Randy, I wanted to talk to you a little more." Raven gripped the sides of the chair, digging in for the coming onslaught. Harry spoke with food still in his mouth, "How long you been playing blackjack? You look pretty young."

"Just a few months. I'm a grad student and I was just passing through town." *And soon to leave, I might add.*

"College student, huh? I never got any formal education myself." Raven hardly considered that a startling revelation. "I got my smarts through the school of hard knocks."

Harry helped himself to the rest of Raven's bread, then continued. "Read some books on blackjack, have you, Townsend?"

Here it was, finally coming out in the open. It seemed odd Harry didn't get into this back in the casino. Maybe he wanted Raven to think it was a free meal only to rescind the comp and charge him when it was over. Raven weighed his options before responding. He was still not far removed from Bible College and it felt wrong to lie to someone face-to-face. But he did anyway. "No, and I'm not sure what you're getting at."

Harry scoffed. "Jack shit! Come on now, don't be coy with me. Who've you read? Wong, Uston, or Snyder?"

Raven was astonished Harry knew so many blackjack authors. It looked like he was cornered, but he was still inclined to admit nothing. *Deny, Deny.* "They don't ring a bell, but maybe I should pick up a couple of books to improve my play. I wouldn't mind winning for a change."

"Horse shit! You university kids think you're so damn smart." Harry shook his head in disgust. "My degree was right here in the trenches. I started out back in Mississippi, dealing blackjack in bars on the gulf coast before you were even born. Worked in Laughlin and as a pit boss in Vegas. I've also been a player, same as you."

Raven didn't flinch. He knew he was trapped, but there were few options of escape available. Harry reached into his shirt pocket for a match and lit up one of the smokes the waiter had brought him. "Randy, I know you read those books 'cuz I did too. I tried for three years in Reno to make a living counting cards. I know that's what you're doing. I can tell by the way your eyes scan the table and the precise amounts you bet, so don't try to bullshit me."

Raven felt helpless and decided to let the conversation run its course. "How'd you do in Reno? I've never been there, but I've heard it's nice."

"Reno's a cesspool of lowlifes and degenerates. Only rats and piss-ants go there."

Raven thought Harry must have fit right in, but decided not to share that assumption with him. "You say you used to count cards. Why past tense? Are you making a lot more money doing this?"

Harry scowled between bites of bread. "I wouldn't call $36,000 a year a helluva lot. I gave it up because card counting doesn't work."

Now this is getting interesting. Raven's hands eased their death grip on the chair. "What about those authors you mentioned. They must have made a lot playing."

Harry rolled his eyes. "All of the money those so-called blackjack experts ever made was off their books, not their play. For card counting to really work, you have to get into the long run, millions of hands. A full-time player gets in 100,000 hands a year at the most. The only people who ever win are the lucky. Even a blind squirrel finds a nut now and then."

Raven recognized a grain of truth in this logic, but it wasn't really necessary to play a million hands to realize your advantage. If a card counter played correctly, he would win about two out of every three days. There might be streaks where he lost more, but overall, he should steadily forge ahead. Raven studied Harry's face to gauge his candor and said, "Seriously now. You don't think the odds can be overcome?"

"I know they can't. Like I told you, I've done it all—deal, supervise, and manage. And seen it all. Been there, done that, and got the damn tee shirt. If it could've been beaten, I wudda done it, but it's impossible to get in ten million hands like those computer simulations do."

A frustrated ex-card counter in charge of a big casino. It's a license to steal! In a way he had underestimated Harry, since he was at least smart enough to read. Yet he exuded an overriding arrogance that left him a few fries short of a happy meal. Raven pushed back his plate and smiled, "Harry, you're probably right."

♣　♦　♥　♠

Day after day Raven camped out at the single deck tables, preferring the middle seat. He always began early, right after a hearty breakfast of bacon and eggs. The pit acted totally disinterested in his play, although Harry did make a comment once about Raven's seat selection. "I see you like to sit in center field."

"Center field? What do you mean?" Raven wondered if he missed some joke about baseball.

"The middle seat—that's called center field. I imagine some book told you to sit there so you can see all the other cards around you to count."

Raven fidgeted, but made no response, since that was exactly what he had read.

Harry bent close and spoke softly. "You know what spot is really the best?"

Raven shook his head.

"Some of them books recommend first base; others say to sit at third base, but they're all wrong. The best is the dealer's spot."

Harry walked away, chuckling at his own humor. His expression indicated a conviction that the young upstart would eventually end up in the land of losers. Raven decided to feed that belief, and stashed black chips in his pocket when no one looked. Later, away from the watchful eyes of the pit, he'd cash out the hidden win. Harry took the bait like a fat rainbow trout latching onto a blood filled mosquito. His face read like an open book whenever he came by, his smirk practically shouting out, "There, you smart-ass punk—I told ya no one can beat the game."

He gladly comped Raven's food but never again joined him at a meal. Raven usually sat alone by the window while dining. The view of the parking lot wasn't exactly stimulating, but it beat staring at the silverware. Several times, the waiter from the first night served him, and one evening Raven struck up a conversation. "Your name tag says Matthew, but didn't Harry call you something else a few nights ago?"

"Wolf. That's what some people call me, but management requires our real names on the tags."

"Well Wolf, my name is Raven, so if we get a couple more animals, we'd have our own zoo," Raven said with a laugh. "Which name do you prefer?"

"Either Matt or Wolf is fine."

"I'll go with Matt then. Anyway, I was embarrassed at the way Harry talked down to you the other night," said Raven.

Matt shrugged his shoulders. "That's just how he is. He could start a fight even if he was the only one in the room. He's as crazy as Rasputin. I just ignore him."

"Glad to hear that. Anyway, a great cut of meat there. Tasted a bit like venison, but I didn't think any was available this time of year. Was it frozen?"

"Nope. Fresh as can be. Just came in off Interstate 10 this morning."

Raven forced a faint smile, hoping the road kill reference was a joke. "Well…what do you recommend for dessert?"

"Try the sugar-free pumpkin pie. I guarantee you'll like it, and it's good for you."

Raven patted his tummy, "No, I don't want to go that healthy. How about the chocolate sundae?"

"Your call, chief—just thought you might be nutritionally conscious," said Matt.

"Me! That's a laugh. What in the name of Frito-Lay made you think that?"

"I noticed your shirt and assumed you were a distance runner."

Raven glanced down. The faded gray tee still carried the logo for Camden High cross-country. "I used to be, but that was a long time ago in another life. I must be twenty pounds heavier than when I ran."

"Then you need some vitamin EX," Matt said with a mischievous grin.

Raven's face contorted in bewilderment. "You lost me again. What's vitamin EX?"

Matt brushed away his jet-black bangs, revealing bright eyes full of intrigue. "Exercise. That's what you need. I run every morning. How about joining me?"

This caught Raven off-guard. In college, basketball kept him in shape, but he hadn't gone out on a serious run since high school. He had been one of the top track stars in Eastern Maine and he couldn't have lost that much, so he figured why not.

♣   ♦   ♥   ♠

The crisp morning air invigorated Raven as he ran with Matt. Familiar memories of running through the woods in Maine came back to him, and a serenade of blue jays and chickadees helped speed him along. A deer browsed in a field nearby. Surprised at his strength, Raven decided to push the pace to show off. He surged up a short hill; Matt easily kept up.

Soon Raven paid the price; his breath came in short gasps and his legs grew heavier with each step. In his mind, the birds' chirping began to sound like a chorus of crows mocking him. Runners talk about a bear jumping on your back the last lap of a race. Raven felt like the bear not only climbed on, but also dug in his claws as each step became more and more difficult. *Pretty pathetic,* he thought. Especially for a guy who used to run over fifty miles a week and had a resting pulse rate of thirty-four in high school—so low, nurses routinely wondered if he was dead. Yet, that all felt like a different planet now as his legs stiffened up and he began to stagger like a punch drunk boxer. Despite his fierce Townsend pride, he finally gave up and slumped under a tree, while his tormented body greedily gulped for air.

Wolf left him to recover and finished his run. He returned with the car, and they rode in silence until a donut shop came into view.

"Matt, pull over here. I really need a maple bar, bad," Raven pleaded.

"No can do," Matt said.

"What do you mean? Just put on the blinker and pull in."

"You don't see the problem, do you? It's what you're eating." Matt shook his head in disapproval. "I'd rather put a gun in my mouth than eat sugar."

Raven gazed hungrily as the donut shop disappeared from view.

Matt glanced at him. "Raven, you ever read the book *Sugar Blues?*"

Raven shook his head sadly and Matt proceeded to tell him why sugar was the greatest curse in the Western Hemisphere, and the source of nearly every evil from slavery to serial killers, and from acne to insanity. Raven felt stupid thinking it only caused tooth decay.

Matt continued his diatribe with a rambling discourse on nutrition with zeal unmatched by many preachers. Raven wondered why he wasn't as excited about his religious beliefs as Matt was about vitamins.

Raven went straight to the casino after showering off the thick layer of sweat. The cards were favorable, and stayed that way for the next couple of days. Harry continued to flash his ugly grin—apparently clueless Raven hid chips.

Winning usually made Raven happy, no matter what else happened. That was no longer the case. The harder and longer he looked at himself, the less he found to like. His athletic body was turning soft. Other than blackjack, he had few disciplines in his life.

He wondered if there was some truth to Wolf's nutritional advice. Casinos were packed with people who rarely said no to any of Earth's culinary pleasures. The majority of customers smoked and drank, certainly speeding their short journey on this planet to an end. At dinner that evening, Raven swallowed his pride and asked to run again with Matt.

The second run felt only a little easier and slightly more successful than the first. But within a week, Raven began striding comfortably as his body acclimated to the workouts. Over a month, he lost twelve pounds and felt good enough to actually chat while they ran—previously Matt had done all the talking.

During one long run, Raven decided to pump Matt for a little info on the Swamp. "So what's the deal with Harry Read? He's not exactly the brightest light on the tree. How'd he ever get to be casino manager?"

"Good question. Most in the tribe see him for what he is—an egotistical know-it-all, who thinks he's a jack-of-all-trades, but is really a master of none," said Matt.

"How did he get hired? He acts like he doesn't even like Indians."

"Nope, every hexagonal-shaped chromosome in his body hates 'em, along with blacks, Hispanics, Chinese, Jews, or anyone else who didn't grow up in the KKK. He got hired because he can bullshit a lot of people into thinking he's knowledgeable."

"But he's not?"

"Not even close." Matt glided along effortlessly despite the hard pace. They were in the middle of a strenuous eight-mile run, yet Matt showed no difficulty conversing.

Raven decided to probe a little further. "Why doesn't the casino hire someone from inside the tribe?"

Matt scowled. "We can't."

"What do you mean? Just fire him and get someone else." Raven worked hard to keep up the pace without showing his pain.

"That's the problem, we gave up control," said Matt.

"To whom?" Raven's sentences became shorter the longer he ran.

"When the Swamp got set to open, no one in the tribe had any gambling experience. So they decided to hire an outside management company to run the operation. We picked some outfit in Mississippi, which turned out to be a big mistake."

"There're a lot of Indians working in the casino," countered Raven.

"Yeah, we have preference on the lower tier of jobs, but none in management. All the bigwigs are good old boys from Mississippi. That's the history of America in a nutshell—whenever Native American tribes get something good going, white men want to step in and take it away."

Raven slowed up to massage his hamstring. "So they take most of the profits?"

Matt chuckled loudly. "Nope, they thought they were going to, but we put in some clauses to prevent them from walking all over us. They're all paid a flat salary."

"So Harry doesn't have any incentive for the casino to make more money?"

"That's right. He gets paid the same every month regardless of how much we make. The entire management team is locked into that for five years. I think they signed the agreement figuring they could take advantage of us, but we weren't the stupid savages they expected to find. Harry only calls me Wolf because he thinks he can tame this Indian like a dog, but he's in for a huge shock someday." Matt's speech accelerated at the prospect of payback in the future.

It all made sense now. Not only was Harry a frustrated ex-card counter, but he also received no percentage of the profits. Even if Raven won a ton, it wouldn't matter and might even make Harry happy, given his racist slant. It sounded too good to be true—Raven had found blackjack heaven.

CHAPTER EIGHT

♣ ♦ ♥ ♠

The morning workouts gave Raven more energy during the day. And he needed it, playing long days in a crowded, smoky casino where it was easy to lose focus. He vowed to implement a diet for life—not just follow a fad to lose a few pounds. Every morning, he promptly did fifty pushups and a hundred sit-ups, followed by a run.

On a typical day he played four hours straight, then stopped for a healthy lunch of free-range chicken and wild rice, followed by a brisk walk outside to get the blood flowing. Matt's running and nutrition regime invigorated Raven. He now realized his taste buds had been dulled by years of salt and sugar from processed foods, and it genuinely surprised him how good some common foods like cucumbers tasted.

After lunch, Raven played another four or five hours before breaking for a dinner of steamed vegetables and fresh grilled fish. If ahead at that point, he would quit. But if he lost, he would play a little longer, hoping to at least get even and salvage the day.

Overall, Raven won consistently and averaged $600 a day. A year ago, he'd never dreamed of making this much money, yet his wins still fell far short of the projected $1,000 a day. He suspected the many slow players drastically reduced the expected number of hands per hour.

The constant flow of new people in and out of the game provided frequent aggravation. It always took them time to fish a crumpled twenty out of their wallet and buy chips. A few always bet odd amounts, probably due to some superstition, which slowed the game to a crawl. Every double down would require some type of chip change or additional buy-in while blackjacks paying 3-2 on the mixed bets of reds and silver taxed the minds of inexperienced dealers.

And the fills were a steady irritation. No matter how many chips rested in the rack, someone always worried they were going to run out. This astounded Raven. The dealer's chip rack would have four hundred in five-dollar chips, and invariably a pit boss would authorize another twenty nickels and some silver be brought to the table. Though this process took only a few minutes, it was repeated a couple times an hour throughout the day.

But the absolute worst part for Raven was the smoke. Having become health-conscious, he didn't know how much longer he could take the stench of cigarette fumes blowing in his face. He tolerated it only because of the high profit potential and lack of heat from Harry Read, who epitomized the saying, "all bun and no hamburger."

Raven preferred playing alone as that was less stressful and offered the best odds. It was a common fallacy that card counters won their money from other players, much like skilled poker pros, but in reality, blackjack experts played only against the casino. Anyone else just got in the way.

Players jumping in and out changed the order of cards, and Raven called it the butterfly theory, since every close decision in blackjack subsequently affected every other hand. He derived that theory from a story about a man who traveled back to prehistoric time and was careful to not disturb anything, yet accidentally stepped on a butterfly and inadvertently changed the entire future of mankind.

Stupid mistakes by tourists always evened out mathematically, but it created great frustration when random decisions by other players helped the dealer and turned Raven's winning hands into losers. In a business where 98% of the time card counters bobbed below their all-time high, any little aggravation flared up like a raging disease to weaken one's resolve.

♣ ♦ ♥ ♠

The next day, Matt's younger brother, Luke, joined them on one of their morning runs.

"Wolf tells me you've got some Indian blood flowing through you," said Luke.

"Sort of. My mother's ancestors supposedly were Native American, but something happened to the genealogical records, so I never knew for sure," answered Raven. "It was like the worst of both worlds."

Luke asked, "How's that?"

"I felt the stigma of being a redskin without reaping any of the financial benefits," said Raven.

Matt scoffed. "You're actually better off that way. The white men give us token payments to ease their guilt, but that only hurts our people. They want us to be dependent on them and never stand on our own."

Luke nodded in agreement with his brother. "Do you have any idea what tribe you came from?"

"Penobscot was the main one in our area," answered Raven.

Luke pondered the name for a few moments. "Never heard of them."

Raven laughed, "They were a pretty docile group and that's why they never made the history books. They tried the matador defense—wave a cape and hope the bull keeps on running. It didn't work and they let the early settlers into Maine without a fight. Eventually the Europeans became more entrenched, and the Penobscots drifted into obscurity."

"Typical," Matt said. "Most Americans preferred the submissive natives who assimilated into the superior society of cities and books. My father named his four sons after the Gospels so we might fit in."

"Did it help?" Raven asked.

"Only with Mark. The other three of us stayed true to our heritage."

Luke turned to Raven, "Are you interested in exploring Native American history?"

"Yes—to some extent. I wanted to become an archaeologist after digging for artifacts in Vinalhaven." Raven described the ruins near the mysterious stone structures. "I wasn't sure of their origins, but my friend, Cynthia Bradford, thought they were Native American."

Matt gave him a quizzical look. "That doesn't sound Native American to me. I'll do some research on the Penobscots, but I'm not aware of any Indian group building like that. And who is this maiden—some girlfriend you've never told me about?"

Raven laughed, "No, nothing like that. The last time I saw her, she was a skinny teenager with braces. Now she's a senior at Yale. We've written a few times, but she's more a pen pal than anything else."

Matt's face radiated disbelief, and he started to speak but Luke interrupted the conversation. He wasn't used to long runs and wanted to stop. Raven marveled at how strong his own body felt during the workout, pleased at his progress in only seven weeks of running. He and Matt decided to finish off their workout with a couple of repeat miles.

A soft barkdust trail wound one mile from the edge of the casino parking lot through the forest to the river. They left Luke to recover by the river and ran bare-foot and bare-chested like deer through the woods. Except for the digital watch marking their time, they could have both been from a different era—two Indians running gracefully through the pristine land before its exploitation. They finished strong and Raven looked at his watch—four minutes and forty seconds for the last mile—his best time yet.

Matt took a deep drink from his canteen. Raven reached out his hand for the container. "How about sharing a little of that H2O with me?"

"You know what's in here?" asked Matt.

"I'm not psychic, but I'll go out on a limb and say it's filled with spring water from the reservation," Raven said with a chuckle.

"And you know why?" asked Matt with an edge in his voice.

"Yes, of course. You never allow chlorine or the other chemicals white men put into their water to enter your body."

Matt nodded and handed over the canteen. "Yet you allow something far worse to enter you."

"And what exactly is that?" asked Raven warily.

"Christianity. I'm not sure that's what you truly believe. If it is, then you are chained to reason and need to release yourself from its bonds and accept new realities."

Matt spoke in a hushed, bedside voice and gently placed his hand on Raven's shoulder. "Not everything can be explained with Western rationality. Why not take a vision quest to peer into your soul?"

"No thanks. I just don't believe God speaks to us that way," replied Raven.

"Really? From what you said, I didn't think your God spoke to you at all. You Christians are all left to guess what your destiny is." Matt paused to watch an osprey circle overhead, preparing to dive for its lunch. "Why do you restrict your God so much? He is too big to put into a box like the white man's Bible. You can't contain His greatness within a book, or only find faith while on your knees in a church. The Great Spirit has much to teach us from nature."

"Not interested," Raven said flatly. "Whenever I hear there's no limits on us, I think of Woodstock."

"The concert?"

"Yeah. Some yahoo gets up on the stage and leads half a million people in chanting 'no more rain.' It still poured and became a mud bowl. That's my image of positive thinking."

Matt wasn't ready to give up. "Did you know scientists have proven that, mechanically, the bumble bee shouldn't be able to fly?"

"No, I've never heard that," replied Raven.

"Yet they do fly—that is a fact. And I think the reason is no one has told them they can't. It is the same with us. We need to open our minds. How about joining Luke on his quest?"

"Listen. I'm not interested in playing Tonto in the wilderness, so let's drop it. Okay?"

He didn't want to admit it to Matt, but there was a certain appeal in some of the mystical aspects of the vision quest. Raven had been taught that only if he rigidly followed the right path, every step of the way, could he be assured of salvation. He pondered the proverb, "physician, heal thyself." He tried to proselyte others yet wondered if he had truly converted himself. As a Christian, Raven was supposed to be the paragon of virtue and kindness, but each day he spent at the Swamp, the further he drifted from those ideals. Many people got on his nerves, since the single-deck table attracted the very worst players. Instead of the ship of fools, it was the table of idiots.

There was one regular named Leroy who always tried to play third base so he could control the table. Whenever he made 21, he flipped over his cards and yelled, "Beat that" to the dealer. His hat said "NO FEAR," but Raven thought it really should have read "NO BRAINS."

Leroy took long, slow tokes on his smoke like someone on death row enjoying his last cig. Once he stood on a pair of 2's because he didn't want to take the dealer's bust card. Despite everyone prodding him, Leroy refused to hit and refused to split—he just stood. The worst part was that it succeeded, which encouraged him to try other stupid plays that didn't work, but his selective memory only recalled the times he won.

Another local named Sammy talked incessantly and called out each number he needed, as if it were possible to change the spots on the cards in midair. Whenever he won— which wasn't often—he turned into a beaming chatterbox, using a loud, wake-the-dead voice. He acted totally self-absorbed and oblivious to the fate of the rest of the table, and always referred to himself in the third person; "Sammy needs a seven" or "Sammy saved the table." If he busted, everyone had to listen to him moan about his bad luck. Whenever someone else got a blackjack, Sammy would complain about how he never got good hands, disdaining the usual table etiquette of congratulations. And when Sammy did get a blackjack, he always went into the same arrogant routine. "Call me Nostradamus, but I just knew I was going to get a snapper that time."

Townsends, by nature, weren't very tolerant, and each additional day Raven spent in the Swamp exacerbated that trait. The hours of blackjack play and the long processions of mathematical calculations and decisions, wore him down and made him even edgier around his fellow patrons.

None of these negative feelings affected his playing proficiency, and the winning sessions continued their steady stream, punctuated by one memorable Monday. He wondered if Louisiana observed some obscure state holiday since none of the regulars like Leroy or Sammy showed up. Raven played one-on-one against the dealer nearly all day long. Twice, he ran the entire single deck, winning all seven hands and finished with his biggest payday yet— over $5,000.

Harry Read also missed Raven's performance. Although it was better for Harry to remain in the dark, Raven almost wished Mr. Read could have been there to witness the slaughter, since the gratification of proving the cocky codger wrong would nearly be worth getting kicked out.

He retired early to his room to count the money. It took him thirty minutes to add up all the C-notes spread out on his bed. When he completed the tally, the amount staggered Raven. Including his earlier wins from Joliet and Minnesota, he now stood over $50,000 ahead—a larger figure than Raven ever hoped possible, even in his most optimistic forecasts. It certainly proved he made the right decision to use all his tuition money for blackjack and it refuted his father's prophetic advice. William Townsend thought gambling was wrong and predicted his son would lose everything.

"You have to work with your hands," he adamantly said. "That's the only way to earn an honest living."

Well, in a way Raven did use his hands—but in picking up chips rather than hay. He would become the first Townsend ever to get a Ph.D. That would show the old man.

Big winning days made the little annoyances in casinos less irritating, though Raven continued to view players around him as pests rather than as God's creation, and started habitually washing his hands after each session to remove germs. He didn't know how much more he could take of the crowded, wearisome Swamp. He needed a dose of the medicine that transformed Matt, but there had to be a better way than pretending to be Crazy Horse under a full moon for four days.

He didn't believe in Matt's pantheist views—but Matt's nutritional advice had proved to be life changing for Raven. He felt great and wondered if his friend might also be right in spiritual areas. How many regrets would Raven have at the end of his life if he always looked in the wrong place and had been too blind to see his real destiny? He decided to observe the ceremony for Luke's vision quest and see if there was any truth to Matt's mystical faith.

♣ ♦ ♥ ♠

The next day, Matt drove Raven to the Indian reservation and explained what would take place. A vision quest consisted of a sacred time of getting out into nature—away from the distractions of everyday life and communing with the wonders of God. It was supposed to bring about change and provide passage into a deeper level of spirituality. Believers anticipated a time of healing and joy upon discovering the interconnection of the earth and sky with all the animals of creation.

The process had three stages. First was the severance and separation from the old. Second came a transformation of healing spirit wounds while listening in solitude for Divine direction. The third stage involved bringing a new purpose, or vision, back in order to make the world a better place.

Wolf added little to Raven's previous knowledge of the subject, so he switched from the theoretical to personal experience. "You ever read Carlos Castaneda?"

"Nope, never even heard of him."

"He's been the greatest spiritual influence in our century and has opened up ancient paths to knowledge hidden to most. Within our minds we have the power to make anything come true and to create our own destiny."

Raven certainly didn't believe in any of this. He saw the world as a place with limitations set on finite man, and no amount of wishful thinking could overcome those shackles.

Matt lowered his voice to a whisper. "Castaneda's writings taught me how to snatch glimpses of the future, my future. My vision quest then confirmed the truth of those images."

This made Raven slightly curious. "You really saw things? All I know is that you were christened Wolf."

"A true vision quest involves communication with a guardian spirit. Most are animals. Mine was the wolf."

"Well, that explains the name," Raven said.

"The wolf fed me and guided me. He's the one who taught me more about holistic health and nutrition than a thousand books. We traveled together to a high cliff. The wolf implored me to leap off the edge with him. I was scared and started to turn back."

Raven gave Matt a skeptical look. "Sounds like a reasonable response to a crazy canine advocating suicide."

"The wolf told me to release the harnesses holding me back and that the only limitation was in my mind. Besides, he said it was a good day to die. Halfway down, he turned into a hawk."

Raven laughed, "Definitely sounds like the dog chewed on some bad bones."

Matt leaned closer to Raven and raised his voice slightly. "No, he was right. My presuppositions were holding me back. I felt a sudden peace and freedom. I ran toward the precipice and lunged into the air. I started falling like a rock but felt no fear. Suddenly, wings materialized on my arms, and I started soaring with the hawk. I was actually flying!"

Raven cautiously sized up his friend. He looked calm and sane, but this nonsense was ridiculous. "Well, the mind can do strange things."

"No, you don't understand. It was real."

"Hallucinations can seem authentic, but I don't think you literally flew," said Raven.

Matt's face lit up. "But I did! I saw the earth clearly for the first time. It changed my life and my beliefs. I came away from that experience with a warmth, and a sense of connection to every living creature."

Raven didn't know what to make of all this. Matt's compassion for mankind certainly wasn't universal—his strong views about white men proved that. Yet Matt displayed a deep inner peace and contentment. Raven's own passion for God didn't feel as intense, and Matt's vision quest both fascinated and disturbed him.

♣ ♦ ♥ ♠

The first phase of Luke's vision quest took place at the sweat lodge. Luke had been ceremonially painted, like a warrior from the Great Plains ready to seek power for an upcoming battle. A holy man, easily in his seventies, sat cross-legged facing him and led chants accompanied by drumbeats, urging those around him to release the bonds entangling them. The steam increased, and Raven understood why they called it a sweat lodge.

A container was passed around and everyone took a deep drink. Raven hesitated and turned to Matt. "Is there any alcohol in here?"

"Just trust me and drink it," Matt said. "It will help open up your eyes."

Raven felt everyone in the room staring at him. Nervously, he took a small sip, then passed it to Matt.

The holy man cried to the Great Spirit. "There are chains in this room preventing us from seeing you. Free us from the bitterness of family hatred. Remove the pride which clouds our vision, keeping us from true faith."

Raven felt extremely uncomfortable. He rationally tried to blame his distress on the heat, which produced huge beads of perspiration all over his body. But something else unsettled him—the old man's words spoke directly to him.

How could he know what was really inside Raven Townsend and about the discord with his father?

The holy man continued, "Cancel out the wrongs hounding one through the short passage on this planet. Forgive the transgression of the fire."

Raven's face flushed. Was it possible he knew about the church fire? No one saw the real truth of that day and the guilt that pervaded Raven's dreams.

The chanting increased in crescendo, and the steam enveloped the room, making it difficult to see. Raven felt a foreboding presence in the dark. He thought he heard sounds, like someone calling him from a distance. At first he couldn't make out any words, then clear as a bell he heard an audible voice.

"Raven, are you looking in the right place?"

The steam momentarily lifted, and Raven looked at Matt who sat motionless with a bowed head. Evidently the message didn't come from him. The voice had been fairly loud, yet it appeared no one else in the lodge heard it. Had he imagined it? If it were real, what did it mean? Was he wrong to be here at this pagan ceremony? Had he searched in the wrong way for God in the past? His head felt light and dizzy.

Then the voice spoke again. *"Do you need forgiveness for what you did?"*

Raven trembled slightly. He closed his eyes, and thought back to the church fire seven years ago in Maine. He had kept a dark secret inside this whole time, not wanting others to see through his outward shell of righteousness.

Now someone or something knew—how he had frantically tucked the offering box money inside his coat and escaped the burning church. Pastor Cook had entrusted Raven with the only key to the box, instructing him to deposit the money each Monday into the bank. But after the building had been reduced to ashes, Raven made the fateful decision to keep the cash that should have perished with the flames. He bought a motorcycle with the stolen money and took a secret step off his chosen path. And although no one saw him, Raven knew what he had done.

He expected his life to have followed a perfect blueprint—but his impulsive theft in the church changed all that. Even though no one else knew, it burned within his soul. He wished the weight of that transgression could be removed as easily as the weight he lost from dieting and running, but he didn't know how to purge the guilt.

The chanting stopped abruptly, and Raven returned to the present as the holy man spoke. "A long time ago, the gods got together and decided to make the search for the meaning of life the most rewarding endeavor for human beings. In order to make it difficult, they decided to hide this wondrous gift. One god said to put it at the bottom of the ocean. Another deity said humans would look there, and it needed to be placed on the moon. Others disagreed, thinking eventually they would look even there. Finally, the Great Spirit came up with the perfect hiding spot. He said, 'Let's put it inside of them; they'll never look there.' And they all agreed."

Luke stood up and approached the holy man.

"Luke, do you have the courage to take this journey deep inside your soul?"

"I do, Grandfather. I am ready to shed these earthly attachments and follow my guide to the other world."

"So be it. Your destiny is now in your hands."

Luke left to begin his quest and the rest of the group filtered outside. The afternoon sun blazed bright and Raven felt queasy. He moved under a huge tree for shade while Matt talked to the holy man. Warm days in September were called Indian summer back in Maine. That name seemed appropriate at a time like this.

Inexplicably, the winds all stopped blowing from every corner of the earth. Not one leaf rustled overhead. Raven heard the shrill cry of a large bird in the tree above him and tried to make out its identity. The bright sun obscured his view, sparkling through the branches. Suddenly, without warning, Raven felt momentarily blinded. His body floated up into the tree, toward the bird and toward the light. He wondered if he was hallucinating, but it didn't feel like a dream.

His vision returned and the bird, a magnificent bald eagle, became visible as it took flight into the sky, instantly pulling Raven upward into the air. Before he could utter a sound of protest, they were soaring over the plains of America. They sailed over the Midwest, and within minutes flew over the Rockies, descending beyond a strangely shaped butte and a deep canyon. Raven landed in an arid desert with sagebrush all around him.

The eagle came to rest on a cactus a few yards ahead and suddenly transformed into a young woman. She had beautiful, long black hair and wore an ornate headband with a single eagle feather protruding from the back. She extended her hand to Raven, but he could never quite see her face as she always kept her head turned away. He tried to cling to the belief it was all being imagined, but her fingers felt warm and her skin so soft it had to be true. *I must be experiencing a vision quest* thought Raven, *and this must be my spirit guide.*

She led him on foot through the desert and through a mysterious rocky terrain she called The Valley of Fire.

They journeyed further until she stopped to dig in the crusty sand. Raven joined her and soon they came across hundreds of scattered coins—some silver, some gold. He grabbed as many as he could stuff in his pockets. She led him to other sites—all laden with so many buried riches, Raven could barely walk.

Fatigued, he lay down to rest for a moment and closed his eyes. At the girl's gentle touch he awoke, and she pulled him up, but the desert had vanished. They now walked along a paved street and people gawked at them. He recognized some of the faces and realized he was back in Camden, Maine. Folks were whispering, "There goes the millionaire."

Raven and his guide walked past them to a beautiful white mansion. They stopped at the front door, unable to get in. The closed door frustrated Raven, but the girl said, "Why do you fret? The key is within you."

Raven reached into his pocket and found a skeleton key. He tried it in the lock and the door opened. They walked through the entry on elegant oak floors, taking in the exquisite beauty of the interior. Each room was beautiful, but contained not a single piece of furniture. The Indian girl beckoned him to follow her through two French doors into the back yard. A huge manicured lawn stretched all the way to the edge of the ocean. As he walked towards the water, the magnificence and splendor of it all overwhelmed his senses.

Is this my house? Is this to be my life?

While still puzzling over this, the waves increased in crescendo, and a huge swell crashed and rolled over the bank, knocking Raven to the ground. He turned to look for the Indian girl—only to see the mansion burning down in flames. He ran to the back porch searching for her. As the inferno grew worse, he fell to his knees, closed his eyes and began to pray.

♣ ♦ ♥ ♠

He awakened as Matt shook him.

"I thought you'd passed out," Matt said with a worried expression lining his face. "Are you okay?"

Raven felt too dazed to respond.

Matt leaned forward and checked Raven's pulse on his wrist. "Is everything all right?"

Raven slowly got up and forced a weak smile. He stared at the huge tree. "No, I must have been dreaming. I'm fine now."

Raven never told Matt about his experience despite numerous probing questions. He vowed never to tell anyone, at least not until he was able to understand exactly what happened and what it all meant.

CHAPTER NINE

♣ ◆ ♥ ♠

Back in his hotel room, Raven still shook from his eerie experience in the sweat lodge. He wanted to believe it had been a dream, but something inside made him question that assumption. After reflecting on his bizarre experience he suspected there might have been peyote in the drink at the sweat lodge. But wherever the voice had come from, it knew the truth of his life.

Raven didn't know how to interpret the strange experience of the previous day and wasn't up to facing Matt until he found some answers. He needed to get away from the Swamp, with its smoke and numerous irritations. Without saying goodbye to anyone, he packed his suitcase and loaded up the Dodge.

He stopped at a tourist booth along the freeway to get information on other casinos in Louisiana. The gal staffing the desk wore gaudy, dangling earrings, and her tight blouse barely contained her overflowing chest. She visually inspected Raven from head to toe.

"So, y'all must be some big time gambler?" she said in a husky voice. "I don't do much gambling myself. Can't get

Herbert away from the tube long enough to get dressed up, let alone go out."

"That's too bad," Raven said flatly. He still hadn't recovered from his recent mystical experience and was in no mood for any banter. "I'm here for maps and directions."

She brazenly licked her lips. "Well Sugar, I get off at five. How about I give you a guided tour so y'all don't get lost?"

Her forwardness stunned Raven. She looked a good fifty pounds overweight and her hair was dyed an odd red shade reminiscent of Woody Woodpecker.

Raven cleared his throat. "Ahem. Very generous of you, but all I want is information on casinos in New Orleans."

"Okay, honey, but y'all really don't know what you're missing. My name's Candy and I might be the sweetest southern belle y'all ever meet." She turned and leaned over to grab some literature, her rear end in a provocative pose. The sight of the huge caboose suddenly made Raven feel very sorry for Herbert.

Candy adjusted her blouse to reveal even more cleavage and handed him two brochures on New Orleans, brushing his fingers during the transfer. "Here's the lowdown on the Big Easy. Several places there for you to lose your money, but y'all don't want to go there," she said.

Raven took the brochures and pulled his fingers away. "And why is that?"

"New Orleans is appealing on the outside, but rotten in the core," Candy explained like a schoolteacher. "The murder rate ranks highest of any city in the nation, and there's widespread graft within the police department."

"Okay, where do you suggest I go?"

"I recommend Lake Charles," she said as she leaned over the counter, inches from his face. "Quaint old plantation town with four rocking riverboats."

Raven backed up and coughed, trying to keep his composure. "How far away is Lake Charles?"

"Just an hour the way I drive," she said with a wicked smile. "I like to do everything fast, if y'all catch my drift."

He definitely caught it—and wanted to quickly get rid of it. "Great. You've been very generous with your time. Now if you could point me towards Lake Charles, I'll get out of your hair."

She sighed. "Straight west on the interstate. They get a lot of weekend traffic from Houston, so it'll be buzzing tonight. Those Texans always have shitloads of money and you'll see some big action there."

He thanked her and quickly escaped.

♣ ♦ ♥ ♠

Lake Charles did have a charming older section with picturesque mansions, but the area near the casinos wouldn't make the cover of any travel magazines. Oil business left an indelible industrial mark on much of the landscape.

However, Raven liked the nice open feel and stylish ambiance of the riverboats. They were much less smoky, not as crowded, and attracted a better clientele than the Swamp.

He mixed up his play between the four casinos and blended well with other big bettors. Each boat had one room with larger table limits set aside for high rollers. They offered no single-deck, but the six-deck games were dealt deeply with $500 maximum bets.

Despite the big action around him, his play still received close scrutiny at the Island casino. One supervisor named Tucker kept showing up to observe him. Raven couldn't believe he was getting heat, since he had lost steadily at their club.

Tucker didn't go away and soon walked over to Raven's table. "Good evening, sir."

"Good evening to you also," answered Raven carefully.

"I'm afraid we're going to have to ask you to no longer play blackjack at either of the two boats operated by Island Management." Several other gamblers around Raven acted shocked upon hearing Tucker deliver this proclamation. Two older ladies gasped and stared at Raven like he was an ax murderer.

Raven truly was surprised. Previously, he only got booted after big wins. "You must be kidding. I've lost four grand here."

Tucker nodded. "I'm aware of that, and we do apologize for not giving you a chance to recover your money. But we feel your play is too strong to allow you to keep playing. Now that the cruise is over, we'd like you to leave."

Raven took the long, lonely walk to his car and hoped they wouldn't communicate with their competition—the two casinos jointly owned by the Lucky Star. He wondered what happened when people got barred at sea. Hopefully they didn't throw card counters overboard. He nervously scouted around. No one gave him any unusual attention, so he settled in and played.

The cards ran much better and Raven won sixteen grand over the next ten days to negate his losses at the Island and push his bankroll to a new high. Curtis, the shift manager, looked old enough to have witnessed Jefferson's signing of the Louisiana Purchase, and probably thought card counters had something to do with formica tops.

Their high roller pit offered a private buffet for big customers, allowing Raven to put in long hours. One local resident named Winston joined Raven there on a Thursday night after work. Winston ran a lucrative construction business, but his gambling activities rarely proved profitable and he bounced around from one club to another, trying vainly to book a winner. The majority of gamblers returned to the same casino each visit. Once they felt comfortable or lucky at one place, they seldom strayed to new watering holes. The player's cards and loyalty programs generally kept most regulars like him from tasting the fruit of other casinos—but Winston didn't care about points. He only wanted to get his money back.

They played side-by-side in silence over several shoes. The high roller pit looked more like a morgue than a casino on weeknights and the only sound heard in the sedate room was the clacking of chips. Winston's luck still ran sour, and his aggressive playing style quickly burned a hole in his pocket. He pressed his bets after each loss and soon tapped out. He took a break to light up a smoke and watched Raven play heads-up against the dealer.

The dealer continued the hot streak through the first half of the next shoe. Raven didn't lose much, since he only bet the table minimum of $25 each hand. Slowly, the count began to rise as several small cards hit the felt. Raven worked his bets up and finished the shoe with the table maximum of $500. He caught a snapper and pulled in the stack of chips as the dealer began the long shuffling process.

Winston whistled in appreciation. "I wish I had your talent, kid. Maybe I'd get even if I could borrow your brain for a night."

Raven nervously chuckled. The last thing he wanted was to be considered skillful. "I wish I could take credit for that nice little run, but you know what they say—it's better to be lucky than good."

Winston gave him a knowing look. "You don't rely on luck. I've seen you in operation."

Raven stared at Winston in alarm, and then remembered playing next to him at the Island—the night he was barred.

Winston turned to Curtis. "You guys got a lot of balls letting this kid play here. Tucker over at the Island said he's one of the best damn card counters they've ever seen."

Curtis slowly removed his wire rim spectacles and warily eyed Raven. "Is that true, Mr. Townsend?"

Raven winced. There was no use hiding. He couldn't believe Winston had ruined a good game for him.

The supervisor continued, "Well, I am very sorry, but we will have to do the same."

Raven didn't get mad at Winston. The local probably wasn't being malicious. He just didn't realize how seriously casinos took violations of their first commandment—the house is always supposed to win. A frustrated Raven Townsend cashed out and headed for the Big Easy.

♣ ♦ ♥ ♠

New Orleans didn't live up to Raven's high expectations. The fabled French Quarter and Bourbon Street failed to excite him. Most shops peddled tee shirts or catered to the twin vices of booze and sex, giving it more the appearance of a seedy den of iniquity than a famous tourist Mecca.

One glance at the local newspapers confirmed Candy's view of New Orleans. A cloud of corruption hung heavy over the Big Easy. Previously Raven kept all his money with him, even when he ran. But carrying so much currency in a crime-infested city didn't seem wise. He placed the bulk of his money into a safe deposit box, taking only enough cash for each day's play.

He tried two different casinos, with mixed results, before finding the River City complex. The classy décor placed it head and shoulders above its competition. One entire level of the casino catered exclusively to high rollers in a serene setting where crystal chandeliers hung elegantly from the ceiling. The waitresses exuded a warm southern friendliness and wore colorful, frilly outfits designed to accentuate their best features. They all looked like beauty queens and must have hand picked from the cream of New Orleans.

Raven experienced several wild swings at the River City, one day being down as much as $15,000. During the losing streaks, the pit bosses practically tripped over themselves trying to be nice to him, offering fancy dinners and a comped hotel suite. The European atmosphere and sidewalk dining of the French quarter restaurants opened his eyes to the unique appeal of New Orleans and Raven's negative image slowly changed.

Losing large amounts always unnerved him slightly, but Raven never once wavered in his confidence. Soon the cards turned and over the next few days, he not only recouped his loss but also won another $20,000. However, the mood of the pit bosses soured. Soon, he received the inevitable tap on the shoulder and was ushered off the riverboat.

They escorted him out to the parking lot and watched closely as he pulled the tan sedan onto the highway. Even though he'd been barred several times now, it still felt wrong to be treated like a king one day, then thrown out the next— simply because he might beat them at blackjack. It had to be one of the biggest injustices in the country.

Raven had driven only a few miles up the freeway when he noticed a black and white police car right behind him, blue lights flashing. A quick glance at his speedometer indicated he was speeding, but only about eight miles over the limit, slow for him. He groaned, wondering what else could possibly go wrong this day, and pulled over.

The trooper swaggered up, maximizing the intimidation value with each step.

"License and registration, please?" The burly officer looked like a Russian weight lifter with his stout barrel chest.

"Yes, sir. Was there a problem?"

"Son, you were exceeding the posted speed limit."

The officer carefully inspected the Illinois license and frowned with his lips tightly pressed together. He returned to his car and radioed dispatch. For several agonizing minutes Raven waited. Soon another trooper arrived in a backup position. As they approached his car, Raven noticed the unlatched holsters—each keeping a right hand near their guns. "Is your name Randolph Townsend?" the first officer asked.

"Yes, it is."

"Would you step out of the car please?" he said curtly.

Raven complied. The second officer frisked him down while the Incredible Hulk stood guard, staring like a raptor about to devour its prey. Convinced Raven had no weapons, the officer inspected the fanny pack.

Raven protested loudly, "That's personal stuff in there."

"Are you refusing to cooperate with an officer of the law, Mr. Townsend?"

"No, I just don't see how any of this relates to speeding." Raven said.

"It doesn't, but you match the physical description of a bank robber we're looking for."

Raven grudgingly gave a tentative nod of his head. "All right, go ahead."

The Hulk turned to the other officer. "The suspect has given permission to search his belongings."

Raven didn't like being called a suspect. He had done nothing wrong.

"And what exactly do we have here?" The police officer's eyes grew large as he pulled several stacks of rubber-banded hundred dollar bills. He turned to his partner. "You guard him, I'm calling for more backup."

"This has to be some incredible mistake," Raven said as he stared down the gun's barrel. "That's cash I use for gambling."

"Sure it is," said the officer. "Then you wouldn't mind us checking out the bills?"

"But I'm not a bank robber. That's ridiculous."

Two more squad cars arrived, one with a police dog. They led the canine to the Dodge Dart and he sniffed the stacks of money. He let out several sharp growls and barked excitedly at Raven.

"Mr. Townsend, for the record, did you give us permission to search you?"

Raven nodded nervously.

"And does the $16,450 in your fanny pack belong to you?"

"Yes, but I already explained..."

"Save your explanation for the judge. None of these serial numbers match the bills stolen from the bank, but our dog has determined several of your hundred dollar notes have drug residue on them. We are therefore confiscating all this currency since you are in a known drug transit area."

"Transit area? How's this a transit area?" Raven asked incredulously.

"Any airport, highway, or port of entry constitutes a drug trafficking area. I suggest you contact an attorney if you have any complaints." He started to walk away, then turned around. "Oh and one last thing."

Furious, Raven glared at the officer. "Yeah, what's that?"

"I'm in a good mood so I'm going to let you off with only a warning on the speeding ticket. Y'all have a nice day." He slapped his partner on the back, and they laughed all the way to the squad car.

♣ ♦ ♥ ♠

The consultation with the attorney didn't help. When Raven angrily explained what happened, the lawyer just shook his head and said. "It might cost between $10,000 and $15,000 just in legal costs to fight them. And there's no guarantee the money would be relinquished. Seizures of suspected drug money has become a profitable business, and the authorities make it very difficult to recover the cash once it's confiscated. In cities like New Orleans, a good percentage of the hundred dollar-bills carry drug residue."

"Are you saying I have no recourse?" asked Raven. "This is just unbelievable."

The lawyer stopped to glance at another piece of paper, coughed weakly, then continued in a dull flat tone devoid of feeling. "It doesn't help your case that the River City casinos claim no one by the name of Randolph Townsend ever gambled there. So, no, I don't think there is any recourse."

Raven wondered if the casino alerted the cops to investigate his cash. He felt totally powerless and got up to leave.

The attorney displayed the compassion of a robot. "Please pay my secretary on your way out." He wrote down the charges for his services on some stationary. "And I prefer cash—no out of state checks."

Raven angrily grabbed the bill and stared in disbelief—it read $150. "Thanks for the empathy. Very helpful twenty minutes," he said sarcastically. He wanted to scream for justice, but it was hopeless. Right now it felt like everyone in the state conspired against him. Completely disgusted with Louisiana, he stomped out of the office and returned to Illinois for his fall semester of grad school.

CHAPTER TEN

Raven dropped his bags on the apartment floor and walked from room to room trying to reacquaint himself with the place. The flat felt much smaller than he'd remembered. He began unpacking and found an old letter from Cynthia in the dresser. They used to write regularly, but this last correspondence dated six months previously.

It included a brochure on an archaeological dig offered fall semester in Israel. At the time he received the letter, Raven didn't think he could afford the University of Chicago, let alone study abroad. But now money wasn't an obstacle—the bulging fanny pack around his waist proved that, and a trip to the Holy Land sounded appealing, so he signed up.

♣   ♦   ♥   ♠

The ancient city of Jericho sprang up like a lush oasis from the barren Israeli countryside. Raven arrived two days late after a grueling trip. A flight delay in Rome thoroughly ravaged his travel connections, and not surprisingly, his luggage had been lost. He'd worn the same jeans and tee shirt for three days. A shadow of stubble darkened his face, and his hair lay matted against his sweltering scalp. Craving nothing more than a cool shower and sleep, he headed for the dig, eager to check in and find his bed. As he walked, the hot sun became intolerable, so he removed his shirt and wrapped it around his head in a makeshift turban. Despite the heat, he relished the clean air, a welcome change after months in smoky casinos.

At the archaeological site, students swarmed over the area like industrious ants working a hill. Raven had no trouble finding the professor in charge. Dr. Richard Cleaver looked commanding even at a distance. Gray-haired, tall and wearing dark-rimmed glasses, he pointed his pencil and notebook in various directions as he barked out instructions to a small group of students.

Raven joined the group just as Dr. Cleaver turned to a nearby young man and shouted, "What do you think you're doing? Digging to China? We're not tunneling out of prison. We're looking for fragile artifacts and you need to slow…"

The professor stopped mid-sentence as his gaze fell on Raven and his absurd headgear. "Well, well. I didn't know the circus was in town."

Raven quickly stepped forward and extended his left hand. "Raven Townsend, sir. I'm the student from the University of Chicago. Glad to meet you."

The professor ignored the gesture and zeroed in on Raven's naked torso like a bull at the sight of a red flag. "Typical self-absorbed American with no respect for other cultures. Get that ridiculous thing off your head and put your shirt back on before the locals decide to stone you."

"Sorry," Raven mumbled. He awkwardly squeezed his arms and head back into the tee shirt, which read "Jesus Saves" in big, bold letters across the front.

The professor's face grew crimson as he glared at Raven, who quickly deduced it wasn't the heat causing the reaction. "And what exactly does Jesus save us from—the Crusades?"

Professors at Chicago were also hostile to Christianity, but Raven thought instructors working in the Holy Land might think differently. However, he didn't see any purpose in rocking the boat the first day and simply asked, "Well, where's my bunk? I haven't slept in two days."

"Great. Just great. First you show up late. Now you want to blow off the rest of the afternoon too."

Raven clenched his teeth. "Okay. Where do you want me to start?"

"Cynthia is the one to blame for dragging you over here—why don't you find her? She should be right over that ridge." He pointed off to the side, barely disguising his disdain. "She'll tell you where to go."

Raven restrained his anger and walked over to the knoll overlooking the area where he expected to find Cynthia. At first glance, no girl looked familiar, but then he felt drawn to one with black, shoulder-length hair. She was down on her knees methodically brushing debris away from a shard of pottery. Her khaki shorts and tank top revealed long, tanned arms and legs. For a moment, she raised her head and shielded her eyes from the bright sun before resuming her work. Though all traces of tomboy were gone, he'd recognize her face anywhere. Raven suddenly felt his fatigue lift as he watched her. Time had transformed her into a Greek goddess in the years since Vinalhaven. He quickly finger-brushed his hair into place as best he could, and then made the short descent down to the trench.

"Hey, Cynthia," he enthusiastically shouted. "I hardly recognized you."

She didn't look up from her work.

Puzzled, he tried again. "Hey, it's me, Raven. I finally got here."

She laid down her pottery and stood to face him. He remembered her being cute, but now Cynthia struck him as drop-dead gorgeous. She flashed a fleeting smile, then it disappeared. Instead of giving him a hug, she formally shook his hand.

"Dr. Cleaver mentioned you signed on late," she said stiffly. "Glad that worked out for you."

Raven smiled. "Yes. I guess I have you to thank you for inviting me."

Her face remained reserved. "No need. I thought this dig might appeal to you, and I know you didn't come all this way to see me—you're here for the archaeology."

Raven actually had prepared a similar speech on the flight over, wanting to make sure she didn't misread his intentions in coming halfway around the world. But that was before he knew she looked like Helen of Troy.

She continued, "So I requested we work with different partners. I didn't want you to feel awkward being stuck with me. I'm with Wendy and your partner is David. He's a great guy, but if it you don't get along, you can always change."

Raven didn't know how to respond. "Of course. I'm sure that will be fine," he said halfheartedly.

Cynthia knelt by her pottery again, and Raven realized the conversation was over. "Guess I'll see you around," he muttered and walked away. *What a day. Coming here looks like the stupidest thing I've ever done.*

♣ ♦ ♥ ♠

The confrontation with Dr. Cleaver ignited a fierce determination in Raven. Years on the farm now paid off as he drove himself to be the first one up each morning and to work through any breaks. After having lived in snow-ravaged, northern states, the heat felt good as it radiated through his veins.

Cynthia shared his Yankee work ethic and also rose early each morning, but she avoided him as if he were a leper. It irritated him that she was friendly and vivacious with everyone else, but froze him out.

One morning as he immersed himself in a particularly difficult portion of the synagogue floor, he heard a student call her, "Hey, Bambi, come check this out." Raven looked up to watch her rush over and excitedly discuss some new find.

Bambi?

Raven turned to his partner. "So David, what's with 'Bambi?'"

David looked surprised. "You don't know Cynthia Bradford yet? I thought you two were old friends."

Raven winced slightly. "Actually I do know her, but I just didn't realize she had multiple names."

"Oh that. She's a bit straight and narrow and the only movie she's ever seen is *Bambi.* So some of the guys started calling her Bambi. Want me to set you up?" David asked with a mischievous grin.

"No, that's all right," Raven stammered. "Her nickname just piqued my interest."

"Just her name?" David smiled calculatingly. "She's pretty cute, although most of the guys think she's a little too conservative. Nice girl though. Sure you don't want me to play Cupid?"

Raven watched Cynthia as she chatted with friends. She had a distinctive way of making everyone around her feel important—except Raven. For a moment their eyes met as she caught him staring at her. She registered no recognition and immediately looked away. Raven sighed, "Thanks,

David, but even if I were the last human being on the planet, she wouldn't have any romantic interest in me."

♣ ♦ ♥ ♠

The 2,000 year-old Jericho synagogue under excavation was the oldest known in the world—a prestigious project. The complexity of a high-profile dig overwhelmed Raven. Besides archaeologists, at various times anthropologists, architects, botanists, zoologists, chemists, soil scientists, numismatists, photographers and geologists dropped by on site. This slowed the overall progress down to a crawl. Some days Raven had to work with a toothbrush and a dental pick, although he would have preferred a well-placed stick of dynamite. He grew increasingly frustrated and believed Dr. Cleaver overanalyzed everything. The strain between them hovered near the breaking point. Ever since his basketball days, Raven liked the feeling of being in control. He enjoyed running the team as point guard and having the pumpkin in his hands late in the game

Raven's headstrong qualities and impatience did not go unnoticed by Dr. Cleaver, who ripped into him during one evening lecture for swallowing Biblical myths and taking accounts like Adam and Eve literally. Many other students apparently agreed and their laughter, at his expense, humiliated Raven.

When the class ended, he quickly slipped outside, wanting to be left alone. Footsteps crunched behind him. In no mood for more abuse, he began to walk faster.

"Raven, wait."

He turned, surprised to find Cynthia running up to him. Breathless, she blurted out, "I can't believe how Dr. Cleaver treated you, but not everyone agrees with him."

Raven frowned. "It sure sounded that way—from the volume of laughter."

"I'm sorry I didn't say anything to support you."

"No need to apologize. He's probably right. My professors at the University of Chicago said the same things. Told me I'm crazy to believe the Bible literally."

"No, he's wrong. If he criticizes you again, I'll jump in."

Women always baffled him, but it looked like he had suddenly been crossed off Cynthia's jerk list. "Well I appreciate the support, but to be honest, I'm still a little puzzled why you've been so cool the last month."

"I guess I do owe you an apology," she said.

"I'll accept that," said Raven. "But I'd still like to know what I did wrong."

"Nothing. The problem was mine. Six months ago, my parents separated."

Raven stopped walking. "Cynthia, I'm really sorry to hear that. It must have been a shock."

"Yes, I always felt we were the perfect family," She looked away and her eyes glistened. "You know that popular book by John Gray?"

"Sure, the one about men and women being from different planets," said Raven.

"Well, my mother renamed it *Women are from Venus and Men are from Hell.*"

Raven laughed nervously. "Sounds like your dad's not real popular with your mother now."

"That's an understatement." Cynthia hesitated and then continued. "And her experience made me a little gun shy around men. Just before I left, she told me the acorn doesn't fall too far from the tree. She warned me about getting involved with anyone from such a different background."

Raven stiffened. "Like a lower class kid from Maine?"

"Exactly, but those things don't matter to me. Still, it'd been so long since we've seen each other, and you could've changed so much in those six years."

Raven swallowed hard. He resolved to prove himself to Cynthia and to find a way to make them equals—no matter what it took.

♣ ♦ ♥ ♠

The following day they switched partners and were constant companions over the next few weeks, working from dawn until evening in the dusty heat. Raven loved the climate, even the triple digit days and dreaded returning to the frosty Snow Belt—where there were nine months of winter and three months of poor sledding. He wanted a future in this land, the most sacred real estate on the face of the Earth. He wasn't alone. Cynthia also shared his excitement and they talked about making great discoveries.

Raven told her how puzzled his friend Matt had been about the Indian ruins they used to explore, unsure they were Native American. Cynthia leaned on her shovel. "Let me guess," she chuckled, "he thought your aliens built them, right?"

"Listen, I never mentioned little green men. Those were your words. Anyway, Matt is a walking encyclopedia on Indian history. He didn't know of any tribes who built sod-walled structures."

"How does he know so much about Native Americans? I didn't think that was a major at the University of Chicago."

"Matt lives in Louisiana—he's Cherokee." He saw no reason to explain how they became acquainted. The gambling part of his life had served its purpose and was best left hidden—at least for now.

His father had always cautioned him against revealing feelings or weaknesses to others, saying one's reputation was not a matter of life and death—it was far more important than that. Raven never liked people probing too deep and that morsel of paternal advice had taken seed. He feared once someone penetrated the outer layers of his life, they might be disappointed with what they found underneath.

Cynthia looked thoughtfully at Raven a moment, as if she suspected he hadn't told the whole story, and then asked, "So who built those buildings on Vinalhaven?"

Raven ran his fingers through his hair. "I hate to bring it up again, but the more I've thought about it, my theory of Vikings makes a lot of sense. I'm starting to think maybe the island was Vinland, and that's how Vinalhaven derived its name."

"I'd forgotten you'd ever said that, but it sounds possible." She returned to work, renewing her efforts with the shovel. Raven's mind drifted to dreams entertained long ago, images of faraway lands and Viking longboats.

The two of them worked together in silence for most of the morning, each content to simply enjoy the other's company. For nearly an hour they attempted to uncover a fragment of mosaic in the floor. It finally dissolved into tiny pieces despite their meticulous efforts. Raven shook his head in frustration. "Days like today make me realize I'm not much of a detail man. I like working hard and discovering ancient history, but this intricate stuff drives me crazy."

Cynthia nodded in agreement. "It's certainly frustrating when the pace is this slow."

Raven wiped his brow, "I think I'm more cut out for exploring expeditions like searching for Noah's Ark than these analytical digs that are scrutinized from every angle. I'm too impatient to sift everything with a fine-toothed comb."

Cynthia agreed. "An expedition sounds a lot more exciting." Wistfully, she looked off into the distance and said, "I've always loved mountain climbing."

Raven shook his head. "No woman could keep up on a trip like that. You've got to be made of steel to climb Ararat."

Cynthia glared at him. She flexed her biceps inches from his nose. "I think you forget who won the Camp Fair Haven Olympiad."

"Your memory is somewhat selective," Raven chuckled, enjoying the fact she still remained as competitive as the sixteen-year old he'd known in Maine. "But the reality is, you only won because my canoe paddle broke."

"Still making excuses? Well, how about a rematch?"

Raven loved her feisty spirit. "All right, I'll take another shot at the crown which should have been rightfully mine—but this time we won't compete athletically."

Cynthia wrinkled her nose. "I see. You couldn't stand the humiliation of losing to a woman again, right?"

Raven knew he was in superb shape and didn't want to trounce her—especially after they just renewed their friendship. "Exactly. I propose we battle on the archeological field. Finding Noah's Ark is out of the question for now. So we start with smaller treasures—whoever finds the most significant artifact in Israel is the victor."

Cynthia smiled broadly. "Okay, but what's the reward? I want to make sure I get a decent prize when I win."

Raven liked the way things were going so he decided to push his luck. "You—I mean the loser—will have to prepare a picnic for the winner."

"Great! I can't wait to see you in an apron." Cynthia said, and they shook hands to seal the bet.

♣ ♦ ♥ ♠

The next morning Raven stood on the embankment and watched the sunrise. As the red globe emerged from the horizon, a silhouetted girl walked in the blazing dawn light.

Raven experienced an eerie rush of recognition—this was the same Indian guide from his vision quest. Though he hadn't seen her face, everything else matched—the shiny, black hair, the graceful way she moved, even the headband. Only the eagle feather was missing. As she walked toward him, the morning rays diffused, and he found himself suddenly blinking at Cynthia wearing a red bandanna, but otherwise dressed as usual in cut-off denim shorts, sleeveless plaid blouse and L. L. Bean hiking boots.

"What are you staring at?" she asked, puzzled. "You look like you've seen a ghost." Raven concluded the bandanna, combined with the blinding sun, changed everything.

"Oh, nothing," he muttered. "Let's get to work."

The rest of the day he thought about how the dawn scene matched his vision quest experience, which he'd nearly forgotten and dismissed as nothing more than a strange dream. *Is there something to it after all?* It couldn't be coincidence, Raven decided. *Do we share some strange destiny?* He watched Cynthia meticulously scrape debris from a wall, hair falling into her face, and secretly hoped so.

♣ ♦ ♥ ♠

The last day before the semester ended, Raven pulled Cynthia aside during a break. "What do you have to show for our competition?"

"Actually, nothing," she said.

Raven reached into his pocket, pulled out the scarab he'd found in the cave during a trip to the Sinai and held it under her nose. "This bears the sign of Pharaoh Thutmosis III—several scarabs with his royal mark were found right here in Jericho at the cemetery by Dr. Wood. I think this might have been left by one of the Hebrews during the Exodus—which makes me the victor. Meet you tonight for that picnic," he said with a dangerous glint in his eye.

Cynthia laughed. "Okay, so you win. I'll try to be a gracious loser."

She picked him up in a rented convertible, reminding Raven again of the difference in their backgrounds. He would have found the cheapest car—she simply got what she wanted. They picnicked on an isolated bluff overlooking the Mediterranean Sea.

"It's been a great semester," Cynthia said.

Raven nodded, "Yes, although I could have done without Dr. Cleaver."

"He never did lighten up," Cynthia agreed.

"I really love Israel and archaeology, but I'm disillusioned with academia," said Raven.

"I know what you mean. What about your dream of finding Noah's ark?"

"Well, that would be the discovery of the millennium."

"Why hasn't anyone found it yet?"

"I believe the whole key to success is the weather," said Raven. "There have been at least thirty eyewitness accounts of people visiting the ark throughout history. Each sighting occurred during unusually warm summers."

Cynthia's blue jay eyes sparkled. "I've got a plan."

He loved her enthusiasm. "Okay, let's hear it."

"The Vinalhaven ruins—on your uncle's property. First, work that land and prove your theory that they're Viking ruins."

Raven looked doubtful. "Sounds simple, except if those really were Viking ruins, I'm sure someone else would've noticed them by now."

"Maybe not. What if we're the only two people who've ever seen them?" Cynthia said excitedly. "Don't you see, Raven? Once our credentials are established, we can get funding for any project. We could even try to find Noah's Ark."

Raven's face softened. She'd given herself away. "We?" he asked quietly.

Cynthia blushed and looked away at the horizon as the flaming sun sank into the water. "I mean, maybe you'd hire me," she said.

She's so beautiful, Raven thought. *I want to be with her for the rest of my life.*

Abruptly Cynthia jumped up. "Oh, I almost forgot. I have a present for you."

She ran to the car and returned with her hands behind her back. "Close your eyes."

When he obeyed, he felt her slip something over his head.

"Okay, you can look now," Cynthia said.

A wooden cross attached to a leather cord hung around his neck. "Do you like it? I got it at the Mount of Olives—it's made out of olive wood," Cynthia said softly.

"I love it," Raven said. "And I'll always wear it."

A warm Mediterranean breeze swirled through her hair and Raven leaned in to gently push a strand away from her eyes. He reached for a strawberry and lifted it to her mouth. Obediently she took small bites until her mouth brushed his fingers. They playfully began feeding each other the rest of the berries. Finally, only one remained. Holding his gaze, Cynthia picked it up and placed it between her lips. Raven leaned closer and hesitated. Then cupping her face in his hands, he slowly nibbled away at the fruit. When their lips met, she wrapped her fingers around the cross necklace and pulled him close. *I know what you're saying with this, Cynthia. Dear God, help me to never betray her trust.*

After seeing Cynthia to the airport, Raven walked along the Mediterranean shore, sorting out his state of mind. He was glad he had come to Israel, but some things were more confusing than when he first arrived. He loved archaeology yet wondered how he'd be able to work with people like Dr. Cleaver. Despite Raven's strong disagreement with his liberal professor's views, some questions unsettled him and old career goals no longer appeared as clear.

As for Cynthia, she complicated things. He hadn't planned on falling in love and wondered how a poor country boy from Maine could make a rich flatlander happy. He scooped up some sand and thoughtfully watched it sift through his fingers. He'd come to the Holy Land seeking clarity, but life was more uncertain than ever.

Chapter Eleven

♣ ♦ ♥ ♠

Raven Townsend rose early and went for a long run his first day back in Illinois. He wanted his body to quickly adjust from the jet lag and a brisk ten-miler would do the trick. Despite bitterly cold temperatures, the trail was crowded—a phenomenon common the first few days of January each year. Raven liked to call these people resolution runners—folks who vowed on New Year's Eve to change their lives, only to give up less than a week later.

The sixty-five minute workout left Raven with icicles on his eyebrows and permafrost in his throat. He dressed and hurried off for the first day of school, still coughing and trying to shake the chill out of his flesh. He carefully navigated the narrow, icy streets near the University of Chicago, looking for a parking spot.

He drove around for thirty tedious minutes. He passed on a few early sites, looking for one closer. None materialized. Soon there were no spaces at all.

The car felt like a jail. The heater didn't work and his breath fogged the windows. Suddenly, without warning, something inside Raven snapped.

He jerked the car around and headed back to the apartment. He packed his belongings, left a note of explanation for Joel and was just leaving, when the phone rang.

"Hi, Son," the voice on the other end said, and Raven winced. Even though the quarrel with his father had been resolved sufficiently for them to talk over the phone, this was bad timing.

"Hey, Dad. How's the weather in Maine?"

"Colder than a mackerel on ice. I just wanted to check in and see how your trip went and make sure you got home safely. You know how I don't trust them airplanes."

His father never traveled outside of Maine, and for all Raven knew, William's perception of flying came from pictures of the Wright Brothers. "Israel went okay," Raven said. "Some great moments and others I'd rather forget."

"That's life Randolph. You ain't always going to be the lead dog. Many times you're back in the pack, with the only view being the other hound's butt."

Over the years, Raven gradually started to miss his father, but not the corny animal illustrations. "Well, funny you should say that, because today I decided to do something about that."

"Like what?"

Raven considered how much to tell. *Can I expect my father to understand?*

"I'm dropping out of school."

"What! How come?"

"This morning I couldn't find a parking spot, and I said the heck with it. Right now I'm tired of all the hoops I have to go through dealing with arrogant professors, and I'm not up for these Arctic conditions." Raven didn't want to get into the real reasons.

His father growled. "Randolph, I think you're making a terrible mistake. What are your plans now?"

"I've decided to gamble full-time for a while." Raven knew this had to be a bombshell, even though his father was aware of his earlier casino forays.

"That's the stupidest thing I've ever heard. All that university learning and nothing to show for it."

"I'm just not the type who can kiss everyone's butt. And that's what I'd have to do to succeed in grad school and in archaeology. If I can win a million dollars in blackjack, then I could pursue my dreams on my own terms." He thought the strongly independent Townsend blood in his father would understand that rationale.

"Just a million, huh. Glad to see you're not greedy," his father answered sarcastically. "Well Randolph, I've got just one last thing to say to you. Never wrestle with a pig. You'll both get dirty and the pig likes it."

Raven hung up. He'd prove his father and other doubters wrong. His special mathematical gift was no different from the genius of talented musicians and artists. He could be one of the best blackjack players in the world. No longer would he deny or fight that destiny. Failure risked ridicule, but Raven dismissed such thoughts. He resolved to succeed, no matter what it took.

Just a few weeks earlier, he and Cynthia shared a vision of great discoveries in the Holy Land. He hoped this detour wouldn't derail those dreams, but might actually give him the financial base to fulfill them. He contemplated going back to the Swamp, but the memory of its crowded tables and smoky atmosphere steered him instead to the numerous riverboats scattered over the state of Mississippi.

♣ ♦ ♥ ♠

The gulf coast of Mississippi with its broad, sandy beaches and sunny skies proved to be a welcome sight. The world's longest manmade beach and its shoreline looked a little dirty, but it still beat Chicago in January.

Raven moved around frequently between the various riverboats, hoping to keep a lower profile and avoid the problems he experienced in Louisiana. His bankroll had dwindled with the expenses of Israel, but he was confident it would soon rise. He remembered how he had taken his $5,000 in tuition money and rode it up to $88,000 before heading to Israel. A serious full-time effort could conceivably turn his eighty grand into half a million in six to twelve months. Then he would only need to double it one more time to reach seven figures.

There was nothing really magical about that goal, but it would be satisfying to return to Maine an actual millionaire. Lately, Raven hadn't given much thought to his impulsive outburst at his high school graduation party, but to go back there and prove his classmates wrong carried a delicious appeal.

He had forgotten so many of the little quirks in casinos—the chatty dealers, the finger flutter all casino employees do when handling money, and his annoyance at the tourists who stop and gawk at everything, unaware they're blocking traffic. After a few days of practice and play, his game was as fast as before.

Slowly, he regained the money confiscated by the New Orleans cops and before long hit a new milestone with $105,000 in winnings. He could now safely bet up to a thousand a hand, the maximum at most riverboats. This enabled him to win more but also brought increased scrutiny from nervous pit bosses.

The Biloxi Belle, however, loved his high-stakes action and the casino manager approached him. "Mr. Townsend, we've noticed you like playing alone."

Raven sized up the bald-headed man with the large ears and groped for a response. "Yeah, I don't like chain-smoking yahoos jumping in and out of my table."

"Well, my name's Reggie and I'm the casino manager here," he said with a fake smile. "Would you prefer having your own private table?"

Raven thought this must be a joke, since only James Bond gambled like that. And with his beat-up sneakers, Raven didn't exactly look like 007 strolling through Monte Carlo. He suspected a trap, but it sounded too enticing to pass up.

The casino set up a separate table with two decks dealt out of a shoe. They used a cut card to insure 70% of the cards would be played before each shuffle. His suspicions melted, and the Biloxi Belle suddenly went from being a loud, poorly lit, musty casino to Raven's favorite. Even the grimy felt and moldy smell of the carpet couldn't dampen his enthusiasm. The place was so seedy and the cards so dirty, wise patrons washed their hands before going to the bathroom rather than after.

None of those things mattered to Raven. He'd play in a barn if the rules were good—and this game was fantastic. A hundred bucks even when the count went negative was new territory for Raven. Usually he switched tables when the house had the advantage, but now he sat through every shoe. However, spreading from $100 to $1000 more than outweighed this small disadvantage.

Raven played twelve hours a day, pausing only for short meal breaks. Reggie told him they could only keep his table open for twenty minutes if he left, so this forced him to fly through the buffet line a couple times a day. Raven didn't mind, since the food choices were severely limited. All offerings swam in butter, and Raven stood a better chance of becoming the next Pope than of finding healthy items like fresh squeezed orange juice.

People often gathered behind his table and the more chips he accumulated, the larger the crowd. Raven enjoyed the attention and power he derived from having so many railbirds watching his every move. He had risen to the top of one of the world's most difficult professions. His counting was fast, flawless and almost effortless after playing long hours every day. He could now count down a deck in eleven seconds—twice as fast as the books recommended, and he wondered if anyone, anywhere, had ever counted fifty-two cards any quicker.

For five straight days Raven shelled the casino. The higher stakes, combined with the speed of playing alone against the dealer created huge swings. One sensational day Raven shot up to $38,000 ahead at one point—before dramatically dumping about half of it back. It was still by far his biggest win ever. Each of the five days at this private table Raven won at least $10,000, and more than $70,000 overall.

Unfortunately, the bubble burst.

The afternoon of the fifth day, Reggie nervously stroked his baldhead as Raven continued the pounding. The pit boss superstitiously called for a new dealer, hoping it might change the luck. A petite gal named Bonnie was quickly brought in. She needed a small box to stand on in order to reach the table. The two decks went through a methodical shuffle, before Bonnie finally offered the cards to Raven for the cut.

The first two hands both ended in a push and used up several small cards. Raven pushed out the max bet of $1000 and won the next six hands in a row, two of them double downs.

Reggie nearly came unglued and finally decided to step in and end the fiasco. Raven could almost detect steam coming out his ears. "Randolph, I think you've been playing us like a banjo here."

"Not sure what you mean, Reggie."

"I mean you're too smart. Almost like cheating," Reggie barked. "You've clipped us for seventy grand and we're not taking any more of your action."

This irritated Raven and he dismissed with the usual pretense of surprise over being detected as a card counter.

"I'm just doing the same thing you guys do—figuring out the odds, so I only play with an advantage. Is using your brain cheating?" Raven asked with an edge in his voice.

Reggie crossed his arms. His face was flushed and his ears bent forward like landing gear on Dumbo. "It's different for us. We're supposed to win."

Raven shook his head at the lack of logic. "Reggie, I appreciated your hospitality, but I don't like being misrepresented. If you can't afford to lose, don't gamble."

He cashed out in a huff, consoled by a bankroll now close to $180,000 and a strong confirmation he made the right choice in leaving the University of Chicago.

Raven pulled over a few miles down the road to call Cynthia. When he first informed her about dropping out of school, she had gotten so upset he never brought up the issue of gambling and just said he needed a hiatus from his studies. Now, with so much money in his pocket, it would be easier to break the news to her.

Cynthia answered on the first ring. She had just returned from spring break and excitedly told him all about her ski vacation in Lake Tahoe with her mother. "The mountains are so beautiful there. It was just gorgeous. Have you ever been to Tahoe, Raven?"

"No, I never have." *Although I plan to be in the future,* he thought.

"Perfect snow, soft and powdery. The only negative was the condo we normally use wasn't available so we had to stay in a casino hotel."

Great, now it'll be easy to bring up the subject.

"That must have been fun."

Cynthia's voice rose. "Are you crazy? Do you know what it's like inside a casino?"

He started to make a joke, but suddenly sensed he'd better tread carefully. "Sure, they're real exciting—non-stop action."

"Get serious, Raven. You've obviously never been in one or you'd know better. The cocktail waitresses wear clothing more appropriate for the bedroom, and the whole environment is built around money, sex, and power."

Raven felt the hair on his neck stand on edge in alarm. "You don't say?"

"They're the epitome of evil. I saw one woman about my age playing slots. She looked like a normal young house-wife, but video poker clearly mesmerized her. She kept losing all her money, but rather than quit, she went to the ATM machine again and again and again. She noticed me watching and started apologizing, promising each time would be the last. It wasn't and she kept dumping buckets of coins down the drain. It was one of the saddest things I've ever seen. God should burn all those wicked places to the ground."

Whoa! This was not exactly going as planned. Raven decided to broach the subject of his current lifestyle later, in person. "Cynthia, I'd like to come see you in Connecticut. There are a few things I need to talk to you about."

"Great! I can get out of school anytime, for you."

♣ ♦ ♥ ♠

Raven headed north through the long Magnolia State, playing the few scattered riverboats along the way. None of the games were particularly good, and he was mostly interested in getting to Tunica and its larger casinos.

Until gambling came to Mississippi, Tunica County had been America's version of the third world. It was frequently cited as the poorest county in the country and Jesse Jackson dubbed it America's Ethiopia. Before the first riverboat opened, more than a quarter of the people were unemployed. In the years that followed, the area became a boomtown with nine casinos, more hotel rooms than Memphis, and millions upon millions in revenue.

The Splash casino was the first and most modest riverboat in Tunica. Raven quickly saw why it was dying. Without a doubt the Splash had the worst layout of any gambling facility in the world—it was crowded, drab, loud, and confusing. Raven meandered around the boat several times before finding his bearings. They packed in so many slot machines that guests had to squeeze through the narrow maze between them to get anywhere. The scattering of tables suggested no rhyme or reason other than a random throw of a dart.

When Raven was acclimated enough to no longer worry about getting lost, he scouted the blackjack games and moved behind one table to start counting. He always watched the cards before playing in a new place since the pit wouldn't perceive him as a threat until he jumped in and made his first bet.

The dealer wore the unusual combination of bowtie and suspenders. He shuffled the cards and began play. A large security guard with an NFL body, and the defiant demeanor of Malcolm X painted on his face, brushed by Raven and stood a few yards away. Another security guard entered the room and positioned himself behind the craps table. Raven nervously glanced around. No one else seemed alarmed. The normal din of happy gamblers and clanging slot machines filled the air, muffling the despair of the far more numerous losers. Raven turned his attention back to the blackjack table.

The count reached plus twelve and Raven unzipped his fanny pack, preparing to jump in with two cash plays of five hundred each. Suddenly, a supervisor with an ugly scar on his throat marched into the pit. Raven hesitated and stepped back, slowly zipping his fanny pack shut.

Could I possibly be getting heat without playing a hand?

While debating this question, he faintly overheard the name Randolph Townsend on one of the security guard's walkie-talkies.

That can't be. No one here has a clue who I am.

He trusted his instincts, and interrupted the dealer. "Sir, where is the bathroom located?"

The dealer straightened his bowtie and pointed to the left. Raven thanked him and headed that direction, although he had no intention of fulfilling any call of nature. He walked rapidly to the stairwell. Once out of sight, he sprinted down the steps and off the boat. He slowed to a brisk walk, as no one appeared to be following him, but halfway to the car, another backward glance confirmed his worst fears. He wasn't just being followed—he was being chased.

Both security guards were running after him. The larger guard looked like he could've played linebacker for 'Ole Miss.' Despite his immense size he was quick on his feet and rapidly closed the pavement between him and Raven. The years of grueling workouts were supposed to prepare Raven for winning some big road race, but now he needed to tap every ounce of speed his legs contained. He pumped his arms furiously and dashed towards the car.

His burst opened up a small gap from his pursuers and he jumped in his car slightly ahead of them. Unfortunately he hadn't parked the car facing out and the few seconds backing up cost him. The colossal guard grabbed the antenna and side mirror shouting, "Stop the vehicle!"

Raven pretended to slow down, but once he had backed up enough, he slammed down the gas pedal and squealed forward. The guard frantically tried to hold the car in place with his enormous strength, but he slid off onto the asphalt with a ripped antenna in his hand.

Raven floored the Dodge Dart and headed for the Tennessee border. He desperately wanted out of Mississippi before any more southern justice waylaid him. Evidently the Gulf Coast casinos shared his name and picture. Possibly other Mississippi clubs also received this information, but Raven didn't want to wait to find out.

He made it to Memphis, fearful the whole way someone had been sent after him. Though he never saw anyone,
the forty miles of hard driving finished off the old car. It
sputtered and belched a dark blue cloud of smoke as the
city skyline came into view. He nursed it to a gas station,
where it was pronounced dead on arrival. He left it for
scrap, caught a cab, and headed to the airport.

CHAPTER TWELVE

♣ ♦ ♥ ♠

It was Wednesday evening when Raven walked out of the Hartford airport. Though anxious to see Cynthia, he didn't want to interrupt her studies midweek, so he headed for the nearby Foxwood Casino to pick up a little money at the tables and hopefully snag a free gourmet meal to surprise her.

None of the previous casinos prepared Raven for the size and scale of Foxwood—a massive complex of slot machines and gambling tables covering more than seven acres. Indians all over the country flocked to gambling, yet none struck riches like the small Pequot tribe. The colossal edifice rose from the midst of a forest—an astounding accomplishment for a tribe numbering less than six hundred members. They dabbled in several marginal businesses, such as raising pigs, before opening a bingo hall. This modest beginning eventually became the world's largest casino—drawing over 50,000 visitors a day and grossing over a billion dollars per year—more than all the casinos in Reno combined.

The huge gaming area nearly required a map to navigate. Raven decided to emulate Marco Antonelli's team approach, yet with no associates to back count, he improvised and did the next best thing. Instead of playing each shoe from the start and making a lot of small bets while waiting for the count to climb, he watched from behind the table and only jumped in when he had a good advantage. Previously he had done this when making his first bets in a new club, but now he used this strategy repeatedly by moving around to different areas of the same casino.

The vast layout enabled him to float inconspicuously around the tables, and he felt a surge of pride over being innovative. In the past, he had only followed the books he read, but stepping out into new territory felt more satisfying. Raven relished adventure and showed no fear taking risks. His father had been just the opposite—afraid to travel outside Maine or try anything new. William dreaded failure and preferred safe, tried routes. He always said, "The early bird may get the worm, but the second mouse gets the cheese."

Raven also started using a false name, Eddie Wilson. After what happened in Mississippi, he didn't want to take a chance giving his real name. Using a pseudonym carried the added bonus of making him feel like a secret agent. He still lacked the tuxedo and elegance of Bond, but he could act like a spy. He looked forward to the expression on Cynthia's face when she learned how successful he had become.

The new technique of back counting worked perfectly. Raven enjoyed sitting less at the tables and being a little more detached from the other players, especially with so many rude big city patrons.

By Friday night Raven had won $12,000 and received a comp to the Fox Harbour, an elegant seafood restaurant. He requested a quiet, romantic spot near a window. Candles crowned each table and soft classical music filtered through the air. Cynthia showed up exactly at 8:00 P. M. and was ushered to Raven's table.

Her eyes danced with excitement as she gave him a warm hug. She smiled easily and often. Raven rarely showed any external emotions, but tonight he couldn't contain the foolish grin spreading across his face.

The waiter brought their menus and Cynthia reached across the table to touch Raven's hand. "Meeting here for dinner confused me since you surely know I dislike casinos." Her gaze scanned the room, drinking in the ambiance of the setting. "But now I see why you brought me here. It's awesome!"

The aroma of grilled salmon drifted over from a nearby table. Raven was glad she loved the place. He desperately wanted to make her happy and soon she would know the real reason they were dining in a casino.

Raven sipped his French onion soup and nervously made small talk, unsure how to shift to more serious matters.

Ironically, it was the maitre d' who broke the ice. "How are we this evening? Everything fine here with you two lovely young people?"

"Absolutely. Exquisite table. Thanks again," Raven answered.

Pierre's lips remained fixed in a plastic smile. "My pleasure, Mr. Wilson. Don't hesitate to ask if there is anything else I can do."

He turned and walked away. Raven stabbed at his swordfish. Cynthia stared straight ahead, not touching her food.

"Raven, why did he call you Mr. Wilson?"

After a long, awkward moment, he decided to break the good news.

"That's the name I'm using," Raven said coolly.

"What? What do you mean that's the name you're using?"

"Downstairs in the casino. I'm playing as Eddie Wilson," he said nonchalantly, as if discussing the day's baseball game.

"I'm not sure I understand all of this." She took a small bite of her yellow fin tuna. "Actually I'm not sure I understand any of this. What exactly is going on?"

Raven proceeded to tell her the whole story. How he got interested in card counting from reading a magazine article on blackjack. He explained the early days in Joliet and how his recent wins dwarfed his earlier success.

Twice he repeated the total amount he now had in cash, confident the sheer amount would convince her he was doing the right thing. Cynthia listened silently. She had always been a good listener. She picked at her salad, choosing only the greens, and finally responded with a nervous laugh.

"Well, you really had me going there. The way you told that story it was almost believable. This is all some sort of joke, right?"

Nothing in Raven's background prepared him for this reaction. He understood cards and numbers, but knew little about women. "No, it's all the truth. It shouldn't be that shocking. Everyone gambles. Thomas Jefferson gambled fanatically at backgammon, and lotteries helped build Yale, Harvard and Princeton. Even life itself is a gamble."

"What's that supposed to mean?" she asked in a forced tone.

"Everyone takes risks and weighs the odds many times each day," Raven said. "Have you ever heard of Gerad Hommel?"

Cynthia shook her head. "No, I haven't, but I'd guess he was some famous card player."

"Nope. He climbed Mount Everest six times, but died changing a light bulb in his kitchen. Fell off a ladder and hit his head on the sink."

"How can you stretch life's risks into an excuse to gamble with money? Don't you see the difference?" asked Cynthia.

Raven remained undeterred and plunged ahead. "I didn't really totally understand all of these things until the vision quest. Then it slowly became clear."

Cynthia's eyes widened in shock, then narrowed with exasperation. "Vision quest? This is getting crazier by the minute."

Raven tried to explain the strange, confusing future he viewed. "At first I thought it was just a dream, but then it gradually made sense. It had to be real. When I got back to Chicago, I knew school needed to wait—at least until I've fulfilled my destiny and made my million."

Cynthia laid down her fork. "I can't believe all the time we were in Israel you never mentioned blackjack. We worked together twelve hours a day for three months and you never mentioned running around the woods with a loincloth on some strange vision quest." Her eyes expressed deep hurt. "How could you hide those things from me?"

Raven looked straight into Cynthia's face. "Listen, trust me here. This is only a temporary detour."

Cynthia's face contorted into a frown. "Have you gone crazy? What about your call from God? You told me in Israel how passionate you were about discovering Noah's Ark."

"I think my future is both. If I take a little time now to pursue this field, I'll be rich enough and never have to work under people like Dr. Cleaver again. I can be an archaeologist anywhere I want."

Cynthia grew silent again. The color drained from her face. Then she spoke quietly. "I expected this to be a wonderful, romantic evening. Do you realize how much I looked forward to seeing you again?" She waved her fork at Raven for emphasis. "How can you do this me? Have you thought about the costs of what you're doing?"

Raven smiled reassuringly. "Yes, that's why I told you how much money I've won so that you can see there's an edge. There's actually a certain nobility to what I'm doing."

"How?" she demanded.

"You see, I'm taking money from the hands of the wicked and..."

"Yeah, you're a real Robin Hood. Raven, I know you're incredibly bright and gifted, but you're gambling with more than just money." Then stressing each syllable she said, "You're gambling with your soul." Her hand slammed down loudly on the table and other patrons in the restaurant stared at them.

Raven tried to calm her down by speaking softly, "Cynthia, don't you see what a difference this money will make. It will give me more control and freedom in archaeology." He reached for her hand. "It'll give *us* more independence."

She pulled her hand away from him. "Raven, with all your talents you're too good for some immoral place like Las Vegas."

She held up her crystal goblet. "Which would you rather drink from? This goblet or a Styrofoam cup?"

"Obviously the goblet," said Raven.

"But what if the goblet was dirty? If it hadn't been washed and there was a bug crawling inside?"

"Then I would use the Styrofoam cup."

"Exactly."

Raven was now totally bewildered. "I don't get your point."

"The point is God uses clean vessels. You can't still expect to be a Christian if you gamble, do you?"

"I really don't see why not. There's nothing in the Bible specifically against gambling."

"What will it take for God to get through to you—a burning bush?"

Now tears flowed down her cheeks. "I don't know you any more. You're not the man I fell in love with."

Raven sat in stunned amazement. He hadn't anticipated this. *I thought she'd want her parents' standard of living. Doesn't she see blackjack is the only way I can get rich?* He wanted Cynthia. He knew that much. But to turn his back on blackjack, now, with so much money rolling in seemed irrational.

"Cynthia, I won over twenty grand in one day in Mississippi. There's no job anywhere on this planet where I could make that kind of money."

Cynthia remained adamant. "You're wrong Raven. You need to choose between me and blackjack, between gambling and God."

Raven always found decision-making difficult. He frequently second-guessed himself and regretted many moments of his life. He had been hesitant to accept the vision quest, but eventually his life seemed to be swept away by a river of fate. To exit now without running the full course didn't feel right. The sudden need for a quick decision confused him.

"Cynthia, I don't know," he stammered.

She was his opposite, decisive and rarely doubted herself. "If you're going to pursue blackjack," she said, tossing her napkin on the table, "forget about any future with me. We're through!" She grabbed her purse and stood up.

Raven tried to speak, but Cynthia stormed out, nearly colliding with the waiter.

He stayed in his chair. *She'll come back after she calms down. It doesn't have to be gambling or God.* After all, he was playing for their benefit, not only his.

Minutes passed. Raven waited nervously. After a while, when he realized the die had been cast, his anxiousness turned to anger. She hadn't even given him a fair chance to make a decision.

He desperately needed to get out of the restaurant and went outside for some fresh air, hoping Cynthia might still be around. She was gone. He considered going up to his room but didn't want to be alone, and he refused to sit by the phone waiting for her to call. Instead, he headed back to the blackjack tables.

The casino swelled with the usual evening crowds. He tried to back count a couple of tables, but for the first time since his initial trip to Joliet, he couldn't keep up with the dealers. The cards looked like a blur, and his mind moved in slow motion.

How did I ever screw up this badly?

The casino host, Alex Littlefield, approached him. "You feeling all right?"

"Yeah, I'm fine. Just a little dazed, I guess," said Raven.

"Was it something you ate?" Alex asked. "I hope the meal we comped for you was okay, Mr. Wilson."

"No, the food was great. I'm just a little unsettled."

"Probably stress from your job," prompted the host. "What do you do for work anyway?"

Raven's brain locked up. He had never thought of a cover story.

Alex continued. "You must have a pretty sweet occupation to be betting two grand a hand. That's more than I take home in a week."

"I'm in Amway," Raven lied. It seemed like a good story and he knew a little about the business from Joel West. Unfortunately, Alex knew a lot about the organization. After several probing questions, it became apparent Raven was lying. The friendly host turned into a suspicious adversary. Within minutes, the atmosphere changed dramatically and Raven decided to leave before they pegged him as a card counter. He wasn't mentally sharp enough to compete with one of the best pit crews in the country. It was a stupid mistake not thinking of a cover profession and one he vowed never to make again.

By the time he arrived at the airport, he'd made up his mind. For now, he needed to get as far away as possible. His destiny lay in the desert. The huge casinos in Nevada offered him the best chance to win his million and prove himself to Cynthia.

CHAPTER THIRTEEN

♣ ♦ ♥ ♠

After Wheaton College, Joel West had tried everything to strike it rich. Amway bombed out and left him with few friends. The commodities trading course left him broke. After so many mistakes, his family pulled the plug on him financially, and he jumped at the chance to drive Raven to Las Vegas.

The long trip halfway across the country gave them their first chance to talk in nearly a year. Raven filled Joel in on the sad state of his love life. "We should have been able to compromise, but when Cynthia demanded I get out of blackjack, something inside me rebelled. People always told me what I could or couldn't do."

"In what way?" asked Joel.

"Such as where to go to college, or that I was too short to play basketball. You've got to be independent enough to make decisions for yourself. I don't like anyone, not even Cynthia, forcing my hand."

Joel readily agreed. "Sure, I understand that. Still seems kind of harsh though, losing sugar that sweet."

"I'm not throwing in the towel yet. Nothing's over until the final buzzer. Look at all those songs that wax poetic over the nostalgia of lost love. After she cools down, things will change and we'll get back together. We have to. It's fate."

Joel shrugged. "Hey, don't get all teary-eyed and drive off a cliff. Besides, from what she said to you, I wouldn't bet on her showing up anywhere except in your dreams."

Raven stood firm. "No, she will."

"Well, don't hold your breath. There are plenty of women out there. Maybe we can even find you a new one in Vegas."

"That's not likely. Women like Cynthia are rare and it's beyond belief to think you'd find a jewel like that in Nevada."

"Just forget about her. Think about all that money in your pocket. Two hundred thou on you...in cash, unbelievable."

Raven laughed. "You think I've hit the big time. Wait until you meet Marco Antonelli. There aren't enough O's in smooth to describe him."

Joel displayed far more interest in Raven's blackjack exploits than in his love life. "I remember you mentioning him from your Minnesota trip. Made a few million, right?"

"That's an understatement. Over a million a year. He burned out so many blackjack games that other pros nicknamed him 'The Terminator.' We'll look him up when we get to Vegas and you'll hear some incredible tales." Raven neglected to share his uneasiness about Marco Antonelli.

"Great. Maybe I could join his team, help keep his girls in line." Joel said with a smirk.

Raven looked at his friend in amazement, wondering how his college roommate could have changed so much since Wheaton. "Are you crazy?"

Joel shook his head. "I got no other options. My parents cut me off and I need to make some money. Might as well follow in your footsteps."

"No way. It's not for you." Raven felt Joel had neither the work ethic nor enough discipline to succeed at blackjack.

"Get off your high horse. Remember how self-righteous you acted when Tim and I grilled you? What's good for the goose is good for the gander."

"It's still different. My memory and ability with numbers destined me to play blackjack."

"So I'm a moron?" Joel asked. "Don't forget how many card games I won on campus. I might not be on par with you, but I'm sharp enough to learn."

Raven worried about his friend. The dark side of gambling preyed on people like him. "It's a tough environment out there and can grind down your values."

"Save the Sunday School speech, man. The only part I care about is you're winning big and I want in."

"What about your parents? They'll die if you get involved in gambling," Raven countered.

"That's exactly why they'll never hear about it."

"You're not going to tell them?" Raven asked.

Joel made a face. "Do I look stupid? They'd react exactly like Cynthia did when you dropped that bombshell on her."

Raven considered his dilemma. Obviously, little would deter Joel once he saw dollar signs. Hoping to steer his susceptible friend away from the morally dangerous waters of Marco Antonelli's world, Raven decided to teach Joel himself.

"All right. Here's the deal. I've thought about putting together a team like Marco. His approach is the most efficient way to make big money in blackjack."

Joel smiled. "I like what I hear so far. Go on."

"I need people I can trust. I'll train you to back count for me if that's what you want."

"Every bee wants to taste the nectar," said Joel. "Count me in."

"Just don't expect to strike it rich," Raven warned. "The funny thing about quick and easy money is that it's never quick or easy."

♣ ♦ ♥ ♠

As they approached the desert Neon City, the temperature steadily soared. Having grown up in the Pacific Northwest, Joel had never experienced such heat. His clothes dripped with sweat. "Man, this is awful. It's like Africa-hot out here. I need to get rid of this clunker and get me a ride with air conditioning."

Raven didn't respond. His eyes fixated on the sign pointing to the Valley of Fire State Park.

"Hey! My Indian guide led me through a Valley of Fire in my vision quest."

"Come on. You don't really believe you've actually been here before, do you?" Joel asked skeptically.

"Yes, how else can you explain it?" Raven asked.

"I don't know, man, this is pretty bizarre. It's like deja-vu all over again."

Raven shrugged. "I'm not sure what to believe about it. Some parts have come true, but I'm still confused."

Joel rolled his eyes. "Earth to Raven! Hello? And you're worried about me shucking my beliefs in Sin City? I'm not the one listening to the Great Spirit in the sky telling us we're all one. I think some of the cheese slipped off your cracker."

They both laughed. Losing their religion was the last thing either of them feared.

♣ ♦ ♥ ♠

Gambling in Las Vegas is unlike any other place on Earth—the imposing strip of luxurious casinos swarm with tourists and the staggering amounts of money changing hands makes it the Mecca for all serious players. Raven loved the place despite his aversion to crowds. He felt like he belonged. He savored the warm dry desert air. Even the West Coast time zone felt right—as if his body had been out of sync all his life until now. Each morning he woke up more refreshed than ever. The nightmare of the burning church rarely tormented his dreams any longer.

The massive casinos were ripe for plundering and Raven hit them hard with his student in tow. Joel watched Raven win eight grand at the Desert Inn. As they left he said, "Man, that was easy. The card gods sure were on your side."

"You're a Wheaton grad and you believe in card gods? Disciplined counting is the only way to beat blackjack. Luck has nothing to do with this business."

"Okay," Joel shrugged. "But what if you doubled your bet every time after a loss? Wouldn't you win eventually?"

Raven shook his head. "That's called the Martingale system. You'd win most sessions, but the wins would all be small and the losses great, making it impractical in the long run."

Joel disagreed. "Why worry about the long run. Just quit when you're ahead every time."

Raven gave an example of starting with five-dollar bets and doubling after each loss. "If you lost seven hands in a row, your bet would now be $640, which is such a jump from the five bucks you started with, that your heart will be pounding loud enough to rattle the chips in the tray."

Joel remained unconvinced. "Come on. You're never going to lose that many."

Raven shook his head. "That's a common misconception. Losing seven hands in a row happens almost every hour. I once lost fourteen hands in a row, all in a positive count. Forget the gimmicks, they're not going to work."

Joel reluctantly agreed and directed his attention to learning how to count cards. Raven didn't expect Joel to become a winning blackjack player right away but hoped he could learn to back count.

After getting settled in, Raven called Marco Antonelli. Marco had something he wanted to talk over with Raven and offered to pick them up. He arrived at noon, an hour later than he promised. The three of them squeezed into the black Maserati for the short drive. Raven sunk into the soft, supple leather seat. He'd never been in such a nice car his entire life. A *ski naked* emblem hung from the mirror. Raven tried to visualize Marco hot-dogging down the slopes wearing only his goggles. Marco noticed Raven staring at it. "You like to ski?"

Raven smiled sheepishly. "Not really. I just couldn't decide which bothered me more—your lack of morals or your tolerance to the cold."

"Well, they're both legendary."

Marco cruised down the Strip pointing out sights. "Welcome to Lost Wages, the city where even tap water comes with a swizzle stick. This place has more unlisted phone numbers and more heart attacks than any city in America—where most conversations end with 'good luck.'"

Joel jumped in. "Is that the reason for your vanity license plate? BIGGER meaning Vegas?"

"Not at all. BIGGER reflects the consensus of showgirls throughout town who consider me to have—"

Raven interrupted, "Okay, we get the picture. I don't think we need the details."

Undaunted, Marco continued the travel commentary by pointing out that fourteen of the fifteen largest hotels in the world were right on the Strip. "Vegas is the epitome of extremes, a city where extravagance and garishness are more important than quality, a common bond it shares with Hollywood. Both cities are an oasis in the desert that feed greedily on mankind's collective dreams and desires. Small doesn't happen in Las Vegas and in this case big is better."

He deftly passed a Volvo, then turned sharply north off the strip and into an upscale part of town. "That gorgeous building on your right is where I go for mass—although it's been a few years. My confessions got too steamy for the priest. Are you guys Catholic?"

"Actually, we're both Baptist," interjected Raven.

"No shit?" Marco asked in a loud voice.

Raven didn't know how to respond to that so Marco continued. "Then you must know the three things Baptists don't recognize."

Raven and Joel both shrugged.

"They don't recognize the Pope as the authority of the church, they don't recognize dancing as proper entertainment, and they don't recognize each other in a Las Vegas casino."

He paused for Joel's laughter to die down. "And surely you know the difference between praying in church and praying in Las Vegas?" Raven shook his head and Marco delivered the punch line. "When you pray in Vegas, you *really* mean it."

Joel again chuckled heartily, while Raven restrained his true feelings and smiled weakly.

They pulled into a circular driveway fronting a massive home built in the Spanish Southwest style. After a quick tour of the interior, they plopped down outside by a huge rock pool and waterfall. A blonde in shorts brought three cold daiquiris and Marco gave her a playful slap on the rump as she left. He gave no introduction, and it was left to speculation whether she was a maid, girlfriend, lover, or wife.

Raven naturally refused to let alcohol pass through his lips and was flabbergasted to see Joel down his frosty drink. Marco asked Raven how he'd been doing in blackjack since they last met. He listened intently to Raven's accomplishments.

"I'm glad to hear you're betting two grand a hand. A lot of beginning players try to get me to bankroll 'em. If those idiots were any good, they'd already have enough money and wouldn't need mine," Marco said.

He finished off his drink and clapped his hands for another. "If you're still betting peanuts, then either you're a losing player or one who doesn't have the balls to bet big. I've got no respect for either."

The conversation next shifted to Joel. "Now, what's your story?"

"I'm just getting started. Raven's teaching me." Joel drained the rest of his daiquiri, ignoring Raven's glaring disapproval.

Marco gave a knowing grin. "Well, good luck. Everyone would be a professional gambler if they could. Next to getting paid for being a gigolo it's the greatest job in America. But only a few make it."

"Why is that?" Joel asked.

"Fluctuation," replied Marco.

"What's so tough about that?" Joel inquired.

"Nothing, as long as it's up. But when the dam breaks and you start losing, that's when you find out what you're made of," said Marco.

"I can handle it," Joel replied confidently.

"Really? I guess you'll soon find out. Do you know the difference between a puppy and a blackjack player?" Marco asked.

Joel looked puzzled over the strange analogy. "No, I don't."

"The puppy eventually stops whining," said Marco. "After you play cards a while, you'll appreciate that joke."

The blonde returned with two new drinks and Marco watched her glide back into the house. "Nice set of headlights, don't you think? Love to see them on high beam."

Joel and Marco laughed robustly, but the innuendo embarrassed Raven. Marco continued, "So Mr. Townsend, how much money you got saved up?"

This surprised Raven and seemed an unnecessary intrusion into his private life. But since Marco had shared so much with him in Minnesota, he felt obligated to return the trust. "About $200,000."

Marco didn't look impressed. Raven assumed he expected more, so he added an explanation. "It would've been much higher except for a little Southern hospitality and government intrusion."

He proceeded to tell Marco about the cash confiscated in New Orleans. The story didn't surprise Marco, since he had a grave distrust of Big Brother.

"And taxes on what I made last year killed me," Raven added.

Marco bolted from his chair. "How could you be that stupid? Filing as a professional gambler is roughly equivalent to dropping your pants in front of the Federal building with a bulls-eye painted on your butt."

"I thought the law required everyone to pay taxes on all income, even gambling," Raven answered defensively.

"Nobody does everything the law says. I don't give any money to relatives and my least favorite relative is Uncle Sam. Someday I'll teach you how to screw the IRS and not pay another nickel to those bloodsuckers," said Marco.

Raven squirmed. He'd been taught to obey the rules. Even though he disliked the IRS, cheating the government was a serious crime.

Joel, however, was enthralled by everything about Marco. He loved the big house, the fancy car, and the huge pool. "Marco, tell us some stories from your career. Raven said you've had some adventures."

Marco nodded heartily. "That's an understatement. I've done it all, A to Z. Made more money than anyone else who ever played the game."

Raven remembered his first impression of Marco Antonelli—humility was not his strength.

Marco continued, "Anyway, it's hard to pick just one story, but the Macao trip stands out."

Joel hung on every word, encouraging Marco with his eyes. "Isn't that the little island off Hong Kong?"

Marco nodded. "That's the place. Easily the dirtiest and scariest city I've ever been to. The casinos there offered special rules where you had almost a one-percent advantage off the top. You didn't even need to count to beat the game. Just had to learn a correct strategy."

Raven's eyes lit up. "I've never heard of an edge off the top. That's amazing."

"Sure was. Almost too good to be true. But none of the locals knew how to play correctly so it lasted a long time. We had a team of four of us, all Americans, and we blasted them for five straight weeks."

"Didn't they kick you out?" Raven asked, surprised they could last that long without getting booted.

Marco laughed. "Nope. That was the best thing. They had a law in their country forbidding casinos from barring skillful players. So they had to let us play."

Joel loved it. This was the man he wanted to become. "Holy smoke. You must have cleaned them out."

"Pretty close. The four of us won $650,000 over the five weeks."

"Why did you quit?" asked Joel.

"They couldn't bar us, but they did everything else to make us miserable. The last week we were there, the casinos spread word for no one to give us food or lodging. We literally slept in bathrooms the last seven nights. Luckily we found one sidewalk vendor in the black market who sold us bananas for twenty bucks a pound. We were nearly starving and sleep-deprived, so we finally threw in the towel."

Joel nodded enthusiastically. "Now that's a story."

Marco said, "You should have seen us leaving the country. We had notes stuck in our shoes, in our coats, under our hats, everywhere."

"Must have been a wild sight. I bet every girl over there must have wanted to marry you with that wad of cash," said Joel.

Marco smirked, "There's a wedding in Vegas every five minutes, but I'm not stupid enough to give up my freedom. Do you know the difference between in-laws and outlaws?"

Joel shook his head. "No."

"Outlaws are wanted." Marco laughed at his own joke. "Anyway, I went there to get rich—not end up with a ball and chain around me. However, there was this one girl that I met who had the largest—"

Raven again interrupted, "That was certainly quite an ordeal. What's your plan now?"

The still nameless girl in shorts arrived with Marco's third drink. She offered everyone a Cuban cigar, but only Marco accepted. He lit it using a twenty-dollar bill, impressing Joel but appalling Raven's New England frugality. Marco took a long, deep puff before answering.

"I gave you my number in Minnesota because I'm interested in you playing on my team," Marco said in a slow dramatic fashion.

Raven raised his eyebrows in astonishment. He hadn't expected this. "I thought you only used girls for backcounters."

"Normally," said Marco. "However, I've been working on something new. Ever heard of shuffle tracking?"

"Nope."

"It's a way of keeping track of the cards as they are placed in the discard rack and then following them through the shuffle," explained Marco.

"Is that possible?" asked Raven.

"It's tough. Some people have done it while others lost their ass trying. It's nearly impossible doing it with only your brain."

Raven looked puzzled. "What other ways could you accomplish it? They certainly won't let you use a pencil and paper at the table."

Marco fidgeted with his drink before answering. "No, but they might let you use a concealed blackjack computer. At least as long as it stays concealed. I've developed a chip to follow every card through simple shuffles. I almost skipped naked down the street when I figured out the last algorithms. Now I want to get a team together and try it in Atlantic City."

Joel jumped in. "Is that legal?"

Marco growled. "You think the casinos care about what's legal? They've experimented with different scents and sights to keep people playing longer. The slot machines use a special grade of metal that makes more noise when coins hit it to exaggerate the winnings. They would prefer customers not leave until every last penny is cleaned out of their bank account or until they die—whichever comes first."

The ambiguous answer increased Raven's suspicions of Marco. "Why are you playing in Atlantic City rather than here?"

"New Jersey's the only state where they can't bar blackjack players. You interested?" Marco asked.

Raven felt uncomfortable with the ethics of playing with concealed computers. Beating the casinos with your mind seemed noble, but this venture scared him. "Sounds too wild for me, but I will think about it."

"No problem. Give me a call when you decide. Maybe we can get some exercise and go out and play golf," Marco said.

Chasing a little white ball wasn't challenging to someone who ran eighty miles a week and ate healthier than most squirrels. Raven tried to be tactful. "Golf doesn't sound like much exercise to me."

"It is the way my partners play when they try to beat me," Marco winked. "It's an exercise in futility."

Marco offered to let them take the Maserati out for a spin. Raven hesitated, but Joel jumped at the chance, and the two took off looking for open road.

♣ ♦ ♥ ♠

Marco remained by the pool and the girl brought herself a drink this time and sat down next to him. Nikki pushed back her long blonde hair and glared at Marco. "Why didn't you tell him the real reason you're not using the computers in Vegas?"

Marco laughed. "Tell him they're illegal here in Nevada? No, the truth might scare him off. Besides, he's a Baptist, and probably thinks he's already got a corner on truth—certainly not your type, Nikki. He probably needs condoms about as much as a blind man needs glasses."

"Why do you want him then?" she asked. "He looks rather young and you usually can't stand narrow-minded Christians."

"Yeah, he's young, but he's hungry. That's the way I used to be, but I'm not anymore. I need someone with a burning ambition to drive this team to success. I think he's that person. And he's good—damn good." Marco finished his drink and watched the sun setting over the mountains to the west. "Besides, he'll shuck his religion after a few months in this town. Before long, he'll be just like us."

Nikki spoke softly in a low husky voice, "Just like you maybe."

Marco took a long toke from the cigar. He hadn't heard Nikki and his mind was already spinning. He flicked the remains of his cigar into the pool. "Call Karl and tell him we're ready to start recruiting and training."

CHAPTER FOURTEEN

♣ ♦ ♥ ♠

The meeting with Marco Antonelli convinced Raven of two things. On the short test drive of the Maserati he decided right then and there to get his dream car—a BMW convertible. He admired the sharp German ragtops so prevalent in sunny Las Vegas; however, he still refused to splurge and chose to buy a used one for a modest price.

Next, he decided to pass on Marco's offer. A large team probably paid an hourly wage or a small percentage of the win, depending on the number of players. Raven wanted to keep control of his money and projected he could make much more by staying in charge. He also never really knew if Marco exposed him in Minnesota. The friendly reception in Vegas made that scenario unlikely, but Marco had a dark side, which still unsettled Raven. He wanted to make his million ethically. The idea of playing with computers bothered his sense of fair play. He wanted to succeed in Las Vegas without compromising his values.

Raven determined to continue with his own team—even if it only consisted of two members. Joel struggled at first,

but slowly got up to speed. After weeks of practice he finally counted the deck consistently under twenty-five seconds and Raven felt confident enough to place Joel behind
a table. There he counted the cards as they were dealt from
the shoe. Raven still handled all the money and did all the
playing. If Joel got a high count, he would fold his arms to
signal Raven to come over. When Raven approached, Joel
would turn away from the table and verbally give him the
count so Raven could jump in and start playing. Then Joel
would go off to start back counting another shoe.

It worked, but after a few weeks, Raven realized they
needed at least one more player to maximize the return.
With only Joel, there was way too much dead time.

A third member soon joined the team.

Raven still ran every day and was in the best shape of
his life, so he entered a local 10-K race, hoping to win the
$500 for first place.

Right from the start, a lanky kid in a green Oregon sin-
glet ran smoothly beside Raven. The two of them quickly
broke away from the rest of the field. Raven normally ran
well in heat and he threw in a small surge at the four-mile
mark to try and break away, but his shadow glided effortlessly along and easily covered the move. As they matched
strides, he spoke to Raven with a strong British accent,
"I've heard that early autumn is known as purgatory in
Vegas because it's not as hot as hell anymore, but it's still
pretty warm."

Raven tried to utter a response, but all he could manage
was a low grunt. Despite being in great shape, Raven soon
felt sapped by the sun and watched the tall, lean runner,
easily pull away down the stretch.

Raven labored home in second and sought out the victor after the race. His name was Duncan Chamberlain and
he had run for the Oregon Ducks on a track scholarship.
He loved the USA, and stuck around after graduation. The

only problem was residency. Being English, he couldn't legally get a job in America. He had been running road races just fast enough to win first-place prize money, but the expenses of traveling around the country were eating him up. Soon he would need to return home, unless he could get a green card.

Duncan planned on staying another week in Vegas before moving on to the next road race in Phoenix, so Raven invited him to stay with them in their rented apartment. They ran each morning, and before the week ended, Raven thought of a way to solve Duncan's problem.

"Duncan, would you be interested in living and working here in Vegas?"

Duncan showed a small flicker of excitement. "Top drawer, mate. I'd love to join you guys in your flat. But there's still one problem."

"What's that?" asked Joel.

"Citizenship. I can't work here. Your country won't let any of the Queen's subjects take a job away from you Yanks."

Raven smiled. "That's the beauty of this situation. It's not a job."

"Come again, mate?"

"You can gamble in our country, right?"

"Sure, nothing wrong with that."

"And you can keep all the money you win, correct?"

Duncan smirked. "You mean if I win. I know this city is built on losers, and I don't intend to part with what little I've got left. No thanks."

"Well, believe it or not, there is a way to win."

Raven explained the basic theory of card counting and invited Duncan to join their blackjack team. They needed another counter and Duncan had all the right ingredients. He possessed a sharp mind, and more importantly, he was the most driven individual Raven had ever met. He approached each track workout with incredible focus. Nothing could keep him from his goals and he ran through pain and difficulty like no one Raven had ever seen. Learning to count would be a snap compared to the discipline he applied in his training.

Recruiting him turned out to be an excellent decision. He spent ten hours a day practicing and soon joined Joel behind the tables back counting for Raven.

The fact Duncan was tall also helped. Early casinos were laid out to be deliberately confusing, built on the theory patrons might get lost and be too stupid to find their way out. The newer mega-resorts employed better designs, but they were still crowded and the height of Joel and Duncan made it easier for Raven to spot them.

It took about two weeks to work out the bugs and turn the team into a machine. Rather than reinventing the wheel, Raven used a lot of the techniques developed by Uston's blackjack teams. The money all came from Raven, as neither Joel nor Duncan had barely enough for a pizza. Uston's formula returned fifty percent of the winnings to the investor who took the risk and the other half to the players.

The team crushed blackjack games up and down the Strip and within a month won over six figures. Raven and Duncan still practiced counting daily to stay sharp, but Joel no longer saw the need and began to deteriorate. He preferred hitting the town and Raven suspected the environment of sex, money, and power was pulling him down.

When they first came to Las Vegas, Joel had ridiculed all the lowlifes. He called them casualties—burnouts done in by the Glitter City. Now he had jumped on the fast track to becoming one. Almost weekly a new chink appeared in his character, as virtues were replaced with vices. Raven suspected Joel had progressed from the social cocktail by the pool to a debauched lifestyle built around nightly drinking sessions. Joel wore a gold chain around his neck and kept his shirts unbuttoned to display his tanned, hairy chest.

One night the growing tension erupted when Raven found empty beer bottles in the garbage. "Ever since you drank those daiquiris with Marco your values have wavered," Raven said accusingly.

Joel's face flushed red in anger. "Like you're so much better than me just because you don't drink. Get real. Those issues aren't important anymore."

"How can you say that? You act like you're trying to create a new proverb—a fool and his money are soon partying," Raven shot back.

"Take a look in the mirror, buddy. Denial ain't just a river in Egypt," hollered Joel.

"What's that supposed to mean? I'm not the one at fault here, it's you."

Joel corrected him in a forceful tone. "Oh really? You're the one who bought a fake Rolex to deceive the casinos. Quit worrying about me and start worrying about yourself."

Raven couldn't control Joel, so he stopped trying. Joel quit hiding his lifestyle and began openly drinking and smoking. The tremendous amounts of money they were winning kept their fragile relationship intact. They doubled the original $200,000 bank in fourteen weeks and a few months later zoomed past $500,000.

Raven employed a hit and run strategy to keep their profile low. They played short sessions at each casino, typically only one or two shoes, then left, hopefully giving insufficient time for the surveillance team to kick in. They used very little bet variation since most shoes were at high counts when Raven jumped in. The result was minimal heat—a welcome change for Raven after getting barred so many times in previous states.

Raven, Joel, and Duncan all dressed in shorts or some type of a sweat suit. This enabled them to literally jog from casino to casino—much more efficient than trying to park a car and get in and out of the huge resorts—a process taking a minimum of fifteen minutes, even for locals. Raven looked like he had just come in off the tennis court, often glancing at his fake Rolex as if he had to rush to make some match.

After Joel or Duncan called him into a shoe, they would take off for the next casino and set up in a predetermined pit. By the time Raven had finished his hot shoe at one club, they would already be in place and hopefully have a high count when he arrived at the next casino.

It became a clockwork operation. By running rather than driving, they wasted very little time. They always set up their route in advance, careful to include alternate meeting places in case something went wrong or they were detected. Neither seemed likely and Raven saw few obstacles to becoming a millionaire in the very near future.

When Raven called his father to brag about his exploits. William remained unimpressed, having belonged to the generation that viewed gambling as a stigma, and unaware times had changed.

"Son, money like that won't do you any good. I read in the paper over seventy percent of the folks who win a million or more in the lottery are flat broke within a year. People don't respect unearned income—getting rich gambling just ain't right."

"Dad, I told you before, it isn't gambling. It's called gaming the way I do it. I'm the favorite when I play."

His father barked back, "Well, the way I see it, if one person calls you a horse, you can laugh it off, but if five people start calling you a horse, then it's time to look for a saddle. It's still gambling to me, Randolph, and it goes against the laws of hard work."

Raven refused to back down. "Hard work alone is never going to make anyone affluent. You have to take risks to make any real money."

"That's another area where we just disagree. Getting rich is a trap. You'd better watch your step."

The conversation left Raven depressed. He thought his recent windfall would convince his father. Instead, William stood as opposed as ever. Townsends were notoriously stubborn. He angrily hung up the phone, silently vowing not to call his father again until his bankroll reached the magic seven-figure mark.

He resented his father wanting him to be perfect. The older Raven got, the less perfection he found. William Townsend once pounded a nail into the wall of the barn and asked his son to pull it out. Next, his father asked him to also remove the hole. Raven was taken aback, and his father explained how mistakes could be corrected, but the scar remained.

He certainly would never admit it to his father, but now Raven needed a way to fill in the hole caused years ago when he stole the offering box money. He wanted to erase his guilt, yet none of his efforts diminished its weight. He could return the $582 to the church. That would be easy. He had lots of cash. But he didn't relish the prospect of admitting his crime to the congregation, the community, and especially to his father. Much of the offering came from hard-working poor people who would be appalled to learn where their sacrificial giving ended up.

Pastor Cook had vaguely alluded to the forgiving power of God, but Raven didn't know how to juggle that with the divine blueprint all believers were expected to follow. And even though Raven's sin ranked relatively low, he had stolen money like Judas, and possibly God the father wouldn't forgive that. He certainly knew his earthly father never would.

Chapter Fifteen

♣ ♦ ♥ ♠

The chips continued rolling in. Profits after eight months totaled a staggering $785,000. Raven finally contacted Marco Antonelli. Calling under the pretext of playing golf, he relished an opportunity to brag about his accomplishments.

The next day Raven and Joel met Marco at his country club. Marco paid for the golf, which impressed Raven. The Townsends were fair but never generous.

A dark-haired man in shorts, carrying two bags of clubs, approached them. With one hand he lifted the newer set of Pings as easily as one might grab a jug of milk from its shelf, and handed them to Marco.

"Is this your caddy?" Raven inquired.

"No, he's more like my slave," laughed Marco. "This is Karl Beck—the point man for my blackjack teams." Marco turned to Karl. "I need to talk business so I'll ride with Raven."

Without a word, Karl brought the two carts around and loaded up the clubs.

Marco said to Raven, "You two should hit it off—you look a lot alike."

"Karl acts more like a lieutenant than a friend," Raven remarked.

"Yeah, we're not exactly close." Marco said. "I've never seen the guy laugh."

"You got to be kidding," Raven said.

"Gospel truth. Even if something is hilarious, he keeps that poker face and says, 'Now that's really funny.' He worked for the secret police in South Africa, so he's accustomed to military relationships. He does what he's told and he gets the job done on our blackjack teams."

"You're not friends then?" probed Raven.

"In this business you don't need friends. That's what dogs are for. You either totally trust someone or you don't work with them."

At that moment Raven noticed Karl using a foot wedge to kick his ball out of the rough and back into the fairway. Marco grinned, "See what I mean about an exercise in futility? Karl can drive a nail and drive a hard bargain, but he sure can't drive a golf ball."

Marco watched Joel take his third shot as he shanked a five-iron into the water. He gave Raven a deadpan serious look. "Are you sure you guys were athletes in college? The only chance of Joel making a birdie today would be if he hits a duck in that pond."

Marco pulled out a fairway wood and sailed his second shot pin high. He hopped back in the cart and headed toward Raven's ball in the sand trap. "I'll give you some free advice, although you and Joel might be better served getting free golf lessons," Marco laughed. "Always remember it's a business and don't worry about being buddies. There's only one reason to play blackjack."

"And that is?" asked Raven.

"Money. And that's more than enough reward. How much are you up now?"

Raven was glad Marco had pried this time, since he couldn't wait to boast. "Our team has made $785,000 over the last eight months."

Marco acted impressed with Raven's achievement and asked, "How is the money divvied up?"

"I took Uston's book as a guide and used his formula. I kept half the winnings as the investor and the other half was split between us three players."

"How much have your two spotters made?" asked Marco.

"Over a hundred grand."

Marco raised an eyebrow. "Each of them?"

"Yep."

Marco shook his head, "You're overpaying them."

"How's that?" Raven got out of his cart and lined up a shot between two cottonwoods.

"If they're only back-counting, they're getting way too much money. Uston's formula was for people playing for investors. They're really not doing that."

"Well, I set up the arrangement when I recruited them, and it would be unfair to change it now."

Marco drained his six-foot putt dead center into the cup. "I admire your ethics, but you're still making a mistake."

"You may be right, but it won't matter. I'm only playing until I get to a million—it's only a matter of time before I hit my magic number."

"The way you're winning, you're probably right. But if things change, let me know. Training this new team to play with computers has been a nightmare. We still won't be up and running for another month or so. In the meantime, I've been doing team counting with some new girls, but I'm anxious to make a really big score the high-tech way."

It surprised Raven so little had progressed since the last time they talked. He was glad he formed his own team, but it was flattering to have Marco still be interested in recruiting him.

♣   ♦   ♥   ♠

Winning big money had little effect on either Duncan or Raven. Other than buying his red "Hello Officer" BMW, Raven had spent little. Duncan likewise practiced frugality to a fault and they both socked their savings away.

Joel, however, loved the money and the fast paced lifestyle of Vegas. When he and Raven played basketball at Wheaton, they were the big stars. They felt significant and important. It was a difficult adjustment to live without that attention. Joel lamented how in a different profession they would be revered like pro athletes who were the best of the best. In blackjack they received no acclaim, no recognition. Joel joked that in a different world, Raven's exploits would make headlines like: "Man from Maine uses brain to drive casinos insane." Instead, their only reward remained financial.

The money was sufficient for Raven. Once he had cherished dreams of changing the world. Now, winning or losing became all that mattered. On one level, the money meant nothing to him. He had developed no lavish tastes, but reaching the magic million-dollar mark slowly became an obsession. He chalked up any day that didn't propel him toward that figure as wasted.

For Joel, the money meant something different. He couldn't spend it fast enough. Throwing cash around bought him the attention he craved and had lacked since college. Against Raven's wishes Joel wanted to play blackjack on his own time, with his own money. Raven disapproved because part of the beauty of their team concept was the anonymity it provided. Nobody knew or noticed the spotters because they never played a hand, but if Joel played on his own, the casinos might recognize him, and that could hurt the team.

None of those arguments dissuaded Joel. He wanted to play, get some comps, and have some fun. Raven asked

Joel to stick to the smaller casinos the team didn't frequent. Joel grudgingly agreed and soon began playing on his own several times a week, usually staying overnight in comped hotel suites.

Joel continued in a downward spiral. His work for the team remained acceptable—he had excellent casino comportment and rarely made mistakes, but his solo play was a different story. Having to handle the chips, make the bets, and do all the other calculations proved his undoing. He wasn't a big loser, but he lost more than he won and got flustered easily. The concept of money management baffled him.

None of which deterred Joel. The huge sums he made playing for the team more than compensated for these losses. So he continued playing on his own, enjoying the perks and attention lavished on high rollers.

♣   ♦   ♥   ♠

The winter months passed and summer once again approached the Desert City. The mercury on the thermometer soared. And Raven's blackjack team had a day in keeping with the temperature. He won nearly every double down. Dealers everywhere busted and Raven's cards were hotter than a pistol. Chips and cash bulged out of all of his pockets. When he added it up, the amount staggered him. He had started that morning with $50,000 on him as the playing bankroll and finished with $153,450. Their team had their first $100,000 day.

After that huge score, Raven became more concerned about being watched. He already knew about the one-way glass mirrors and cameras high above in the ceilings. The surveillance department of a casino remained a closely guarded secret, with a high-tech mission control room monitoring the vast gambling floor. The amounts Raven won surely attracted intense scrutiny overhead.

Despite their financial success, the team still had many trying moments. They typically won two out of every three days. They had about a 75% chance of being ahead after one week and over 90% after one month. Yet, even a few sporadic losing sessions still drained a lot of emotion. Raven remembered the negative swings far longer than the big wins. The expectancy now stood at $1500 an hour, or nearly ten grand a day, but many days Raven struggled riding the wild waves of fluctuation.

Because their strategy involved moving from casino to casino, it took eighty hours of time to get in thirty actual hours of play. Raven decided to cap their bets at $5,000, since that was the maximum allowed at most of the big clubs. His impressive action attracted many casino hosts, who fought like vultures over the few big hitters in the gambling world. Called whales, these super-affluent players had the capacity to win or lose a million dollars.

With never enough whales to go around, most hosts were constantly on the lookout for the next level of gamblers—the ones who could win or lose $20,000 per trip. These players constituted only five percent of the gamblers but accounted for nearly half of the casino's win.

The hypocritical smiles of casino hosts reminded Raven of sunning snakes waiting to strike. Their philosophy consisted of giving someone a free room—hoping he ended up paying for the hotel. They preyed on the tremendous egos of these high rollers, flattering them by catering to their every whim—and gambling really brought out the arrogance in these people. Raven didn't need insincere men bolstering his vanity. He turned down all their offers and quietly refused to give his name or get rated.

♣ ♦ ♥ ♠

Howard Goldberg had worked on the other side of the tables for years and the worst part of his new job was throw-

both ing out card counters. He still admired their skill and knew how tough it was to beat the game. However, some casinos considered them no different than common thieves, and naturally viewed Howard as an expert in rooting out these vermin. He preferred dealing with other aspects of financial drain for the casinos, well aware how few truly gifted card counters existed in the whole world. It was because of a card counter, or at least the threat of one, which got Howard summoned to the Nugget on a Friday night.

Phil met Howard in the cramped monitoring room. The compartment was unusually cluttered by Vegas standards, hardly surprising, since the Nugget lagged far behind the bigger casinos in modernization and high-tech surveillance. Phil switched the image on the middle monitor to show a tall blond player on table five.

"Got a young guy here been playing blacks for three hours. Charlie downstairs swears the kid's a counter," said Phil.

Howard smiled knowingly, "Charlie, huh? That's not exactly a vote of confidence. Remember the guy he threw out last December?"

Phil chuckled, "Yeah, some guy betting green, got lucky, and won two grand. Charlie kicked him out thinking he was a card counter—turned out to be the brother-in-law of the hotel manager just visiting for Christmas. I'm still surprised Charlie didn't get canned for that fiasco."

"Knowing Charlie, he's probably got compromising pictures of the owner tucked away for job security. Let's take a look and see what he's found this time. You got a name?" asked Howard.

"Calls himself Joel West. Don't know if that's real. Nothing turns up in any of the books and the Griffith Agency's never heard of him."

"Okay, let's watch Mr. West and see for ourselves," Howard said as he slid his chair closer to the screen.

They monitored the situation for nearly an hour. Howard had a gift of reading people quickly. Having been a pro himself, he could usually determine if they were counting cards within five minutes. But something about Mr. West puzzled him. Phil had never seen Goldberg take this long to make a decision, and was startled when Howard finally spoke.

"Let him go," Howard said simply.

"Really? Don't think he's a counter?" asked Phil.

"No, he's a counter all right."

Phil gave Howard a puzzled look. "Then why let him walk?"

"Because he's not a very good one. He steams when he loses and he doesn't raise his bets high enough to get an advantage. But most of all, he lacks discipline. See how intoxicated he is with that waitress and the Coronas she brings him every twenty minutes?"

Phil chuckled again. "Yes, the kid's eyes looked like saucers. Hard to blame him, though, Rochelle could make even a monk have second thoughts."

Howard got up to leave. "That's not the point. In the long run the kid's a losing player. Got too many bad habits and no focus. Let him play and tell Charlie he's gonna have to start paying the light bill here if he kicks out any more losers."

♣ ♦ ♥ ♠

Two days later Howard received an urgent message to come to the Dunes. Slowed by congested streets, he arrived an hour later. Jack put the phone down when Howard walked in. He never liked Howard and was still miffed that management had gone over his head to hire outside help.

"Nice of you to finally get here. For what you're paid, you ought to at least make us a priority."

Howard remembered why some employees referred to their boss as Jack-the-Jerk behind his back. "Stuff it, Jack.

I got tied up on Flamingo. Some tourist tried to do a U-turn and the wreck backed everything up from Eastern to Paradise."

Jack just grunted, obviously not believing the excuse. He walked over to the racks containing thousands of surveillance videotapes and pulled out the most recent one. He plopped it in the VCR and grabbed himself some coffee. He always drank his brew black, never with cream or sugar and never offered anyone else around him, especially Howard, a cup.

He backed the tape up to where a young, dark-haired kid wearing a blue Reebok jogging suit started playing at table twenty-nine. Jack and Howard watched together in silence as the subject on the video made a string of $5,000 bets, won a little over $22,000, then left at the end of the shoe—walking out of the casino.

Howard spoke first. "That's it? Five minutes of play?"

"Yeah, he didn't stay long."

"How'd you expect me to get over here within five minutes of being beeped?" Howard asked.

"When we beeped you, we anticipated he'd be playing more. He's been coming here off and on for the last three months. He usually plays a little longer, but seldom more than thirty minutes."

"What's his name?"

"Never gave one. Said he didn't want to be rated."

"That sounds dubious. What's his overall track record?"

Jack acted slightly embarrassed as he pulled out a card. "That's the problem. He's hit us hard."

"How hard?"

Jack read from the file. "Sixteen visits total and a win of $177,000."

"Holy shit! How come you're just now calling me?"

Jack shrugged. "At first we had no reason to be suspicious. He rarely spreads his bets up and down like normal card counters and he materializes out of nowhere to jump in the middle of shoes with big bets. There's no way he could know the count of the cards played before he got there."

"Not by himself, but he could with a team spotting for him."

"We thought of that but we're convinced nobody at the tables passed him the count."

Howard remained skeptical. He didn't consider Jack to be the brightest can in the six-pack. "How do you know that?"

"Take today for example. The only other player at the table was the fat bald guy with the unbuttoned bowling shirt, right?"

"Okay," said Howard.

"His name's Floyd. He's from Cleveland. Owns a muffler shop. Floyd's been coming here twice a month for six years. Always bets green and always loses big. There's no way in the world he's smart enough to hook up with any team."

Howard studied Floyd's pudgy image on the screen and readily agreed. "That makes sense. Any other way he could be getting the count?"

"None I can see. We've given up on counting and now we're trying to determine if there's collusion between him and some of the dealers."

Howard nodded. "Let's back the tape up and watch it again."

They rewound it and viewed it two more times. Nothing looked wrong except the amount of money the kid won.

"Does he always play with the same dealer?" asked Howard.

"Don't think so. I'd have to pull some old tapes on him to check, but I'm pretty sure he's jumped all over the casino."

"Then it's unlikely he's working some cheating scam," said Howard, "unless all of your dealers are in on it."

Jack didn't like that implication or Howard's smugness. He rewound the tape one last time. He slightly overshot the starting point and started fast-forwarding to the high roller's first bet. Howard stopped him. He noticed something on the screen. He had Jack back it up again to just before the young man in sneakers showed up at the table. "What is it? What do you see?" said Jack.

Howard's face took on a knowing look. Standing behind the table, but not playing, was Joel West. "See the tall kid. I watched him the other night at the Nugget. He couldn't win when he had to bet and make all the other decisions, but he's certainly competent enough to have passed the count to the high roller."

Before long Howard had isolated the part of the tape where Joel verbally gave the count to the big player. They could even read Joel's lips as he turned away from the pit boss, but still within view of the overhead camera. Howard had absolutely no doubt he had discovered a new blackjack team in operation. The only remaining pieces of the puzzle were whether there were other members involved and how to catch them.

Jack theorized it wouldn't take long. "They've been treating us like a bank, dropping by a couple times a week to make withdrawals. I can't wait to get my hands on those cheats."

Howard knew they weren't cheats in any sense of the word—just highly skilled players who used their brains. But it wouldn't do any good to argue with Jack; he came from the old school and anybody winning money deserved cement shoes.

♣　♦　♥　♠

Raven had no inkling his operation was plunging into jeopardy because of Joel's sloppiness. Things looked great and the stacks of money completely filled his safety deposit box.

Joel's frequent late nights forced the team to start their play after lunch. This upset Raven, but he resigned himself to taking whatever he could get from his declining friend. They had worked out a system where Raven no longer cashed out chips. Duncan would cash them out later. This sped things up, and limited Raven's exposure in the casinos.

The next day, they lined up eight casinos for play and then split up to start the blitz. The first two sessions went well, both modest wins. The third casino on the schedule was the Dunes.

Joel and Duncan were already in place when Raven arrived. Each had found a freshly shuffled shoe and had casually begun counting behind the table, trying to look like interested tourists who liked to watch, but didn't play. Raven lurked behind a bank of slot machines and scanned the pit, awaiting his call. Duncan still used the crossing of the arms while Joel had switched to putting a cigarette in his mouth when the count reached a high number. Both Raven and Duncan detested smoking, but it was a good signal. It had the advantage of being different from Duncan and also easy for Raven to spot.

The first call came from Duncan. Raven quickly came out of hiding and moved towards Duncan's table. He covered the ground fast, but without running, as that would attract attention. Duncan turned as he approached and told him the count. Raven made a couple of $4,000 dollar bets, and then moved to $5,000 near the end of the shoe. He got lucky on a $10,000 double down, winning on 12 when the dealer busted.

He felt the familiar feeling of exhilaration when suddenly he noticed two security guards slowly moving in behind Joel on the other side of the pit. Raven quit playing and signaled to end the session. Joel was totally oblivious to any heat and continued counting the shoe. Raven tried again to get his attention, but with no success.

With no time left to warn Joel, Raven headed for the exit. A quick backward glance showed two people following him. He darted through the slots and angled for the door. Two new security guards stopped that route. Minutes later Raven and Joel were sitting on hard folding chairs facing Jack in the backroom.

Raven fumed. *How could Joel have been so dense?* They both could have escaped if Joel had paid attention.

And Raven also got mad at himself. He had frequented the Dunes far too often over the last few months, thinking the hit-and-run strategy would allow them to play with impunity, clearly a miscalculation.

Security tried to take pictures, but Raven and Joel both refused. Next Jack wanted to view the contents of Raven's fanny pack. Raven didn't budge. Legally, he didn't have to show ID or allow them to invade his privacy. He had committed no crime.

Jack glared at his quarry. "Okay, let's start with your name."

Raven wasn't the strongest man physically in the world, but few matched his mental toughness. He stared Jack straight in the eye, showing no fear.

"You gotta give me a name or we'll never let you out of here," Jack said.

"The name's Fred," answered Raven coolly.

Jack smiled. "Now we're getting somewhere. All right, Fred. What's your last name?"

"Flintstone. Fred Flintstone."

Jack's face flashed red and he forcibly grabbed Raven's fanny pack and dumped its contents on the table. He found an Illinois driver's license for Randolph Townsend.

"You can't do that," Raven protested.

Jack found two big wads of cash in rubber bands, which he estimated to be twenty grand each, and a smaller stack of loose hundreds. What really caught security's attention, however, was the large assortment of chips. There were thousand-dollar tokens from several local casinos, showing Jack exactly where the team had played. Raven knew his rights were being trampled, but he could do nothing to stop them. In one fell swoop his team had crashed and burned.

A new person walked into the room. He introduced himself as Howard Goldberg. He looked at Raven's wrist and asked if he bought his Rolex in Hong Kong. His perception surprised Raven, but somehow he felt safer with this man in the room. Reluctantly, he gave his usual left-handed handshake.

Howard took one glance at the chips and cash on the table and called Jack out of the room.

"What do you think you're doing? You can't search his personal possessions like that."

Jack snapped back. "Like hell. He's been stealing us blind. I can do anything I want to that punk. Let's take a good picture of him and a photocopy of his ID."

"Forget it. I'm not going to work with any casino that's involved in illegal actions. Give him his stuff back, now," Howard commanded.

"Are you crazy? I'm not giving him his money back. That's only a pittance of what he's won here over the last few months."

"Jack, if you don't, you'll get your butt sued. Bar him, read him the trespass act, but let him leave with his money or you'll never hear the end of it." Howard was adamant.

Jack stormed back into the room and angrily stuffed the cash and chips back into the fanny pack. He read Joel and Raven the trespass act and warned them they would be arrested if they ever returned.

Jack asked if they understood the trespass act. They gave a halting nod.

Raven spoke up. "Is there a reason we've been brought back here and treated like criminals?"

Howard answered, "Look, you guys know the score. We didn't catch your other buddy, but we've got a good picture of all three of you from the overhead camera. Do us a favor. Don't come back here and we won't send your pictures around to those other casinos you've been playing."

Raven sized him up. He sounded honest and looked sincere. Raven wasn't sure if they really could get pictures from their overhead cameras, but if word of their team spread around town, it would be all over. He agreed and they were escorted to the door.

They met up with Duncan at the alternate emergency site; happy he had at least succeeded in getting away. They called it a day, none of them in any condition to continue after that ordeal. Only one question remained—would they get heat from other casinos, or did Howard tell them the truth?

♣ ♦ ♥ ♠

They took a few days off to recover and then hit the strip again. The first day back they were kicked out at two places. The following week several more clubs either barred them or gave them so much heat they had to flee.

After kicking Raven out, the shift manager at the Hacienda called the Dunes. "Jack, thanks for the tip on that team. We just caught all three of them and threw their sorry asses out."

Jack smiled on the other end of the phone. "Good for you. I'd like to have broken their legs, teach them punks a lesson. I guess this is the next best thing."

"You got that right. Anyway, I owe you one."

"No problem. Howard may be too wimpy to send their pictures around town, but I'm not. I hope they realize there's no way they're going to get away with that crap here in Vegas. Not as long as guys like you and me still work this town."

♣ ♦ ♥ ♠

The next night Raven and his team got booted from the Palace when Howard Goldberg showed up.

Does he work for more than one casino?

Either way, Raven had trusted Howard, but apparently he'd been burned. The management read all three of them the trespass act.

They were now too hot for Vegas, having been barred at nearly every casino. Duncan had grown discouraged from the harrowing recent turn of events and threw in the towel. The Olympics were coming up in the next year and he headed back to England to concentrate on running. He received his portion of the huge win, leaving Raven still up a hefty $813,000.

Joel and Raven also choose to leave town, but to keep playing. Raven wanted to reach his million-dollar goal, and they headed north in search of new casinos.

CHAPTER SIXTEEN

♣ ♦ ♥ ♠

The drive through the interior of Nevada meandered through some of the most barren countryside in America, the landscape as desolate as the moon with treeless mountains surrounded by sterile plains. Joel swerved the BMW to avoid a jackrabbit. "God must have really hated this state," he remarked "This place has got to be the ugliest spot on the face of the earth."

The terrain reminded Raven of the Sinai, and his thoughts drifted to an evening he and Cynthia sat in the entrance of a Bedouin tent gazing at the glittering, black satin sky. On that dark night in the desert, a panorama of brilliant stars danced overhead. He remembered impressing Cynthia with his knowledge of the constellations as they discussed fate and destiny. She listened attentively and extracted more personal information from him in an hour than most people learned in years.

Raven adjusted his car seat to a reclining position, stretched out and replayed every vivid detail of the night he'd fallen in love. He would never forget how Cynthia's eyes had sparkled in the starlight and the thrill of holding her hand for the first time. A faint smile appeared on his face.

Joel glanced over and asked, "What're you thinking about?"

"The Sinai," Raven said simply.

"That's where you met that dude on the camel, right?"

Raven nodded. "When we left, Cynthia noticed the Bedouin admiring my tee shirt, so I took it off and gave it to him. Always wondered what happened later. The phrase 'Jesus Saves' on the front of the shirt must have been a great ice-breaker with any English-speaking Arabs."

Joel laughed. "Wish I could have been there."

"Yeah, you should have seen Cynthia that day. She looked so good. Her features always made me wish I were a painter. Her face is truly striking."

Joel rolled his eyes. "Wake up and smell the coffee. She's ancient history."

Raven shook his head. "How can a romantic match seemingly made in heaven evaporate so rapidly into nothing."

"You've got a better chance of comprehending black holes than the mind of a woman. Either way, you need to move on and stick a fork in that relationship—it's done."

Raven didn't appreciate the brusque uncompassionate style of Joel and they rode in silence until they cut through the mountains and entered Tahoe. The change in the landscape astonished them. With its surrounding trees and boulders, the cobalt blue lake provided an incredible contrast to Vegas—where every structure competes to be the largest, tallest or grandest. Here, the casinos blended sensibly into their surroundings, instead of overwhelming them.

These casinos also differed from Vegas in the blackjack games they offered—almost all single-deck. With no shoes to back count, Joel and Raven needed to split up and work individually. Raven had already conquered the nuances of one-deck at the Swamp but Joel had played only shoes. Reluctantly, Raven agreed to bankroll his friend, this time paying him by the hour, rather than a portion of the win.

Right from the beginning nothing went right. The casinos were classy and the surroundings beautiful, but both Raven and Joel simultaneously hit losing streaks—almost in inverse proportion to how successful they'd been in Vegas. Their bankroll experienced violent fluctuations as they each returned nightly with horror stories of cold cards and hot dealers.

Raven fought to stay disciplined and in control, without succumbing to the temptation to overbet when losing big. Most gamblers remembered their big scores and conveniently forgot all the losing sessions. Pros like Raven were different. They accepted the wins stoically, since they had the advantage and were expected to come out ahead. It was the losses that embedded themselves in their mind.

The error most casino patrons make, when they win, is to think it's free money because they're playing with the house's chips. Raven never felt that way. Once it entered his pocket, it was his money. It didn't matter whether he won it on one hand of blackjack or by working all year flipping burgers.

A true pro understood this. He didn't think about what he could buy after a big win. Instead, Raven dwelt on the losses. At times he felt as if on a roller-coaster ride—sometimes climbing to new heights, sometimes plummeting to new lows. Raven played many sessions where his drop could have paid for a cruise around the world or a chartered Lear jet to the Riviera. But the longer he remained in blackjack, the less he desired short-lived pleasures. If he have could bought anything with his money, it would have been another chance to sit down with Cynthia and try to explain his decision—to somehow reverse the wrong turn in their relationship. But he knew Joel was right—the odds were slim she'd ever play a part in Raven's future.

The losing streak challenged Raven to improve—he no longer simply followed what he read, but tried to become more innovative. He developed his own three-level count to squeeze out an even bigger edge for single deck play.

Joel, however, remained unconcerned no matter how much he lost.

"Raven, don't sweat it, man. The cream always rises to the top."

This was Joel's pet phrase; normally used to gloat during the rare times he beat Raven at backgammon or cribbage. He began to blame everyone around him for his losses, complaining that his good play became a magnet for morons.

"I know I'd be winning big time if I could just get a table to myself, but every time I win, a crowd shows up. Those damn Asians are the worst. Always jumping in just when I get hot," Joel whimpered. "I try to discourage them from joining me, but they always say, 'you have rotsa ruck.'"

"Come on, they're not affecting your cards," said Raven.

"Guess again. They take gambling superstitions to the highest levels. Whenever they double down, they inevitably slap their hand on the table and yell 'monkey' hoping to catch a face card." It amused Raven when people actually believed calling out for a particular card could possibly make any difference.

"Your superstitions aren't a whole lot different," Raven said, unable to resist the dig.

Joel ignored the comment and continued his tirade, "You know, it really fries me the way they all play in groups. When they place their chips on their friends' bets, almost every other hand results in an argument over how to play it."

"I've seen what you mean," Raven said, "And unlike us, they don't have a matrix to tell them exactly how to play each hand, so they have to guess."

"It's obvious none of them ever worked on the Psychic Friends Network. It must be a cultural stigma to not hit stiffs and then they've got the nerve to turn around and criticize other players at the table. The way they cluck over what they perceive to be bad plays drives me crazy. I tell you Raven, they wouldn't know what a good play looked like if it crawled off the table and bit them in the butt."

Raven wondered if his friend was really that prejudiced or if he just needed a scapegoat to soothe his wounds over losing. "Quit worrying about everyone else," Raven said. "Just focus on your play and getting back what you've dumped."

Joel's losses had increased almost daily. However, Raven knew that eventually they *should* get their money back. But there was a big difference between *would* and *should*.

Joel calmed down. "I guess you're right. What do you think is wrong? You suppose that single deck's the problem?"

"No, the games are good here and we can beat them." Raven said.

"Then what's keeping us from winning?"

Raven suspected Joel's level of play to be part of the problem but decided not to address that issue now. Instead he shared some personal lingering doubts. "I feel like God is somehow going to keep me from reaching my goal."

Joel threw his arms up in the air. "Wait a minute. You're the one who said playing blackjack was kosher."

"I know, and I still believe that. But, somehow I've become more fatalistic."

"Forget about it. You're just having a few bad days. You'll get it back. You always do."

Joel was right—Raven always got his money back. Scanning through the previous entries in the logbook comforted

Raven. It showed he was indeed way ahead overall despite recent setbacks.

However, Joel was a different story. He had never proven himself as a player and Raven had compounded the mistake by paying him by the hour for single deck play, rather than a portion of winnings. Joel was ecstatic to make a hundred bucks an hour, bragging that only lawyers and hookers made that kind of money. His losses and hourly wages put a huge drain on the bankroll.

Raven grimly realized it would be up to himself to stop the bleeding and right the ship. He grabbed three rubber-banded wads, each with twenty grand, and headed for the tables.

♣ ♦ ♥ ♠

It didn't take long before his renewed confidence was stripped away. At one point he lost nine hands in a row. Then he got a lucky break when the dealer miscounted and incorrectly paid him on his 18 even though the dealer had 19. There might have been a time earlier in Raven's blackjack career where ethically he would have felt compelled to give the money back. He certainly would never take money from a store-clerk who erroneously gave him too much change.

But this was different. Blackjack had become a battlefield where he took advantage of every little weakness in his opponent. So Raven didn't even hesitate in grabbing the thousand-dollar chips. Unfortunately, just as his fingers reached the bumblebees, an obnoxious player to Raven's right spoke up.

"Wait a minute. You've got 19." He pointed to the dealer's cards and Raven shot him a deadly look. The dealer hesitated, recounted her five-card hand and pulled in Raven's chips. Raven sarcastically thanked the helpful player for correcting the mistake and angrily left the table.

He hadn't gone far when another dealer, with a nametag reading "Don from San Jose," called to him. Most dealers become rather blasé about their jobs, but Don acted like a high-energy carnival barker trying to get players to come to his table—not to increase business for the house, but because he aggressively hustled tips.

He called to Raven like an old friend. "If you could see yourself in a mirror, you'd be amazed how lucky you look today. Now sit down. I guarantee you'll win the first hand, so bet big."

If the player did win, then Don naturally expected a tip for his psychic advice. And if they lost, he shrugged it off by saying he just needed a few hands to warm up.

Raven found the act mildly amusing and sat at the empty table. Don had the high, raspy voice of someone who either smoked all his life or worked around cigarette fumes daily. Raven could usually judge the age of people by looking at their appearance. Dealers were the exception—the nature of their job often left them jaded and old before their time.

Don continued his running dialogue. "You're going to be glad you sat down here. They call me the dump truck cause I lose so much. It's amazing they haven't fired me yet. Especially today. I've been busting like crazy."

Raven took this banter in stride. He knew there was no such thing as hot or cold dealers—that was just another casino myth. Don began dealing the cards. He made a big issue out of every hand won—irking Raven since he had lost steadily for several days. Now when he finally eked out a small win somebody wanted a piece of it.

Few other businesses exist where months of gain are wiped out in a couple of hours. Most players routinely tip as an offering to appease angry gods, but not Raven. So despite the dealer's strong hints for a handout, he wasn't about to part with his chips now that he finally won some back. Besides, it was against his principles to finance the dealer's jewelry collection.

Don finally realized this and shuffled the cards whenever Raven raised his bet. To outwit him, Raven began raising his bet on negative counts, causing Don to unknowingly shuffle away the bad cards. This went on for a while until Don soured when he recognized how Raven had turned the tables on him. When the relief dealer replaced him, he whispered something to her and glared at Raven.

Most players don't notice the body language that occurs during the changing of dealers. The departing dealer uses hand signals to point out who tipped generously, players they call a "George," and who was a "Tom Turkey," or a big stiff.

It was obvious which category Don placed Raven. The new dealer's nametag read "Shirley from Topeka." Woman dealers were a late addition to the gambling world, having been instituted during World War II because of the shortage of men. Female dealers helped fuel the gambling boom by bringing an element of trust to a shifty business. Usually Raven liked playing against the fairer sex, but this scowling woman unnerved him. Shirley looked like a battle-ax and hardly evoked trust. Her lips had an unnatural downward curl, resulting in a perpetual pout and her eyes reminded him of Halloween cats.

He decided to stay for just a few more hands. The cards ran normal for about ten minutes, then came the hand that Raven would never forget. He'd always tended toward a fatalistic view of life, feeling like a pawn in some cosmic game; fearful someday he'd lose everything. And this was judgment day.

Raven bet $3,000 and was dealt two 8's. The dealer showed an ace up. Normally insurance is a sucker's bet, but with so many face cards left in the deck, Raven took insurance and lost that $1,500. The correct strategy called to split the 8's. He did, placing another three thousand on the felt, even though that was a play he hated to make. Raven had memorized almost two hundred numbers to guide him on nearly every hand, but none covered this situation. There was never a count high enough to deviate from the correct basic strategy play to split the pair and Raven always followed the rules even on difficult hands like this one.

The first card was a 7 for 15. He hit and pulled another 7 and busted. Now he had already lost $4,500 and still had another hand to play. The second hand received another 8. He had to split again. Haltingly, he plunked three more bumblebees on the felt. The dealer dealt him yet another 8. *Unbelievable.*

Time stood still. The moment felt surrealistic. He slowly pushed another three thousand out for the new hand, his fourth. He received a 3 on the second hand, which required more chips in order to double down. He caught a 7 for 18. The third hand drew a 9 for 17. He stood. The fourth 8 also got a 3. Raven doubled again catching a 9 for 20—his best hand.

Already, he'd already busted one $3,000 bet and lost $1,500 more on insurance. He had another three grand riding on one hand, along with two double downs for $6,000 each. His three remaining hands totaled 17, 18 and 20—not real strong, but a dealer bust would salvage everything.

The dealer turned over her hole card. It was an ace.

Good. At least she's not pat.

She hit it with a third ace for a soft 13. Raven knew he had used up all four 8's, so there was no chance the dealer would pull another one for 21. The next card was a jack for a hard 13.

Yes! Come on now. One more big card is all I need.

The dealer paused and grimly compressed her lips. Raven knew most dealers don't mind losing. It wasn't their money

and if players won big the dealers usually received large
tips. This dealer was different. She wanted to beat Raven,
although he didn't know why.

She twitched her nose like a witch and confidently pulled
out the next card. A deuce for 15.

*Even better. Just flip over that bust card and give me
my money.*

Now there was real hope. The next card was yet another ace for 16. Raven's face tightened. All four aces
and eights were used on this one round. *With so many
cards on the table she'll need all her toes and digits to
add them up.*

The dealer blinked her eyes three times as if summon-
ing magical powers of darkness. She reached for the final
card. A six or greater would bust her and net Raven a win
of over ten thousand on one hand. The odds were in his
favor with about a 65% chance for a bust.

The last card was a five.

Twenty-one.

Raven stared at the five of hearts in stunned disbelief.

The dealer cackled and removed all of his chips with
one fluid motion. He had lost a total of $19,500 on one
hand—Raven's face bore the look of the first soldier to hit
the beach on D-Day.

As the dealer put away the last chip, she asked Raven if
he'd like to hear a joke. Raven was certainly in no mood
for humor.

She proceeded anyway. "Do you know the difference
between a card counter and a canoe?"

Raven's face flushed with anger. He gave no verbal re-
ply, only a shrug to indicate no.

"Sometimes a canoe tips."

Now he got it. Normally dealers act friendly when they
hustle tourists. Don had apparently told her Raven was a
pro who never tips away his winnings.

Raven staggered back up to the room, dazed at the dizzying sequence of hands. *Twenty grand on one turn of the card,* he moaned.

Joel stood on the bed, sipping Dom Perignon straight from the bottle and playing air guitar to a Joe Walsh tune between swigs. Raven grabbed the champagne from Joel's hands and poured its contents down the sink.

Joel yelled at Raven. "Are you out of your Vulcan mind? That stuff costs $150 a bottle."

"Did you pay for it?" asked Raven angrily.

"No, of course not. I charged it to your room since you're on full comp."

"Then it's mine, and I'll do whatever I want with it."

"Man, you must've had a bad session down there."

"Let's just say that champagne cost more like five grand a glass."

Joel's eyes grew large as Raven recounted his hand from hell. "I'm telling you Joel, it was unbelievable how all four eights and all four aces came out. The moment seemed beyond belief; I had to wonder if God didn't arrange the whole thing to punish me for getting into gambling." Raven slumped on the bed. "Sometimes I feel like a puppet on strings playing out a hopeless part, crashing miserably in the end with no money and no dignity."

"Here we go again. Mr. Fatalism. God doesn't care about your cards," Joel said.

"I don't know. I feel like I'm under a microscope sometimes. Even the mundane decisions like when to break for lunch are agonizing. I lay in bed at night thinking about each time I stayed just a few more minutes and it cost me a couple of bumblebees."

Joel shrugged nonchalantly. "That's just life in the fast lane. You know how wild this business can be."

"Yes, but it still feels like a cosmic game sometimes. Even which table to play—it's like deciding on a supermarket checkout line. No matter which one I choose, there's always another that moves quicker. That's how I feel about life—that maybe I'm stuck in the wrong line."

"Don't get so worried, you just had a bad run," said Joel.

"Well, I am worried. Pack it up. We're blowing these mountains and heading to Reno. Maybe things will get better there."

CHAPTER SEVENTEEN

♣ ♦ ♥ ♠

Reno appeared stark and drab compared to the beauty of Tahoe—like a cheap painting hung next to a Rembrandt. The city, once famous as the divorce capital of America, exhibited few reminders that the *Biggest Little City on Earth* once ruled the gambling world.

Pushed out of the number one spot in 1950 by Las Vegas, Reno slid to number three when Atlantic City revived casinos thirty years later. The arrival of the Chicago riverboats followed by the Connecticut tribal casinos sent Reno tumbling even further down the list.

This steady decline created edgy pit bosses all over town who nervously fretted any losses. Raven's arrival into town hardly came as a welcome event. Many casinos in Reno routinely sweated five-dollar action and when two young guys betting bumblebees showed up, they nearly suffered heart attacks.

Reno's clientele tended toward blue-collar, scruffy-looking types, who bet only a few bucks a hand—unless they lost control, a frequent event in this town. The Vegas crowd typically consisted of tourists, while Reno attracted a lower-income crowd who often viewed gambling as an investment opportunity to pull them out of their financial quagmire. The typical answer to "when did you get here" for most people was "about a hundred dollars ago."

Many gambled with money they couldn't afford to lose—a fact written all over their faces. Raven noticed the blackjack tables were often as enticing as lottery tickets to these people. As he wandered through the crowds, he witnessed an older man betting nickels at blackjack and losing steadily. Suddenly the man slapped down five twenties on the green felt. When he lost the hundred bucks, his face contorted in anguish as if his retirement was now in jeopardy. The man quit the table and announced he was going home. Ten minutes later he returned, played two hundred dollars and lost again. He jumped up as if a scorpion had stung him, ran from the table, then returned again and with shaking hands placed four hundred bucks in the betting box. Again he lost, and now completely broke, bolted for the door.

The dealer scooped up the chips with smooth, one-handed dexterity and commented on the man's bad luck. The dealer adjusted a cuff link and casually remarked, "There are no bad cards, only bad card players. He's just another loser."

"How can you tell which players are losers?" Raven asked.

"Anyone I see here more than once," he smirked.

Raven learned from basketball that sports didn't build character—it only revealed the character underneath. He came to believe gambling operated much the same way, stripping away the veneer and baring the inner soul. And no one modeled this truth better than Joel West.

One night, Raven slipped into Harold's club to scout it out for future play, when he noticed Joel sitting alone at a quarter table. Raven decided to silently observe his partner in operation. Joel wore a Chicago Cubs baseball cap backwards and his shirt opened halfway down his hairy chest. Raven moved in a little closer and was shocked to see Joel gripping a cold Heineken with his left hand. A scantily clad cocktail waitress came over with a new bottle and Joel paused in mid-hand to run his eyes up and down her body.

"Hey, little Lady, know what I do for a job?" Joel winked. She said no.

Joel proudly pointed to the blackjack table and said, "This is it, babe. I gamble for a living."

She acted impressed with that confidential information as well as the twenty-dollar tip. Raven, however, was shocked Joel would so carelessly blow his cover.

Later he confronted his friend over this incident. "What's the deal with you telling that cocktail waitress you're a pro? That's got to be the stupidest thing I've ever seen."

Joel bristled. "It's not any worse than you spying on me. What's up with that? I thought we were friends."

"We are, but this is different. This is business," Raven said.

"So friendship is out the window here? You've become the plantation owner and now I'm just a slave. What's next? You going to fire me?"

Raven didn't like confrontations. He wished it were just a business relationship so he could can Joel and be done with him. "No, but you've got to pull yourself out of your losing streak. You're getting more superstitious everyday."

"Just because I wear my lucky Cubs hat?" Joel asked.

"That's only the start. You routinely ask dealers if they're hot and I've seen you slapping your palm on the felt calling out for face cards on your double downs—just like the Asians you criticized."

"Well, at least I don't carry a rabbit's foot around."

"Not yet, maybe. But you do wear the same shirt the next day whenever you win."

"So what's the problem there?"

"Joel, wearing the same shirt isn't going to help your cards. It's only going to affect one thing."

"And that is?"

"It'll make you smell."

Joel refused to listen and left the room. *He's fading fast,* Raven thought, and it made him reflect on his own life. He was skeptical of people who made outlandish claims, such as seeing aliens or spaceships. Yet such encounters often proved life changing, and Raven wished he had the zeal and passion those folks demonstrated.

He wondered if he had indeed met the real God of the universe. Lately, winning had become the sole yardstick for measuring his life. He still believed in a creator but spent little time contemplating the deeper questions of life.

The only real soul-searching he did involved Cynthia. The women on display in the casinos didn't interest him. In his mind he'd already met the best. He thought of Cynthia every day and wrote her twice right after Connecticut, but she never responded. Since then he'd composed nearly a dozen more letters but had torn up each one, knowing his words fell on deaf ears until he proved himself to her.

♣ ♦ ♥ ♠

The next night Raven went to a concert at the Nugget casino. The joy he felt through the early tunes vanished when America played *Lonely People,* a sad song about the elusive nature of love.

He lingered in his seat to compose himself and didn't leave as quickly as usual. Finally, he rose and headed out behind the rest of the herd. There was still a crowd of people and Raven followed ant-like through the narrow exits. Time was money and Raven hated the minutes lost day after day trying to get around slow-moving tourists.

Eventually he broke free and found an empty blackjack table. He liked to play alone since it was faster and less aggravating. Usually, as soon as he opened a game, other players swarmed in. They acted as if safety was found in numbers. Raven tried to avoid eye contact with others since that only encouraged them to join him. He also incorporated body language by spreading a leg or coat across a chair or setting down a drink to block several spaces.

He bought in for six thousand in chips and just started to sit down when he noticed a tall, dark-haired athletic gal in blue jeans and a yellow top across the casino. Raven froze. It wasn't only her striking beauty that caught his eye—the resemblance overwhelmed him.

He couldn't quite see the face, but she glided gracefully through the crowd, and even though her back was to him, a chill ran down his spine. It had to be Cynthia. He abruptly grabbed his chips and left without even an apology to the bewildered dealer.

He wormed his way through the thick crowd, struggling to keep his eye on the target. He wanted to see her face and hoped she would turn around for a moment. If only he could only catch a glimpse of those baby blues. Raven always considered Cynthia's eyes her best feature. But perhaps those alert eyes had already noticed him and she wanted to get away without being seen. He picked up the pace, nearly pushing people over trying to reach her.

An older couple in front of him waddled side-to-side like a pair of ducks, making it difficult to pass. He finally tried to squeeze between them, but the rotund lady bumped him as she swayed back towards her mate. The minor collision cost him, and he lost sight of the black-haired beauty.

The next hour, he frantically scoured the casino, wondering if he'd seen a ghost or the real thing. He remembered the Bradford family often vacationed in nearby Tahoe. It was haunting to think Cynthia might be out there somewhere.

Finally, Raven gave up the search and glanced at his watch—nearly midnight. He pulled out the faded, wallet picture and stared again at Cynthia in a blue summer dress sitting on a porch swing. One edge of the photo was frayed, but it was his only picture. Like so many men before him, he realized too late what he had. Perhaps love and not the lover eluded him. Reluctantly, he returned the picture to his wallet and decided to check into the Nugget.

♣ ♦ ♥ ♠

The simple task of getting a room was anything but simple for Raven. The stressful lifestyle of blackjack made sleep difficult. In addition, casinos differ from normal hotels. They have no thirteenth floor because that's considered unlucky. The windows are designed to prevent any distraught customers from leaping to their deaths.

Those things were unique quirks, but for Raven the rowdy guests posed the greatest problem. He did everything possible to minimize disruptions. If the room lay too close to the elevator or ice machine, he returned to the lobby and asked for another. He rarely took the first room offered.

When the suite at the Nugget finally passed the test, Raven followed his usual bedtime routine. First, he checked under the bed and all the closets for intruders. Next, he disconnected the phone; twice some drunken casino patron who misdialed had wakened him in the dead of night. He used safety pins to fasten the curtains together. A towel laid at the bottom of the front door muffled outside noise. Then he propped a chair against it to deter thieves.

To lessen the chance of hearing the rude neighbor who decides to shower at five in the morning, he shut the bathroom door. Finally, after slipping under the covers, he put in a pair of earplugs and pulled blinders over his eyes.

Raven lay on his back and contemplated the ironies of his life. His nighttime routine once included Bible reading. Now he ended each day with a reflection on money. If he won, it was a good day; if he lost, the day had been a waste of time. *How strange my life has changed so much in such a short period of time.* The stress ate at him. At times he almost wanted to tap out and end the misery. Some days seemed destined for losing no matter what, and it almost felt better to get it over with rather than continue the battle. He had to remain disciplined enough to overcome the urge to rush the megabucks slot machine in hope of recovering his losses with one quick pull.

Raven fidgeted under the sheets, worried over the recent losses. He used to dismiss stories of blackjack players unable to sleep, but now rest escaped him. Since their arrival in northern Nevada, they had lost over a hundred grand, most dumped by Joel. Raven had recovered from his disastrous beginning and began to win, but the pressure and despair took its toll. His work required quick, accurate decisions with thousands of dollars on the line. Although extremely gifted at this, he began second-guessing himself. In the long run no one could know exactly where or how long to play. Raven didn't believe in hot tables or breaking dealers. But so many times a random decision went the wrong way and tore at the fabric of his soul.

Sleep never came, so he got up and spent the rest of the night writing a letter to Cynthia. He explained his position and suggested their relationship simply suffered from a misunderstanding. She probably would not respond, but he still went through seven drafts before calling it quits.

After his morning routine of fifty pushups and a hundred sit-ups, he skipped the morning run and staggered downstairs. At the last minute he decided to trashcan the letter and left to meet Joel for breakfast.

♣ ♦ ♥ ♠

After several weeks in Reno, many faces began to look familiar—locals appeared again and again, especially the slot players and their favorite machines. One somber looking woman brought dolls and rubbed them in a pattern across the glass video poker face before playing. Raven routinely observed people happily losing their chips. He overheard two ladies talking about losing all they brought. The older gal was excited because her money had lasted five hours instead of five minutes. Raven thought such logic absurd. *What difference did that make?* He never understood an entertainment mentality towards gambling and knew many gamblers lived in denial. Like prisoners who never committed a crime, few gamblers believed they lost overall. They remembered the big wins and minimized their losses.

But not all gamblers in Reno were hopeless losers trying to overcome impossible odds. One confident face kept cropping up—a short Hispanic player—with sharp piercing eyes, who often crossed paths with the team. Even though the player wasn't counting, Raven sensed right away something different about him—he didn't act like other gamblers. When they finally met, Raven discovered more ways to win at blackjack existed than he thought.

Diego Chavez sported closely cropped dark hair and stood only a tad over five feet. He bumped into Raven and Joel outside Circus-Circus, and soon they knew all about the talkative little man.

He had grown up in Mexico City before working in the States as a news correspondent. One assignment took him to Las Vegas, and his life changed forever. Fascinated by gambling, he soon devoured books on how to beat the casinos, learned to count cards and quit his job.

The three of them took advantage of the summer weather and walked the path along the Truckee River through the heart of downtown Reno. Diego explained that although he'd been successful in those early years, he constantly sought out new ways to win and gain a bigger advantage. "I started chasing all sorts of casino promotions," Diego said, "like blackjacks paying 2-1 or slots which paid double time a few minutes an hour in Laughlin."

"Why would casinos play double on blackjacks instead of 3-2?" asked Raven.

"To stimulate business, boost their visibility," explained Diego.

"But wouldn't that give players about a two percent edge, even without counting?" asked Raven.

"Yes, but most players are still bad enough to lose, despite that bonus. Never lasts though—always too many pros flocking in to bet big money on those deals. So I always had to look for new horizons." Diego stopped to toss a rock into the surging river below them.

"Evidently you found them?" asked Raven.

"If I dug hard enough. For a while I played the Lady Luck in Vegas. Had a great coupon book there."

Raven raised a skeptical eyebrow. "I did the coupon books when I first hit town, but they're only worth a few bucks each and seemed like a waste of time to me."

Diego gave a sly smile. "Most are, but the marketing people at Lady Luck made one oversight. They put in a free insurance coupon, figuring most people using them would be betting peanuts. But if you bet $500 a hand, each coupon is worth about $240. I went through garbage cans to find extra ones and used a few each day."

Raven admired his resourcefulness. "Very clever. How long did that last?'

"Longer than I expected, maybe a couple of months. After that ended, I moved up here and stumbled across the Canadian money exchange," said Diego.

Joel liked Diego right away. He always paid rapt attention to anyone who discovered ways to make fast money. "How did that one work?" Joel asked.

"Many casinos in this town give chips to Canadian customers at par, even though their dollar is only worth about seventy cents. So I watched a movie with the McKenzie Brothers, worked on my 'eh' and began making almost three hundred bucks every time I bought in for a thousand with the funny money from up North. I'd play just a little, then cash out for American dollars."

Joel turned to Raven. "Man, we've got to start doing that. Sounds better than our method."

Diego shook his head. "Too late. Already burned."

"So what are you doing now?" asked Joel.

"Decided to look for something more permanent. I finally came up with the seventeen-card cut." He explained how at a full seven-spot table, each player received two cards, including the dealer. After the cut, a dealer would burn one card and then deal two cards to each player. So the seventeenth card would be the dealer's hole card. Despite his slight accent, Diego spoke very precise English, and could have easily been mistaken for a college professor.

Joel cut in. "What's the big deal there? Doesn't matter if it's the seventeenth card of the seventh card."

Raven agreed. "That's true. There's no advantage unless you could somehow know the value of the seventeenth card ahead of time."

Diego gave a crafty grin. "You're both right, but I developed an ingenious method to manipulate that card. In some casinos when the deck is offered to the players for cutting, the bottom card of the deck is exposed. I practiced and practiced until I could precisely place the cut card seventeen cards up from the bottom of the deck. If I hit the correct spot, I knew the bottom card would be the dealer's hidden card."

Raven admired the audacity of such a feat. "So with a full table dealing two rounds before shuffling, you would know the dealer's hole card half the time. Wow! That's a big edge."

Joel still looked confused and threw his hands in the air. "The whole technique sounds pretty shaky to me. Must be extremely difficult to do."

Diego said, "True, but it can be done if you commit yourself to practice. But if that's too hard, I've got another one for you."

Joel smirked, "If it's easy, I'm all ears."

"Have you two heard of hole card play?" asked Diego.

They both shook their heads and Diego continued. "It's a technique where you view the hole card of the dealer. Hole card play comes in three flavors—front loading, spooking, and first basing. Because of my height, I front load. I get down very low to the table and am able to catch some sloppy dealers exposing their hole card before they tuck it away."

Raven frowned. "I can't believe any trained dealers would allow that and if they did, isn't there some law against it?"

Diego said, "Nope. If the dealer accidentally turned over their bottom card and everyone at the table saw it, would that be wrong?"

"No, I guess not," Raven said.

"Same principle here. If the dealer isn't skilled enough to keep it from view, anyone can take advantage of that information."

Joel mulled it over. "I like that technique better than the other one and it sounds like a strong edge, but would it work for someone tall like me?"

"No, not a chance." Joel looked crestfallen, but Diego continued, "However, you would make me a great partner for first basing. To do that, a tall guy stands up in the first spot and is able to see the hole card when the dealer checks for blackjacks under tens and aces. Only about a third as strong as front loading, but more common."

Joel lit up again. "Well deal me in."

Raven said, "Not so fast, Joel. I think we need to talk about the ethics a little more."

Joel retorted, "Ethics get checked at the door whenever you enter the casino. Besides, you can't expect to make an omelet without breaking a few eggs."

Diego's innovative nature and keen eyesight made him the king of front loaders. His style fascinated Raven, but in his mind, trying to see the dealer's cards smacked of cheating. Even though Diego insisted it was legal, it still felt wrong to him. However, he liked the seventeen-card cut technique and quickly became adept at it.

Joel gravitated to the easier concept of first basing and soon joined Diego. Raven shunned the ethics of hole-card play and stuck to either counting or the seventeen-card cut whenever it was available. Before long, every casino in Reno changed their procedure and covered up the bottom card. This effectively ended that game, and Raven reverted back to counting.

Joel, however, never returned. He found a home in hole-card heaven and finally started winning, having discovered a game much less taxing on his brain.

When the Reno games completely dried up, Raven decided to return to Vegas, but Joel had other plans. He chose to stay and play hole cards on his own money with Diego. The fact he had lost $112,000 plus received another $26,000 in wages incensed Raven. He insisted Joel play for the bank until he at least won Raven's money back, but Joel didn't care—his only priority was himself. Remembering how his father always told him if you're riding a dead horse the best thing to do is dismount, Raven gave up and left his longtime friend in Reno.

CHAPTER EIGHTEEN

♣ ♦ ♥ ♠

When he approached the outskirts of Las Vegas Raven still was unsure where he'd play blackjack next. He stopped at a grocery store. The clerks were decked out in Halloween costumes and inspiration hit—he would return to the Strip—but in disguise.

He received a makeover transforming him into a blond Californian. Hopefully, the change would allow him to again play casinos that had given him the boot. After a quick stop at his apartment, he went out to test his new disguise, battling traffic all the way down the strip until he found a parking spot, the last one available, on the top floor of the Palace's parking garage.

An hour later he returned to his BMW carrying his blond wig, furious over the evening's events. He had been caught again by Howard Goldberg and faced the sober prospect of no future in Las Vegas. Depressed and disillusioned, he drove home pondering his dilemma. Impulsively, he changed directions and headed for Marco Antonelli's house.

Marco listened attentively to Raven's tale and nodded his head in agreement. "It's that damn technology that's doing us in. Years ago, all we had to worry about was the pit bosses' memory. If you stayed away long enough, they forgot you. Now with computers and faxes, we're virtually marked for life."

Raven appreciated the sympathy. "So what's happening with you? I thought you'd be long gone by now, doing the high-tech shuffle tracking."

Marco exhaled a long sigh. "I vastly underestimated the training time required, but we're finally ready to head out to Atlantic City."

"When?"

"Hopefully next week. Karl's been there for almost two months scouting and waiting for the rest of us." Marco took a long pull on his cigar while sizing Raven up. "Any chance we can get you involved?"

Raven had convinced himself months ago to avoid any financial dealings with Marco. The way he treated women, his arrogance, and complete lack of ethics placed them worlds apart. However, now Raven faced an uncertain future. Because of Joel, his bankroll had slipped down to $650,000. He could quit now and go home victorious, but the million-dollar figure still drove him—deep down he still craved the approval of his father and old classmates. He didn't see any way he could reach his goal in Nevada—he was too well known and too good.

"What do you pay players for this venture?" Raven asked tentatively.

Marco responded, "Fifty bucks an hour plus expenses. Karl gets the hourly wage plus five percent of the win because he also organizes the logistics of the teams. The remaining profit gets split between the investors."

Raven mulled this over. Fifty bucks might be good pay for a lot of people, but after Reno, it would hardly make a dent in his quest. "I'm flattered you want me, but I couldn't go for that," he said firmly and stood up to leave.

Marco let the conversation lay dormant for a few moments, then spoke. "Good, I didn't think you would."

Raven stared in surprise. "Then why even invite me? I don't get it."

"Because I'm not looking for another player— I'm looking for a partner," Marco said. This startling revelation set off a battle in Raven's conflicting emotions—fear competing with greed.

Marco pulled out a notepad and began writing. "What I'm proposing is the two of us each put up half a million. With this large a team we should carve up Atlantic City like Sherman plowed through Georgia. I project a win of nearly $300,000 a month for each of us. And it's illegal to bar skilled players in New Jersey. We can't lose."

The huge potential had a strong appeal to Raven after his recent setback, but the flip side meant his money, almost all of it, would be out of his control. "Isn't it hard to monitor everyone? I lost a ton of my money letting Joel West play for me in Reno."

"Not a problem. Joel was a rookie. Everyone we've picked is a competent pro or they wouldn't even have gotten through my door. I'm telling you, we can't lose."

"Then how come you need me? My money I mean. You must have that much just under your pillow."

Marco laughed, "No, actually I hide it in the liquor cabinet." Marco laid down the notepad with the figure $300,000 circled in red ink. He toyed with the pen in his hand and stood up to face Raven. "Right now I've got most of my money tied up offshore, and more importantly I want another person to help drive the team—someone who has a vested interest in their success."

Raven took a long look at the notepad. He suppressed the small voice of protest saying he was making a deal with the devil and shook hands.

♣ ♦ ♥ ♠

The technological devices Marco developed consisted of a small computer chip embedded in a special shoe with switches operated by the toes. The player punched in various combinations of four keys to input the value of each card played and the CPU would then send a signal up a wire to a transmitter taped to the sensitive part of the thigh. The skin received pulses instructing the player how to play the hands, how much to bet, and where to cut the cards after the shuffle.

Wires connected to their skin intimidated many people, but Raven had no qualms. He quickly grasped the complexities that baffled many other trainees. Some gave up using the shoe computers and switched to simpler hand keypads inside false pockets. These were considerably easier to master but more likely to get spotted by casino personnel.

Within a week Raven caught up to those who had practiced for months. He personally still disliked the notion of using machines instead of his brain to beat the casinos but trusted the group wouldn't get involved in such a huge venture unless everything was legal. A confident Marco Antonelli packed up all the equipment and the entire team flew to New Jersey to begin the onslaught.

♣ ♦ ♥ ♠

The very name Atlantic City conjured up romantic images for Raven. He'd grown up playing monopoly and dreaming of the real Boardwalk. That nostalgic glow died a quick death once they reached the city limits.

Atlantic City had once been a slum by the sea. Now it was a slum with casinos by the sea. Some sectors resembled a war zone. Evidently the huge profits generated flowed directly into the pockets of casino owners and did nothing to revitalize downtown.

Karl Beck arranged for them to set up camp in a big rented house and Marco showed Raven around. It was an ancient colonial structure with weathered clapboards and a poor man's view of the ocean.

"What do you think?" asked Marco.

"I think the house needs to be remodeled—with a bull-dozer," said Raven.

Marco laughed. "Yeah. I know what you mean. It's close enough to walk to the casinos, but with so much crime in the area, nobody wants to."

Karl clearly was used to running Marco's teams and being in charge. Raven had difficulty stepping back and allowing so much of his money to be controlled by others, especially when they soon sank into a deep financial hole.

Mistakes and screw-ups happened frequently in the casinos, despite the long training period. The bankroll swiftly went south and losses of fifty grand a day became commonplace. Computer malfunction and glitches occurred daily. Marco hung around the house and dealt with hardware problems while the team split up into two groups—Karl heading up one, and Raven the other.

Before long, Karl and Raven formed an uneasy alliance that slowly evolved into mutual respect. They admired each other's competence and also discovered a common interest in running. Each morning they jogged a few miles up the Boardwalk and along the beach while talking over the team's problems. Karl often ran bare-chested, even on cold days. With an extraordinary physique, he looked like a competitive body builder, his arms and stomach rock hard muscles. He and Raven shared similar facial features and hair color, but beyond that the resemblance ended. Raven usually kept his shirt on.

One morning they returned to the house and Karl remarked, "You're certainly a paradox."

"What do you mean by that?" Raven asked, by now used to Karl's South African bluntness.

"Well, for someone who professes to be a Christian, you're an enigma. I mean, there can't be too many professional gamblers in your church, are there?"

"Religion is about truth," Raven said. "That's why I base my life on the Bible—not on what other people think."

"Back in my choir boy days I might have agreed with you."

"Why not now?"

"I've read too much of Nietzsche to see any meaning in this world anymore."

Raven answered, "Nihilism doesn't work. Logically, there's got to be some measure of right and wrong—and the Bible is the only source that gives us those absolutes."

Marco walked in as Raven answered. Carving up fundamentalists was his second-favorite sport, so he jumped into the argument. "Have you guys ever heard the one about the agnostic, dyslexic, insomniac?" Karl and Raven both shook their heads no. "Tragic story, really. Stayed up all night wondering if there really was a dog."

Raven frowned. "Aren't you a bit flippant about God?"

Marco snickered, "If there is a God, he's either dead or asleep. The archaic absolutes of the Bible are a joke. No intelligent person thinks a book can impose right and wrong on us."

"Why not? Everyone has absolutes whether they realize it or not. It's just a question of where you draw the line."

"What do you mean by that?" Marco demanded.

"For instance, you think sex is okay?"

"No," Marco grinned, "I think sex is great. Last night, for instance, I spent a very satisfying evening with a hard-bodied blonde vixen. What could be wrong with that?"

"So you think sex anytime, anywhere and with anybody is okay?" Raven asked. "What about rape and murder?"

"Come on. That's a totally different issue," Marco snapped.

"Really? It just depends on where you draw the line. Do you have any basis for saying you're better than Ted Bundy?"

Marco turned to Karl for support. "Help me out here, Karl. Tell this religious quack there's a big difference between sex and serial killers."

Karl quietly stared at the floor. Then he raised his eyes and faced Marco. "No, he's right. There's no difference between you and Bundy. You both just take whatever you want."

At Karl's intense stare, Marco stepped back, unsure what to make of this outburst. He turned to Raven. "Well, that's why I like evolution. It gives me the right to do whatever I want. The strong survive. There's no God who steps in and saves the weak."

Karl asked, "What's your take on that, Raven? Even you must believe in evolution."

Raven shook his head. "Evolution is just a theory, not a science. Look at the world around you, there has to be a design."

"How so?" asked Karl.

"When I was a kid on Vinalhaven, I used to find arrowheads in the dirt. Wouldn't you agree these were shaped on purpose rather than some chance, chaotic erosions of a rock?"

"That makes sense," Karl agreed. "Even though I believe in the Big Bang, I've always wondered who lit the fuse."

"It's the same with life. There's far too much complexity just in the human eyeball for all the parts to have evolved independently by chance. Every piece needs to be present to work, just like a mousetrap, except infinitely more complex," Raven said. "It clearly shows design."

"Then why do all the scientists believe in evolution?"

"Actually I read in a magazine that over half don't and that nearly 90% of astronomers believe in God," Raven said.

"That's bullshit," roared Marco. "I never read that in any magazine."

Raven suspected Marco's literary tastes rarely rose beyond *Playboy* or *Hustler.* "High school biology teachers may think evolution is fact, but the top people who study the universe and its mysteries every day know better."

"That's a bunch of baloney," Marco said. "All of it could've happened given enough time."

"Do you believe that monkeys could have typed *The Iliad?* It's all too amazing a tapestry of complexity out there. No amount of time could account for the intricate mosaic painted right before our eyes, and it's infinitely more detailed than some epic book by Homer. Had to have an intelligence behind it." Raven still firmly believed in creation, even if some of his other views had waned over the years.

Marco scoffed, "You're just deluding yourself."

"No, this is the one thing in life that I'm sure of. Furthermore, you probably didn't know Darwin was a racist."

Marco's eyes widened, incredulous. "Now I know you've flipped."

"It's true. That's where Hitler got a lot of his views and rationale for the superiority of one race over another. He considered Jews and blacks inferior byproducts of evolution. He logically built on Darwin's premise seeing no reason to keep the strong from wiping out the weak."

Marco exploded. "Now you're blaming the holocaust on evolution? That's ridiculous. I never want to discuss religion with you again."

He stormed out of the house. Karl shrugged his shoulders and shook his head. "How you two ever got hooked up is a bigger mystery than the origin of life."

Karl grabbed a bagel and plopped the team logs on the kitchen table. Raven whipped up a wheat germ shake the color of peat moss and studied the results of the previous night's play. The bankroll had taken another hit, the fifth in the last six nights.

Raven took some comfort in knowing his group had won. Karl's group, however, had been a disaster and stood almost two hundred grand down. Raven attributed the difference to fluctuation since playing with computers removed the variable of human skill. Possibly some of the players on Karl's team were making operational mistakes but more than likely it was just bad luck.

Everyone assumed the poor run of cards would end soon, but the losing days continued. A week later the deficit sunk to a quarter of a million in the hole. Players new to computers began to doubt the technology and wondered if they really had an edge. The nerves of everyone were frayed and two members quit.

Marco made a rare appearance to observe the team in operation and to discover what might be wrong. He watched Raven's team pull slightly ahead after a long battle when a member of Karl's group came over from the other part of the casino. They had gotten hammered. Marco cut the session short and joined Raven out front to retrieve their car and head home.

The preppy-looking parking attendant with a goatee gave a big smile with his canned greeting of "How we all doing tonight?"

Marco answered. "How the hell do you think we're doing? We just lost forty thousand in your damn casino. So how about we just skip the clichés and get the car."

Raven started to speak, but Marco cut him off. "Forget about him. We need to worry about our money."

"I'm glad to hear you're finally concerned. You haven't played one hand of blackjack since we arrived. What do you think we need to do? Won't we win it back?"

"Normally yes, but something's funny here. Down $270,000 after six weeks of play is unbelievable. Almost impossible," Marco said grimly.

"You think players are incompetent?"

"No, I think players are skimming."

Raven digested that sentence. Skimming evoked seedy images of the mob. "Get serious. Surely no one in this group could be stealing. Didn't you hand-pick them all and scrutinize their credentials?"

"I did, but cold cash can do strange things to people. And the lure of easy money has a very strong appeal."

"Okay, so that's a possibility. How do we find out?"

"Do you know how to make holy water?"

Raven didn't see the reason for another religious joke.

"No, I don't."

"You boil the hell out of it. That's how you make holy water." They got in the car and Marco explained. "With enough heat we can bring any scum to the surface."

"How's that going to help? If someone's cheating us I doubt they're going to admit it even under pressure."

"No, they might lie to us, but not to a polygraph machine."

"You have one of those?" Raven asked.

"No, they're too expensive to own and difficult to administer. We need to hire an agency to come in and do the testing."

"Does everyone get tested? Because my group is slightly ahead, so I'd think Karl's group needs the testing."

"Not necessarily," Marco said. "Skimming happens most frequently when someone is winning. They feel entitled, and it's easier to rationalize that the investor will still make money. It could be someone in your group."

"So everybody gets the electrodes?" Raven prided himself on being a tough guy, but inwardly even he didn't relish the prospect of getting wired.

"No, because if the cake is missing, you always check the fat people first. The money is ours, so there's no reason we'd steal it."

Raven didn't mention the obvious fact that Marco hadn't even got around to playing so testing him was a moot point. "That makes sense. But what about Karl?"

"Karl had training in South Africa that taught him how to control his blood pressure and pulse to fool the machine. Besides, I've worked with him long enough to fully trust him and his main incentive is the five percent of the bankroll."

Raven agreed. They arranged for the tests and everyone eventually complied, although several members complained vehemently. Raven made a mental note of the protesters, assuming one of them was the thief.

When the results came back, everyone passed. Not one of them had stolen any money from the team.

With this reassurance, they renewed the attack. Atlantic City remained one of the few places where skillful blackjack players couldn't be barred. The New Jersey Supreme Court had ruled casinos couldn't throw out card counters just because they were smart, so the team stood a good chance of retrieving their losses.

Raven's group continued to win and Karl's team finally started turning things around. The next two weeks produced mostly winning sessions and the bankroll edged back to only $200,000 in arrears. Then, just when things looked promising, the wheels came off.

The first setback came in the attitude of the casinos. Initially all the casino hosts practically fought each other trying to get the business of these new high rollers. They extended lavish offers of flying to the city by private helicopter to watch the Yankees and invitations to play golf with celebrities. Soon, these extravagant perks began drying up and the hosts became as approachable as a Doberman with hemorrhoids.

Evidently some pit bosses had become suspicious of Raven's team. They weren't aware of the computers, but they suspected some form of shuffle tracking. Even though they couldn't be kicked out, the team soon found conditions deteriorating. They rarely got any comps and the cards were often reshuffled early when the team placed their huge bets.

Coupled with this setback, Karl's team began losing again—this time even bigger than before. The bankroll dived to minus $330,000 and the conditions for good play evaporated.

Marco normally remained unflappable over the losses; always saying "no one is dead until their ass is cold" and insisting things would turn around. But now the numbers began to wash away his optimism. When the deficit reached $400,000, he decided to pull the plug.

Raven was furious. "We're just going to walk away? I don't think so. Half of that bankroll is my money and I want to get it back."

"We can't," Marco countered. "The casinos are tightening up and changing the shuffles. Besides, there's something seriously wrong here. There's just no way we should still be losing."

"Yeah, thanks again for getting me involved in your computer venture," Raven shouted. "Next time I'll stick to using my head."

"No, it's not the computers. They can beat the game. I know that."

"How would you know? You never even played here."

Marco put up his hands. "Calm down, it ain't over until the fat lady belches. I think we can still get it back."

Raven quit pacing the room and sat down. "What do you mean? I thought you were throwing in the towel."

"Just on Atlantic City. I think you and I can still win the money back elsewhere."

"You and I? That's an even bigger joke. You haven't exactly led by example here and joined your troops in the trenches."

"There's a reason for that," said Marco coolly.

"Oh yeah? What's that?"

"I'll tell you later."

"Great. Another one of the Antonelli secrets." Raven rolled his eyes.

"One of the things I learned from dating girl scouts was to always be prepared, so I've got a backup plan," Marco smirked.

"Okay, where do you propose we recover our money?"

"The Caribbean."

Raven's mood improved immediately. It was almost Christmas and the weather along the Jersey coast worsened by the week. Sun and beaches did have an exotic allure. But the most important consideration was the money. He desperately wanted to get it back. "So we move the team down there and set up shop?"

"No, just you and me."

"Really?" This surprised Raven, but he liked the idea of only the two of them working together—the control would be back.

"Let's face it. Something is faulty here. I'm sure the computers are working fine, but it's our money. So let's can everyone else and pack our toothbrushes. There's some good games down there, and I could use a little bit of Caribbean eye candy."

Raven considered suggesting a sugar-free diet to keep Marco in line. "Are you really going to play?" he asked.

"Of course. I want to get the money back as much as you."

Raven hoped he spoke the truth.

CHAPTER NINETEEN

♣ ♦ ♥ ♠

Marco was no stranger to the Dominican Republic. From the moment they touched down in Santo Domingo, he knew exactly where to go. He confidently worked his way through a gauntlet of hawkers and guides, then selected the cleanest driver and car for hire outside the terminal, a blue Olds Cutlass—modest by American standards, but a luxury automobile on this island.

"All those drivers inside will try to rip you off. And many of their cars will be lucky to make it to Santo Domingo without breaking down," Marco explained.

Marco carefully watched to make sure their luggage ended up in the trunk, then got in. "Karl got sick down here once and had to go to the hospital in an ambulance. It stopped three times on the way. Twice to check the radiator and once to get gas."

"That's unbelievable," Raven said. "I'll try to stay healthy."

"Good luck. Besides the usual worries about dysentery, Montezuma's revenge and the Tijuana trots, you've also got to be careful of tuberculosis. It's an epidemic down here, and you could get it just from some greaser breathing on you."

Raven shot a glance at the driver and quickly opened the window to let in fresh air. Marco noticed him staring at the long string of shacks lining the bumpy road, and spoke up. "The first time I came here, the level of poverty shocked me too."

Raven continued to take in the haunting images. "I can't believe a country could be this third-world, yet be so close to America."

"Depressing nation for sure, but it does have a great upside," said Marco.

"Let me guess—sun and surf."

"No. The casinos and the senoritas. That's what makes this place appealing. The blackjack games are incredibly easy, and so are the women. They're both *mucho* hot."

Raven hoped Marco came to the islands to chase their losses rather than native women. "Isn't it difficult meeting locals with the language barrier?" Raven asked.

Marco let out a lecherous laugh. "Are you crazy? My perfect girl is a dark-eyed Latin who speaks little or no English. The less talk, the more I like 'em."

It turned out Marco was at least right about the gambling. The casinos were small, dingy, and poorly lit, but their blackjack offered great rules. They were patrolled by anxious pit bosses whose motto seemed to be "when in trouble, when in doubt, run in circles, scream, and shout."

Marco and Raven pounded the simple shuffles with their computers while the bosses watched in bewilderment. They had no idea why they were getting beat. They neurotically tried changing the cards, then the dealers. It didn't help. They tried standing on different sides of the table, but it made no difference. The two American high rollers crushed them day after day.

The only difficulty stemmed from playing in pesos. Normally, Raven would place a bet at a certain count, such as $500 at plus three. Here, he needed to figure out the true count and then convert the dollar amount to Dominican pesos—a difficult task even with a calculator. The amounts they won were staggering because of the exchange rate. After a few weeks, they accumulated millions in small bill denominations and rented four safety deposit boxes to store them.

Raven expressed concern over when and how they would switch it back to dollars. Marco assured him he would handle it, having dealt with the black market on previous trips.

The mention of the black market unsettled Raven, but at least they were winning. He and Marco had won back nearly a hundred grand, despite the small limits at most of the Dominican casinos.

And Marco actually played this time, although his pleasure-seeking mentality remained in constant conflict with Raven's Maine work ethic. One night, Marco quit after a few hours of play while Raven continued toiling late into the evening. On returning to the hotel room, he found the door dead bolted. He knocked and knocked but got no answer.

Eventually, after several minutes of pounding, he heard some faint voices. A sheepish-looking Marco cracked the door slightly and peered out at Raven. He wore only a towel and his hair looked like Einstein on a bad day.

Raven started to enter, but Marco blocked the door. "What's the deal here?" Raven demanded. "Let me in. I just played over twelve hours and I want to hit the sack."

"Just a few minutes, okay? Let me get rid of the hookers first."

"What!" Raven exploded. "You brought prostitutes into our room?"

Marco made a funny face, "Prostitutes? Damn. I thought they said they were Protestants and you'd approve." He laughed and sauntered back into the room leaving the door slightly ajar.

Raven fumed while in broken Spanish Marco haggled over the price with his two *dates*.

The girls finally left, each gleefully clutching a Ben Franklin.

Raven ripped into Marco. "Don't you have any morals at all?"

"I used to, but I had them surgically removed. Didn't even have to use an anesthetic," Marco said with a smirk.

Raven just shook his head. "You're hopeless."

Marco scoffed. "Get real. What could be wrong with what we just did? We brought each other a great deal of enjoyment."

"Well, for two hundred bucks they ought to have been ecstatic. That must be a fortune down here and a real waste of your money."

"Yeah, but it was worth it. Besides, it wasn't just my money."

"What do you mean?" Raven asked.

"It's standard procedure to charge all hookers to the bankroll," Marco said without a flicker of emotion.

Raven's jaw dropped. "Surely you're kidding. Tell me you're joking."

"No joke. That's the way we've always done things. Anyway, it's a fair investment to keep me happy and working."

"You're disgusting."

Raven's indignation amused Marco. "Look, I didn't realize you'd react this way. I'll tell you what. Next time this happens, why don't you hide out on the balcony and watch? That way you can at least get your money's worth."

"You're sick," Raven shouted.

His blood boiled. For a long time he had been willing to turn a blind eye to Marco's shady side, but this situation took the cake. He threw his suitcase on the bed, packed his stuff and left without a good-bye.

♣ ♦ ♥ ♠

Because high rollers rarely visited the Dominican Republic, it worked out better to split up and keep a lower profile. The operation in Atlantic City involved rotating in a number of different computer operators standing behind the table and tracking the shuffle. They signaled the big player at the table through an electronic transmitter on his thigh. He would then place the bets and cut according to instructions sent him by the concealed computers.

On this island, none of that stealth seemed necessary. The level of expertise in surveillance proved pitiful, and Raven and Marco played individually—a far more efficient style.

Despite his misgivings about Marco, Raven's confidence in the computers soared—as he finally saw the strength of shuffle tracking. They won large amounts and it baffled him why they performed so poorly in Atlantic City.

Raven typically played alone at a private table. Many of the dealers were careless in their procedure, but almost all were fast, and Raven easily averaged over two hundred hands per hour. One night at the Conquistador Casino, a dealer named Hernando challenged Raven like a Spanish matador. His cards flew out of the shoe, and after each bust he scooped them up in one quick, sweeping motion. Hernando dealt nearly twice as fast as any other dealer in the house, and Raven struggled to keep up with the maniacal pace.

Intent on catching all the cards before Hernando buried them in the discard rack, Raven didn't hear the voice behind him at first. When he felt a soft tug on his elbow, he stopped playing and turned around, stunned to see a grinning Butch Jackson standing behind him.

The shock of seeing his high school classmate again left Raven speechless. A flood of childhood memories rushed through his mind.

Butch extended his hand. "It is you, Randy Townsend."
Hearing his name aloud brought Raven to his senses.
He quickly turned and cast a wary glance at the pit bosses.
Did they hear my real name? Marco had insisted they use
false ones in this country—although it hardly seemed necessary. Since most pit bosses didn't even speak English, he
doubted they noticed the discrepancy. The two of them now
whispered something in Spanish, but Raven couldn't get a
bead on the context.

He hastily grabbed his chips, whisked Butch out of ear-
shot, and suggested a walk outdoors. They stepped into
the bright sunlight and strolled down the cobblestone streets
of the New World's oldest city.

Remembering their last tense encounter, Raven felt awkward being with Butch, yet at the same time it delighted
him to see a face from his past. Almost a decade had gone
by since he last set foot in Maine.

Butch ordered a cup of coffee from a sidewalk vendor
and poured in a generous portion of cream. "I couldn't
believe it when I saw you in the casino, but I'd recognize
that jet black hair anywhere—though it's a bit shorter now,"
he said. "You've bulked up some, too—not the skinny runt
I remembered."

"I've been doing a lot of push ups and sit-ups, but I'll
never look like you, Mr. Universe," Raven said, grinning.
"How's everyone in Maine?"

"Great. A lot of people ask about you, wondering if
you'll make it home next year for the high school reunion."
Then with a knowing glace in the direction of the casino
Butch said, "Looks like there've been a lot of changes in
your life."

Raven didn't want their conversation to work its way
back to gambling. "Yeah, but nothing interesting to talk
about. What about you? Did you and Jennifer Ross end up
together?"

"Nope, things just didn't work out." Butch looked contemplative for a moment, then continued. "This may sound stupid, but I think she always liked you."

"Yeah, right," Raven said sarcastically.

Butch was animated, happy, talkative and friendly—completely different from the redneck teenager Raven remembered.

Butch couldn't stop beaming. "Fancy meeting you here in this country. What a shock. And in a casino no less. What's the story with that?"

Raven didn't want the tale of "devout Christian turns to gambling" to be blabbed all over Camden. *Hope Butch didn't notice how much money I was betting.* He adroitly changed the subject. "Just down here on sort of a vacation. How about you? I never pictured you as the type who'd stray very far from Penobscot Bay."

Butch took the bait and dropped his inquiries. "I started a maple syrup business after high school. It took a few years, but after a while it really exploded. We sell it to all the tourists who come up for the fall foliage. It's kind of a nostalgia thing."

Butch had become successful, cosmopolitan and likeable—completely the opposite of what Raven expected from anyone who stayed in Maine.

"Great. Sounds like you're doing well," Raven said.

"Unbelievably well. I take three months off every winter to sail and dive down here in the Caribbean while my partner holds down the fort. You might know him."

"Really? He a Camden boy?"

"No, he's from Rockland, but I never held that against him," said Butch with a hearty laugh. "His name's Garren Horne."

Raven's eyes registered recognition. "Of course I remember him. He's the only guy who ever beat me in the mile. State champ two straight track seasons."

"That's the guy. Thought you'd recall those days," said Butch.

"Hard to forget. How's he doing now?"

Butch kept talking while Raven's mind drifted back to his high school running career—how he never quite fulfilled his promise, always ending up just short of his goals. He snapped back to reality when Butch mentioned the name Cynthia and interrupted, "Excuse me? What did you just say?"

"I said Garren might be marrying some flatlander gal—a Cynthia something who used to summer in Vinalhaven. Met her once—a real knockout but not my type—too prim and proper."

Raven hardly heard another word Butch said. The longer he traveled down the road of blackjack, the more he realized how much Cynthia meant to him. And now, the dream appeared dead.

He continued to float in a fog until Butch, glancing at his watch, said, "Wish I'd run into you a couple days ago. We could have gone diving together. But I've got a flight to catch home tonight."

After Butch left, Raven sat down on the stonewall overlooking the ocean. His mind spun like reels on a slot machine. The shock and finality of the news overwhelmed him. He'd always clung to the hope of a future with Cynthia, but evidently he'd just been dense. Her final words had been clear enough; apparently he simply hadn't wanted to hear them.

The fiery, orange sun blazed as the vast ocean swallowed up its dying rays. It reminded him of the picnic with Cynthia on the bluff overlooking the Mediterranean Sea. They had shared a kiss—a common event, hardly unique for two college students. Yet, Raven knew what she had implied with that act. Her lips would not be offered to anyone but the man of her dreams.

He'd basically thrown her love away—for blackjack. Now any chance of reconciliation had vanished. Over and over Raven berated himself for letting Cynthia go without more of a fight. The last trace of the sun sank into the Caribbean and he felt darkness settle in. He always wore the wooden cross necklace Cynthia had given him. Now he gently lifted it to his lips, then stood up and walked back to the casino.

The Conquistador had given him a reserved table in the main pit, or "solo privado" as the sign said in Spanish. Now Raven slipped back into the same seat and began to play but found it increasingly difficult to focus. With his mind in a haze, he decided to call it a night and left to cash out his chips.

The casino manager quickly showed up at the cage and, in rapid Spanish, spoke to the cashier. Raven couldn't make out the gist of the conversation but noticed the mood had changed.

They finally handed over the money and he felt a measure of relief. The feeling was short-lived. He barely tucked the bills into his fanny pack when the shift manager called him by his real name. Raven nervously rubbed his nose and pretended to not understand.

The manager continued. "That is your real name, is it not Senor Townsend?"

A year earlier perhaps, the Wheaton College grad would have been hesitant to lie. He wasn't anymore. "No. What are you talking about? You know my name is Peter Brooks."

"I don't think so. While you were gone with your big gringo friend we contacted the Griffith Agency in Las Vegas. They confirmed your photo and identified you as Randolph Townsend, also know as the Raven. Seems you've been barred from many casinos in Nevada."

Raven didn't respond. No denials or subject changes could save him here.

"You can add our country to your list. You are no longer welcome to play anywhere on this island. We will notify all the other casinos. Furthermore, your hotel comp is rescinded and we want you out of your room immediately."

Raven quickly packed and left. It was almost midnight and he wasn't in the mood to look around for a new place. He took a cab to Marco's hotel and was glad to find no hookers in the room this time. He explained what happened and they both agreed it was time to exit the country. Marco would exchange the money and then they would leave.

♣ ♦ ♥ ♠

Two days passed without Marco taking care of the currency conversion. He claimed a mild case of tropical fever, but a skeptical Raven grew increasingly agitated. On the third day when Marco again slept in till noon, Raven had enough. He collected all the Dominican pesos and set out for the black market on his own.

He found the general area of the market, but it took a long time and several inquiries before he found the correct merchant—a Cuban family who handled all the financial dealings for the local business community. When he saw their home, a square concrete block structure with black iron bars over the windows, Raven doubted they would have the amount of cash necessary. The humid day accentuated the stench of dog urine in the barren dirt yard. He immediately regretted choosing this route rather than settling for a lower exchange rate at a bank.

The two brothers sitting at the kitchen table eyed him warily while a young woman rocked a crying baby on the other side of the room. Raven carefully laid the Dominican currency in stacks on the table. The heat felt even more oppressive inside and he was drenched in sweat. This was unlike any banking experience he'd ever known.

Despite the language barrier, they agreed on an exchange rate written on a piece of paper and Raven relaxed a little. It was a good rate, considerably higher than the banks offered. *I don't think I'll walk out of here with a free toaster, but netting an extra eight grand should make up for it.* The Cubans began the task of counting pesos. Suddenly the older brother jumped up and began screaming in Spanish. Raven had no idea what happened, but clearly something had gone wrong. The younger brother ran into the other room and returned waving a gun. He pressed the cold, metal barrel against Raven's head. Then, the older brother grabbed Raven by his tee shirt and dragged him into the next room. Suddenly, the man's grip came loose. Raven crashed face-first onto the concrete floor. The older brother stared at the wooden cross necklace left in his hand.

As Raven laid on the floor with blood pouring out his nose, the Cubans bickered loudly. He didn't know what the argument was about and didn't dare move. The older brother finally left and the younger kept the shiny Smith and Wesson pointed at his quarry.

Minutes later, the older brother returned with a priest. The priest spoke softly and the gun was put away. He leaned down to Raven. "Are you American?"

Raven couldn't express how glad he was to hear English. "Yes."

"That's what Pedro thought. He brought me over to translate. Evidently there's some type of problem."

"That's putting it mildly. I thought they were going to kill me—I'd consider that a problem." Raven rolled onto his side. Pain shot through his shoulder and face. He suspected his nose was broken, but that was the least of his worries at the moment.

The priest conferred with Pedro who nodded his head. Raven noticed the priest's disposition change. "Pedro says you tried to pass off some counterfeit bills."

Raven thought quickly. That explained why the brothers became so excited. They believed he was cheating them. "I had no idea any of those bills were bad," he said. "They all look the same to me."

The priest translated. They looked unconvinced. Then Raven remembered the last casino that barred him. The manager had said something to the cashier at the cage. It dawned on him where the bogus bills originated. He explained this and hoped they would buy it.

The brothers argued more. Evidently Pedro believed him while the other brother preferred homicide. Raven's heart pounded as his fate hung in the balance. Pedro kept holding up the wooden cross and pointed at the priest.

The clergyman joined the conversation and calmed the brothers down. Slowly the mood changed. He turned to Raven. "Why were you wearing this cross? Are you Catholic?"

Raven wanted to lie. The wrong answer could end his life. Yet as easily as he lived deceptively in the casinos, he couldn't bring himself to deny his true faith. "No, I'm not."

Tensions again filled the room as the priest translated. The situation was precarious. Raven sat up and reached for the cross. Surprised, Pedro released its grip and Raven said, "But I am a Christian. This cross was carved from olive wood in Jerusalem. I studied in Israel and believe in the same God as you."

Spanish once again filled the air as the brothers spoke rapidly. Finally, Pedro disappeared into the next room and returned with American dollars for Raven. After deducting for the counterfeit bills, he counted out the exchanged amount.

The priest leaned over with a towel and helped clean up Raven's bloodstained face. He examined the swollen nose and determined it wasn't broken. Then he held up the necklace. "Well, my son, this cross probably saved your life. When you say your prayers tonight, you should be very thankful because you are indeed a lucky man."

♣ ♦ ♥ ♠

When Raven returned to the hotel, he found Marco entertaining a senorita by the pool.

"I thought you said you were sick," Raven said tersely.

Marco gave the girl a quick kiss and shooed her away. "Yeah, they must have mixed something therapeutic in those pina coladas—tasted like real coconut juice. I feel great now."

"Amazing recovery," Raven snapped.

"Indeed." Marco put a little more lotion on his nose. "Did you take care of our money?"

Raven came unglued. "I nearly got killed while you cavorted with another one of your conquests. There is no 'we' in this partnership. You're a hedonistic jerk."

Marco removed his sunglasses. "Calm down, man. What went wrong?"

He told him what happened at the black market. "Listen, I want out of this country right *now*, before anything else happens," Raven demanded.

Marco played with the little umbrella in his drink and appeared unconcerned over Raven's ordeal. "I kind of hate to leave so quickly. That girl promised me a tango lesson tonight."

Raven glared at him. "You don't have a single regret over what happened to me, do you?"

Marco shrugged. "Okay, if it's that important, we can catch an evening flight to the Bahamas. We were going to play there next anyway—we'll just go a little earlier."

Raven angrily left the pool and began to obsess over one thing—how to make Marco pay for his near-death experience.

CHAPTER TWENTY

♣ ♦ ♥ ♠

Marco Antonelli continued his recovery by drinking heavily during the short flight. He made comments about every girl near him on the plane. "See that brunette over there, Raven? She looks sexy, but I'm guessing she's not real bright, kind of a foxy moron—the type who thinks Nassau is where they launch the space shuttle. And that blonde with the big hooters in row two probably told her travel agent to book a seat away from the window, so it wouldn't mess up her hair."

Marco's obnoxious behavior further strained their tenuous relationship. As the plane circled the airport, Marco pointed out the banking section of Nassau. "I never did finish filling you in on the details of how I screw Uncle Sam, did I?"

Raven stiffened. "I'm really not interested."

"Nonsense," said Marco. "You're going to love this arrangement."

"All right, go ahead."

"I set up an offshore account based in the tax haven of Antigua. Twice a year, my lawyer flies from the Caribbean to Las Vegas. I give him a briefcase full of cash from my gambling winnings."

Raven nodded, "I follow you so far."

"The attorney returns to Antigua with the money and deposits it in my offshore corporation. Then it's transferred to an international business corporation domiciled in the Cayman Islands to give it another layer of privacy."

Marco paused to return his seat to its full, upright position after a third warning from the stewardess. "Then the lawyer invests most of the winnings in a Swiss annuity held in Zurich under my name. The annuity accumulates tax-free, and I can borrow against it anytime. The corporation pays my attorney and me each $100,000 a year in salary. In addition to the salary, the corporation also pays all of my housing expenses and car payments."

The plane touched down and slowed to a stop. Marco stood up, ahead of everyone else, to grab his bag and drew one more glare from the stewardess. "So," Marco explained, "I get to keep almost all my hard earned money away from those bloodsuckers in Washington. Pretty clever, huh?"

Raven admired the elaborate system for its ingenuity, but by now Marco thoroughly disgusted him. He figured that anyone cheating the government would probably take advantage of his business partners.

A revelation hit him. *Maybe that's where all the money went in Atlantic City.*

Raven was fed up with using computers, with Marco's laziness, the heavy losses, the hookers, and he resented the harrowing black market experience.

With those things weighing heavily on his mind, he made a fateful decision. Rather than be victimized and possibly even cheated by Marco, he decided to strike first. He would hide his winnings to make sure Marco held up his end of the team. When the bank got back to even, he'd mix the money back in, then pull the plug and end the relationship. If Marco wanted to retrieve his losses he'd have to begin carrying his own weight and play more.

Soon chips flowed into Raven's pockets. Within a week he had set aside sixty grand. Even though Marco worked the same casino, they played at separate tables, so he suspected nothing. The only suspicions came from casino personnel mystified by huge losses.

All went well—until the evening Raven felt a warm sensation in the lower part of his abdomen.

At first he attributed the heat to his spicy dinner, but soon the burning intensified. Focused on playing, he failed to notice the source of pain—or the smoke rolling out from under the cuff of his pant-leg.

From across the pit, Marco recognized the problem instantly. During a team play in Monte Carlo, some faulty wires connecting the chip had ignited. Now, fearing disaster, he rapidly walked over to Raven and tapped him on the shoulder.

Startled, Raven gave Marco a puzzled look. "Your transmitter wires are on fire," Marco whispered. "Get out immediately!"

Raven glanced at his leg. A steady stream of smoke now poured out. They both hurried to the bathroom. Raven quickly stripped and tore off the red-hot wires. The hair on his thigh was singed, but otherwise he'd sustained no serious damage. Marco smothered the device in wet towels and frantically wrapped the computer in his sport coat. Suddenly, the bathroom door opened and two pit bosses walked in. They coolly took in the comical scene—Raven Townsend, wearing nothing but his boxers and Marco Antonelli, furiously trying to hide a tangle of wires.

They were not amused.

Security handcuffed the two Americans, who just hours earlier were living large as high-rolling guests of the casino, and forcibly escorted them to a windowless room in the basement. The guards pushed Raven and Marco into two hard-backed chairs, and a lanky casino supervisor arrived to grill them.

Raven became defiant. "You can't hold us here. We're American citizens. Contact our embassy. Now!"

The supervisor just laughed. "This is our country, gentlemen. There's no Hawaii 5-O to call for help here on this island." He paused to peel the cellophane off a cigar. "And the way I see it, playing blackjack with concealed computers is a crime. I'm guessing you boys are looking at some serious jail time."

Marco took a swing at his interrogator. He missed, but the security guards didn't. They pummeled him, twice knocking Marco out of his chair.

The supervisor said, "We're going to leave for a few minutes and let you two think about your predicament."

When their jailors had filed out of the room, Raven glared at Marco. "What's this about computers being illegal? You never mentioned that."

Marco swallowed blood from his lip.

"I thought they were legal here, but these banana republics can pretty much do whatever they please. My guess is they want a bribe to let us out. I think five grand will spring us."

The creak of the door as the three men returned interrupted them. The supervisor carried a clipboard. He glanced at Marco and Raven and read some numbers from the pages. He lit up his stogie and made a sweeping motion with his cigar at Marco's nose. "Here's the deal. You guys return all you've won and you're free to go."

Raven jumped up. "That's ridiculous. You have no right to our money. We haven't committed any crime."

The guard slammed a hard punch into Raven's gut, yet he hardly flinched and gave the supervisor an icy stare. Years of sit-ups had paid a dividend, and he wasn't about to cave in to this browbeating. "You'll never get away with this," Raven said defiantly.

"Yes, we will. You tried to cheat us. We don't like cheats down here. Neither will your roommates in the jail cell."

One of the guards chimed in, "Yeah, you know what they say about cute guys like you in prison. You go in as a tight end and come out a wide receiver." Both guards laughed and Marco's face turned white. The supervisor immediately took advantage of this sign of weakness and turned his attention to Antonelli.

He held his smoldering cigar up to Marco's face and said, "This makes perfect little circles. Unless you want tattoos on your neck, I suggest you come up with the money by the time we return."

They left again and shut the door. Raven didn't classify Marco as a friend. And he wished Marco had never talked him into this venture. But despite all that, he couldn't idly watch him get branded like a bull. "Marco, we've got to do what they want even if we're didn't cheat them."

"You're probably right, but I hate to see these bastards get anything," Marco said through clenched teeth.

"I know. But we don't have any choice, do we?" Raven felt he could hold out but sensed Marco was fading fast.

"No, we don't. We're in deep shit here," Marco said. "My butt puckered up tighter than a drum when he waved that hot stogie in my face."

When the supervisor returned, he was delighted to hear the two cocky Americans had thrown in the towel, but the two security guards looked disappointed the evening's entertainment ended prematurely.

They unlocked the handcuffs and allowed Marco and Raven to empty their pockets. They stacked all the chips on a desk and counted it up. One of the guards confiscated the safety deposit box key and soon returned with the drawers and their cash contents. The supervisor twice ran his figures through the calculator. "Nice try, guys," He said. "Now, where're the rest of your winnings?"

Marco shot back. "What are you talking about? This is it. The only other money is the fifty grand in cash we each put up in the cage."

"I know about the front money, and at this point, you two shouldn't expect to see that again either," threatened the supervisor.

"What?" Marco exploded. "Now wait a minute. You said if we gave back all our winnings, we could go."

"Too bad. You guys picked the wrong people to scam."

Marco's face now turned beet-red and his eyes pleaded. "For the last time. I don't know what you're talking about."

"Well, our records show a win between the two of you of $96,000. What you have on you and what we got out of your safety deposit boxes is about sixty grand short. No more games now, what did you do with the rest of the chips?"

The guard leaned forward and gave Marco a kick in the knee to encourage him to respond. Antonelli dropped to the floor clutching his leg. Raven yelled, "Wait. No more violence. I have it."

The supervisor smiled. "Good. Now, we're getting somewhere."

Marco propped himself up against the chair and looked at Raven, perplexed. "What are you talking about? There isn't any more money. They made a mistake. We only won $36,000 between us."

"No, we didn't. We won $96,000. The rest is hidden up in my room," Raven said in a low, quiet voice.

Marco still looked confused. "What? How's that possible?"

"I got mad at you and kept my winnings separate until I knew you would come through."

Marco now redirected his rage at Raven. "Then you're the one who skimmed in Atlantic City," he shouted.

"No," countered Raven.

"Bullshit!" Marco screamed. He began flailing at Raven with his fists. The guards pulled him off as the amused supervisor chuckled at this unexpected turn of events.

They marched Raven upstairs to his room where he produced the missing chips. Under guard, the two Americans quickly cleaned out their rooms. The supervisor confiscated their fifty grand in front money, and like exiled criminals, shipped them to the airport.

♣ ♦ ♥ ♠

Marco and Raven sat in the back seat during the short drive and not once looked at each other, let alone speak. Unceremoniously dumped off at the terminal, Marco and Raven were told to be out of the country within two hours. They needed no encouragement and caught a prop plane to Miami. Their partnership finished, each booked separate flights for the return to Vegas.

Raven waited in the terminal reflecting on the bizarre path his life had taken recently. He'd barely escaped death and jail time. His money had been seized with no hope of return. Worst of all, Raven realized he'd crossed new ethical boundaries. Despite the protests from his conscience, he had used computers to play blackjack. He had skimmed money. Somewhere along the way, the lines between good and evil became blurred. He'd been judgmental of Marco for taking whatever he wanted. Now Raven saw himself becoming like his partner and it scared him. *How do you know when you're morally bankrupt? It's common to have a CPA to keep you liquid, an attorney to keep you legal, and a doctor to keep you alive—but what about a spiritual audit?*

Even after God miraculously spared his life in the black market fiasco, he'd still continued down the same path, never stopping to think. Raven had never felt lower, sure he'd hit rock bottom.

His inner turmoil created a desire to speak with someone. He found a pay phone and wondered whom to call. He thought of his dad. It had been a long time since they last talked. But he couldn't envision telling him about his failures. A Townsend never admitted wrong, and it was unlikely his father would be very sympathetic, especially since he had considered gambling and the pursuit of riches a mistake to begin with.

The only person with whom Raven felt he could share his emotional distress was Cynthia. Though she never responded to his letters he decided to chance rejection. No one else knew his heart the way she did.

He dialed her old number from memory; his heart rate accelerated with each ring.

Raven was ready to hang up when a faint, female voice answered. He glanced at his watch and groaned. Through the confusion of his harrowing night in the Bahamas, he had lost track of time. It was only 6:30 in the morning. He thought of hanging up.

"Hello? Who's calling, please?" She sounded more awake.

Raven decided it was now or never. "Cynthia, it's me, Raven." A long silence followed.

The voice returned. "Raven Townsend?"

"Yes." He was relieved that at least he'd reached the right person.

"Why are you calling me?"

The relief evaporated.

"Cynthia," he pleaded. "I've just got to talk to you."

"What do you want from me?"

"I just don't know who else to talk to. We both had the same dreams once—but I've really screwed up."

"Raven, if you're looking for forgiveness, call God, not me. He isn't up there keeping score. He's interested in how we respond to situations in life, not how perfect we live."

Forgiveness sounded like a foreign word to Raven. "I know, but I feel like damaged goods." Raven proceeded to tell how he skimmed money from his partner. He waited for the shock to settle in—the man she once loved had become little more than a common thief.

"Raven, I read the novel *Deadline* recently. The book convinced me externals aren't that important. It's never too late to change your life no matter how big the mistakes. The important thing is your legacy in life."

Raven never heard of that book. For two years he had lived and breathed blackjack, rarely taking the time for anything else. "Cynthia, there's more." He hesitated. Not a soul on the planet knew what he was about to share. "Do you remember when the Camden church burned down?"

"Of course. How could anyone forget that?"

"Pastor Cook put me in charge of counting and depositing the offering and had given me a key. Big responsibility for a high-school kid."

"What's that got to do with the fire?" Cynthia asked.

"I was the first one on the scene. I ran into the building and saw it was out of control, but I saw a chance to save the money from the offering box since it hadn't been taken to the bank yet."

"What's wrong with that?" Cynthia asked.

"Two things. First, I didn't even check around the church to see if anyone was trapped inside. I grew up so poor, all I cared about was the money."

"I read in the paper no one was hurt in the fire."

"True, at least no one but me," said Raven quietly.

"What do you mean?"

"The other wrong thing I did involved the money. It never made it to the bank. After I thought about it, I decided to keep it. I rationalized that everyone would assume the money vanished in the flames." Raven hesitated. "I've never told anyone."

"That's serious, but—"

Raven interrupted, "After than, I felt like I'd blown any shot at heaven and needed penance to release my guilt."

"That's ridiculous theology. You can't buy your way out of sin."

Raven continued. "I wanted to be like Billy Graham and instead I turned out like Judas, but I kept up an outward façade of piety—like the false front of a casino."

"Everyone has fallen short, Raven. The whole rigid list of rules we were taught is not what God is like. He's more concerned with your heart," Cynthia said.

"I'd like to believe that. I just don't feel good enough anymore."

"Nonsense. You're too good for Vegas. You're gambling with more than just money and the stakes are too high to treat your life like just another chip."

"Cynthia?"

"Yes?"

"When you walked out of that restaurant, I should have come after you."

"What's done is done, Raven."

An eternal silence followed. Then she said, "I'm sorry. I really have to go now," and the line went dead.

On the long flight to Vegas, Raven replayed the conversation over and over in his mind. Maybe it was better Cynthia ended up with Garren Horne. At least they shared the same social class.

Raven reflected on Cynthia's comments on forgiveness and her challenge to do something meaningful with his life. His recent harrowing experiences in blackjack certainly dimmed his enthusiasm for the business. *It's time to exit,* he decided.

CHAPTER TWENTY-ONE

♣ ♦ ♥ ♠

One of Marco's friends looked after Raven's apartment while he was gone—a colossal mistake, he soon realized. The place looked like it had been used as party central, but everyone left before garbage duty. A note on the counter explained the two dents on his BMW. Raven rushed out to the carport to examine the damage to his prized red convertible.

Back in the apartment he slumped on the couch, wondering if life could get any worse. A friendly, stray cat wandered in through the open door. The black feline reminded him of his cat in Maine, except it bore a small scar on one ear. He petted her soft fur and thought about his legacy. His was a sorry one. He stared at the wall where he had tacked four white posters in the shape of a thermometer to track his winnings. The high point had been $813,000, right before he went to Reno. Now he had fallen all the way back to $263,000, far short of the mark but still a significant chunk of money. He stroked the cat's ears and made plans to leave blackjack behind.

Two days later, Raven had stuffed all his possessions into four boxes and was looking for the packing tape when the phone rang. It startled him because he had already called to disconnect service. The voice on the other end surprised him even more—it was Karl Beck.

"Raven, I'm glad I caught you in. I've got a foolproof way to make some really big money in blackjack. I just need a partner. Would you be interested?"

Karl must have known what happened in the Bahamas, but Raven saw no need to bring it up. "Why me? I thought you always teamed up with Marco."

"Let's just say I'm not going to be working with him in the future. There's a ton of money to be made with this venture and I think someone with your ability is the perfect choice," Karl said.

It flattered Raven to be praised again for his blackjack prowess. He knew only a handful of players in the world matched his skill. He stared at the thermometer on the wall. Raven felt little desire to do any more gambling, yet it pained him to fall short of his goal, especially when he had won well over a million—only to watch incompetent players and teammates flush most of it down the toilet.

"How much money are we talking?" he asked cautiously.

"If things go as planned, your share would be at least half a million, maybe more. And it should take less than a month."

Raven suddenly became very interested. He wanted to get out of blackjack once and for all—he knew that would please Cynthia. But in his mind, that foolish telephone confessional had blown any chance of ever getting back together with her.

He figured it couldn't hurt to at least hear Karl out. "Okay, let's get together, but your apartment, not mine." Raven didn't want Karl to see all the packed boxes—the image of a defeated loser.

♣ ♦ ♥ ♠

Karl opened the door and greeted Raven. "Good to see
you again, mate. I'm really excited about us working together and making some serious money. When you and
Marco hooked up in Atlantic City, everyone on the team
thought your partnership looked like a bad chemistry ex-
periment."

Raven relaxed a little. Maybe Karl hadn't heard about
the skimming incident in the Bahamas. "Yeah, he's a piece
of work. I kick myself for not finding out about computers
being illegal. I'd have never gotten involved if I'd understood the whole story."

"You don't know the half of it. Marco is such a smart-
ass he probably can tell the flavor of ice cream just by sitting on it," said Karl.

"Sounds like your friendship has soured as well," Raven
said, chuckling.

"Absolutely. I'm tired of being used. That guy's been on
so many ego trips he ought to get frequent flyer miles."

Raven felt free to proceed. "Yeah, he took advantage of
me too. I made money while he chased women. So you're
totally done with him?"

"Definitely. I should have quit before Atlantic City. There
was a near mutiny on the team. That's why none of the girls
went. I had already gone ahead to Jersey to set up the house,
and the most practical course was to finish what I started."

"What happened?" asked Raven.

"One night when you were in Reno, Marco threw a big
kegger by his pool for the team. Things got a little out of
hand—not unusual for his parties. But then things escalated.
Marco got sloshed and started ripping the bikinis off every
gal he could grab—including my sister Nikki. He always
treated women like objects before, but this night the bugger
went way overboard and tried to rape one of them."

"That's not too shocking after how I've seen him operate," Raven said.

Karl clenched his fist. "I wanted to nail the bloke when I heard the news, but after thinking it over, I decided to stay in Atlantic City and turn the tables on him for a change."

The last statement puzzled Raven, but he decided not to probe. "No wonder things looked strained between you two in New Jersey."

"Yeah, he shows up there a month later like nothing ever happened. All the girls quit his team and he didn't even get it. But I believe in karma and I think he'll get the smug look wiped off his face any day now," Karl said with a cold, calculated expression.

Raven nodded, "So what's the plan? And how's it possible for the two of us to make that much money. We had almost twenty people for three months in Jersey playing with computers and we still lost."

"Like I said on the phone, I've got a surefire way to win."

Raven raised one eyebrow. "Come on Karl, nothing's for sure in gambling. Even the best card counters in the world can still lose in the short run. And a month's not that long."

"Agreed. However I have something different in mind." Karl walked over to fidget with the air conditioner.

"If it involves computers, count me out right now. I've had it with those," Raven said.

"We won't be using any electronics. Tell me, how much do you know about casino credit?"

"A little. I heard it's easy to get, especially compared to a normal bank loan. All you need is a few dollars more in your checking account than the credit line you're requesting and typically you're approved. Once it's activated, you sign markers at the tables, get chips up to your credit limit, then I think you have up to thirty days to pay them back."

"That's mostly correct, except only the larger accounts get the thirty day grace period. Average players are expected to settle before leaving town."

"How's any of that impact us?" asked Raven.

"Did you know casino gambling is outlawed by some states' criminal code and the casinos have no legal recourse outside their home state?"

"I didn't know that, but it makes sense, although today's global economy must negate those antiquated laws." Raven welcomed the first cool blasts as the air conditioner finally kicked in.

"Partially. Nevada adopted the 1865 British stature governing the enforcement of gaming debts. It wasn't until 1983 that a Nevada casino could legally enforce a gambling debt," said Karl.

"Maybe they couldn't legally enforce collection, but I'm sure they had a couple of tough guys around to make sure you paid."

"Back in the fifties and sixties that happened. Now the casinos are all legit with big corporations owning them and their stock traded on Wall Street," Karl explained. "They don't use physical force and consequently fail to collect about eight percent of the unpaid markers."

"That's a lot. All because Guido can't break your legs anymore, huh?" The room was slowly cooling down, but Raven still roasted and considered taking his shirt off.

"That and recent court rulings. A Florida gambler a few years ago put a stop payment on his $100,000 check to the Tropicana Casino in Atlantic City. A judge ruled he did not have to repay the money."

"I bet that fried their bean-counters," Raven said. "So your scheme is to move to the sunshine state, run up huge gambling debts, then stiff them?"

"Not exactly, although my first strategy wasn't much different."

Raven got up from his chair. "If you're talking about cheating someone, even the casinos, you can count me out right now."

Karl smirked. "Don't get so self-righteous and let me explain." At that moment the front door opened and a girl walked in, holding a key. Raven recognized her as the same blonde who served drinks at Marco's pool.

Karl said, "Let me introduce you to my sister, Nikki Beck."

Built like a model, she stood a couple inches taller than Raven. This made him feel a little awkward in her presence, but she quickly put him at ease with a warm handshake. "I'm very pleased to meet you—finally," she said. "I've heard a lot of interesting things about you." Nikki cast Raven a parting glance, then sashayed into the kitchen to put away groceries.

"Karl, the whole time we were in Atlantic City, you never mentioned a sister, but that's not surprising, since blackjack players always carry some secret no one else knows," Raven said.

"Some more than others," Karl said. "Anyway, the plan doesn't involve cheating. It simply takes advantage of a flaw in the system."

"Okay, I'm still listening. What exactly is the plan? I hope it's not Amway, because I hate that even more than cheating."

Raven laughed at his own joke until the puzzled look on Karl's face made him wonder if they even had Amway in South Africa.

Karl answered, "The plan is to get a huge bankroll by obtaining high credit lines from several different casinos."

"How big a line?" asked Raven.

"In the neighborhood of a quarter-million."

"That's a pretty good neighborhood."

"If we got that much credit at say four places, we'd have a million bucks to play against."

Raven quickly did the math. "With that we could bet up to ten grand a hand."

Karl nodded. "Correct. And our expectation tips in at over three thousand bucks an hour."

"So we use the casino's money for our bets," said Raven. "I have to admit that's very resourceful. But what if we lose? Do we just skip town and grow oranges in Florida the rest of our life?"

"First of all, we're not going to lose."

Raven interrupted. "Karl, don't give me that, I'm a mathematician. I know how brutal this game can be."

"So do I." Karl paused and made room on the couch as Nikki joined him. "I also know you and I each have strong work ethics. Unlike Marco, we both work at least ten-hour days. In a month we'd be able to get in 300 hours, which qualifies for the long-run."

Raven fed those numbers through his mental machine. "That many hours at three grand an hour would theoretically net close to a million in winnings. And the odds of being ahead after that period of time is extremely high— possibly close to 98%. But that still leaves a small chance of losing."

Nikki joined the conversation. "I know we're going to win, because Karl has told me you're the best blackjack player on the planet." Raven blushed slightly.

"Nikki will work with us," said Karl. "We're going to use all ten of the girls who back counted for Marco's team. None of them want to work for him anymore."

"Can't blame them there. He mowed a pretty wide path down in the Caribbean," Raven said.

"He's always been like that. He was a great blackjack player once," said Karl. "Now all he wants is to get laid. I think it's safe to say he never walked out of a brothel saying 'I wish I had a V-8.'"

The room had finally cooled down to a pleasant temperature, but Raven now felt new warmth from the exciting potential of the scheme Karl placed before him. "Okay," he said, "but you still haven't answered the question about what we will do if we lose. I don't want to end up owing a bunch of casinos, even if they don't break your legs anymore."

"Here's where the real beauty of the plan kicks in," Karl explained. "We set up a fictitious identity on an offshore island to get the credit line. In the unlikely event we're still behind at the end of the thirty days, we simply burn up his identity."

Nikki spoke, "So in essence, that person never existed and the casinos have no one to collect their debt from."

Karl looked at her, then at Raven. "Like I said, it's foolproof. There's no downside since there's absolutely no way to lose. The casinos would have difficulty collecting anyway, but setting up your ID in the Caribbean rather than Florida makes it impossible."

Raven considered the ramifications. It involved some borderline moral principles at best. But Karl correctly pointed out that in almost all cases, they would win and there wouldn't be any problems. Even the worse case scenario of a billion-dollar mega-corporation unable to collect a small debt didn't sound too bad. "One question, Karl. If it's so foolproof, why do you need me?"

Karl got up and turned off the air conditioner. "Two reasons. As Nikki said, you're the best damn player I've ever met. And secondly, we need your money. Working for Marco didn't exactly make us rich. To get a credit line of $250,000 requires someone who has at least that much in his bank account. We don't have it—I'm guessing you do."

Raven wondered if Karl was psychic since his savings weighed in just over a quarter million. "That makes sense. However, there's one major flaw in your plan which will sink it."

"What is that?" asked Karl.

"I'm too well known in Vegas. There's absolutely no way I could get a credit line in this town under any name—let alone play 300 hours without detection. I've already tried a disguise and that didn't work."

Karl shook his head. "I've thought of that. Do you know what I did in South Africa?"

"Not really. I've heard bits and pieces."

"I worked for BOSS."

"Big deal. Everybody works for a boss."

"No. In South Africa, BOSS is the Bureau of State Security. I worked as an undercover agent."

Raven thought that fit in with Karl's clandestine personality and the background snippets Marco had mentioned.

Karl continued, "My biggest assignment involved infiltrating the ANC."

Nikki noticed Raven's puzzled look and clarified. "ANC stands for African National Congress—Mandela's political party."

Karl nodded. "Right. They inherently distrusted whites. The only way to get someone inside was to use a black man. We tried a couple of people, but none proved very reliable. Then we concocted a bold scheme."

Raven said, "I don't think I'm going to like this."

"We used a special pigmented makeup to pass off one of our white agents as black."

"I was afraid you were going to say that. Did it work?"

Karl waffled. "For a while. Eventually they detected him and…well, you probably don't want to hear how it ended."

Raven winced slightly. "No, I don't think so. And it must be obvious I'm not stupid enough to volunteer for that."

Karl shrugged. "Sorry, but that's it, mate. But I know it'll work this time."

"Why?"

"Three reasons. It's for a much shorter time and you're never actually coming into close contact with the enemy."

"That's two—you mentioned three."

"The third reason it will succeed is the prejudice inherent in the casino culture. These people thrive on money, power, and sex. If you're black, you've got it made. They're all such racists; they'll never give you a second look. And by using women back counters I guarantee you'll play without any heat."

Raven requested a day to think things over and left. Elements of the scheme made sense. Other parts alarmed him. The money tempted him, but there were drawbacks. Walking away from the entire gambling world still seemed the most prudent choice.

Yet, the chance to achieve the destiny revealed in his vision quest rose like the promise of the proverbial pot of gold at the end of a rainbow. He'd never be this close again. All night he wrestled with his conflicting feelings and barely slept. In the morning he made the phone call.

"Karl, I hope I didn't wake you up."

"Of course not," Karl said. "You know me—I get up at dawn for an hour run. Been doing that ever since my BOSS days."

"Yeah, I do remember that. I should get out there with you," Raven said. "My life's grown so frantic these last few months, I rarely run anymore."

"Well, it's never too late, you know."

"You're right. That's why I called."

"You want to go for a run?" asked Karl.

"No, I think I want to be part of your plan. Just have one question."

"Fire away."

"How do you propose splitting the money?" Raven asked carefully.

"You're putting up the capital to get the credit line, so you're entitled to half the win as the investor. Then we pay the girls their hourly wage and split the remaining half between us. You'll end up with nearly 75% of the win with the other 25% going to Nikki and myself. Should be fair compensation for having to be a black man for a month."

The deal was far better than he expected. Raven set the process in motion with two simple words. "I'm in."

♣   ♦   ♥   ♠

The plan, as Karl called it, had been well thought out. Randolph Townsend's new name was Victor York, a black businessman from Zimbabwe. Raven memorized a fabricated background of high school and college in Florida to account for Victor's American accent.

Karl collected a favor from an old friend in BOSS to set up a bogus history for Mr. York. The key piece of the puzzle involved putting together a fabricated history of Victor gambling at the Sun City casino in South Africa with a hefty $500,000 credit line. Without this background, Karl knew that most Nevada casinos would never grant an unknown player from a foreign country such a large credit line.

The next step required Raven to fly to the Cayman Islands where he deposited his entire bankroll of $263,000 into Barclays Bank in cash. From there he wired the money to a Swiss Bank in Anguilla to an account set up under the name of Victor York. After the four casinos each approved his new $250,000 credit line, Raven simply reversed the process. He switched the money back to the Caymans, then overseas to another account in Luxembourg, before finally returning it to his own account in Las Vegas. With such a complex paper trail, Raven felt confident no one other than himself could ever touch his money.

Karl arranged passports and identity papers and taught Raven a new handwriting style for signing markers in Vegas. They ditched the fake Rolex watch and anything else that might identify him as Randolph Townsend.

They didn't seek credit at any properties with newer surveillance and chose four clubs—the Sands, Hacienda, Marina and the Dunes.

Karl said, "These places employ many older pit bosses who couldn't count even if they wore sandals and used all their toes."

The make-up Raven wore to darken his skin worked better than he expected. Only applied on his face, neck, and hands, it washed off easily at the end of the day. The hands created the only difficult area and required several applications a day to look convincing.

Raven, or Victor as he was now called, dressed like a tourist, typically carrying shopping bags with him as he approached the tables. Having ten different girls back counting gave a wealth of choices and created the illusion that Victor's decision to gamble had been an impulse on his way through the building.

Winning came easy—converting the huge amount of chips to currency created the only difficulty. When Victor took out fifty thousand in markers, the casino wouldn't let him cash out without first redeeming the marker, but he needed the money in hand to play at different casinos besides just the four where he had credit.

Karl found a solution. He used the girls to cash out the chips for them, a few thousand at a time. They had no markers to pay off, and were unknown in the casino, so this wasn't a problem. Karl tossed them extra comps in addition to their hourly wage for this service.

As a result, Victor owed more and more on his credit line and the cash horde grew larger. Raven trusted Karl but still preferred handling the money himself, so Karl set up a safety deposit box at a private Vault Company which could only be accessed by Raven and Nikki simultaneously. Raven agreed, but as an added precaution, declared he alone would keep the key.

He'd grown fond of Nikki—she brought a fun side to the team that offset the serious stoicism of the two men. Raven loved her cute accent, although it sounded much different than Karl's South African one. It was refreshing to be around a woman who admired him for his blackjack prowess and ability to take risks and regretted Cynthia could've been more like that.

CHAPTER TWENTY-TWO

♣ ♦ ♥ ♠

After two weeks of long, grueling days, the team had won more than $600,000 with virtually no heat. They constantly rotated the ten girls and so many fresh faces fooled the casinos. Karl played at a separate table and mentally shuffle tracked the aces so Raven could occasionally push out a huge stack of chips off the top for cover. If a hand contained an ace, the player had an advantage of about 50% over the house. Tossing out ten grand on the first hand from a freshly shuffled six-deck pack also confused the pit bosses, who knew card counters only raised their bets later in the shoe.

Raven's share of the win totaled over $400,000, and for the first time in months he allowed himself to imagine being a millionaire. Nikki suggested they take a day off to recharge. Karl acted reluctant to slow down the money train, but Raven said, "I'm with Nikki. I could use a break from wearing this make-up."

Karl relented. "Okay, maybe a little sun might be good for us. I can borrow a sailboat from a friend. Let's hook up at Lake Mead tomorrow morning."

Raven had never sailed before and felt inept around Nikki and Karl. Their experience showed in the way they navigated through the maze of boat traffic. Both of them looked extremely buff in their swimsuits and Raven imagined they took great pride in their sculpted bodies. With his dark hair and eyes, Karl could have passed as Raven's brother—except his rippling rows of muscle contrasted sharply with Raven's leaner frame.

The popular lake was crowded with jet-skis and motor-boats. The noise dampened the experience somewhat for Raven, and he didn't like how these gas-powered toys polluted the environment. When Karl guided the boat onto a quiet beach, Raven was relieved.

Nikki set up a picnic lunch and the three of them stretched out on a blanket, gazing at the vast lake. Karl took a long drink from a cold Australian beer, then turned to Raven. "So, how do you like sailing?"

"I think I'd like it more without all these people. In Maine, it's more pristine, with clear water and no trash."

"Yeah, these Yanks don't seem to care where they throw their empties," Karl agreed. "Next time we'll pick a better spot—maybe buy our own private lake after this month is over."

"Now that sounds appealing," Nikki cooed

Karl nodded. "Not too improbable if we can keep it up for two more weeks. You two did an inventory in the box last night?"

Nikki answered, "Besides the $612,000 we've won, there's close to $700,000 in cash from the million in credit."

"Pretty fair sum," Karl said. "Ought to at least get us a down-payment for a yacht, don't you think, Raven?"

Raven took a sip from his bottled water. He still allowed no liquor to pass his lips. "More than enough," he
said. "There's one thing I don't understand, though."
Karl stiffened. "What's that?"
"Since we're up so much money, why do we need to
keep tapping deeper into our credit line? We've got plenty
of cash right now."
Karl said, "Because things can change fast in this business. You know that better than anyone. It's smarter to have
the money available if we need it. We have thirty days to pay
them back, so I see no downside to keeping it until then."
"I guess you're right," Raven said tentatively. "It just
makes me a little nervous."
"That's because you won't drink any of this Fosters. A
few cans will cure any nerve problems."
Karl whispered something to Nikki, then got up. "I need
to return the sailboat. You're parked not far from here.
Would you mind giving my sis a ride home?"
Nikki flashed Raven a playful smile.
Raven said, "No problem—it's right on my way."
"Thanks. See you two later," Karl said.
Raven began packing up, but Nikki stopped him. "Let's
enjoy the sun for a while. I've spent so much time in those
casinos lately I must look as pale as a ghost."
Raven agreed. "I could use a little natural tanning my-
self. Maybe if I stay out here long enough, I won't have to
use the make-up tomorrow."
She laughed and rolled over on the blanket facedown.
"Raven, could you put some suntan lotion on my back?"
Raven fumbled through her beach bag and found the
Coppertone. Nikki untied her bikini strap. Raven stared at
her bare back and hesitated. He had spent countless hours
in casinos around beautiful, often scantily clad women. Yet
he had never been this close—actually touching.

"Oh, that feels purr-fect, Raven. You should've been a masseuse."

It felt even better to him.

He'd never fully noticed her stunning figure before. In the casino she deliberately wore baggy clothes to look less conspicuous. Out here in only her bikini, Raven became acutely aware of her long shapely legs and smooth skin. Her blonde hair flowed nearly to her waist, and Raven needed to push it aside to work on her back.

Nikki propped up slightly and looked back at Raven. "It's amazing that we've worked together every day, and I know so little about you. Karl said you grew up really poor in Maine. Is that true?"

"Yeah, maybe that's why I value money so much today."

"Tell me about your childhood."

Raven shrugged. "I don't want to bore you..."

"I want to be bored by you. Please tell me."

Her eyes twinkled, and Raven actually thought for a moment she might be flirting with him. He dismissed the possibility. "Well, starting in second grade I had to either run or bike to school every day. Three miles each way, with a couple of killer hills."

Nikki looked impressed. "What about the winter? Doesn't it like freeze in Maine?"

"Down to forty below once, but my father made me go everyday, no matter what the weather."

"Wow, that must have been tough," said Nikki.

"Not really. Pain never bothered me. I remember having a couple of warts on my fingers in sixth grade. Other kids in school made fun of me, so I wanted to get rid of them. My family didn't have the money to go to a doctor for something like that, so I burned them off."

"No way! How did you do that?"

"I went back into the woods behind our house and lit matches, setting fire to them one at a time, until they were all gone."

Nikki's face expressed astonishment. "That's incredible. You must be immune to pain. Didn't you cry?"

"Real men don't cry."

"Amazing. A man who never cries teamed up with my brother who never laughs. You two must have shells over your hearts like a turtle."

"I guess the only thing that hurts is losing money. That bothers me."

"Money? What about love? Don't you have a girl-friend?"

Raven's mind drifted briefly to Cynthia. "No, I don't."

"No one at all?" asked Nikki.

"No. None."

Nikki re-attached her strap and rolled onto her back. When Raven stretched out on the blanket next to her, she reached over, removed his sunglasses and said, "It's not fair for you to see my eyes and to hide your own."

Raven felt his pulse quicken. *This really looks like flirting.* Then she removed all doubt. "I've got plans tonight, but let's spend some evening alone together." She placed a hand around his neck and pulled him in for a quick, soft kiss. The expression in her eyes mesmerized him. She whispered, "No one else—just us."

"Sure," he stammered. He'd always considered himself fiercely independent, but now he felt drawn to this beautiful woman like a fish on a hook. He fought to retain control, but no will for resistance remained.

They returned to the city in Raven's convertible. He loved how Nikki's yellow hair blew in the wind. They spoke very little, but every so often she smiled at him and he felt intoxicated. He dropped her off at Karl's apartment and drove home marveling at the turn of events. He had failed to see any of this coming. But in a way he deserved it. At twenty-eight years old, perhaps the time had come to move on. After all, *how could something be wrong when it felt so right?*

Raven hoped the budding romance between them wouldn't upset the team's chemistry. His worries were needless, because the next day Nikki acted totally aloof—as if nothing had happened. He shrugged it off as another example of how little he understood women, and the team continued the financial onslaught.

They were winning everywhere, but the biggest payday came at the expense of the Sands. Even though they'd barred him the year before, no one recognized the black man with glasses and kinky hair. The game was good with less than one deck cut out of play, and the pit bosses responded like Karl predicted—completely oblivious to Victor's threat.

♣ ♦ ♥ ♠

The swing shift surveillance supervisor at the Sands, Kenneth Wentworth, grew increasingly agitated over Victor's success and finally phoned Howard Goldberg. The clubs employing Howard called him in whenever they took a big hit. Most of the time, the drop was just bad luck, a negative fluctuation. When cheating occurred, it normally took place on the inside. Since no one on the floor usually knew Howard, he was an ideal source to sniff out such problems.

Howard arrived and immediately went to the monitors. "Okay, Kenneth, what we got here?"

"Nothing for sure, just a JDLR."

"You called me over here for a Just Don't Look Right?" Howard asked. "The way you spoke on the phone I thought you had a major problem here."

"I think we do. That's why I need your help."

Howard liked Kenneth. Wentworth was a straight shooter and one of the few supervisors who didn't resent someone else pointing out mistakes. Howard turned to the screen. "Which guy are we talking about?"

"The black gentleman at table twelve. Dressed like he's going to a barbecue and betting up to ten thousand a hand."

Howard let out a soft whistle. "That's big action. I'm surprised you guys increased the limits that high for him. How's he doing?"

Kenneth grimaced. "He's been here for a couple of visits over the last three weeks and he's up about two hundred grand."

Howard gave Kenneth an incredulous look. "Get out of town. Are you serious?"

"Serious enough to have called the Griffith Agency."

"Kenneth, why would you ever call those clowns? I've told you before they're going to go down in a big lawsuit someday for selling a book with card counter's pictures lumped together with crooks. It's got to be unconstitutional to use those photos without a signed release, yet they go ahead anyway."

"You're probably right, but I got a little desperate," Kenneth said sheepishly.

"What'd they say? They probably think anyone who wins is a cheat."

"They had no pictures of this guy in their book, they'd never heard of a Victor York, and I didn't need to worry."

"Easy for them to say—it's not their money." Howard took off his coat and grabbed a chair next to Kenneth. "Do you think he's a counter?"

"Could be, although his play is different than the modus operandi of normal professionals. He bounces around between tables so much, you'd think he was a pinball. Unless he's got a lot of confederates calling him in, there's no way he'd know the count at every table in the club."

"A team operation's not that difficult to do, although I've never seen one that big. Let's take a look and see what we've got."

They studied the monitors for a while.

Finally Howard spoke. "There's something about him I don't like. I can't put my finger on it, but the way he handles his chips reminds me of someone."

"You know him?" asked Kenneth hopefully.

"Possibly, but it's hard to tell from here. I'm going to go down for a closer look."

♣ ♦ ♥ ♠

Howard caught Victor between tables and tapped him on the shoulder.

Despite the many times Raven had been barred over the years, the routine tap on the shoulder still spooked him. When he slowly turned around, the stern face of Howard Goldberg proved even scarier than he could have imagined. Raven feared no one in the casino world more than this eagle-eyed nemesis.

"Hi, I'm Howard Goldberg, and I just wanted to welcome you to the Sands."

Raven froze like a deer in headlights before he haltingly offered his left-handed shake. "Victor—Victor York."

Howard's gaze scanned every inch of his quarry. An unmistakable feeling of familiarity hung in the air. "I know most high rollers in town," he said, "but I don't think we've met before."

Raven began to recover his composure. "No, I'm sure we haven't. I mostly play in Africa. First time here in Vegas."

"Really? Your English is quite good. Didn't detect an accent at all."

Raven felt the sweat running down his back. He needed to end this conversation fast and get out of Dodge. "I went to high school in Miami and college at Florida State. Guess I got Americanized a little too much." He was glad Karl made him learn a background identity in case of scrutiny.

"No kidding!" Howard exclaimed. "I grew up in Miami myself. What school did you go to?"

"Miami Jackson," said Raven as he self-consciously rubbed his nose. Howard's body position blocked a quick escape. "I went to Coral Gables myself. Almost right next door to Jackson." Raven had no idea if Miami Jackson was anywhere near Coral Gables. He couldn't tell if Howard was simply being friendly or fishing. It didn't matter. Danger signals pulsated through him. He had to get out fast. "Excuse me, but I have an appointment with my banker and I'm already late. Perhaps we could catch up later."

"No problem. One question though." Howard placed his hand on Raven's elbow in a friendly way, but in such a manner as to make it very awkward to leave.

"When we met, you shook with your left hand," said Howard. "Yet earlier I watched you handling all your chips with your right hand. Are you ambidextrous?"

Raven again nervously pinched his nose to remove the beads of perspiration. "No, that's an old African custom. I'm right-handed, but I shake left-handed because that is the side our heart is on, and it demonstrates sincerity and friendship." Raven faked a warm smile, but Howard didn't appear to be buying his story. Instead, he stared intently at Raven's nose. Raven didn't know why until he looked down at his fingers. Fresh, black stains smudged all over his hand. *Oh crap!*

Without another word, Raven turned and hurried to the exit. He didn't look back until he stepped outside. Then he sprinted for his BMW convertible, and without stopping to open the car door, leaped into the driver's seat. He gunned the engine, burning rubber all the way out the parking lot.

Arriving separately, Karl and Nikki showed up about twenty minutes later at the pre-arranged emergency meeting site. Karl jumped out of the car. "What happened? You were killing them and Nikki had a plus thirteen count for you. Why did you bolt?"

"Didn't you see who I was talking to?" Raven shouted. "That was Howard Goldberg. The one person I wanted to avoid. We didn't play the Palace or the Mirage because I wanted to stay away from him. Then he shows up at the Sands." Raven still felt his heart racing.

"Not the end of the world, mate. He's probably an outside man and works for several properties."

"That's not all. Look at my nose. The color came off."

Nikki laughed at how comical Raven looked with a black face and a large skunk-like white spot on his nose. "Big deal," Karl said. "Still doesn't mean he recognized you."

"I know he did. This guy's sharp. And I'm sure he remembered my stupid left-handed handshake," said Raven.

"Okay, okay. Maybe he's on to you. Still be a while before he puts it all together. The credit line setup was pretty elaborate."

"You might be right, but I don't want to take any chances. We're up almost seven hundred thousand—let's shut down and get out of town."

Karl looked thoughtful, then slowly nodded his head. "Agreed. I'll take some of the hired help with me to cash out the chips while you and Nikki clean out the safety deposit box."

He left and Nikki and Raven stood alone in the parking lot. She ran both hands through her thick, blonde hair and gave Raven a mischievous look. "You ready to do it?"

Raven's face flushed brightly. "Do what?"

Nikki giggled. "Boy, you are slow on the uptake, aren't you? Get the money, honey—what else?" She placed her hands on her hips in a questioning posture. "Now where would that little key be to unlock all those beautiful stacks of Franklins?"

"I don't have it on me. It's over at my place."

"Well, how about we waltz on over there and get it? All this time I've known you, I never did get to see your apartment. This might be our last chance. What do you say?"

She moved in and placed her hands gently on Raven's shoulders, her face just a few inches from his.

Raven never understood women. How could this gal be so friendly at the lake, then so cold, now so affectionate? It didn't make any sense. He said, "We really don't have time with the heat coming down. Besides, my place is a mess right now."

"Relax. The bean counters won't figure things out for a few days, at the very least. We have plenty of time. I'll even swing by the store and pick up a bottle of Cristal champagne to celebrate and give you a chance to tidy up."

Without waiting for an answer she embraced him and gave him an unexpected kiss. "Here's something to think about until I get there. And there's a lot more where that came from—a whole lot more." She gave him a sultry wink, climbed in her car and drove away.

Raven stood rooted to the pavement a moment, confused. He contemplated recent events. The gig was up, but at least it had been profitable. Now he had a difficult choice to make. If he didn't take advantage of this chance for romance, perhaps he'd have regrets the rest of his life.

Undoubtedly, very few men could resist the allure of a beautiful woman like Nikki. Yet Raven had never crossed that line. His father told him five things to avoid in women—older, taller, fatter, different values, and having a man's name. Nikki fit four of those criteria. But she wasn't chunky. Her body would cause accidents at any busy intersection in America. It was definitely the best Raven had ever seen, and in his mind, that was enough to negate the other four.

Raven returned to his apartment with the decision made. He quickly cleaned up and covered the packed boxes with a blanket. He grabbed the wallet-sized picture of Cynthia off the mantel and stared at it a moment. Then he lit a match and burned it in the fireplace, watching her blue dress turn to ashes.

The doorbell brought his thoughts back to the present. Nikki strolled in carrying the champagne. "Oh, I just love that smell, is that incense burning? Nice thought."

Raven cringed at the irony.

She took off her sunglasses and popped the cork. Raven made no objections, already past the point of no return. The last few taboos, which he had observed a lifetime, were about to be broken.

For the first time in his life he lifted a glass of alcohol to his lips. The bubbly tasted like fog, smooth and sweet. Raven staggered from its impact, feeling the sugar rush through his body. Nikki giggled loudly and her face began to fade in and out of focus. Whatever the joke was he must have missed it.

Nikki put on some soft music and began dancing with him—another first. He had no resistance—his legs felt like rubber. She droned on and on about sailing or some subject Raven couldn't quite catch. She kept chuckling and something didn't feel right. She no longer acted sultry—instead she looked like a doctor examining a patient. He didn't know a lot about sex, but he didn't think it would be this weird.

It must be the alcohol. I feel like I'm floating.

Nikki became blurrier by the moment. She said something about taking another drink, followed by more laughter as she slid a huge a diamond ring on her finger. Then everything went black.

♣ ♦ ♥ ♠

Nikki and Karl met Marco behind his house on the private putting green. Marco put away his golf club and asked with a crafty smile, "Successful mission?"

"No problems," Nikki answered. "He must be awfully tough, because it took him almost thirty minutes to pass out. The supplier said he'd be out cold in ten minutes. And I gave him a double dose to make it quicker. Anyway, I found the safety deposit box key, and we got all the money."

"He never suspected you two were married?" Marco asked.

Karl spoke, "No, not once. He bought the brother-sister act with no suspicions."

Marco chuckled, "With the incentive of a little romp with Nikki I can see why. Did you have to use plan B?"

Nikki glared at him and raised her hand as if to slap his face. Karl intervened. "We got the cash, all of it. Almost seven hundred thousand in winnings and the million we scammed from the credit lines."

"Good," Marco said.

"That ought to even things up for all the money that bastard stole from us. I got a private plane that'll be ready in two hours at McCarren. They'll fly us to Mexico where we catch a regular flight to the Bahamas. Once there, we'll split the money. After that, I think it'd be best for you two to take a long vacation and to stay out of sight for a while."

"That's exactly what we have planned," Karl said with a smile—the first Marco had ever seen. "But what about Raven? He could be dead. Nikki put enough animal tranquilizer in his drink to knock out a horse."

Marco sneered, "Who cares? The thought of him taking the money I worked so hard to win still fries me. I bet he skimmed over three hundred grand. Nobody, I mean nobody, cheats Marco Antonelli."

♣ ♦ ♥ ♠

Nikki spoke first in the car. "We should never have gone to Marco's house. I almost hit that pig—then he might have known something was up."

"Relax, babe. I wanted to see his face one last time—before he finds out what it feels like to be the one who gets screwed. It was worth it to hear him say 'nobody cheats Marco Antonelli.'"

Nikki laughed. "Nobody. That is nobody except us. And you skimmed more like four hundred thousand in Atlantic City, didn't you?"

Karl nodded. "Yes, and every damn dollar I stole from him made me even angrier—thinking of the way he treated you. Now, I think things are even."

Karl and Nikki had no intention of meeting at the airport or of ever seeing Marco and America again. They switched cars at a warehouse in Henderson, carefully placing the two duffel bags of money in the trunk. In five hours they would be leaving on a sailboat out of San Diego.

Nikki snuggled close to Karl. "It feels good to be a couple again."

"I know, but I do feel bad about Raven. He didn't deserve this," said Karl.

"Hey, don't go soft on me now," said Nikki.

Karl merged onto the freeway. "The way I see it, Marco had it coming. He's a swine who couldn't keep his hands off any woman, even my wife. But Raven worked hard and was the best blackjack player I ever saw. To walk away not even knowing if he's still alive doesn't seem right."

"Didn't you tell me what a self-righteous hypocrite he was?"

Karl set the cruise control, then looked at Nikki. "That's the way I felt once, but many of the things Raven said made sense. I'm not sure if we really did right by him."

"Relax, Karl," Nikki said. "On some of the South Sea Islands where we're headed, treachery is considered a virtue. We'll fit right in."

♣ ◆ ♥ ♠

Raven stirred for the first time in hours. He tried to open his eyes but they remained shut. A strange darkness enveloped him.

I must be dead. And what have I accomplished with my life? Hardly anything. I won a little money, nothing else. A moist sensation on his cheek broke through his semiconscious state. The cat was licking his face and he realized he wasn't quite dead yet.

It took him nearly an hour to get his bearings. The apartment looked like a tornado hit it. Numerous items lay overturned. His head felt like a lead balloon. *I will never drink again. What a sick feeling. Why would anyone want to go through this?*

He felt nauseous, disoriented. *I need to get to the hospital.* He struggled to get up, dragged himself out to the car and drove at a snail's pace to the emergency room.

The doctor gave him some medication to restore his equilibrium, asked some questions, then shocked him by saying, "You were slipped a mickey in your drink. You're lucky to be alive. If you had vomited while out, it could have killed you."

What a way to die—choking on your own puke.

Now Raven felt even worse. He'd been betrayed. The champagne hadn't done this to him. *What a fool I've been. Why didn't I see this coming?* He returned to his apartment and went straight to the clock where the safety deposit box key had been hidden.

The clock had been knocked over and the key was gone.

And with it all his money.

Karl must have passed for me at the vault—we resemble each other enough. And Nikki—what a fool I was.

He had actually believed she cared about him. Perhaps even Marco had been involved. At any rate, they were gone, and so was the cash.

He remembered the other dramatic incident in his life involving a key—the Camden church fire. Perhaps he was being punished for his theft. If so, this was fitting. Just a few weeks earlier he thought life couldn't get any worse. But it had. In spite of good intentions, he slipped back into selfishness, thinking the world owed him more. Well, he had finally gotten what he deserved. Raven had always considered himself better than others but now realized he was as flawed as the next guy.

He sat on the couch and stroked the stray cat while weighing his options. He still had his $263,000 tucked away in the bank account. That was safe. But all of the last few weeks' winnings were gone. Up in smoke.

After some time he realized his situation was even worse—he owed the casinos a million in markers from his credit line.

Actually, Victor York owed the money, not Raven. That comforted him somewhat, but Howard Goldberg most certainly recognized him. In that case, Raven could be guilty of fraud with no means to pay back the debt. Buying something on credit and being unable to pay isn't illegal, but buying on credit with no intention of repaying is a crime.

How ironic. I wanted to leave Vegas a million ahead and instead I'm a million behind.

There were really only three options. The first was to leave town and hope no one ever traced the transactions to him.

The second possibility was to leave the country. With the leftover money, he could start a new life. But if he did, there'd be no turning back. He'd never be able to return home.

The third option seemed the most implausible. If he came up with a million by the end of the month, he could pay off all markers before they went into default, avoiding charges of fraud.

His father used to say "the easiest way to double your money is to fold it over once and put it in your pocket." If only it were so simple.

Ten days to come up with a million. Might as well expect to take a bus to the moon.

The one common denominator all three options shared involved getting out of Nevada. Tracking down Karl and

Nikki would be fruitless. They could be anywhere. Maybe they weren't even from South Africa. The only thing Raven knew for sure was the sooner he escaped Sin City, the better his chances of surviving. He drove to the bank, converted the remaining $263,000 balance into cash, closed the account and left town.

CHAPTER TWENTY-THREE

♣ ◆ ♥ ♠

Raven had no idea where to go or what to do, so he just got in his BMW and drove. The more distance he put between himself and Vegas, the safer he felt. Eight hours later, right outside Albuquerque, a bold scheme came to him.

He stopped for gas and a bean burrito at a new, clean-looking collaboration between Texaco and Taco Bell. He located a pay phone and hoped that Harry Read still worked at the Swamp. An ornery guy like Harry could have easily been canned since Raven last played there.

Minutes later, and nearly out of coins for the phone; he heard the familiar raspy voice of Harry Read.

Raven launched into his stratagem. "Harry, I've recently come into a large sum of cash."

"No kidding. I thought you'd be broke by now. What'd ya do? Rob a bank?"

Harry's laughter crackled over the phone and Raven held the receiver away from his ear. "No, nothing dramatic like that," Raven said. "Anyway, I'd rather not get into the story."

Harry made a new sound, and Raven couldn't tell if it was a snicker or a belch. "Must be a woman involved if you don't want to give me details. Am I right?" Harry asked. "Yes, there most certainly was a woman involved," sighed Raven. "But here's the deal. If I report all the money now, taxes are just going to kill me. So I've got a proposition for you."

Raven fed the phone his last two quarters and proceeded to explain his bold plan. He wanted Harry to set up a special private blackjack game for him. Single deck, no other players. The table limits would be raised to a maximum of $10,000. Raven would play until he either won a million dollars or lost a million dollars.

Harry let out a long, low whistle. "That's asking a lot, I'd have to get approval—but I doubt they'd go for action that big."

Raven decided to work on that huge ego by rattling the chain of the bigot on the other end. "Come on, Harry, I thought you were the big chief. Don't tell me you're lower on the totem pole than all those Indians. Your motto was always 'ride hard or stay in the barn,' remember?"

Harry snapped back. "Yeah, but even giants like me still have to report to a boss. Call me back in a few hours and I'll let you know." He slammed down the phone, sending a loud clang through the line.

Raven drove on, hoping Harry had enough clout. Even if he did, the whole venture was riddled with danger. First of all, Raven didn't have a million. He could put up $250,000 in cash and pray that he didn't need the rest.

Secondly, even if the Swamp miraculously went for the freeze-out proposition, it had a very high rate of failure. Normally with optimal bet sizing, he had a 95% chance of doubling his money. If Harry approved this game, Raven would be severely over-betting his bankroll and faced a very real chance of tapping out.

The Aztecs were fanatical gamblers, sometimes betting all they owned to test fate. Raven wondered if he was any different. Nevertheless, this was a chance he had to take. If he could win a hundred top bets over the next week, he'd have the million to pay off the credit lines for Victor York before the thirty days expired.

Raven waited until he got to Amarillo before he called again. Harry sounded chipper on the phone. "Surprise, surprise. We got it authorized. They've already had a killer year here, but there's always room for another million," he chuckled.

Raven didn't know whether that was good or bad news. "Great. I'll be there tomorrow morning. And Harry?"

"Yes?"

"I'd like to get started right away," said Raven.

"We'll have our best-looking dealer ready and waiting. Only one condition."

Raven feared anything Harry might require. "What's that?"

"We need the money in cash. You do have the money don't you, Randy?"

Raven avoided answering the question. He really wanted to change his life and end the lies. "How about I deposit a quarter million initially?"

Harry paused dramatically. "I guess that'll have to work. When you get here, I'll take care of the money. See y'all in the morning."

Raven had no intention of letting Harry handle the cash. He didn't trust him in the least and suspected Harry only set up the game for the opportunity to get his fat little fingers in the pie.

Next, Raven called Matt and discovered that he'd moved up in the organization and now worked as supervisor in the cashier's cage. *That's good news,* thought Raven and his mind began whirling. *Maybe Matt can take care of the money and keep it away from Harry.*

He looked forward to seeing Matt again, although Raven remained unsure whether his eerie experience at the sweat lodge was real, just a dream, or a peyote-induced hallucination. But Raven's life had convinced him he couldn't control destiny. That was a fallacy. And he wasn't sure how to express those insights to Matt without offending him.

♣ ♦ ♥ ♠

The next day at the Swamp, he greeted Harry with his signature left handed shake. "You still look the same," Raven said.

"Quit sucking up to me, I've gained another ten or twenty pounds." Harry patted his ample beer gut. "Of course it doesn't show so much on us husky masculine types. You still look like a preppie, although your hair's darker than I remembered. Almost looks like a damn Afro."

Raven hadn't done anything about the dye or kinks in his hair. Right now that remained the least of his worries. "When can we start?"

Harry grinned wickedly, "Can't wait, huh? Must be a hole burning in your pocket. Well, get your cash and come with me to my office."

"Sorry, Harry. I already talked it over with Matt, and he's going to handle all my money."

"Helluva way to treat me after I put my ass on the line to set up this game for you," Harry fumed. "Going behind my back—with an Injun no less. Some nerve."

Raven didn't want to alienate Harry any further, since he still needed his help to pull off this caper, so he tried to calm the waters. "I just thought it might be simpler that way..."

Harry interrupted. "Listen. I don't dance unless I hear some music, and you're burying yourself by not throwing me a bone." Raven started to answer, but Harry shook his head disgustedly and walked away.

Raven desperately needed allies, not enemies. The whole venture seemed dangerous to begin with, and now it looked even more difficult. He wearily carried his satchel of money to the cashier's cage.

♣ ♦ ♥ ♠

Matt's face lit up when he saw Raven. "Great to see you again, my friend. As I said on the phone, I'm ready to help in any way possible. You know how I feel about this white management team."

"It's good to be back." Raven paused to reflect on his financial predicament. "And I really do need your assistance."

Matt's expression turned somber. "My brother Luke..."

"Hey, I feel horrible about not keeping in touch with you guys after I left so abruptly. I really look forward to seeing him again," Raven said.

"Well, you won't. At least not in this world. He's dead."

Raven stared in disbelief. "What?"

"His vision quest became an obsession. Eventually Luke thought he could literally fly. Two months ago he jumped off a cliff."

"I'm so sorry," Raven said, groping for words to express his feelings.

Matt struggled to keep his composure, then continued. "It's a shame. We wanted to unleash the incredible powers within our minds and become like the Mayans, who received visions of future events. But we went too far in believing there were no limits."

Raven agreed. "I also found out the hard way that life does have restrictions."

"Yes," Matt nodded solemnly. "Luke and I took positive thinking too far."

Raven didn't have all the answers to the hard spiritual questions of life. He saw no easy formula for riches, fame, success, and especially one's salvation, but he clearly saw the tragic consequences of placing faith in the wrong reality. He feared his own life also had spiraled out of control, and within a few days, he too might crash.

♣ ♦ ♥ ♠

Harry led Raven to the private table and went over the rules. Raven could wager up to $10,000 as long as he always bet at least $1,000 minimum. That gave a one-to-ten spread, yielding a fat edge, as long as the penetration stayed decent. The Swamp always dealt single decks down to near the bottom, so Raven's confidence climbed for the first time in days.

He took out a marker for fifty grand and dug in. He requested a new deck be brought out at the start of every session to keep the game honest. Raven cut the cards and placed a thousand-dollar chip in the betting square.

This was it.

Everything on the line.

What started with a few hundred bucks back in Chicago long ago now was ready to be played out to its finality. Raven would need an Olympic performance from his brain over the next six days. He normally kept a side count of aces with his feet, but here he also mentally tracked the deuces and sevens to squeeze every last ounce out of his edge.

The first cards hit the felt and the game began. It took less than an hour to lose the initial fifty grand. With a certain amount of apprehension, he tapped into the next fifty. Those chips lasted only two hours.

By the time his third fifty thousand arrived from the cage, a small crowd had gathered, bustling over the amounts of money wagered. Raven overheard one of them muttering how Raven had lost more in ten minutes than his job paid in a year. Another commented that Raven recently won the lottery. Harry obviously blabbed to anyone who would listen about the young high roller at the table.

So much for trying to keep a low profile.

The situation unnerved Raven slightly, although he was far too disciplined to let it affect his play. When he reached a deficit of $120,000, he took a short break. Now he only had fourteen top bets left. The game was good, but he just couldn't catch any cards. He stepped outside and walked around the building to clear his mind.

When he returned, Harry was cackling to some high official in the tribe on the phone. He obviously enjoyed this moment. It made him look good and confirmed what he already thought about Raven—just another loser. Harry's arrogant smirk reinforced Raven's desire to win.

I'm going to prove you wrong, Harry. I'm not going to tap out—I'm going to wipe that smug grin right off your ugly face.

Once again Raven saw a battle pitting good against evil. A casino that sent charter buses around to nursing homes and senior centers needed someone to teach them a lesson.

Raven looked over the fresh deck of blue cards and settled in, determined to turn things around before he ran out of money. He asked the security guards to rope off the area behind his table, creating breathing space from any on-lookers vicariously wishing they were playing ten grand a hand, or hoping for crumbs falling to the floor.

It didn't happen very rapidly, but eventually, over four, nerve-wracking hours, Raven crawled back to even. By midnight, he had turned a likely disaster into a winning day of $88,000.

The onslaught continued the next day. The crowd behind the rope swelled as stacks of chips rose higher and higher in front of Raven. By the end of the second day, he had won over $200,000, leaving him up nearly three hundred grand for the first two days.

The penetration deteriorated slightly on the third day, but he still continued crushing the casino. He picked up $174,000 more and closed in on the halfway point of his goal.

The fourth day proved the most momentous yet. Raven experienced several wild, gyrating swings—twice winning more than eighty thousand, before quickly losing it back. Shortly after lunch the fluctuations ceased and the roller coaster only went up. In an incredibly short period of time he won twenty top bets, leaving him ahead nearly $650,000 in less than four days.

Harry grew noticeably more agitated and less cocky each day. Now frustration showed in every line on his weathered face. When Raven returned from dinner, Harry greeted him tersely at the table.

Harry ran his palms methodically over the felt like some superstitious ritual and forced a smile, displaying two crooked rows of yellowed teeth. "Randy, my boy, I'm afraid we gotta make some changes here. From now on all your bets gonna be the same. Whatever you wager on your first hand will be what you bet the whole deck. Got it?"

This infuriated Raven. "What do you mean? We had a deal. You can't change the rules in the middle of the game. You told me I could bet anywhere from $1,000 to $10,000. Now it's got to be one or the other?"

Harry haughtily dismissed Raven with a wave. "Don't tell me what I can or can't do. I've got a boss, a mother-in-law, and a teenage daughter for that. Flat bet. Take it or leave it. I need your advice like I need another hole in my butt."

Raven took an hour break to fume. *I should never have trusted that redneck*, he thought. *No way he'd ever play fair.* With no other options, Raven reluctantly returned. He played one spot at a thousand bucks a pop for the rest of the evening, losing back nearly thirty grand. He still had a small edge flat betting, but it was so slim, he doubted now whether it was worth the battle.

♣ ♦ ♥ ♠

After a fitful night's sleep he came up with a stroke of genius. He got up early, spent a few hours practicing, then went into the casino with a trick learned long ago in Reno— the seventeen-card cut. If done properly, he would get a big edge on the first hand each deck by knowing the dealer's hole card. The downside was the huge amounts of money involved. To make it work he'd have to play all seven spots.

Seven thousand dollars each round.

Fourteen grand in action every deck.

It was the riskiest thing Raven had ever contemplated.

He played every spot on the entire table all morning. The rustiness in his technique showed and numerous times he cut the wrong spot. By noon he had lost eighty thousand and now stood only $540,000 ahead. He retreated to his room to practice harder. A couple hours later he felt ready and headed out of the room towards the elevator. He didn't see either of the two men lurking by the ice machine until a huge muscular arm had buried its fist in Raven's gut.

Raven staggered from the blow and the second man rushed him. Raven struggled to fight back, but the two men hustled him into a room and proceeded to add a few more kicks to his ribcage. He fought back as best he could before finally giving in to the inevitable and reluctantly handed over his wallet.

The tall, smarter looking one laughed while manipulating a toothpick back and forth across his mouth. "Keep your small change, kid. We ain't here for that."

Raven regained his breath and a little of his composure. "Who are you then and what do you want?"

That elicited another laugh. "What we want is what we will get. Your name wouldn't happen to be Townsend would it?" Raven didn't answer as the tall man with the crew cut stared at the driver's license in the wallet. "Don't speak if you don't want. That's okay kid. We know who you are. And who are we? You shouldn't have to think too hard."

He strolled around the room for a while, letting the element of fear sink in. "You ever play at the Dunes Casino in Las Vegas?"

Raven stroked his chin to indicate deep thought, then shook his head. "Not since Elvis died."

This earned him another boot in his already aching ribs from the stout brute who looked like Popeye the sailor man. "Smart-ass. I think you know why we're here. One of the guys at the Dunes is a friend of ours. Maybe you remember him. Name is Jack. Sure remembers you."

Raven certainly recalled the unpleasant backroom encounter with Jack.

"Jack don't like people making him look stupid. That chickenshit Howard Goldberg tried to convince Jack that you were an honest guy and would pay the $250,000 in bogus credit you took out, but Jack don't see the need to wait for the due process of law and justice." He removed the toothpick and replaced it with a Marlboro. "It took a while to track you down, but we got bird-dogs all over the country. Finally, we heard about some kid named Townsend betting ten grand a pop in this god-forsaken toilet of a casino. We're here to collect."

Raven didn't see any use denying it. It certainly wouldn't do any good to explain how the credit really wasn't his debt; that Karl had run off with the money and Raven was actually doing the honorable thing to try and win it back. These clearly were dangerous people and none of those things mattered now. "I can't pay it," Raven said.

"And why is that?"

"All my money is in the cage. I got nothing on me." Raven got up off the floor, counting his ribs to make sure they were all still there. "I can't touch any of it until Friday."

Popeye threatened another kick. "You're lying."

"No, it's the truth. I'm doing a freeze-out. Everything's downstairs."

Popeye looked at his partner for approval to continue the pummeling. After a few puffs the tall man answered. "I'll give you twenty-four hours. If you don't have the money by then, you're a dead man. We'll watch you every second, so don't even think about making a run for it. Am I clear?"

"Crystal. Now can I go?" asked Raven.

"Sure, kid. Just don't try anything stupid."

♣ ♦ ♥ ♠

Deeply shaken, Raven made his way downstairs. He ate first to calm his nerves and recover some before playing. He always considered himself a tough guy, almost impervious to pain—but this situation scared him. He felt like someone clinging to the edge of a cliff by his fingernails—not sure how much longer he could hold on or how much more he could take.

Raven turned his attention from his fear to the task at hand. Worry wouldn't help his dilemma—he needed money, and lots of it. He grimly marched like a condemned convict on death row over to his private table, hoping for better success with the seventeen-card cut. The practice immediately paid off. Now he smoothly hit the spot on almost every cut and finished the day up just a shade over a hundred grand. Tomorrow, he'd need another big win to reach a million, but at least now it looked possible.

Raven asked for security guards to escort him to his room. Safely there, he dead-bolted the door and slid the desk against it as an additional blockade.

Exhausted, he sank to his knees and prayed earnestly for the first time in years. He'd blindly followed a set of rules and had totally misunderstood that God had been trying to guide him through a minefield, rather than place restrictions on him.

Like the story his father told about the nail in the board, Raven's guilt left a hole that could be hidden but not removed—no more than MacBeth could clean the blood off his hands. But Raven had missed one key element—God's ability to forgive.

The loud ringing of the phone cut into his meditations. He got up and answered it. Raven recognized the gravely voice on the other end—it was the tall Vegas thug.

"Cute move with the security guards, kid. Afraid you might trip on the way up to your room?"

Raven grimaced. He didn't relish any encounter with these guys, either in person or on the phone. "Just wanted some company for the long walk. I'm a lonely guy."

"So that's it? I thought you might have been a little scared of me and Jimmy."

"Of course not," Raven said. "We've got a deal right?"

"Sure kid. We do. Just as long as the money ends up in our hands by noon tomorrow. You will come up with the cash by then, right kid?"

"Absolutely. I'd hate to even think about wasting it on myself," Raven said. He kept his voice even, unwilling to convey even a hint of fear.

"Glad to hear that. But just in case you have any thoughts at all about changing your mind, take a look out into the parking lot."

Raven grabbed the handset and walked over to the window.

"Can you see your shiny red BMW from there?"

Raven's stared at his prized possession. His body tensed in alarm. He had parked the car at the edge of the lot to avoid door dings, and it stood alone by the woods. "Yes?"

"Good. Take a last look and remember what will happen if you don't play ball."

At that moment his convertible exploded into a ball of flames. Raven froze in horror.

The menacing voice continued. "Meet us tomorrow in that same parking spot with the cash. And no security guards or your fate will be worse than your Beemer."

Then the line went dead.

Raven hung up the phone. He didn't know if he had the reserves left to continue this fight. Now the smoldering remains of his BMW symbolized his life. He had lost nearly everything. But many people had their hopes squashed and didn't give up, and no way would he quit tomorrow. Win or lose, he resolved to do the right thing.

Raven's commitment to finish the fight revived his courage, and he no longer feared the beginning of the next day and its uncertainty. Perhaps he'd finally tap out. Even if he somehow won the required million, there was no guarantee all would end happily ever after. But God never promised personal peace or prosperity—only hope for those broken enough to receive it.

Raven pulled a shiny, black Gideon Bible from the drawer. The date stamped on the inside cover placed it in service over two years ago, but its cover looked untouched. He slowly flipped through the crisp white pages, pausing every so often at a familiar passage. The Bible had once been his very existence for living—now the book felt distant and foreign.

He pored over its words for three hours before one verse struck him like a thunderbolt. "For what shall it profit a man, if he shall gain the whole world, and lose his own soul?"

Raven suddenly realized his mistake. He had always been so good at seeing the flaws in others, but hadn't noticed how greed crowded God out of his own life.

He laid several pages of hotel stationery on the desk. The casino logo taunted him from the top of the page, making it an unlikely choice for a confessional. Raven didn't care. He felt compelled to write Cynthia one last time.

Dear Cynthia,

I don't know where I'll be when you receive this letter. I might be in jail or I might be dead.

I'm sorry I wasn't honest with you about black-jack and should have told you in Israel. I apologize for getting involved in a business where duplicity is a strength. I can see clearly now—I was wrong in many areas and my morals slowly eroded.

I thought you would never be happy married to a poor man. How foolish to think someone like you ever needed riches for contentment. Please forgive me for the anguish I caused in your life. I knew the price of everything, but the value of nothing.

I still don't understand destiny or fate, but I guess those areas are beyond my mortal comprehension.

Even though my life has hit rock bottom, I know God is still gracious—even to self-righteous hypo-crites like me.

Whatever happens tomorrow, I'm ready. I'm fi-nally letting God have control. I've quit fighting Him and have accepted His mercy and hope you will for-give me also.

Raven sealed the envelope and felt an incredible peace. He finally understood the saying "confession is good for the soul." He had tried so hard to eradicate the stigma of sin through his own actions that he overlooked simply asking for forgiveness.

He used the remaining stationery to wipe the slate clean. Raven wrote another letter to Pastor Cook and the entire Camden Baptist Church congregation explaining his theft. Leaving the envelope open, he tucked it into his back pocket. He then wrote his father, and with no excuses, confessed his transgression.

He experienced a cleansing forgiveness for the first time in years. The bitterness finally was released. Raven gazed out the window and watched the first diffused rays of white light appear on the horizon. The most important day of his entire life was about to begin—but he now felt ready.

Serious issues still remained. Once he turned over the money to the thugs, they might do him in anyway, keep the cash and say he disappeared. He couldn't trust them. He needed to win and also get away. After some thought, Raven devised a brilliant game plan. He picked up the phone, hoped it wasn't bugged, and called Matt. After a short discussion explaining his predicament, they worked out a strategy, and Matt made the other calls to arrange his end.

Sleep was out of the question, so Raven pulled himself together and went downstairs to mail two of the letters, before heading to the tables for his date with destiny.

The casino hadn't expected him to begin play so early and they scrambled to ready his private table. They pulled the glass cover off the chip tray and systematically removed the smaller denominations, replacing them with several racks of thousand-dollar chips. Many of the bumblebees shined, looking like they had never seen the light of day before.

Next, the pit boss opened a new pack of cards and discarded the jokers. The dealer fanned the red deck over the felt. She carefully checked the fronts and backs of all fifty-two cards for imperfections. Raven also scanned the pack, making sure no cards were missing. Today of all days, he needed to stay alert, think clearly, and play like his life depended on it—because it did.

The dealer mixed the cards together and shuffled them thoroughly before offering them for the cut. Raven only had a few hours left to resolve his predicament. Despite the risks, he decided to play ten grand a spot, putting seventy thousand into action each round. He needed a big day and didn't have much time left. The dealer wished him good luck and the battle began.

The fluctuations proved enormous, triggering a buzz in the growing crowd behind him. Twice, Raven reached a point where he saw his goal within reach, only to drop back to half a million. Harry had been called in out of bed and didn't look too happy to be there. He stationed himself right on the edge of the felt, watching Raven's every move. The two thugs prowled strategically close, waiting like vultures for the inevitable death, their eyes riveted on his play.

An hour before noon, Raven caught fire. He counted the chips—$622,000 in winnings. Even after that flurry, Raven still needed a miracle and he needed it now.

Harry brought in a new dealer named Nancy in hopes of stopping the run. She flashed Raven a nervous smile and seemed ill at ease with all the attention focused on this game. Harry thoughtfully stroked the stubble on his chin and downed his sixth cup of black coffee. His hair was a mess, but his eyes were alert and intent as he watched the table.

Raven placed ten thousand in each of the seven spots while she shuffled the deck. As Raven reached across the table to cut the cards, Harry grabbed him firmly by the wrist.

"Not so fast, college boy," Harry said suspiciously. "I think I'll cut this deck."

Raven felt like a kid with his hand in the cookie jar. He had underestimated Harry and tried the seventeen-card trick too long. Now he had been found out. The gig was up.

Raven never liked to make a bet unless he had the advantage, so he reached to pull his bets back, but Harry had other plans. He instructed Nancy to deal the cards before Raven could react. Now an angry Raven Townsend had seventy grand riding on the seven spots. Win or lose, he would still be far short of the million-dollar debt.

The first hand took four hits to reach 18 and the second hand totaled 17. He stood on both of those against the dealer's ace. *A couple of losers there,* he grimaced. The next hand wasn't any better and he hit his 14, pulling a 4.

The fourth hand totaled 12 and he drew a 7 for 19. *My best hand yet.*

Next, he stood on a 17 and then the sixth hand required two hits to make 18. *Not quite so bad,* he thought. *Six hands with sixty grand on the line and no busts.*

The crowd pressed in, eager to follow the play. Raven picked up his last two cards. Harry folded his arms defiantly; confident a catastrophe would soon strike. He looked like a wizard, trying magically to will the dealer's hole card into a 9.

Raven picked up his last hand and stared in disbelief at the two cards.

A pair of 8's.

The memory of his disastrous 8 split against an ace in Tahoe remained firmly etched in his mind. But there could be no turning back now. The correct play was to split, so he slid out another ten thousand. He pulled a king for a total of 18 and breathed a little easier.

Harry nervously lit up another cigarette, forgetting he already had one in his mouth. Harry's job hung in the balance and his Adam's apple bobbed, betraying his anxiety.

The next card was another 8. Raven shook his head in amazement. He had to split again. He caught a 3 on the first 8 for 11. He doubled, putting out another ten thousand and caught a 7 for another 18.

Incredibly Raven drew another 8 on his remaining hand. He split again, consoling himself with the knowledge that at least all four 8's were finally removed from the deck.

Now he caught a 9 on the first 8 for 17, followed by a 2 on his last split. He doubled down and Nancy dealt him a 9 for a total of 19 matching his best hand.

Raven surveyed the table. He now had an incredible $120,000 riding on one turn of the card. He had not busted any of his hands, but none were very strong with three 17's, five 18's, and two 19's.

If the dealer has a 9 in the hole for 20, I'm dead meat.

Harry, normally impassive, sweated visibly and anxiously awaited the dealer to reveal her hole card. The crowd pressed in closer. It was another ace.

I can't believe this is happening. Is it possible to go through the same nightmare hand twice?

Some players believe in mysterious card gods altering the laws of chance—but not Raven. Whatever happened next would not be the product of metaphysics or positive thinking. There had to be a Creator in control of the universe. Raven closed his eyes and silently prayed—not for a winning hand but for more faith.

The next card was a 3, followed by another ace. *A soft 16. Either a 4 or a 5 would kill me now—I'd lose all $120,000. But I'd win everything if the dealer busted.*

Nancy flipped over the next hit—a queen of diamonds for a hard total of 16, increasing the dealer's chances of busting. Raven's countenance brightened until Harry commented on how he hadn't seen any 5's played.

Raven tried to remember. *He's right—they are all left in the deck.* Suddenly the odds looked bad again.

Raven nervously rubbed his nose before standing up to accept his fate. The next card would determine the rest of his life. If it were a 4 or a 5, he'd possibly be a dead man.

Nancy started to flip the last hit card over, then paused in midair. She looked delighted. Raven didn't know if that was good or bad since many dealers detested counters and you never knew whose side they were on.

He soon found out.

She tossed the last card onto the felt. It was a 6 for a total of 22.

The dealer had busted.

Raven collapsed into his chair. Harry slammed his fist into the table so hard it knocked over Raven's chips and muttered "Damn" over and over.

The crowd roared its approval. Even the two Vegas thugs looked happy. The only distraught person was Harry, whose career at the Swamp was history.

Raven quickly rearranged the stacks of chips and added up the total. That one bust card meant a difference of $240,000. If the dealer had made 20 or 21, he would have lost all his hands. Now he found himself up nearly $750,000. He gathered up his chips and turned to Harry.

"I'm done," Raven said simply.

The shell-shocked pit boss didn't answer—they both knew it was over.

Even though he hadn't won a million, Raven quickly realized that if he added the front money in the cage to his winnings, he'd have barely enough to pay off his bills.

Raven requested two security guards walk him to the cage and strategically used them to block any view of the transaction from the two thugs. Popeye and his boss stood a couple yards away, arms folded across their chests, watching Raven like a couple of hawks.

Matt carefully counted out the chips. He leaned over the counter and whispered to Raven. "Once I add your

front money on deposit here and the other cash you brought with you, the total comes out to $1,006,875."
Raven did some quick math. "I want you to keep five grand for your help," Raven said quietly. "And put another $800 into this envelope."
Matt put eight Franklins into the letter addressed to Camden Baptist Church. "I'll make sure this gets mailed. And the rest?"
"Give me $75 in cash and use the rest for this." Raven slid a list of instructions across the counter, which Matt quickly read, then nodded.
Raven stuffed the seventy-five bucks in cash into his pocket and headed for the door with a large shopping bag of money that had taken Matt several minutes to fill.
The two thugs quickly fell in behind and followed him out to the parking lot. As requested, Raven went alone with no guards.
The blackened asphalt still had the strong smell of smoke from the previous night's car bombing. A strong breeze swayed the treetops in the nearby forest. Raven neared the edge of the parking lot when Popeye called for him to stop.
He turned obediently, facing his adversaries. They had picked this spot, far away from the casino, in order to deal with Raven privately. Their car stood parked close by with the trunk open.
"You got the money, kid?"
Raven glanced apprehensively at them and cautiously lifted the bag high. At that signal, a pickup came screaming around the corner with Matt at the wheel, pounding on the horn.
Raven added to the distraction by throwing the bag of money into the air, letting its contents fly with the wind. The bills swirled like confetti in the breeze.
Popeye and his confused partner scampered to grab the money while Raven bolted for the woods. He gambled they

would go for the cash rather than chase or shoot him. He put his head down and ran furiously along the trail he used to race with Matt. With arms and knees pumping, he speedily covered the mile between the parking lot and the river.

He hoped it took the two thugs that long to figure out the bag of cash was filled with only one-dollar bills—one thousand of them. The remaining million was in Matt's possession and on the way to the bank.

At the river, Matt's youngest brother, John, waited for Raven with a canoe. The two swiftly paddled three miles down stream to the edge of a bayou, where a jet boat sped Raven to the nearest town. From there, a car took him to the bus station where he bought a one-way ticket to Maine.

Next, he called Matt. "It worked. I got away perfectly. What's happening at the casino?"

"I got the money to the bank and wired as per your instructions," said Matt. "Sent $250,000 to each of the four casinos in Vegas under the name of Victor York. With our sovereign tribal status, no one should ever trace the money to you."

Raven breathed a deep sigh of relief. "What about my two friends from Vegas?"

Matt laughed. "It was like a Kodak moment watching them scrambling for all those loose bills. Looked like two kids chasing butterflies. Should have seen their faces when they realized they'd been had. I thought they were going to choke each other."

"No chance of them finding me?"

"Nah. When they get over their shock, they'll reluctantly call their employer and find out you no longer have any debt. Nothing left for them to do except go back to Nevada and try to take the glory for getting you to pay. You're home free, although I wouldn't recommend vacationing in Vegas for a while."

Raven thanked his friend for his help. His plan had really worked. He sat in the back row of the bus and prepared for the long ride to Maine.

CHAPTER TWENTY FOUR

♣ ♦ ♥ ♠

When the bus crossed the Maine border, Raven sat up straighter and stared intently out the window at the familiar rocky shore. It hardly seemed possible he'd been gone ten years. As the scenery passed by, so did recollections of his childhood. The white New England clapboard homes and laundry fluttering on clotheslines stirred something in him he could not at first identify—long-buried memories of his mother. He pictured her standing in the kitchen and remembered the smell of her fresh baked biscuits.

The driver maneuvered the bus into the Camden depot and Raven abruptly returned to the present. He had no luggage or possessions, having left everything in his room when he fled, so he walked the last couple miles home. The wallet in his back pocket felt thin—and Raven hardly felt like the same person who played cards for ten thousand a hand. Strangers in oncoming cars waved and smiled—nowhere in all his travels had he experienced this sense of community. He knew now, somewhere deep in his soul, he had never stopped loving Maine.

As a teenager, he had grown somewhat contemptuous towards these unsophisticated country folk. Now, he only saw kindness in their weathered faces and he finally understood the unique bond shared by mankind.

The sun broke through the clouds as he ambled along the road, but he became more and more preoccupied with one thought—soon he'd be face to face with his father. Mentally he braced himself for the inevitable I-told-you-so routine. Raven had vowed to come back as a triumphant millionaire. Instead he was returning beaten and contrite, lucky not to be a million in debt or in prison. His reputation certainly was shot, but he felt cleansed and ready to face the music.

A myriad of familiar sights bombarded him each step closer to home. He gazed at the creek where he used to catch turtles and noticed a blue heron patiently waiting on the bank, looking for lunch. He recalled happier times when his father used to take him hunting and how he praised his son for always being the first to spy game.

He passed the last house before his father's place. The familiar howling of the neighbor's barking dogs greeted him and the broken down, corroded car still sat in their front yard.

Up ahead stood the Townsend home. The paint had worn off the house and it looked more gray than white. A solitary figure sat in a rocking chair on the porch. Raven hesitated a moment, watching his father swat flies. When the elder Townsend saw his son, he struggled to stand up.

"Randolph," he gasped, steadying himself on his cane. His left arm hung limply at his side and he shuffled a few steps forward.

Raven had never seen his father look so feeble and vulnerable. This shock caught him off guard and he couldn't swallow the lump in his throat.

"I'm sorry, Dad, I didn't know..."

"Didn't want you to," William said.

They stared at each other in silence for a moment. "Dad, I'm sorry I held a grudge so long—I should've come home a long time ago."

William leaned heavily on his cane and looked off into the distance for a moment. His voice husky, he said, "You're here now. That's what counts."

He tottered toward the steps and Raven rushed forward to assist him. William gripped his son's arm and clung to him with a fierceness that spoke more than words. In that act alone Raven read all the loneliness and pain he had caused his father. He had traveled to all fifty states while his father never once left Maine.

"I should have been here for you, Dad," Raven said regretfully. "I made so many mistakes."

William nodded. "I know. I got your letter."

"You must be very disappointed in me."

"That's part of growing up," said William. "Even a bear gets stung sometimes getting honey. It's how they learn."

"Well, I learned the hard way. Spent my life chasing the wrong things."

William grabbed his son's arm tighter. "I'm still proud of you, Randolph."

Raven looked at his father in surprise. "You are?"

"Yes, I am. I put too much pressure on you to be perfect. I've been wrong too, Randolph."

Over the years, Raven had honed a stoic exterior by watching Spock on Star Trek, but now the mask dropped off his face. He fought to hold back his tears and stared intently at his father.

"Son, I was wrong to try and be a lone goose all my life, everyone needs a flock. Look at me now. Since this stroke I can't even tie my shoelaces." Raven hugged his frail father. For the first time in his memory, tears flowed down his cheeks.

William returned the hug. "We all need each other. I probably never said this before—but I do love you, Randolph."

♣ ♦ ♥ ♠

Raven spent a few quiet days at home enjoying his father's company. He wondered if he should visit Jennifer Ross. The high school reunion was only a week away, but he dreaded facing the inevitable questions classmates would ask about the last ten years of his life. He wasn't quite ready to deal with that.

Instead, he decided to revisit the site of his happiest childhood memories. He got his old bike out of the barn and took the ferry to the island of Vinalhaven. The warm summer air and the splendor of the sapphire ocean waves invigorated his spirit.

Maybe it's not too late to recover some of the dream and vision I once had. If I could prove the ruins I used to explore were from the early Vikings, I might be able to return to archaeology. After that perhaps I could tackle the Noah's Ark project.

The decade had hardly changed the idyllic island. He pushed his bicycle off the dock and pedaled towards the far end of the landmass, where the mysterious ruins stood. His aunt and uncle would have to wait—first he wanted to explore.

The place looked exactly as he remembered it. The field was a little overgrown, but the tall oak trees still stood majestically behind the huge stones. A bald eagle soared just above the stand of hardwoods, shrieking for its mate and riding the shifting winds. Its white tail feathers gleamed a brilliant white in the sun.

Raven parked his bike and took a deep breath of the salty Penobscot Bay air. It felt great to be back.

Raven had only gone a little ways when he saw the unthinkable. Piles of dirt. Neatly organized—not some vandal or gravedigger, but the methodical work of an archaeologist.

Someone beat me here!

The dig didn't look like a big commercial project, but he could tell someone had been busy for a while. He located one worker, only the back of the head visible from a deep hole.

Raven considered it maddening to find someone else here, working on his discovery, but he could do nothing now. Curiosity replaced his resentment, and he walked over to inquire about the work.

When he reached the edge of the hole, a shovel of dirt flew through the air and landed on his feet. "Hey, watch out," he yelled, and then froze when he saw the culprit. Cynthia Bradford looked equally shocked at his sudden appearance.

"Raven Townsend! What are you doing here?" Cynthia quickly climbed out to meet him.

"I could ask you the same thing," Raven answered, recovering his composure.

"Your uncle gave me permission to work here," she explained. "He didn't think you'd ever return."

"I didn't either until a few days ago. I had to work out a few problems before I could come home."

"Yes, I know. My mother forwarded your letter and it arrived at my grandmother's yesterday. It meant a lot to me," she said quietly, "and I really appreciated your honesty."

"Well, I owed you an apology."

Cynthia shrugged. "Raven, you know I didn't think gambling was the wisest course for your life. You could have done so many other things with your talent. But I shouldn't have reacted so impulsively and walked out on you. I'm also to blame."

Raven held her gaze for a moment. "No need to apologize—I've made a real mess of my life. But God has forgiven me and I hope, with time, you will too."

She nodded. "I already have."

They walked over to the old, fallen oak tree. "So you never did make your million?" Cynthia asked.

"Well, I did make more than that, but I'm not a millionaire." They sat down on the tree and he explained the bizarre twists his life had taken in blackjack. He expected her eyes to grow wide with shock, but her expression never changed during the lengthy story.

He concluded with the dizzying end to his gambling career at the Swamp. "So I escaped Louisiana with just grocery money left in my wallet."

"That must have been a big disappointment."

"Yeah, it was tough at first. But I paid off the million in credit to the casinos and also returned the money I took from the church—with interest." He reflected a moment. "I think getting rich would've been the worst thing for me."

"Really?" Cynthia asked.

"Yes, I mean that. I'm just happy to be home and I feel at peace for the first time in a decade. That's a feeling you can't put a price tag on."

He struggled to hold in strong emotions. "So what's your story?" he asked.

"I came here in early May. Decided to find out once and for all who built this place."

Raven surveyed the impressive amount of work she had accomplished in such a short time. "And what did you conclude? Was I really crazy?"

"Well, I always thought you were crazy, but that's a different subject," she said with a sly smile. "Anyway, you and I shared the same dream here."

She adjusted her bandanna. "First, all I could find was more Indian stuff—arrowheads, a few pots, nothing exciting."

Raven had forgotten how striking she looked, even with dirt in her black hair. "Then?"

"Then, I discovered some iron nail fragments—which was pretty exhilarating, until I found this." She pulled a worn coin from her pocket and leaned closer to Raven. "This is a Norse penny commonly used for trading by the Vikings." She paused dramatically. "Around 1000 B. C."

Raven could feel his heart pounding and he wasn't sure if was from the coin or his proximity to Cynthia. "Amazing, but it could have been brought here much later."

She grinned and her blue eyes sparkled. "I wondered the same thing at first. After that, I found several old iron tools. I haven't had anyone else look at them yet, but there can be no doubt—they're Nordic tools."

She got up, walked to her tent and returned with another object. "The clincher came in finding this. A soapstone spindle wheel, just like they discovered in Greenland. The Vikings were here. Right here in this place."

Raven stood up to take in the scene. He had been right. "Cynthia, I'm so happy for you. This will make headlines all over the world. Especially if you can prove a connection between Vinland and Vinalhaven."

Cynthia laughed softly. "I'm not going to."

"What do you mean? Now I think you're crazy. You've got to finish the job here," said Raven.

"Oh, I will. I just meant I'm not going to do it alone."

Raven studied her face. "You must be planning on working with your husband, Garren Horne, then?"

"What are you talking about? I never married Garren."

"You didn't?"

"No, Raven. I never found anyone who..."

Her words trailed off as she turned away. Women always baffled him, and he didn't want to misread this situation.

He reached for her hand and decided to take one last gamble. "Cynthia, is there any hope for us?"

Her eyes were moist. "Raven, I never stopped caring about you. You're still the first thing I think of every morning."

He pulled her close and said. "I made a big mistake back in Connecticut when I let you leave."

He felt the warmth of her fingers closing around his.

Their lips met, and a gust of wind blew in from the sea. Overhead, the eagle landed in a nest at the top of a tall pine tree.

GLOSSARY

basic strategy The optimal way to play each hand of blackjack based on the dealer's upcard.

blackjack The game of twenty-one—or an ace and a ten dealt on the first two cards.

blacks Chips in the hundred-dollar denomination are commonly colored black.

bumblebee Chips in the thousand-dollar denomination were traditionally black and yellow, thus earning the nickname "bumblebees" in some casinos.

bust Whenever the total of any hand exceeds twenty-one, the hand loses.

bust card The individual card which brings the hand's total over twenty-one.

buy-in The transfer of cash for chips at the table.

cashiers cage The casino money transaction area where chips are cashed out.

chip tray The rack which drops into the blackjack table to hold the various rows of chips for the dealer to distribute to the rare players who win.

chips The tokens, unique to each casino, which are used for making wagers.

comp Complimentaries offered by the casino to players.

discard rack A clear, plastic device screwed into the table to hold the used cards after play.

double down Doubling the original bet and receiving only one additional card—typically done on a total of ten or eleven.

eighty-six Barring any individual from playing in the casino.

fills Bringing additional chips when the rack is depleted.

first base The first seat at the blackjack table to the dealer's left.

heat Whenever the pit bosses or surveillance become suspicious a blackjack player is a card counter and start scrutinizing his play.

hit When a player scratches or signals the dealer for an extra card for his hand.

insurance If a dealer shows an ace up, any player can take insurance if they think the dealer might have blackjack.

matrix A mathematical chart of index numbers showing the correct number to deviate from basic strategy for card counters.

nickels Chips in the five-dollar denomination.

outfield Players in the middle of the table sitting directly opposite the dealer.

pat A hand which is seventeen or higher and doesn't need a hit.

press During a hot streak, many gamblers increase or "press" their bets.

quarters Chips in the twenty-five dollar denomination.

reds Five-dollar chips are generally colored red.

shoe The device positioned to the left of the dealer used to hold multiple decks of cards.

silver One-dollar chips are often silver-colored metallic tokens, evoking the days when actual silver dollars were used in the casinos.

snapper Slang for a blackjack—when the first two cards consist of an ace and a ten.

split Players, but not dealers, have the option to split any two equal valued cards by matching their original bet. Then each hand is played separately.

stiff A hard hand totaling twelve to sixteen—a common sight for the author.

third base The last person dealt to at the blackjack table to the dealer's right.

toke A tip for the dealer.

wonging Only placing bets during positive counts.

BUY ADDITIONAL COPIES
OF THIS NOVEL AT THE
AUTHOR'S WEBSITE

www.kevinblackwood.com

OR

Send $14.00 by check or money order
for each book to:

Wooden Pagoda Press
1056 Green Acres Rd., Suite 102-132
Eugene, OR 97408

*Shipping and handling is free if you mention special code
PREVIOUS BUYER. Be sure to include your name, address,
and phone number.*